INTRIGUE

Seek thrills. Solve crimes. Justice served.

Tracking Down The Lawman's Son
Delores Fossen

Twin Jeopardy
Cindi Myers

MILLS & BOON

TRACKING DOWN THE LAWMAN'S SON
© 2024 by Delores Fossen
Philippine Copyright 2024
Australian Copyright 2024
New Zealand Copyright 2024

First Published 2024
First Australian Paperback Edition 2024
ISBN 978 1 038 93897 8

TWIN JEOPARDY
© 2024 by Cynthia Myers
Philippine Copyright 2024
Australian Copyright 2024
New Zealand Copyright 2024

First Published 2024
First Australian Paperback Edition 2024
ISBN 978 1 038 93897 8

This is a work of fiction. Names, characters, places, and incidents are either the
product of the author's imagination or are used fictitiously, and any resemblance to
actual persons, living or dead, business establishments, events, or locales is entirely
coincidental.

MIX
Paper | Supporting
responsible forestry
FSC® C001695
www.fsc.org

Published by
Harlequin Mills & Boon
An imprint of Harlequin Enterprises (Australia) Pty Limited
(ABN 47 001 180 918), a subsidiary of HarperCollins
Publishers Australia Pty Limited
(ABN 36 009 913 517)
Level 19, 201 Elizabeth Street
SYDNEY NSW 2000 AUSTRALIA

Cover art used by arrangement with Harlequin Books S.A.. All rights reserved.

Printed and bound in Australia by McPherson's Printing Group

Tracking Down The Lawman's Son

Delores Fossen

MILLS & BOON

Books by Delores Fossen

Harlequin Intrigue

Saddle Ridge Justice

The Sheriff's Baby
Protecting the Newborn
Tracking Down the Lawman's Son

Silver Creek Lawman: Second Generation

Targeted in Silver Creek
Maverick Detective Dad
Last Seen in Silver Creek
Marked for Revenge

The Law in Lubbock County

Sheriff in the Saddle
Maverick Justice
Lawman to the Core
Spurred to Justice

Visit the Author Profile page at millsandboon.com.au.

Delores Fossen, a *USA TODAY* bestselling author, has written over a hundred and fifty novels, with millions of copies of her books in print worldwide. She's received a Booksellers' Best Award and an RT Reviewers' Choice Best Book Award. She was also a finalist for a prestigious RITA® Award. You can contact the author through her website at www.deloresfossen.com.

CAST OF CHARACTERS

Deputy Luca Vanetti—When this Texas lawman's infant son goes missing, he has to put the past behind him and team up with his ex to find their baby and keep them all safe.

Bree McCullough—Even though she's vowed never to get involved with Luca again, their son is her top priority, and Bree soon learns Luca and she must work together to stay alive.

Gabriel Vanetti—Luca and Bree's son. He's only two months old and too young to understand the danger around him.

Brighton Cooper—A woman whose murder might be the reason that someone now wants Luca and Bree dead.

Dr. Nathan Bagley—He's obsessed with Bree, and that obsession could have led him to take desperate measures to get her. That could include kidnapping her son.

Tara Adler—A bartender with plenty of dark secrets, but is she trying to cover up a murder?

Manny Vickery—Tara's boss, who had a connection with the murdered woman. Maybe he killed her, or maybe he, too, is a target.

Chapter One

Deputy Luca Vanetti ran through the ER doors the moment they slid open, and he made a beeline to the reception desk. The nurse on duty saw him coming and got to her feet. Luca figured the concern on her face was a drop in the bucket compared to his.

He tried to tamp down the worry and fear that were firing through him. Tried not to jump to any bad conclusions, but Bree and his baby boy could be hurt.

Or worse.

No, Luca couldn't deal with *worse* right now.

He just needed to see Bree McCullough and his two-month-old son, Gabriel, and then try to get to the bottom of what'd happened. Bree and he might barely be on speaking terms, but they both loved Gabriel, and Bree would know what a gut punch it was for Luca to get a report that she'd been in a serious car accident.

"Where are they?" Luca demanded before he even reached the reception desk.

The nurse, Alisha Cameron, was someone he'd known his whole life. Something that could be said about most people in their small hometown of Saddle Ridge, Texas, where there weren't many degrees of separation.

Alisha motioned toward the hall. "The exam room on the right. Slater's already here."

Slater McCullough was not only a fellow deputy at the Saddle Ridge Sheriff's Office, but he was also Bree's older brother. Luca had expected him to be here since Slater was the responding officer who'd arrived on the scene of the single car accident, only to learn his sister was the driver.

"Gabriel wasn't in the vehicle with Bree," Slater said the moment he spotted Luca. "I just got off the phone with the nanny, and Gabriel's with her."

Some of the tightness eased up in Luca's chest. Some. His baby boy wasn't hurt. "And Bree?" Luca managed to ask.

"She's in with the doctor now," Slater said after he swallowed hard. "She has a head injury, and they're examining her."

"How bad?" Luca wanted to know.

Slater shook his head. "I'm not sure. When I arrived on scene, she was trying to get out of the car, but her seat belt was jammed, and she couldn't reach her phone. There was blood," he added. "Some scrapes and cuts, too, on her face, but I think most of those came from the airbag when it deployed."

"What happened?" Luca wanted to know. "Why did she crash?"

"I'm not sure what caused the accident." He paused, his gaze meeting Luca's. "Her car went off the road right before the Saddle Ridge Creek bridge, and she slammed into a tree. If she hadn't hit the tree, her car would have plunged into the creek."

Hell. That was where his parents had been killed, so Luca knew firsthand that a collision like that could have been fatal because the creek was more than twenty feet deep in spots. But crashing into a tree could have killed her, too.

Luca studied Slater's eyes that were a genetic copy of not

only Bree's but of Gabriel's. "Why did she go off the road?" he pressed.

Slater shook his head again. "I don't know. Like I said, she was woozy, and I arrived on scene only a minute or two before the ambulance got there. The EMTs loaded her right away and brought her here."

Because Luca knew Slater well, he could see that Slater was worried. And troubled. "You said Bree has a head injury. How bad?" Luca asked.

"I don't know," Slater repeated. He scrubbed his hands over his face. "Other than what I've told you, the only other thing I know is a delivery driver traveling on that road spotted Bree's car and called it in. There were tread marks nearby, but I have no idea if they were from her vehicle or not. The delivery driver didn't see any other vehicles around."

So, maybe she'd gotten distracted or something and had lost control of the car. That wasn't like Bree, though. She was usually ultra-focused. A skill set she needed for her job as legal consultant for the Texas Rangers. But she was also the mother of a two-month-old baby, and it was possible lack of sleep had played into this.

That possibility gave Luca another gut punch. Because he could see how this would have played out. Even if Bree had been exhausted, she wouldn't have asked him for help. In fact, he was probably the last person in Saddle Ridge she would have turned to. Ironic, since they had once been lovers.

Had.

That was definitely in the past, and as far as Bree was concerned, it wouldn't be repeated. Luca was learning to live with that even though they'd had an on-again, off-again thing since high school. The *off* had become permanent eleven months ago when they'd landed in bed after Bree's father had been murdered.

That brought on gut punch number three of the day.

Because Bree's late father, Sheriff Cliff McCullough, hadn't only been Luca's boss, he'd been his surrogate father after Luca's parents had died in a car crash when Luca had been just sixteen. Luca had been grieving and on shaky emotional ground following Cliff's murder. Bree had been, too, and they'd spent the night together.

The night when she'd gotten pregnant with Gabriel.

Bree hadn't told him that though until four months ago when she'd moved back home. Only then had Luca learned he was going to be a father. Luca hadn't quite managed to forgive Bree for shutting him out like that, but she apparently didn't want his forgiveness.

The door to the exam room opened, and Dr. Nathan Bagley stepped out. Another familiar face but not an especially friendly one. Well, not friendly toward Luca anyway. Luca knew Nathan had always seen him as a romantic rival. During Bree and Luca's off-again phases, Nathan and she had dated.

"How is she?" Luca immediately asked.

The doctor didn't get a chance to answer though. "I'm fine," Luca heard Bree say.

Nathan's sigh indicated he didn't quite agree with his patient, but he stepped back out of the doorway, and Luca saw another nurse who was in the process of washing her hands.

And Bree.

Her short dark brown hair was tangled and flecked with powder from the airbag. And she was pale. So pale. She was also getting up from the exam table. Not easily. She was wobbling a little, and Luca immediately went to her, took hold of her arm and steadied her.

There was blood on her cream-colored shirt. A few flecks

of dried blood, too, on her right cheek by her ear. That had no doubt come from the cut on her head that was now stitched up.

Bree dodged his gaze, but that was the norm for them these days. "Thanks," she muttered, and stepped out of his grip. "I'm fine," she repeated, her gaze pinned to Slater.

"You're sure about that?" Slater questioned. He went to her, gently cupped her chin, lifting it while he examined her.

"Sure," she insisted at the same moment that Nathan added his own comment.

"She doesn't appear to have a concussion, but I'd like to run some tests," the doctor said. "I'd also like to admit her for observation for the head injury."

All of that sounded reasonable to Luca, but Bree clearly wasn't on board with it. "I'm fine. I want to go home and check on Gabriel."

"Gabriel's okay," Slater assured her. "I called the nanny just a couple of minutes ago."

Now it was Bree's turn to study her brother's face, and it seemed to Luca that she was making sure he was telling her the truth.

What the heck was going on?

Slater and Bree were close, and Slater wouldn't have lied to her. Well, not under these circumstances anyway. And not about Gabriel. Slater might have downplayed the truth though if Bree had been in serious condition, but that wasn't the case.

"I need to go home," Bree repeated. "Can you give me a ride?" she asked, and then moved away from Slater. She went to the small counter where the nurse was now standing and picked up her purse.

"Hold on a second." Slater stepped in front of her to stop her from heading for the door. "What happened? Why did you wreck?"

Her pause only lasted a couple of seconds, but it was

enough to make Luca even more concerned about her. "A deer ran out on the road in front of me," Bree said. "I swerved to miss it and lost control."

There were indeed plenty of deer and other wildlife in the woods around the creek, and drivers did hit them from time to time. But something about this still felt, well, off.

"Why were you on that road?" Luca asked. It wasn't anywhere near Bree's place. Her house was one she'd inherited from her grandparents when she'd turned twenty-one, and it was on the outskirts of the other side of town.

"I was going to Austin for a business meeting," she said.

That didn't seem off. Bree was a lawyer who did legal consultations for the Texas Rangers and some state agencies. Most days, she worked from home, but she sometimes had meetings in nearby San Antonio or Austin.

"I thought I was going to end up in the creek," she added in a mutter.

Now she looked at Luca. Or rather glanced at him, and he saw the apology in her eyes. She no doubt knew it always hit him hard to be reminded of his parents' deaths.

"A deer," Slater muttered, a question in his tone.

"Yes," she verified, and Bree suddenly sounded a whole lot stronger. She didn't look it though. She still seemed plenty unsteady to Luca. "And now I need to go home and see my baby."

This time, it was Nathan who maneuvered in front of her. "You hit your head. You really should stay here for observation. You need to have medical supervision."

"I can get someone in my family to stay with me," Bree insisted right back. "I need to check on Gabriel."

Nathan huffed and turned to Slater to plead his case. "Head injuries can be dangerous. She shouldn't be alone."

A muscle flickered in Slater's jaw, and he volleyed glances

at both his sister and the doctor. Slater must have seen the determination on Bree's face because he sighed.

"She won't be alone," Slater told Nathan. "I'll make sure someone is with her for the next twenty-four hours."

Nathan repeated his huff, but his obvious objection didn't stop Bree. "I'll phone in a script for pain meds," he called out as Bree headed for the door. Slater and Luca were right behind her.

"Where are you parked?" she asked without looking back at them.

"By the ambulances," Slater provided. It wasn't far, but Luca's cruiser was closer.

"I'm right by the ER door," Luca said. He'd left his cruiser there when he'd been in a near panic to check on Bree and their son.

"Your cruiser then," Bree said, and her glance was just long enough for Luca to confirm she was talking to him.

She was obviously shaken to the core so Luca understood her urgent need to see Gabriel. The baby would likely steady her nerves. Again though, it seemed like more than that.

"Slater, why don't you ride with us, and I can give you a statement about the accident?" Bree asked when they stepped outside. She fired glances around as if looking for something.

Or someone.

"Sure," Slater said, sounding as concerned and skeptical as Luca was. He opened the passenger's side door to help Bree in, and he slid into the back seat.

"Drive," Bree insisted the moment Luca got behind the wheel.

Luca didn't press her to explain what the heck was going on. He pulled out of the hospital parking lot while he, too, glanced around.

"All right, what's wrong?" Slater demanded once they were on the way.

Bree dragged in a quick breath and squeezed her eyes shut for a moment. "Someone ran me off the road." Her voice cracked. "I think someone tried to kill me."

Chapter Two

Bree knew she had plenty of explaining to do. No way could she just drop a bombshell like that on two cops and not tell them more.

Especially these two cops.

Slater, because he was her brother, and Luca, because of their history together. Of course, their history was playing into their present since she'd given birth to Luca's son.

"Drive slow," she instructed Luca since it would normally only take about five minutes to get to her house. She needed a bit more time than that. "I don't want to talk about this in front of Coral." Coral Saylor, the nanny. Bree trusted her, but she needed to keep this just between the three of them.

For now, anyway.

Because it was possible anyone she involved in this could end up being in danger.

She hated that. Hated that she had to bring them into this, but after today's attack, Bree didn't see a way around it.

"Who ran you off the road?" Slater asked. "Who tried to kill you and why?"

The first part was easy to answer. Well, the info was easy anyway. Reliving it sure as heck wasn't.

"I didn't see the driver," Bree admitted. "He came flying out from the dirt turnoff by the bridge and rammed into me. It was a large silver truck with heavily tinted windows." She shook her head and winced, which caused the fresh stitches to pull. "I didn't get a chance to dodge him or see the license plates."

"Had you ever seen the truck before?" Luca asked.

"I don't think so, but, uh, for the past couple of days, I've had the feeling that someone was watching me."

Both Slater and Luca cursed. "And you didn't think to tell one of us that?" Slater demanded.

"No." She stretched that out a few syllables, annoyed that he was using his big brother tone. "Because it was only a feeling. It happened twice when I was in town. First at the grocery store and late yesterday when I went to the post office. I glanced around, but I didn't see any unfamiliar faces."

Still, she should have trusted her gut. If she had, she would have been more careful. That had to stop. Careful had to be at the top of her priorities because of Gabriel.

"All right," Slater said a few moments later. He was making a visible attempt to rein in the big brother stuff. "Tell us why you think this truck driver maybe followed you and then rammed into your car."

Bree dragged in a long breath. Where to start? There were so many pieces to this so she decided to go back to the beginning.

"I've been investigating Dad's murder," she said, knowing that in itself wouldn't be a bombshell. They were all investigating her father being gunned down by an unknown assailant eleven months ago.

A date that she had no trouble recalling.

Because it was also when she'd gotten pregnant with Gabriel.

She'd ended up at Luca's that night, and they'd both been in shock and grief-stricken not just over her father's murder but her mother's disappearance. Her mother, Sandra, had simply vanished without a trace, and there was the worry that she, too, was dead. Or that she'd killed her husband and fled. That theory had some juice since her mother's wallet, phone and car had gone missing as well. None of the items had yet been recovered.

Both of those possible scenarios had shaken Luca and her to the core, and with their defenses down, they'd fallen back into their old routine of landing in bed.

"What does Dad's death have to do with what happened to you today?" Slater pressed.

"Getting there," she muttered and returned to the beginning. "As you know, Dad called me the day before he was killed. I was a legal consultant for the state prosecuting attorney back then, and Dad wanted me to check through my resources to see if I could find any info on one of his cold cases."

"Brighton Cooper," Luca readily supplied. "The young woman who was murdered five and a half years ago."

She made a sound of agreement. It didn't surprise her that Luca would remember that. Or know how much the unsolved murder had troubled her father. Luca had been a deputy for over a decade and had been on duty when the twenty-three-year-old waitress had been found stabbed to death in her apartment in Saddle Ridge. The case had gone cold, but the sheriff's office, and especially her father, had continued to investigate it.

Her mother, Sandra, had done some unofficial investigating as well since Brighton had been the daughter of Sandra's late friend, and Sandra knew that Brighton was often impulsive and prone to getting into trouble. Brighton also had a track record of getting involved with the wrong men.

Something that Bree could definitely relate to.

"Dad was frustrated that he hadn't been able to find anything new on Brighton," Bree went on, "and he knew I had access to a lot of different databases and law enforcement resources. He wanted me to see if anything about Brighton popped. *Anything*," she emphasized.

"Did you find something?" Luca asked.

"Not then. And maybe not now, either," she added in a mutter. "After Dad was killed, I continued to dig though."

It was hard for her to spell out, but the digging felt as if she was helping to fulfill her father's last wish. Added to that, diving into work temporarily helped her set aside the grief and her worries about her missing mother. Well, it had when she wasn't using those databases to hunt for her mom. Something she did at least weekly in case anything new turned up.

"For months, I did facial recognition searches, a lot of them, looking for any sign of Brighton," Bree went on. "And yesterday, I saw a woman I believe could be her on security camera footage of a fight outside a bar in Austin. The footage was recorded two nights before she was murdered, and the only reason it hadn't been erased was because the footage was used in a civil lawsuit."

"Brighton was assaulted in this bar fight?" Luca immediately wanted to know.

"No, if it was indeed her, then she was a bystander, along with about a dozen or so people who were trying to break up the fight that started inside the bar and then moved out onto the sidewalk. It was one of the men involved in the fight who filed the lawsuit."

A lawsuit he'd lost and then had posted the footage on social media.

"I contacted the officers who were called in," Bree continued, "but neither of them took a witness statement from anyone matching Brighton's description so I'm guessing she left before they arrived on scene. The man who filed the lawsuit didn't remember her either."

Bree's phone rang, and she groaned when she saw her sister's name on the screen. Joelle would have almost certainly heard about the accident by now and would want to know how she was doing. And Bree would tell her. First though, she had to finish filling in Slater and Luca so she let the call go to voicemail.

"Using facial recognition, I matched another face in the bar crowd footage to a bartender and contacted her," Bree went on, trying to hurry since they'd be at her house soon, and she had so much to tell them. "She didn't recall seeing Brighton so I dropped by the bar and spoke to the owner to ask him to give me receipts for that night. He said it would take a while since it was years ago but that he'd get them for me."

"We checked Brighton's credit card," Slater reminded her. "And she hadn't recently charged anything at a bar."

Bree made a sound of agreement. "I wanted to see if I recognized any names of customers who might link to Brighton."

"Did you?" Luca asked.

"I don't have the list yet. But this morning I got a call from the bar owner, and he said someone tried to run him off the road."

Both Slater and Luca cursed. "I want his name," Slater demanded.

"Manny Vickery," she quickly provided. "He owns the Hush, Hush bar in downtown Austin. It's one of those not-so-secret trendy gin joints. Not seedy though, and I didn't uncover anything illegal going on there."

"But someone tried to kill both him and you," Slater was equally quick to point out.

Hearing it spelled out like that gave her a new jolt of fear and worry. Bree wanted to believe it was all a really bad co-incidence. Or an accident. If it'd only been Manny's incident, she could have believed that, but coupled with hers, both attempts had to be intentional.

But who had done this?

It was something she needed to find out and soon.

"What did Manny say when he called you this morning?" Slater asked.

It wasn't hard for her to recall it since she'd mentally gone over the conversation several times. "Manny told me he was driving to the bar from his house, which is apparently in a rural area about twenty miles outside of Austin. He was on an isolated road when a silver truck rammed into his car from behind. The truck had one of those rhino bumpers and tried to push him off the road. Manny said he managed to keep control, and the driver of the truck sped off when another car came along."

"Did he get the license plate?" Luca wanted to know.

She shook her head. "He said he was too shocked by what'd happened to even think of looking at the plate."

"Was he hurt?" Luca pressed.

Bree shook her head again. "And his car only had some minor damage. He reported it to the local cops," she added since Bree knew that would be Luca's or her brother's next question. "Manny said he'd spoken to the cops right before he called me. He wanted to know if someone was after him because he was gathering those receipts for me. I said I wasn't sure. And I'm not," she quickly tacked on to that. "I'm not sure of a lot of things."

"You were on your way to see this Manny Vickery when someone tried to run you off the road?" Luca pressed.

Bree nodded. "And, yes, I've considered that Manny knew

I was coming so he could have said something to someone who was waiting for me. Or he could have done it himself if he lied about being attacked and wants me to back off the investigation."

They sat in silence for a moment, all of them obviously processing this. "I'll need to check your car," Slater finally said. "If the silver truck broadsided you, there could be some paint flecks we can use to try to trace the vehicle. I'll need to check the bar owner's vehicle as well."

Luca stopped the cruiser at the end of her driveway, and he turned in the seat to face her. "I'll also make some calls and see if anyone's brought in a vehicle like that for repair. I could ask around, too, to see if anyone spotted it in the area." He paused. "You didn't want to say anything about this in front of Dr. Bagley. Why?"

She had so hoped not to get into this, but Bree doubted Luca was just going to drop it, and if she tried to stonewall him, it might make him dig for the answer on his own.

"Because Nathan has been pressuring me to go out with him, and I didn't want to give him any excuse to…insinuate himself into my life."

She stopped, groaned, and knew she obviously had to spell that out a little better.

"As you know, Nathan and I briefly dated a couple of years ago when I was home for the summer, and when I broke things off, he didn't take it well. He kept calling and texting, kept sending me flowers. When I went back to Dallas, he showed up at my office there, and I had my version of a showdown with him. I made it clear he'd better back off."

As expected, Luca and Slater cursed. It was Luca who responded though. "And you didn't tell us he was stalking you?"

"No, because it stopped." Bree locked gazes with Luca's

intense brown eyes and went ahead with her explanation. "Added to that, I wouldn't have felt comfortable blabbing to you because of our history together."

Luca's jaw tightened. "It's not blabbing. It's reporting a stalker to a cop." He stopped, muttered more profanity. "If you didn't want to tell me, you could have gone to one of the other deputies. Or to the Dallas PD. You should have said something both back then and today. By that, I mean, you could have asked for another doctor instead of being treated by a man who stalked you."

She'd considered doing that. Mercy, had she, but Bree had just wanted to get the stitches and get out of there. She certainly hadn't wanted to dish up any of what'd happened since it would have ended up being juicy gossip. Even though she had no idea what was going on, Bree figured it was best to work this quietly behind the scenes.

"There's more," Bree went on, and this part was not going to be easy. "After I saw the woman I believe was Brighton on the video, I expanded the search to other cameras in the vicinity. Of course, most had been erased since it was over five years ago, but I found this."

She pulled up a picture on her phone and realized her hand was shaking when she held it up for Slater and Luca to see.

"It's footage of that same fight outside the Hush, Hush, but it was filmed by another customer who also posted it on social media." She paused. Had to. "I examined the footage frame by frame and saw this." She used her fingers to enlarge the still image she'd culled from the video.

"Hell," Slater said, and he not only moved in even closer, he took the phone from her, repeated his single word of profanity and then handed it to Luca.

Luca shook his head. "That's your mother."

Yes, it was, and when Luca handed her back her phone,

she took yet another look at it. Because she was in the mix of the other bystanders, only her face was visible, but it was enough for Bree to see the familiar short brown hair, and the eyes and mouth that were so much like Bree's own features.

Either her mother had a doppelgänger, or that was indeed Sandra McCullough.

"I don't recall Mom ever mentioning going to a bar in Austin," Slater muttered.

Nor had Bree. And their mother hadn't seemed to be the bar-going type. Then again, maybe she hadn't actually been in the Hush, Hush. It was possible she had just been walking by and had been filmed.

But it didn't feel like that.

This felt like some kind of important clue. But what? This had happened five and a half years ago, long before Bree's father had been murdered and her mother had disappeared.

"This morning, I went back through Mom's old credit card statements," Bree added. "No charges to the bar or anywhere else in Austin. And since Mom's not around, I obviously can't ask her about it."

"You're not thinking Mom had something to do with Brighton's death?" Slater questioned.

"I can't think that," Bree admitted in a whisper.

She couldn't wrap her head around her mother committing a crime of any kind. But then, Bree knew she wasn't impartial about this.

"I'd like to check on Gabriel now," she murmured.

Luca stared at her. And stared. She wasn't immune to that look. Nor to him. And that caused her to silently curse. She couldn't handle another on-off with Luca. No bandwidth for it. Even though she couldn't deny that the heat would always be there between them.

"You two can go in and see Gabriel," Slater suggested.

"I'll drive the cruiser to the crash site and look around. And I want to check out Bree's car. After I get back, we can figure out how to handle the rest of this."

Yes, *handling* was indeed required, and it wouldn't be just the three of them for long. They'd need to brief Joelle and her husband, Sheriff Duncan Holder. And Bree's other brother, Ruston, who was a San Antonio cop. All of them would want to know what'd happened and if it was connected to Brighton's and her father's murders.

Luca drove along the driveway to the house and parked near the porch. A reminder that he didn't want her to be out in the open any longer than necessary. And that was a reminder that she could be in danger. Bree wanted to hang on to that "could be," but she didn't plan on taking any unnecessary risks either. That's why she hurried into the house after she used her phone to unlock the front door.

"It's me," Bree immediately called out to let Coral know she was there.

As soon as Luca and she stepped in, Bree closed and relocked the door. Moments later, Bree heard footsteps coming from the laundry room.

"Didn't figure you'd be back this soon," Coral said, coming into the entry. She was carrying a clothes basket, and the baby monitor was on top of the folded pile of laundry.

As usual, Coral was wearing loose sweatpants and a T-shirt that was equally loose, and she'd pulled up her dark blonde hair into a messy ponytail. She had one of those faces that made her look a good decade younger than her thirty-eight years.

"Oh, hi, Luca," Coral greeted. "Gabriel's still napping," she said, smiling. At least she was smiling until she saw Bree's face.

Coral gasped. "You're hurt."

"A minor car accident," Bree was quick to say. "I'm fine, really."

But she would need to say plenty more because she wanted Coral included in that better-safe-than-sorry mode. It sickened her to think of that truck driver coming here, but it was too risky not to prepare for it. That meant locked doors and using the security system. The house was rigged with one, but normally Bree only turned it on at night. That would change.

"You're sure you're okay?" Coral pressed.

"Yes. It's just a few stitches." Which were starting to sting now that the numbing meds were wearing off.

Bree glanced at the baby monitor and checked the time. Since she'd put Gabriel down for his morning nap before she'd left, that meant he'd been asleep for nearly three hours. That was slightly longer than his usual, but then his sleep pattern was nowhere near consistent.

"I was going to put this laundry away and go take a peek at him," Coral explained, and she handed Bree the camera monitor.

Gabriel was indeed still asleep in his crib, and just seeing that precious face performed some magic. Bree felt some of her nerves start to melt away.

"He'll probably want a bottle soon," Coral remarked. "You want me to go ahead and fix that so Luca can feed him?"

That had more or less become their routine. Luca had been coming over daily to give Gabriel at least one bottle, sometimes two. Bree hadn't been able to nurse because of a nasty bout of mastitis when Gabriel had only been a week old, so that meant she hadn't needed to be in the nursery during those feedings.

A good thing.

She'd learned the hard way that too much time with Luca triggered the memories of their last night together, which in turn triggered memories of her father's murder. It was ironic that her son didn't have that same effect on her despite Gabriel being the spitting image of Luca.

"Yes, please make the bottle," Bree instructed, and she was about to head to the nursery when Luca touched her.

She jolted when his fingers brushed over hers, but then she realized he wasn't actually touching her. He was taking the monitor, and he had his attention pinned to it and not her.

Her nerves returned in full force. "Is something wrong?"

Luca shook his head, but the gesture didn't seem very convincing. "Look," he said, pointing to the screen. She saw a bird zoom past one of the nursery windows.

"A blue jay," she muttered and was about to dismiss it. Then, a few seconds later, a bird flew past again.

No. Not "a" bird. It appeared to be the same bird, flying at the exact speed and angle. This wasn't live feed but rather a recorded loop.

Bree bolted toward the nursery. Luca was right behind her, and he actually passed her before she reached the nursery door. He threw it open, and together they rushed into the room.

And her heart stopped. Just stopped.

Because the crib was empty.

Chapter Three

Everything inside Luca froze. At first, his mind couldn't register what he was seeing, and then the reality slammed into him.

The baby was gone.

"Where is he?" Bree asked, the panic rising in her voice. "Where's Gabriel?" She ran to the crib, and since there were no toys, pillows or blankets, it was easy to see it was empty. Still, Bree felt around the sheet as if she expected him to be there.

The cop in Luca kicked in, and he took hold of Bree to pull her back. If someone had taken Gabriel, then he needed to try to preserve any evidence.

If someone had taken Gabriel.

Those words knifed into him, robbing him of his breath and nearly sending him to his knees. But none of those reactions were going to help this situation, and he tried to focus on fixing this. On finding his precious son.

"What happened?" Coral asked as she ran into the room. She gasped and put her fingers to her mouth when she saw the empty crib.

"Where's Gabriel?" Bree demanded. "Why isn't he here?"

Coral frantically shook her head. "He has to be here. You put him in the crib and left for your meeting."

Luca fired glances around the room, taking it all in, but

other than the missing baby, he didn't see anything out of place. There were no signs of a break-in, and the windows were all closed.

While Coral and Bree ran to search the closet, Luca looked at the baby monitor again. On the screen, Gabriel was exactly where he was supposed to be, and the sickening realization hit him. This was a loop, a repeated recording of when Gabriel had actually been sleeping in the crib.

And that meant someone had hacked the monitor.

"We need to search the rest of the house and the grounds," Luca insisted, taking out his phone to call the dispatcher. "This is Deputy Vanetti. I need backup." He rattled off Bree's address. The next part wasn't nearly as easy to say. "Issue an Amber Alert."

He heard the sound, not footsteps, but a heart-crushing moan, and he knew it had come from Bree. She wasn't crying, not yet anyway, but that would no doubt soon happen.

"Search the other bedrooms," he told her and then shifted to Coral. "You look through the rest of the house. Check to see if any windows are open." Since it wasn't a huge place, that wouldn't take much time.

The grounds though were another matter.

This wasn't a small city lot by any means. The house that had once belonged to Bree's grandparents was situated on about a dozen acres with a barn and pastures for horses. He would need backup to cover the entire area, and every minute counted right now. Especially since there were two country roads within a quarter of a mile of the place.

"Coral, were the doors all locked?" Luca called out as he headed toward the kitchen so he could access the back porch.

Coral hurried into the kitchen with him, but she was clearly still in shock, and it took her several seconds to answer. "I think so. I don't know," she amended with a sob. "Where is he? Did someone take him?"

Someone clearly had, but Luca didn't voice that. Wasn't sure he could. He definitely didn't want to think of his son in the hands of someone who might hurt him.

"What about keys?" Luca pressed, trying to tamp down his own building panic. He drew his gun but prayed he didn't need it. "Who has keys to the place?"

Coral shook her head again, and their conversation must have gotten Bree's attention because she, too, hurried into the kitchen. "Me and my family," Bree said. "Coral, too, of course."

Since her family members were all cops, they'd likely kept the keys secure. He'd need to make sure Coral had done the same. For now though, Luca checked the back door for himself. His gut clenched, and he cursed under his breath.

Because it was not only unlocked, it was slightly ajar.

"Did you leave this open?" he asked.

"I didn't," Coral said.

"Neither did I," Bree insisted, "but I can't swear it was locked either. I had my coffee out there this morning, and I got distracted by the phone call from Manny."

Now, the tears came, flooding her eyes, and Luca wished he had time to comfort her, to try to reassure her that they would find their baby. But time was critical now so he used his elbow to open the door wider in the hopes he wouldn't destroy any prints that might have been left there. Then, he hurried out onto the porch.

He understood why Bree would want to have her coffee out here. The October temps weren't scorching hot as they could sometimes be in this part of Texas, and there was a picture-postcard view of the still green pastures, a pond and two grazing horses. But there was nothing picturesque about it for Luca at the moment. He took it in like a crime scene.

And he cursed again when he saw nothing out of the ordinary.

He needed clues. Evidence. He needed anything that would point him in the right direction to where his son had been taken. Then, he could catch up with the kidnapper and get Gabriel back.

"Don't go in that part of the yard," he instructed when Bree headed down the porch steps. "There might be footprints."

Since it probably wasn't a route a kidnapper would have used, Luca ran to the side of the porch and checked the yard below. As expected, there were no indications anyone had recently walked here so he vaulted over the railing, dropping down the three or so feet to the soft ground.

"Did you get any visitors this morning?" he asked while he searched that side of the house. Nothing visible there either, but there were shrubs so he had a close look around those.

"No," Bree answered. Luca heard the sound of footsteps behind him and saw that she, too, had jumped over the porch railing. "I only got that phone call from Manny."

Yes, that. Luca certainly hadn't forgotten about it. Or about Bree's, and possibly Manny's, run-ins with a truck driver who might or might not have wanted them dead. It was probably all connected.

But how?

If those attempts had been some kind of threat to ward them off, then why hadn't they gotten a lesser warning? A *back off or else*. Maybe because their attackers and the kidnapper hadn't wanted to alert them as to why this was happening. As a cop though, he had to believe this was connected to Brighton's murder. It didn't seem like a coincidence that all of this had started shortly after Bree had come across that video.

"Coral, did you see any vehicles near the house after Bree left?" he called out while he ran to the front porch so he could check it. Bree was right behind him.

"No," the nanny was quick to say. "I swear, nothing happened, and I didn't see or hear anything."

He believed her, but she had obviously been in the laundry room, and it was on the other side of the house from the nursery. If the washer or dryer had been going while she was in there, Coral might not have heard someone come in through the back door and take the baby.

There was a problem with that theory though.

A stranger would have had to search through the house for Gabriel. Of course, that search could have happened by peering through the windows, but Luca wasn't seeing any signs of footprints to indicate that. There was also the question of where a kidnapper would have parked so that Coral wouldn't have noticed.

Luca immediately shifted his attention to the barn.

"You think Gabriel's in there?" Bree asked, obviously following Luca's gaze.

"I can't rule it out," he settled for saying. "I want to check the other side of the house first," he added and headed in that direction just as his phone rang.

Because his mind was narrowed in on Gabriel, his first thought was that this was the kidnapper with a ransom or some other demand. But it was Slater's name on the screen.

"What the hell's going on?" Slater immediately demanded. "There's an Amber Alert?"

"Gabriel's missing. I don't know who, why or how," he added while he combed the side of the house for any potential clues. "When Bree and I went inside her house, he was gone, and it's possible he was taken as long as three hours ago."

Bree made another of those ragged sobs, and Luca knew she

was thinking the same thing as he was. If it'd been that long, if the kidnapper had taken Gabriel within minutes of Bree leaving the house, then their baby could be anywhere. Three hours was a lifetime when it came to something like this.

"I'm on my way," Slater insisted. "I'll call Duncan, Joelle and Ruston and fill them in."

That meant the four of them would also soon be on their way here, too. Well, maybe not Joelle since she was on maternity leave and had a baby of her own. Still, she would likely find a way to join the others. So would any available deputy. And Luca had to believe that would be enough help for them to find and recover Gabriel.

"Uh, how's Bree?" Slater asked. "Never mind. She's a wreck. I'll be there soon," he added before he ended the call.

Bree was indeed a wreck. She was strong and had survived going through hell and back, but that didn't mean she couldn't break. This was enough to break even the strongest person. That's why he needed to help her focus on the things that could be done rather than letting the fear take over. Luca tried to do the same for himself.

"Look for any signs of footprints," he instructed. "Especially beneath the windows."

She did, pinning her gaze to the ground as they hurried along the side of the house, but there was nothing to indicate the kidnapper had been here.

"Stay right behind me as we go through the backyard," he told her. Because there was a strong possibility of footprints being there.

"We're going to the barn," she muttered.

They were, and Luca knew it wouldn't do any good to ask Bree to stay in the house while he did that. If their situations had been reversed, he sure as hell wouldn't have stayed put and neither would she.

But it could be dangerous.

If they cornered a kidnapper, then Gabriel's captor might do anything and everything to escape. Still, there was no other option, not even waiting for backup. Luca intended to do everything possible to find his son now, and then he'd have to deal with whatever they were about to face.

"Look for tracks," he reminded her.

Luca did the same, but he didn't take the direct route across the yard. He stayed on the perimeter, hurrying, while he made his way through the flower beds and shrubs and toward the barn. They reached the wide metal gate, and Luca slowed down to check for footprints.

And he saw something.

Of course, that something could be Bree's own tracks since he knew she tended her two horses. Still, Luca skirted around them, climbing over the fence and approaching the barn from the side.

"Are the barn doors usually shut like this?" he asked Bree in a whisper.

"Yes. I open them if bad weather is coming."

Since there was no such weather in the forecast, then this was the norm, but Luca hoped Gabriel's abductor had ducked in and shut them. That way, his son would be nearby, and he'd be within seconds of finding him.

The horses whickered and lifted their heads, but they must have picked up Bree's scent because they went back to grazing. Luca and Bree went past them and ran to the barn. There were no footprints on the side of it. None that Luca could see anyway, but there were also enough patches of grass that anyone could have used them like stepping stones.

When he reached the door, Luca lifted the latch to ease it open, and he winced at the creaking sound it made. No way to sneak it with that noise. Then again, the spears of sunlight would have alerted anyone inside, too.

They stepped in, and Luca paused so his eyes could adjust to the dim light and so he could listen for any sounds. Nothing.

Not at first anyway.

Then, he heard something or someone rustling. It came from the far corner of the barn where there were some stacks of hay bales. Bree must have heard it as well because her attention zoomed in that direction while she took hold of a muck fork rake that was propped against the wall. It wasn't a gun, but it could be an effective weapon if it came down to it.

Luca was praying it didn't.

Keeping his footsteps as light as possible, he made his way toward those bales. Not approaching them directly where Bree and he would be easy targets. Again, he kept them to the side of the barn so he could approach from the side.

Of course, there might not be a kidnapper. The sound could have come from a mouse or some other critter that had gotten inside. Still, Luca moved as if their lives depended on it.

Since they could.

Luca stopped when he heard another sound. More rustling. Followed by what could be a whimper. That got Bree and him moving even faster, and he had his gun aimed and ready when they reached the stack of hay bales. Bree moved to his side, the muck fork raised.

And then they both froze.

There, seated on the floor was a woman, and she had Gabriel cradled in her arms. Not a stranger. Far from it.

Because the woman was someone who'd been missing and presumed dead for nearly a year.

Bree's mother.

Chapter Four

Bree's breath stalled in her throat, and the only sound she managed to make was a strangled gasp of raw shock. That shock anchored her feet in place. Her mind, too. She just couldn't grasp what she was seeing.

Her mother.

With Gabriel.

What the heck was her mother doing here in the barn, and why had she stolen Gabriel?

Her mother didn't say anything. She just stared at Bree with her own stunned silence. She was pale. No color except for some red scratches on her right cheek. Her hair looked as if it hadn't been combed in a very long time.

Gabriel made a sound, a soft whimper that yanked Bree right out of her stupor. Her maternal instincts kicked in. Mercy, did they. The boiling anger and urgent need to protect her baby slammed through her, and despite who was holding him—a woman she'd once loved and trusted—everything inside her screamed for her to get to her son.

Bree flung the muck fork aside to hurry to Gabriel. She didn't even acknowledge the woman holding him. Bree just reached down and took him.

Her mother didn't resist. Just the opposite. Her grip on Gabriel melted away as Bree's own grip gathered him into her arms. Cradling Gabriel against her chest, Bree stepped back.

Luca moved in front of Gabriel and her. Protecting them. And giving Bree a jolt of a different kind. Luca and she were a unit. Parents. Together. For this nightmare anyway. Even though she was holding their son, the fear of him being kidnapped was causing adrenaline to fire through her, and the only person who could understand what she was feeling right now was Luca.

Or rather, he could understand what she was feeling about finding their son.

He probably couldn't grasp what she was going through over seeing her mother. Then again, Bree couldn't quite grasp it either.

"You're hurt," her mother said. "Were you attacked?"

Bree had forgotten about her fresh stitches and the nicks on her face, and it definitely wasn't a high priority for discussion right now. "You took my son," Bree managed to say.

Her mother nodded, and tears spilled from her already red eyes. "Yes. To protect him."

Nothing about this felt like protection. But Bree immediately rethought that. Just an hour or so ago, someone had run her off the road and had possibly tried to kill her. Was that connected to her mother?

"To protect him," Luca repeated. "Explain that," he snapped, and it was obvious from his tone that he was still getting some adrenaline jolts of his own. Equally obvious, too, was that he wasn't just going to dole out a welcome home to the woman who'd stolen their child.

Her mother opened her mouth but didn't get a chance to answer before there was the sound of running footsteps. "Bree?" Slater called out. "Luca? Where the hell are you?"

"Here," Luca said.

That brought on more running footsteps, and he wasn't alone. Coral was with him.

"Did you find…" Slater's words trailed off when he saw them. He, too, had his weapon drawn, and his gaze swept from Gabriel to Luca and Bree.

And then to his mother.

Slater shook his head, clearly not able to process what he was seeing. Coral was having a similar reaction. The nanny didn't know Sandra well, but it was obvious she recognized her.

"What are you doing here?" Slater asked Sandra.

"Sandra's the one who took Gabriel," Luca supplied.

"I did it to protect him," her mother insisted. She moved to get to her feet, a gesture that caused Luca and Slater to take aim at her.

"Are you armed?" Luca demanded.

Luca and Slater were clearly treating her mother like a kidnapper, and Bree didn't object. Too many things weren't clear right now, and she didn't want Gabriel in any more danger than he might already be.

Her mother shook her head, and she lifted her hands while she stood. She staggered a little but kept her hands raised.

"I don't have a gun, and I wasn't going to hurt Gabriel," her mother said. Her face was a mix of shock and fear. "I'd never hurt him or any of you." She added that last part when she shifted her attention to Slater.

Slater swallowed hard. "What are you doing here? Where have you been all this time?"

Those were both very good questions, but Bree had another question of her own. "Why did you feel the need to kidnap my son to protect him?" She didn't ask it nicely either, not with the terror of nearly losing her son still coursing through her.

The sigh that left her mother's mouth was long and weary. "Because someone else was going to take him."

"Who?" Luca and Bree asked in unison.

Sandra shook her head. "I don't know." She repeated that while she shook her head again and continued to cry. She took a step toward them, staggered a little and caught onto the barn wall.

"Are you hurt?" Slater asked. He lowered his gun but didn't holster it.

"Just my ankle." Sandra squeezed her eyes shut for a moment. "I twisted it when I escaped."

Bree was trying to grasp each word her mother said. Trying to examine her body language, too. But *escaped* flashed like a neon sign in her head. Luca picked right up on it, too.

"Escaped from who and from what?" Luca still sounded like a cop interrogating a suspect.

Again, her mother didn't get a chance to answer because there was a shout from outside the barn. "Bree?" someone called out.

Joelle.

And judging from the sound of more footsteps, her sister wasn't alone. Bree was betting Duncan was with her. Moments later, she got confirmation of that when Joelle and Duncan hurried in. Since they didn't have their baby with them, Bree figured they'd left Izzie at home with the nanny.

"We came to help look for Gabriel," Joelle said.

Bree looked back at her sister. Their gazes connecting, for a couple of seconds anyway, before Joelle saw Gabriel in her arms. Relief flooded her face, but it, too, passed quickly when Joelle's attention landed on Sandra.

"Mom," Joelle muttered on a rise of breath. Unlike the rest of them, Joelle didn't stand back. Just the opposite. She hurried to their mother and pulled her into her arms.

"She could have a gun," Bree was quick to point out.

Joelle's shoulders went stiff, and she shifted from worried daughter to cop in a blink. She stepped back, way back, volleying glances at Slater and Bree. "What's going on?" Joelle asked.

Bree wanted to know the same thing. Clearly, so did Duncan, Luca and Slater, but Slater obviously wanted to make sure they weren't about to be attacked.

"I'll check her for weapons," Slater volunteered, stepping forward.

Joelle's mouth dropped open, and it seemed as if she was about to object to their mother being frisked. She didn't though. It must have occurred to her that they needed a whole lot of answers before they could trust the woman who'd given birth to them.

"She's not armed," Slater relayed. "She doesn't have a phone or a wallet. Just some keys." Slater lifted out the keys and held them in the air. "There's one here marked with a B."

Bree was pretty sure that was the key to her house. Her mother had had one like that anyway. But Bree didn't recognize the rest of the keys. Or the clothes her mother was wearing. Loose jogging pants and a baggy T-shirt. Definitely not her mom's usual fashion choices, especially since she was barefoot. And she'd clearly lost some weight. All possible signs of, well, Bree couldn't be certain, but she wanted to know.

"What happened?" Duncan demanded. "Is Sandra the one who kidnapped Gabriel?"

Luca nodded. "She hacked into the baby monitor—"

"No," her mother interrupted. "I didn't do that. The kidnapper did."

That got their attention, and all of them pinned their attention on Sandra. She sighed again. "Eleven and a half months ago, I was kidnapped, and I've been held all this time."

Bree had to admit that fit with her mom's appearance. Well, maybe it did. But it could also fit with someone who'd been on the run.

"Did you kill Dad?" Bree came out and asked.

Her mother's eyes widened. "No." She sounded stunned but adamant. "Of course not." The tears began to spill again, and a hoarse sob tore from her throat. "I think the person who took me killed him."

"And who would that be?" Slater demanded.

Sandra shook her head. "I don't know."

Bree and Slater both groaned, but Duncan cursed. Maybe because of Sandra's answer but also because his phone dinged with a text.

"Someone reported seeing a silver truck that matches the description of the one we're looking for," Duncan relayed. "It was near here."

Bree automatically pulled Gabriel even closer to her. Oh, mercy. Had the hit-and-run driver come back for another attack?

"I drove a silver truck here," her mother volunteered.

Again, that got their attention. Not that it had strayed too far from her mother. "You're the one who ran me off the road?" Bree asked.

Her mother flinched. "No." She used that same adamant tone. "I drove the truck here, that's all, and I parked it on a ranch trail." She pressed trembling fingers to her mouth for a moment. "Did someone try to hurt you?"

"Someone did hurt me by running me off the road so I'd crash into a tree," Bree clarified. "And that someone was driving a silver truck."

Sandra staggered back and sank down onto the floor.

"I didn't do that. I wouldn't do that," she amended. "But my kidnapper would."

"I'll want to hear all about the kidnapper," Duncan stated. "For now, tell me where you parked the silver truck."

Sandra fluttered her fingers toward the pasture. "It's on the old ranch trail just on the other side of the fence. I left it there and walked to the house."

"Because you didn't want the nanny or Bree to spot you?" Duncan pressed.

"No, because I didn't want the real kidnapper to see me," her mother was quick to say. "I wanted to get Gabriel away from the house before she had a chance to show up and take him." She stopped, her forehead bunching up. "I should have figured out another way. I shouldn't have scared you like this."

Bree glared at her. "Yes, you should have figured out another way. If you thought Gabriel was in danger, you should have called me."

Sandra shook her head. "I didn't have a phone, and when I didn't see your car in the driveway, I figured you weren't home."

"I wasn't here, but Coral the nanny was," Bree was equally quick to point out.

"Coral," she repeated, and her gaze drifted to the nanny. "The woman in the laundry room. I only saw her back so I didn't know who she was. I wasn't sure I could trust her so I decided better safe than sorry. I took Gabriel, sneaked out the back door and waited in the barn, hoping you'd show up and start looking for him."

Bree mentally went back through that. "You said you'd been held all this time so how did you even know about Gabriel?"

"From her. From the woman who held me," Sandra clarified. "I overheard her talking to someone about Bree and her baby. I don't know who she was talking to, but it was clear they were planning on kidnapping Gabriel."

"Who is this woman?" Duncan pressed.

"I don't know. I don't," Sandra insisted when Duncan groaned. "She always wore a mask whenever she was around. I didn't even know where I was until I escaped."

Now it was Bree's turn to groan when her phone rang, and she yanked it from her pocket and answered it without taking her attention off her mother. She instantly regretted not looking at the screen for the caller's ID though when she heard the man's voice.

Nathan.

"Bree," he said, and there was a frantic edge to that single word. "I just heard about your son being missing. I can come and help look for him."

"No," she couldn't say fast enough. She definitely didn't want to have to deal with the clingy Nathan right now. "We found him. He's safe."

And she hoped that was the truth. Hoped that her little boy wasn't still in danger. But if what her mother was saying was true, then he possibly could be.

"Oh, thank God," Nathan said, punctuating that with what sounded like a breath of relief. "Are you all right? You must have been shaken to the core when you realized he was missing."

"I was. And I'm fine," Bree added, ready to hang up.

Nathan spoke before she could. "I can come over and give the baby a checkup. You know, just to make sure he's really okay."

That gave her another jolt of fear. She hadn't checked Gabriel after she'd taken him from her mother, but she intended to do that now.

"I have to go," she told Nathan, and she ended the call so she could put her phone away and open Gabriel's onesie.

Her movements must have been frantic because Luca holstered his gun and moved closer to help her with the onesie zipper. Gabriel objected to that by frowning and whimpering, but other than that, there appeared to be nothing wrong with him. She wanted to do a more thorough check soon. First though, she needed to deal with her mother.

"I didn't hurt him," her mother insisted. "I wouldn't. I stopped him from being hurt. If the kidnapper had taken him…" She stopped, dragged in a few clipped breaths. "I don't know what would have happened. And I couldn't risk it." Sandra paused. "We should take the baby inside the house and I can tell you how I ended up here. I can tell you what happened to me."

Bree very much wanted to know that, but she didn't budge. Neither did the rest of them.

Duncan's phone dinged again, breaking the silence. "The CSIs are going with one of the deputies to locate the silver truck. If it's where Sandra says it is, then we should know within the hour if there are paint flecks on the truck that match Bree's and Manny's vehicles."

"Do you mean Manny Vickery?" Sandra asked. "The owner of the Hush, Hush bar in Austin?"

Once again, they all turned toward her mother. She had managed to surprise them once again. "You know him?" Luca asked.

Sandra nodded. "I talked to him when I was helping your dad investigate Brighton's murder." She stopped, gathered her breath and opened her mouth to continue.

The sound stopped Sandra cold. A loud blast. And Bree instantly knew what it was.

A gunshot.

Gabriel jolted from the sound and began to cry. Bree instinctively pulled him back to her body while she stooped to go to the floor.

Luca helped her with that. He got her down in a blink, positioned himself over them and drew his gun. Joelle, Slater and Duncan did the same, and they took cover behind the hay bales.

"Move away from the wall," Duncan told Sandra, and the woman scrambled closer to Joelle. Duncan then called for backup. "Carmen and Woodrow were already on their way out here to look for Gabriel," Duncan relayed to them a moment later. "They'll be here in less than five minutes."

Carmen Gonzales and Woodrow Leonard, both veteran deputies. Good. Bree wanted all the help they could get.

There was another blast, but it didn't seem to hit anything. At least Bree hoped it hadn't.

"I think both shots came from the direction of the road," Luca muttered. His gaze met Bree's for a split second, and she saw the renewed fear that was there. Fear for their son's safety.

She doubted the shots had come from a hunter who'd strayed too close to her place. Not with everything else that had gone on. Someone was after her, and that someone didn't care if they put her baby at risk. That both sickened her and terrified her. Bree could deal with someone coming after her. She was a cop's daughter after all. But she didn't want her baby involved in this.

Keeping low, Slater made his way to the barn door that was still open, and staying to the side, he peered out. "I don't see anyone, but if the shots are coming from the road, the shooter could be hiding in the trees."

There were certainly plenty of those by the country road. So many places for a gunman to hide. But maybe Carmen and Woodrow would be able to see the shooter when they arrived. Maybe they'd even be able to arrest him, and Bree might be able to get those answers she so desperately needed.

The seconds ticked by, and her heartbeat and breathing had just started to level when there was another gunshot. This one blasted through the wall of the barn, creating a hole where light speared through it.

Another shot.

This one tore through the barn as well and smacked into the wall on the opposite side. The shots weren't low but rather at the height if the target had been standing. That changed though because the next shot came in low. It ripped through yet more wood, sending splinters flying.

Bree ducked her head, putting her face right against Gabriel's to shelter him. He continued to cry, loud wails now because he was obviously afraid.

In the distance, she heard another sound. A police siren. Obviously, Carmen and Woodrow weren't going with a silent approach. Part of her was thankful for that because it might cause the shooter to stop. But it might also cause him to run.

Duncan's phone rang, and he answered it while he ran to the barn door next to Slater. "The deputies don't see a shooter or a vehicle on the road."

The vehicle could be on the ranch trail. Perhaps even the one where her mother had left the silver truck. But there were trails that threaded all through this area. What likely hadn't happened though was the shooter had come on foot. Her place was too far off the beaten path for that.

The wailing of the sirens got closer. But there were no more gunshots.

"Luca and Joelle, wait here with the others," Duncan instructed. "Slater will come with me. Stay put," he added to Bree.

She didn't ask what Duncan and her brother were doing. Because Bree knew. They were going to go in pursuit of the person who'd just tried to kill them.

Chapter Five

Luca set the bag of baby supplies on the floor next to the sofa in the break room of the sheriff's office where Coral was feeding Gabriel a bottle. Bree was right there, clearly not wanting to take her eyes off their son, but Luca also knew she would soon have to do that. Because there was no way she would miss her mother's interview.

Bree, her siblings and every cop in the building—including Luca—wanted to hear what Sandra had to say. It could be critical for not only the events of the past eleven months but also for what'd happened today. Bree being run off the road, Sandra taking Gabriel.

And the shooting.

That was at the top of Luca's list of things he needed to know. Since Duncan and Slater hadn't been able to find the shooter, it meant there was a possibility it could happen again. This time, they might not get so lucky, and someone could be hurt. Luca didn't intend to let that happen, and it was the reason he hadn't let Bree and Gabriel out of his sight since those shots had been fired into the barn.

Of course, he'd have to allow it eventually because he didn't want the baby in the interview room where tempers might flare, but Coral would stay just up the hall with Gabriel. No baby monitor, not after what'd happened to the one at Bree's. But if there was any trouble, Luca would be able to get to Gabriel in a matter of seconds.

"It's time?" Bree asked him.

Luca nodded. After they'd all arrived at the sheriff's office, Duncan had told them to take thirty minutes so they could get Coral and the baby settled. So they could settle their own nerves, too. That would also give Duncan time for an EMT to come in and give Sandra a quick exam. Other than some cuts and bruises and the sore ankle, Bree's mother hadn't seemed injured, but if she was telling the truth about being held captive for eleven months, then she needed at least a cursory exam that would no doubt be followed by a complete physical once she'd given her statement.

"Your mother, Slater, Joelle and Duncan are already in the interview room," Luca added. He knew that because he'd glanced in the room after he'd retrieved the baby supplies from Carmen, who'd picked them up from Bree's place. Everyone was sitting and waiting for the EMT to finish. "Ruston is on his way from San Antonio, but he said for us not to wait for him."

Since Ruston was a San Antonio detective, he understood the urgency of getting any and all info. In this case though, there were plenty of emotions mixed with that urgency. Yes, Sandra could possibly give them answers, but she was still Joelle, Bree, Slater and Ruston's mother. A woman who'd been missing for almost a year.

A woman who, despite her denial, could have murdered their father or at least have knowledge of that murder.

Yeah, no way to take the emotions out of that.

Bree brushed a kiss on the top of Gabriel's head. Luca did the same. And after giving their son one last look, they left to go to the interview room. Luca stopped just outside the closed door and looked at Bree to gauge how worried he should be about her.

Worried, he decided.

She looked exhausted and no doubt was. Spent adrenaline was a bear to deal with and sapped plenty of energy. Added to that, she still had those stitches from her car crash. There'd been way too little time for her to process that before they'd realized Gabriel was missing. Then, the gunshots had added to the hellish day.

And it wasn't over.

Bree still had to deal with her mother, and the nightmarish memories the woman's reappearance would stir up for her. Then, there was the part he'd go ahead and tell her now.

"I'm staying with Gabriel and you," Luca spelled out. "You can consider it protective custody, but I'm staying." He steeled himself for an argument where she could point out that one of her siblings could provide that protection.

But no argument came.

"Good," she muttered. "No one will protect Gabriel better than you."

"I feel the same way about you," he assured her.

Their gazes connected. Held. He saw the faith she had in him about this. And he hoped she saw the same in him. They would indeed do whatever it took to keep their son safe. But like a hit of adrenaline, there'd be a price to pay. The close quarters were going to test barriers that Bree likely didn't want tested. Still, no price was too high to pay for their little boy.

The door opened, breaking their connected gazes, and Luca and she stepped back so the EMT, Shaun Gafford, could come out. Luca knew him well since they'd been in the same grade at school.

"She's got some bruises on her arms, hands and legs,"

Shaun explained, "but other than that, she's good." He paused, looked at Bree. "How about you? You got meds in case those stitches start to throb?"

Bree nodded. "Dr. Bagley phoned in a script."

At the mention of Nathan's name, Luca remembered the call Bree had gotten from him shortly after they'd found Gabriel and her mother in the barn. Maybe Nathan had just been concerned about Bree and Gabriel, but after what Bree had revealed about the doctor's stalking, Luca made a mental note to keep tabs on Nathan to make sure he didn't resume those stalking attempts.

They stepped into the interview room that was a decent size, but usually there weren't this many people present. Duncan, Slater, Joelle, Sandra, Bree and him. Then again, there was nothing "usual" about this situation. Sandra was seated with Joelle by her side, but Duncan and Slater were standing. Bree and Luca stayed on their feet as well.

"I just got a call about the silver truck," Duncan said. "Woodrow and Carmen found it where Sandra said it would be. And they saw paint flecks on the bumper. It's being taken in now for processing. According to the plates, the vehicle belonged to a man named Alan Smith, but Woodrow says the guy's been dead for nearly a year now, and that his son sold the truck to a woman who paid cash for it. Woodrow has the buyer's name. But it's Ann Wilson so it's probably bogus."

Probably. But it was something Luca would check for himself.

"Still no sign of the shooter?" Bree wanted to know.

Duncan shook his head, and the frustration of that was all over his face. "But there were other tire tracks on the trail so it's possible the shooter parked there and then escaped after he or she fled." He made eye contact with Luca. "There were some indications that someone had tried to set fire to the silver truck."

Hell. Luca hoped no evidence had been destroyed. They needed anything and everything in that vehicle to help them make sense of what'd happened. He was hoping though that the making sense would start right now with Sandra.

"I'm going to Mirandize you," Duncan said, shifting his attention to Sandra.

Sandra didn't object. She only sighed as Duncan recited the warning. He followed that up by stating his name, the time and the names of others who were present. All very official, but it didn't mean Duncan was anticipating that he might have to arrest Sandra for anything. This was just a legal formality and a way of covering themselves.

"I didn't kill my husband," Sandra said the moment that Duncan had finished. Her voice cracked, and more tears filled her eyes. Joelle handed her mother a box of tissues that she took from the table. "Cliff was alive the last time I saw him," Sandra insisted.

"Start from the beginning," Duncan instructed as he took the seat across from her. "You said you were kidnapped. When and how were you taken?"

Sandra gathered her breath. "It was November first of last year. Cliff had already left for work, and I went to my home office to try to do more searches on Brighton. She'd been dead for four years by then, and Cliff was frustrated that he hadn't been able to find her killer. He wanted me to search through old social media posts to see if I could come up with something."

Cliff had asked Bree to dig as well. And Luca. So, Luca could attest to his former boss being frustrated. It was understandable, too, that he would ask his wife to help since Sandra and Brighton's late mom had been best friends.

"Someone knocked at the door while I was working," Sandra went on. "At first, I thought it was Cliff, that maybe he'd locked himself out or forgotten something since he'd only been gone about twenty minutes so I opened the door without looking. A woman wearing a ski mask jabbed me with a stun gun. She dragged me out of the house and into a car, and then she gave me some kind of injection in my arm that knocked me out."

Luca thought back to the scene of Cliff's murder. There'd been no signs of a struggle. No signs of Sandra either, and her purse and phone had been missing.

"Describe the woman and the car," Duncan said.

Sandra nodded, but then paused for a couple of seconds. "Like I said, she wore a mask so I never saw her face. But she was tall, maybe five foot ten, and she had an athletic build. She didn't have any trouble dragging me to the car. She just put me in and drove off."

"But she took your purse, keys and phone?" Luca questioned.

"Yes. I had my phone in my pocket, and she got that right away and took out the SIM card. But she also grabbed my purse, and it had my keys in it." She paused again. "I've had a lot of time to think about that, and I think she took my purse to make it look as if I'd voluntarily left. I didn't," she insisted. She repeated that while she made direct eye contact with Joelle, Bree and Slater.

"What happened after this woman kidnapped you?" Duncan pressed, clearly anxious to get some answers.

"I'm not sure how long I was unconscious," Sandra admitted. "When I woke up, I was in a bedroom with log walls, and it was attached to a small bathroom. There was a window in the bedroom, but it'd been boarded up." She stopped, shook her head. "Believe me when I say I tried to tear off those boards, but I was never able to do that."

"Where was this place?" Duncan asked.

Sandra pulled in another of those long breaths. "I didn't know at the time, but after I escaped in the silver truck, I realized the cabin was only about twenty-five miles from here. It's off an old farm road between Bulverde and the Guadalupe River." Her eyes went wide. "It'll be in the GPS. I didn't know where I was, but the GPS was working so I told it to navigate to Bree's address."

Duncan took out his phone and made a quick call to Woodrow, instructing him to check the truck's GPS right away and then to have local cops go out to the scene immediately.

"Okay," Duncan said to Sandra when he'd finished with the call. "Go back to the kidnapper. You're sure you never saw her face, never got any indications as to who she was?"

"I'm sure," Sandra insisted. She stopped, and it seemed as if for several moments, she got lost in the memories of what'd happened. "She only came in every three days or so, and one time she brought me a newspaper with the article about Cliff. That's how I learned my husband was dead." Her voice broke. "I read about in a newspaper that horrible woman brought me. Did she kill him?" Sandra asked.

Most of them shook their heads. Bree went with a verbal response. "We don't know. We're all investigating it. Did the woman ever say anything about Dad?"

"Nothing. Just that article. I asked…no, I begged her for more information. I begged her to let me go, to tell me why she was holding me. She never answered." There was a world of genuine heartbreak in her words, and Luca didn't think any part of it was fake.

"Did your captor stay there with you the whole time?"

Duncan asked, obviously shifting the interview back to the abduction.

Sandra shook her head. "No, she wasn't around that much. Like I said, she'd come every two to three days and always had on a mask. She'd put a bag of groceries in my room. Sandwich stuff and chips mainly. Toiletries, sometimes." She wiped away more tears. "A couple of times, I tried to jump her when she came in, but she always had the stun gun with her and would hit me with it."

"Not this last time though," Luca reminded her.

"No," Sandra murmured. She stopped when Duncan's phone dinged with a text.

"Woodrow called the county sheriff's office, and they're sending out deputies now to check the cabin," Duncan relayed after he read the message.

Good. The sooner they got there, the better, and with any luck, the kidnapper would still be there so they could arrest her.

"You were telling us about how today's encounter with your captor was different from other times," Duncan prompted.

"Yes," Sandra verified. "A couple of times before today, I'd heard her talking on the phone to someone. It sounded as if she was getting instructions or orders because she said things like, 'I can do that' and 'Understood.' The call I heard today though was different." Her voice cracked again.

"How?" Duncan pressed.

"She said she was worried about someone noticing the damage to the truck, that she didn't want to be pulled over by some local yokel when she went after the kid. Then, I heard her say Bree's address, like she was repeating it to make sure she had it right." A bite of anger trickled into her voice. "She said she'd get out there and get the kid before Bree was back from the hospital." Sandra shifted her gaze to Bree. "I didn't even know you'd had a baby."

Bree nodded. "Gabriel. He's two months old, and Luca's his father." She didn't add more, but Luca could see for himself that Sandra was working this out in her head. Especially the fact that Gabriel had been conceived shortly after Cliff's murder.

"Duncan and I have a daughter," Joelle said. "Elizabeth Grace. We call her Izzie. You can meet her after, well, after," she settled for saying. "For now, we need to know how you ended up at Bree's and anything else you can tell us about what happened to you."

Sandra stared at Joelle for a moment, and there was another flood of emotions. One that looked as if it might cause Sandra to lose it, but she reined herself in and continued. "When I overheard the woman saying she was going to take Bree's baby, I knew I had to do something. I couldn't let my grandbaby be taken and locked up like I was."

Now the rage flared in Sandra's eyes. Luca had rarely seen any show of temper from her over the years, but it was there now.

"I crammed everything I could into the last plastic grocery bag she'd dropped off two days earlier," Sandra explained. "My shoes, toothpaste, even the bar of soap, and when she came in, I bashed her upside the head with it. She fell, the stun gun clattering to the floor so I used it on her. While she was jittering and flopping around, I ran. The truck was parked out front, and the keys were in the ignition so I got in and drove away as fast as I could."

"You didn't think to take off her mask and see who she was?" Duncan asked.

"No. I just ran. I had to get to Bree's. I had to save her baby."

Duncan shook his head. "But if you took your captor's truck, then why did you believe she would still come after Gabriel?"

"I thought once she was able to move, she'd call her boss or partner and that he or she would rush to Bree's and take Gabriel. I couldn't risk that." Sandra stopped again to wipe away more tears. "If she killed Cliff, I didn't want to think what she could do to a baby."

Neither did Luca, and if all of this was the truth, then Sandra had stopped something horrible from happening. Luca was beyond thankful for his son's safety. But without the identity of the kidnapper, there could possibly be another attempt to take him.

But why?

Did someone want to use Gabriel for leverage? If so, that brought Luca right back to another why? It was possible someone wanted to use him to sway the outcome of an investigation, but at the moment, there were only two unsolved murders on the books. Cliff's and Brighton's. So, did that mean one of them was connected to this?

"Why do you think this woman kidnapped you? Why did she want Gabriel?" Bree asked, taking the questions right out of Luca's mouth.

"I don't know," Sandra said through a hoarse sob. "I've obviously had plenty of time to think about it. To think about losing my husband, too. Did he suffer?" she asked Slater. "Did your dad suffer when he was killed?"

Slater shook his head. "The ME said death was almost instantaneous after he was shot."

Almost. Like Slater and the rest of his family, Luca had read the ME's report countless times, looking for anything that would lead them to his killer. So far, all they had was that someone had gunned down the sheriff, and he'd bled out.

"If the woman kidnapped me," Sandra went on, "she must have had something to do with Cliff's murder. Did she try to frame me? Did she do something to make me look guilty?"

"With you missing, you became a suspect," Duncan admitted. "But we also had to consider that the killer had murdered you as well."

Sandra flinched a little. "But she didn't kill me. Why?"

Again, the big question. Too bad they didn't have a good answer. But maybe there'd be clues in the cabin where she'd been held. Maybe in the silver truck, too.

"You said you used the stun gun on the woman who kidnapped you," Duncan continued. "So, she would have been incapacitated for a while. For at least five minutes. Was there another vehicle at the cabin that she could have used to come to Bree's and fire those shots?"

Sandra's forehead bunched up. "Maybe. I didn't look behind the cabin. I guess a car or motorcycle could have been parked back there. You think she's the one who tried to kill us?"

Duncan shrugged. "I'm considering it." He glanced down at a notepad. "Tell me about Manny Vickery," Duncan threw out there, obviously trying a different angle. "How well did you know him?"

"Not well at all. In fact, I've never met him. I just knew the name because I talked to Brighton a couple of weeks before she was killed, and she mentioned she'd been going to the Hush, Hush. She was upset, but the only thing she'd say about it was that things weren't going well with some man she'd been seeing. She was very upset," Sandra emphasized. "So, I went to the bar to see if I could find out what was going on."

"That's how you ended up on the video outside the Hush, Hush," Luca commented.

"Video?" Sandra questioned.

"Several people posted recordings of a fight, and I saw you on one of them," Bree explained. "I saw Brighton on another. It's possible though you weren't there at the same time, that Brighton left before you showed up." She stopped, gathered her breath. "Did you find out what was going on with Brighton when you went there?"

Sandra shook her head. "No. I talked to a couple of people, just to get a sense if anyone there knew Brighton. I talked to a bartender, Tara..."

"Tara Adler," Bree provided. "I spoke to her, too," she added when her mother gave her a questioning look. "She said she didn't know Brighton."

"She told me the same. I tried to talk to Manny, but he had Tara tell me he was too busy to see me. And there was that fight. A regular brawl, and it scared me so I left." She squeezed her eyes shut. "If I hadn't, if I'd stayed and found out what was going on with Brighton, she might still be alive."

"Wait," Sandra said a moment later. "You think Manny's the one who had me kidnapped? You think he had something to do with your father's murder?"

"We're looking into that," Duncan assured her. "We're looking into a lot of things. But in light of what happened to Bree and to you, I want you in protective custody. I could arrange for a safe house." Now it was Duncan who paused, and he looked at Joelle as if maybe confirming—or questioning—something they'd discuss.

Joelle nodded and turned to her mother. "You can go home if you'd like. Duncan, Izzie and I live there now."

What Joelle didn't spell out was that it was the place where her father had been killed. If Sandra had read the article about his death, she would know that, and it might not be easy for her to deal with it.

There was another side to this situation though. Luca believed Sandra was telling the truth about her abduction, but there were still plenty of blank spots as to what had happened. And why.

Especially why.

Sandra apparently wondered that as well, and she came up with the same concern that Luca and Duncan had. "I want to be there with you. All of you," she amended, glancing at Slater, Duncan, Bree and Luca. "But what if that woman comes after me again? It'd put you in danger."

No one could dispute that. As long as her captor was at large, the threat was there. And not solely for a kidnapping either. Those shots were proof that this person could and would kill. If the woman hadn't been the shooter, then the likely suspect was the person she'd been talking to on the phone. So, two people who could come at them anytime, anyplace.

"We'd have to take precautions," Duncan said. "Lots of them."

"One possibility is that Slater and I could be at the ranch with you," Joelle explained. She glanced at Slater, and he nodded, indicating this was something they'd already discussed. No doubt when Bree had been in the break room with Coral, Gabriel and him. "We could also ask one of the reserve deputies to stay with us as backup."

Duncan's attention shifted to Bree. "But you're in danger, too. Which means so is Gabriel."

Yeah, Luca had already gone there. Obviously, so had Bree because she made a quick sound of agreement.

"We could all be at the ranch," Joelle spelled out. "All," she emphasized, glancing at Luca. "We could conduct the investigation from there while putting security measures in place."

Luca thought of the McCullough ranch and the house.

It was big, with five bedrooms, but there were a lot of adults and two babies. Added to that mix would be Sandra, a woman he wanted to trust but wasn't sure he could.

Bree turned to Luca, and she lifted her eyebrow. "Well?"

"I'll be wherever Gabriel and you are," he assured her.

Bree nodded. "All right. Then, we'll all go to the ranch."

He heard the worry in her voice. Saw it even more on her face. And he knew something else. Bree hadn't been back there since her father's murder so this was going to be an emotional avalanche. Then again, the same could be true for Sandra.

Slater took out his phone. "I'll make arrangements for Gabriel's baby things to be moved to the ranch."

Luca would need to pack a few things as well, but before he could even consider a mental list, the door opened, and Ruston came in. His gaze fired around the room and landed on his mother. Unlike Joelle though, he didn't rush to pull her into his arms.

"Does she know anything about Dad's murder?" Ruston immediately wanted to know.

"No," Sandra said at the same moment Bree, Duncan and Joelle indicated with headshakes that she didn't.

The disappointment seemed to wash over Ruston. Obviously, he'd hoped his mother would be able to give them that closure.

"We have a lot to fill you in on," Bree said, going to Ruston and giving him a quick hug. Their gazes met. "There's trouble."

"Yeah, I heard. Are you all right?" Ruston asked.

"I've been better," Bree muttered. She took in a breath through her mouth. "I'm going to check on Gabriel."

Luca moved to go with her, but before they made it to the door, Duncan's phone rang. "It's Woodrow," he relayed, taking the call. He didn't put it on Speaker, but after just a couple of seconds, Luca knew Duncan was getting bad news.

"What?" Duncan asked the caller. "You're sure?" He paused and a moment later muttered, "Hell." Duncan scrubbed his hand over his face and repeated the single word of profanity when he ended the call.

"The local cops went to the cabin," Duncan explained, "but it was on fire. The fire department's on the way, but they won't get there in time."

Luca groaned, and it blended with the other negative reactions in the room. With the cabin gone, they'd lose any critical evidence that might have been inside.

"There's more," Duncan added a moment later. "Woodrow checked, and the cabin was on a two-year lease to someone local." His gaze met Bree's. "Dr. Nathan Bagley."

Chapter Six

Bree watched from the back seat of the cruiser as the house came into view. She'd never thought of her childhood home as cramped quarters, but it certainly felt like that now. Still, she knew this was their best chance at keeping everyone safe.

Well, hopefully it was.

Until they had answers about her mother's kidnapper and the shooter, they'd never actually be safe. And some of those answers might come from Nathan.

It twisted at her to think of her former boyfriend having a part in this. Or rather *maybe* having a part in it. Woodrow had verified that Nathan's name was indeed on the lease for the cabin, but so far, they hadn't been able to question Nathan about that since he was tied up with a patient in the ICU. Once that was finished though, he'd be given the message to contact Duncan right away.

Rather than wait at the sheriff's office for Nathan's response, Duncan had proceeded with the move to the ranch. No easy feat with plenty of moving parts. Literally. She watched as Duncan's cruiser stopped in front of the house, and Joelle, Slater, their mother and Duncan all got out. Izzie's nanny, Beatrice Walker, opened the door for them.

Luca pulled up behind Duncan's cruiser, and as Ruston and he had both done on the drive over, they glanced around, looking for threats. Bree did as well, but she didn't see anyone other than some ranch hands milling about.

Luca's gaze met hers in the rearview mirror, and she saw the concern in his eyes. She was no doubt sporting plenty of concern of her own, but somehow they had to make this situation work. They had to do whatever it took to keep Gabriel safe.

Even share a bedroom.

Yes, that was the plan. The house had five bedrooms, but one was being used as a nursery and another had been converted to the live-in nanny's quarters. Joelle and Duncan had the main bedroom attached to the nursery. That left two rooms, and since her mother would need one of them, Luca and Bree would be roommates along with Gabriel.

That way, they wouldn't have to be far from Gabriel.

Thankfully, Luca and she wouldn't actually have to share a bed. Ruston had come ahead of them to set up a cot for Luca and a portable crib for Gabriel. Since Ruston was recently married and had an adopted daughter, he wouldn't be staying at the ranch but rather at his own house on the outskirts of San Antonio. Slater, however, would and had claimed the sofa in the family room. Coral had offered to use a cot or sofa as well, but since the nanny hadn't actually been threatened, Bree had decided to give her some time off.

"Go ahead and get Gabriel out of the car seat," Luca instructed while they were still in the cruiser, and Bree understood why he wanted that. It would minimize their time outside.

She unbuckled a sleeping Gabriel who stirred when she picked him up. It was at least another hour before he would normally want another bottle, but with his schedule thrown off, Bree wasn't counting on much of anything being normal today.

Ruston and Luca gathered up the diaper bag and baby supplies they'd brought with them and got out of the cruiser. Bree steeled herself for the punch of grief from seeing the spot where her father had died. And it came. It came with a vengeance and momentarily robbed her of her breath. She didn't give in to it, though. Couldn't. Because even a slight hesitation could turn out to be a deadly mistake. Gathering Gabriel close to her, she hurried inside.

Joelle and Duncan had kept the furniture. In this part of the house anyway. But for the time being, they'd turned the large formal living and dining areas into a makeshift squad room. Someone had moved in small tables that were serving as desks, and there was even an incident board, and Slater was in the process of pinning up three photos.

Brighton's, Sandra's and Bree's.

There'd no doubt soon be other photos and notes, and the visuals might help them better connect all of this. Duncan was already in work mode, too. He was talking on the phone while he gathered up papers that were churning out from a printer. Luca set down the diaper bag to go help him with that while Ruston carried their things upstairs.

"I've put Luca, Gabriel and you in your old bedroom," Joelle explained to Bree. She was holding her infant daughter who was fussing and clearly ready to eat because she kept turning her mouth to Joelle's breast. "And Mom will be in Ruston's old room. Beatrice is up there now, getting everything ready."

Her mother actually seemed relieved about that. Maybe because Sandra had thought she might end up having to sleep in the room she'd shared with her husband.

"You holding up okay?" Joelle asked their mother.

Sandra's nod was shaky and not very convincing. "So much happening," she muttered.

Yes, and Bree figured this was just the start of it. There were five veteran cops in the house, and she knew Duncan was thorough. This would be a *leave no stones unturned* kind of investigation.

"I could cook if anyone's hungry," her mother volunteered.

"Food is on the way from the diner. Lots of it," Joelle clarified. She studied her mom's face for a moment. "But if you could put out paper plates and cups in the kitchen, that'd be great. Also, maybe make a fresh pot of coffee."

Sandra nodded and seemed eager for something to do. Or maybe she was just eager to get a moment to herself to try to wrap her mind around all of this. She certainly didn't waste any time heading toward the kitchen that had once been hers.

Though technically it still was.

Even though the ranch and the house had belonged to their father, Sandra was his primary beneficiary. Bree knew that since she'd been the one to prepare his will. There'd be legalities and such to work out later about that, but Bree didn't want to deal with it now.

"Once Duncan finishes with his latest call to Woodrow, he wants to do a briefing," Joelle added to Bree. The baby's fussing became more insistent. "But I might be late for that since I need to feed Izzie."

Joelle hurried upstairs, and Bree glanced down at Gabriel to see if she would need to feed him as well, but he'd gone back to sleep. So, she made her way to the sofa and watched Slater as he added Nathan's picture to the board. Slater looked back at her.

"You know him fairly well," Slater remarked. "Is Nathan capable of something like this?"

Bree took a couple of seconds, trying to picture Nathan orchestrating her mother's kidnapping and the shooting. Also arranging for Manny and her to be run off the road. She couldn't quite make herself see that.

"Nathan might have the means and opportunity," she said, "but I can't figure out a motive...unless maybe it all goes back to Brighton."

She realized Duncan had finished his call, and along with Slater, both of them were listening to her.

"As far as I know, Nathan has no connection to Brighton," Bree said. "But this is a small town so he likely knew her."

"Trust me, I'll be asking him about that when he's available," Duncan assured her. He walked to the board, and sighing, he put up a picture of what she realized was the burned-out cabin. "There's good news and bad news. I'll start with the good. Two people came forward and said they'd seen a woman driving a silver truck in the area of the cabin over the past couple of months. They're working with sketch artists right now."

That was indeed good news. Even if they didn't recognize the woman from the sketch, they could put it out to the media and maybe get some hits.

"Now, for the bad," Duncan went on. "The cabin's owner never met Nathan or the person posing as Nathan. The rental agreement was all done online and secured with a credit card that has Nathan's name on it, but it can't be traced to him. It's linked to an offshore account under the name of a dummy company."

Bree groaned. Not only was that sort of account hard to unravel, it also meant Nathan probably hadn't actually been involved. If he had, he wouldn't have used his real name. Well, unless this was some kind of reverse psychology deal.

"So, someone wanted to set Nathan up?" Bree asked.

Duncan shrugged. "Maybe. Or it's possible the kidnapper

just used his name. Maybe because the owner of the cabin wouldn't think twice about renting the place to a doctor."

Yes, that made sense as well. Then, if things fell apart— like the victim escaping—there'd be nothing to point back to the real culprit. Yes, they'd interview Nathan, but with no actual proof to link him to the crime, he wouldn't be arrested.

Duncan shifted his attention to Bree. "I need to interview Manny, but since the incident with his vehicle didn't happen in my jurisdiction, I can't force him to come here, not without a warrant. I thought maybe since he already knows you, you could talk to him."

"Of course," Bree readily agreed, already taking out her phone. Though she wasn't sure Manny would actually be willing to come to Saddle Ridge. Still, he might if he thought it would prevent him from being attacked again.

"See if Manny will agree to having the call on Speaker," Duncan added. "That way, I can hear if he has anything to say about his attack."

She nodded and made the call. However, it wasn't Manny who answered with a "Yeah?" It was a woman.

"Tara Adler?" Bree questioned.

"Yes," she verified, and she paused. "Who is this?"

"Bree McCullough. I spoke to you, remember? I asked you about Brighton Cooper."

"I remember." There was plenty of uneasiness in her voice. "Like I told you, I didn't actually know her. You're calling for Manny?" she quickly tacked onto that. "Because I can get him for you. He left his phone out here on the bar so that's why I answered it."

"Oh, I didn't realize you were open this early," she commented.

"We're not. I'm training some new waitstaff. Let me get Manny," she insisted.

Tara hadn't been exactly friendly when Bree had spoken to her before, but the woman seemed on edge now. Maybe because of Manny's attack? Tara might be worried she could be at risk, too. And she might be if this was indeed connected to Brighton's murder.

"It's that lawyer who asked about the dead woman," Bree heard Tara say, and several moments later, Manny came on the line.

"Bree," he said, sounding just as uneasy as Tara. "Did they catch the guy who tried to kill us?"

"No, not yet. Manny, I want to put this call on Speaker. Is that okay? I'm with Sheriff Duncan Holder and some of the other deputies from Saddle Ridge. They're all looking for the person who attacked us, and anything you can tell them might help find him or her."

"Sure," Manny said after a brief hesitation. "But I've already told the Austin cops everything I know."

"Yes, and they're looking, too," Bree assured him, switching to Speaker. "But the more people searching, the better."

Manny made a sound of agreement. "All right. But I don't know what more I can say. Someone in a silver truck rammed into me, that's it."

"This is Sheriff Holder," Duncan said. "And we believe we've found the truck. It's being examined now by CSIs to see if there are any paint flecks on it that match your vehicle."

"You have the driver?" Manny quickly asked. "You know who tried to kill me?"

"No, we don't have the driver, but we might have a description soon that'll help with that," Duncan explained. "What will help, too, is if we know why the attack happened."

"I don't know why." Manny's voice took on an agitated edge. "But since the same thing happened to Bree, I have to figure it's got something to do with all the questions she was asking about the dead woman."

Duncan didn't confirm that. "Who else knew Bree was asking questions about Brighton Cooper?"

Manny muttered some profanity. "Well, I didn't exactly keep it a secret. Anyone who works for me knew. And my financial guy, too, since I asked him to get the old credit card statements Bree wanted."

Bree sighed. She'd hoped that Manny and Tara had kept this close to the vest, which would have significantly narrowed their pool of suspects. But when Bree had spoken to them, she hadn't known there'd be attacks. If this was all connected, then someone had gotten spooked and wanted to silence Manny and her.

That, however, still didn't explain her mother's kidnapping.

"It's possible I'll soon have sketches of your attacker," Duncan told Manny. "I was hoping you'd be willing to come to Saddle Ridge and have a look at them and so I can get a statement about what happened to you. Then I'll compare it to Bree's statement to see if it can help with an arrest."

Manny certainly didn't jump to agree to that. "I guess," he finally said. "I can't get there today though, but I can come in the morning, maybe around ten. I should have those old credit card statements by then and can bring them with me."

"Good," Duncan said just as his phone dinged with a text. "We'll see you at the sheriff's office in the morning."

Bree thanked Manny, ended the call and kept her attention on Duncan while he read the text he'd just gotten.

"The CSIs have found no prints other than Sandra's in the silver truck," Duncan explained. "There was a box of plastic disposable gloves on the passenger seat."

So, the kidnapper had gloved up. That shouldn't have

surprised her, but Bree had hoped the woman had left some part of herself behind. And maybe she had. It would likely take the CSIs a while to go through the entire truck and then process whatever they found. Including those paint flecks that Woodrow and Carmen had seen.

Luca walked toward her and sank down on the sofa next to Bree. "It's been a hellish long day," he pointed out. "If you want to try to get some rest, I can watch Gabriel." He brushed his fingers over Gabriel's hair.

It had indeed been hellish, and since she was exhausted, Bree didn't want to turn down his offer, but she figured Luca was worn-out as well. Plus, she didn't want to pull him away from the investigation.

"I'll put Gabriel in his crib for the rest of his nap, and then I'll lie down," she said to offer a compromise, though both knew Gabriel might wake up the second she tried to put him down.

Luca sighed and went with her out of the room and toward the stairs. "Are you okay about being here with your mother?" he asked, keeping his voice barely above a whisper.

"Yes." That was the truth. Mostly, anyway.

"You believe everything she said about what happened to her?" he pressed.

She considered her answer while they went up the stairs. "I want to believe her. That's not the same thing."

His quick sound of agreement told her they were of a like mind on this. "Sandra had no obvious motive to kill her husband. No reported marital problems. No history of violent tendencies."

"All true. But that doesn't mean the unthinkable hadn't happened. An argument that went horribly wrong. An affair that none of us knew about." She stopped. "But that doesn't feel right."

Luca made another sound of agreement. "This is a wild what-if, but what if your dad learned your mother had something to do with Brighton's death? That could have spurred a violent confrontation."

She considered it and dismissed it just as Luca added, "But that doesn't feel right either. Your mother was looking out for Brighton. She was almost like another of her children."

Again, that was true, and hearing it spelled out like that helped convince Bree that her mom had been a victim in all of this. Just as her father. And it was connected. It had to be. She just didn't know how yet.

Luca and she were halfway up the stairs when she heard a flurry of movement on the ground floor. She turned to see Duncan and Slater moving fast toward the front door.

"What's wrong?" Luca asked.

"One of the hands alerted me that Nathan just drove up," Duncan explained.

Bree's first reaction was to groan. Or curse. She was beyond exhausted, but Duncan needed to question Nathan about the lease on the burned-out cabin. She hadn't figured though that the interview would happen here but rather over the phone or at the sheriff's office. Still, since he was here, she'd be able to listen while he gave his statement.

The nanny, Beatrice, appeared at the top of the stairs, and she'd obviously heard they had a visitor. "Joelle and your mom are with Izzie so I can take Gabriel if you like," she offered.

Bree glanced down at her sleeping baby and then over her shoulder out the sidelight windows of the front door. Nathan was pulling his car to a stop in the driveway.

"Yes, thank you," Bree said, and she eased Gabriel into the nanny's arms.

"You don't have to deal with Nathan," Luca let Bree know after Beatrice had taken Gabriel upstairs.

Bree nodded. "But I might be able to tell if he's lying." Of course, that was a long shot. She certainly hadn't picked up on any overly possessive behavior until it'd started to happen.

"Still," Luca said, "you don't have to put yourself through this."

"I never had sex with him," she blurted out and then immediately wanted to take it back. Good grief. Luca didn't need to know that.

Luca didn't seem pleased. Or surprised. Then again, Luca and she had dated for nearly four months before they'd had sex the first time. Nathan and she had only gone out for a couple of weeks.

"I think that's why his possessiveness was such a shock," she went on. Since she'd launched into this uncomfortable subject, she might as well get some things clear. "We weren't lovers, and I certainly hadn't made any kind of commitment to him. I never mentioned anything about being exclusive. I was just testing the waters, that's all."

He nodded. "That happened when I was dating Shona Sullivan. And, yes, I know your dating Nathan had nothing to do with that," he was quick to add. Maybe because he saw the flash of annoyance in her eyes. "I mentioned it because of the timing. Nathan might have thought Shona and I were in a 'together forever' kind of deal, so that could have been why he thought he had a clear path to a long-term relationship with you."

The annoyance vanished because Luca was right. Everyone knew Luca and she were an item. Heck, they even thought it now. Bree could see the *aha* look in people's eyes now that Luca and she had a child together.

She pushed all that aside for now when Nathan knocked at

the door, and Duncan opened it. "I got your message that you needed to talk to me right away," Nathan said. "I went by the sheriff's office, but the dispatcher told me you were home."

Nathan looked past Duncan, his gaze settling on Bree as she came down the stairs.

"Are you hurting?" Nathan asked her. "Is that why Duncan called me?"

"This isn't about anything medical," Duncan was quick to say. "Come in." He stepped back, his cop's gaze focused on Nathan as he came in. Like Luca and Slater, Duncan was probably checking to see if there were any signs Nathan was about to try to attack them.

Bree certainly didn't see anything like that. If she had to put a label on his expression and body language, it'd be moony-eyed. Nathan always managed to seem as if she held his heart in her hands. She definitely didn't want that or the look he was giving her.

"Are you sure you're all right?" Nathan asked her. "I called the pharmacy on the way over, and they said you hadn't filled the prescription I wrote you for the pain meds."

She certainly hadn't forgotten about the pain but didn't intend to fill the prescription. She didn't want her mind to be numbed. "I'll take something 'over the counter,'" she settled for saying.

Nathan opened his mouth, probably to advise her to get the prescription, but Duncan motioned toward the living room. "In here. Slater, will you turn the board around while we talk to Nathan?"

Slater nodded, hurried ahead of them, and she heard the movement as Slater did as Duncan asked. There wasn't a lot on the board at the moment, but Duncan still probably didn't want to display an investigative road map to someone who was still technically a suspect.

"Is this about Bree's accident?" Nathan asked, looking and sounding very concerned.

"Not exactly," Duncan said once they were in the living room. "I need to ask you some questions, but I'm going to read you your rights first. It's just a formality," he insisted when Nathan snapped back his shoulders. He didn't give Nathan a chance to voice his defensiveness. Duncan just proceeded to Mirandize him.

"You can't possibly think I'd have something to do with Bree's car accident," Nathan said when Duncan had finished.

"Are you familiar with a hunting cabin about twenty-five miles from here?" Duncan asked, obviously not addressing Nathan's comment. Duncan then provided the exact address.

Nathan's forehead bunched up. "No. I don't hunt, so I don't usually go to places like that. Why?"

"Because it was leased in your name," Duncan supplied while he watched for Nathan's reaction. Bree, Luca and Slater did the same.

"What?" Nathan snapped. He reached into his pocket, causing Duncan, Luca and Slater to all put their hands over their weapons.

Nathan froze, and his eyes widened. "Obviously, you think I've done something wrong. I haven't," he assured them. "If someone used my name to lease the cabin, then my bank account has been hacked or something. I was just going to take out my phone and see if any money was missing."

"Do that," Duncan instructed, but he didn't take his hand from his gun until he saw for certain that Nathan was pulling out a phone.

Nathan muttered something under his breath and started typing in something on the app he pulled up. It took him at least a minute before he shook his head. "No. There are no missing funds, no fraudulent charges on my credit card. Who said I leased that cabin?"

"The owner," Duncan answered. "Someone used a credit card in your name to secure it and paid for the lease."

Nathan cursed. "Well, it sure as hell wasn't me. Someone must have stolen my identity." He groaned, cursed again. "I need to report that. Do you investigate it or is that something my bank does?"

"We'll be investigating it," Duncan said, tipping his head to Slater and then Luca.

Judging from the sudden tight set of his mouth, Nathan wasn't a fan of having Luca dig into his financials. "I'm guessing something illegal happened at this cabin?" Nathan snarled.

"We're investigating that, too, but yes, something happened there," Duncan verified. He didn't add any specifics though. "We're also looking at a Ford F-150 silver truck that was involved in several incidents. Have you ever owned or driven a vehicle like that?"

"No. I drive an Audi." Nathan looked at her again. "Bree, what's going on?" he asked, but he didn't wait for her to respond. "Certainly, you've told them I haven't done anything wrong."

She hadn't meant to give him a flat look but it came away. After all, Nathan had stalked her. Nathan not only noticed her expression, he also responded. His mouth tightened. His eyes narrowed. And he aimed a glare at Luca.

"I don't appreciate you trying to turn Bree against me," Nathan said. "If you're jealous of her and me—"

"I'm not," Luca interrupted and stepped to Bree's side. "And Bree can make up her mind for herself how she feels about you."

Nathan's scowl stayed in place, but it was obvious he didn't have a good comeback for that. "All right," Nathan said through clenched teeth, indicating that things were far from all right. His expression softened a bit when he shifted back to her. "Bree, if you need me for anything, you have my number. And remember, I care about you. I wouldn't do anything to hurt you."

He reached out as if he might try to hug her, but Bree stepped back and landed right against Luca. The impact put her off balance just enough that Luca's arms came around to steady her.

That intensified Nathan's glare. "Remember what I said," he muttered. "I care about you."

With that, Nathan walked out. Or rather, he stormed out. And Bree found herself releasing the breath that she'd been holding. She hated that Nathan could still annoy her like this. Hated, too, that it had felt so reassuring when she'd landed in Luca's arms. She eased away from him and stood on her own two feet.

"I swear, I've told Nathan many times that nothing will ever happen between him and me," she muttered. "And, no, I don't need to do a restraining order," she added to Slater. "Nathan hasn't called or texted me in months."

But she was worried that Nathan would use her injury and this interrogation to try to wheedle himself into her life again.

"I plan on doing a deep background check on Nathan," Luca said, going to the front door to lock it. "It's possible he has a history of stalking women. Maybe other things, too, that he doesn't want us to know about."

"You believe he could have been the one who leased that cabin?" Duncan asked.

Luca shrugged. "On the surface it wouldn't be the smartest move to use his own name. But criminals aren't always smart. And sometimes that sort of move might have us thinking he's not guilty."

That was true, and Bree tried to play out that scenario. "Even before I went out with Nathan, he was obsessed with me. I didn't see that until afterwards," she added. "But I know now, it's an obsession. It might be far-fetched, but maybe he kidnapped Mom to try to punish me."

"Or maybe he hoped you'd turn to him while you were vulnerable and grieving," Slater supplied.

That settled like a fist of ice in her stomach. Because it didn't seem so far-fetched at all.

"I'll do that deep background check," Luca repeated. He looked at her. "You want to try to get some rest now?"

She would have definitely agreed to that, but Duncan's phone dinged again. "It's Woodrow," he said, glancing at the screen. "The artist just finished with the first sketch of the woman seen driving the silver truck." He looked at it, shook his head and then turned his phone for them to see. "I don't know her."

Bree went closer. She didn't get an immediate jolt of recognition, but it came the longer she studied the image. "I think I might know who that is," she muttered. "She looks like the bartender at the Hush, Hush bar. I think that's Tara Adler."

Duncan, Slater and Luca all exchanged glances. "Do you have her number?" Duncan asked.

She shook her head. "I can call Manny and ask to speak to her."

"Do that," Duncan said. "I want to see if I can get Tara to come in with him tomorrow morning for an interview."

Bree called Manny and put it on Speaker. She thought Tara might answer again, but this time it was Manny.

"This is Sheriff Holder again," Duncan said. "I'd like to speak to Tara Adler."

"Tara?" Manny questioned. "Why?"

"It's routine," Duncan answered, which, of course, wasn't an actual answer at all. "May I speak to her?"

"You could if she was here," Manny grumbled. "Right after I got off the phone with you, Tara claimed she was sick and had to leave."

Bree couldn't believe that it was a coincidence. Was Tara really the one behind her mother's kidnapping and the attacks? If so, this had to be connected to Brighton's murder. And maybe her father's.

"She didn't look sick to me," Manny added in a snarl. "You want her number so you can talk to her?"

"Yes, I do," Duncan verified.

Once Manny had given them the number, Bree ended the call with him, and Duncan used his own phone to call Tara. Or rather, to try to call her. Bree's stomach sank when she heard the recorded message that she didn't want to hear.

Tara's phone had been disconnected.

Chapter Seven

Luca hurried in the shower. Along with not wanting to hog the bathroom, he also didn't want to leave Bree and Gabriel alone for long. Added to that, there was plenty of work to do, and a long shower was a luxury he couldn't afford.

He turned off the water and listened to make sure everything was well in the adjoining bedroom. The bedroom he'd shared with Bree and their son the night before and would continue to share as long as there was a potential threat. He could hear Bree murmuring something to Gabriel, but that was it. No sounds of distress or phone conversations that might or might not deliver more bad news.

So far, the bad news was winning out over the good. There was no sign of the gunman who'd fired those shots into Bree's barn. No sign of Tara either, which meant they couldn't question her about the sketch that matched her description. Since Manny didn't have any idea where she was either, it could mean Tara had gone on the run. It was possible she was the one who'd held Sandra captive, but it could also point to Tara meeting with foul play.

When Duncan had shown Sandra a photo of Tara, Sandra had said she recognized her from the Hush, Hush, but that she had no idea if Tara had been the one who'd kidnapped her. That wasn't much of a surprise since Sandra had been adamant about not knowing who'd been responsible for taking her.

The bad news had continued on the forensic side of the investigation as well. Other than the gloves and Sandra's prints, the CSIs hadn't found anything in the silver truck. Manny might be able to help with that though during his interview if he could tell them anything else about the truck or the driver. Especially if the driver could possibly be Tara.

There had been some good news though in the burned-out cabin. No DNA results yet, but there was evidence to support Sandra's account of the boarded-up window and multiple locks on the interior door where she'd been held. That was a huge validation for Bree's mother.

And a relief.

There were enough unknowns in this investigation without adding Sandra to the mix. Now, she could be ruled out as a suspect, and they could focus on Tara. Nathan, too, since Luca was keeping him on the list. Maybe that had more to do with Nathan's history with Bree, but Luca wasn't dismissing Nathan's possible involvement in all of this.

Luca dressed in the clean jeans and shirt he'd had brought to the ranch, and he went into the bedroom to find Bree sitting with a very alert Gabriel who'd obviously just finished a bottle. Bree had the baby against her chest and shoulder and was patting his back, no doubt to get him to burp.

Bree's gaze immediately went to Luca's, and he saw the tension in every bit of her expression. It was understandable and wouldn't be going away until they had a suspect in custody.

Or as long as they had to share such close quarters.

That was definitely causing her some stress. Him, too. They'd been on-and-off lovers for a long time now. Over a decade. His body couldn't forget that kind of history and neither could Luca. He still wanted Bree. Still cared deeply for her. And that must have shown on his face.

"It's not you," she muttered. Then, she shook her head. "I mean, you're not the reason I get this slam of memories about my dad."

He was glad to hear that, but there was a flip side to this particular coin. "You get them though," he said.

She nodded. "So do you."

Luca had to go with a nod as well and admit it was true. In fact, he'd had a dream about her father's murder in the handful of hours he'd managed to sleep. Judging from some of the things Bree had muttered in the night, she'd done some dreaming as well.

He wanted to say more. A whole lot more about hoping that one day they could look at each other and not see the past. But the sound of an approaching vehicle had him going to the window.

"It's Coral," he relayed to her.

Luca sighed. "If you're still going to the sheriff's office for Manny's interview, we'll have to leave soon."

He already knew though that Bree hadn't changed her mind about this. If she had, she would have already called Coral to cancel. But like him, Bree wanted to be at the sheriff's office to hear what Manny had to say. Bree wouldn't actually be in the interview room though. Duncan had made an exception when they'd questioned Sandra, but with Manny, they had to play by the rules.

Bree stood, giving Gabriel a kiss before she handed the baby to Luca so he could do the same. They made their way downstairs where Duncan was already letting Coral into the house. Coral immediately went to Bree and hugged her.

"I've been so worried about you," Coral said, but she

conjured up a smile when she looked at Gabriel. "And I've missed this little man. How is everything?" she asked.

"The investigation's still in progress," Bree said. It was the standard response cops often doled out, but in this case, it was the truth. And about all that could be said since they couldn't voice suspicions about a local doctor. Not without proof anyway, and at the moment, they didn't have that.

Joelle, Sandra, Slater and Ruston were all downstairs, and Sandra was holding Izzie. Woodrow was there, too, and he was no doubt waiting to make the drive with them to the sheriff's office.

"I made Mom an appointment to see her doctor at the hospital clinic," Joelle volunteered. "I talked to him, and he wants to run some labs on her just to make sure she's okay."

Luca and Bree both made quick sounds of agreement. Not Sandra though. She was obviously reluctant.

"Woodrow can stay with Sandra at the hospital, and Carmen will meet them there," Duncan explained, glancing at Luca and Bree. "Then, the three of us can go to the sheriff's office."

It'd be a snug fit in the cruiser with five people, but it was better than making two trips. They were leaving backup at home with the babies, too, since Joelle, Slater and Ruston would be staying behind.

Luca wished they'd had a dozen cops available to guard his son and Izzie. Not enough manpower for that, but the ranch hands had been put on alert to keep an eye out for anything suspicious.

Sandra handed Izzie back to Joelle and kissed Gabriel as Luca was passing the baby to Coral. Bree's mother patted Luca's arm in a gesture she had done many times before she went missing. He muttered a thanks. Then silently said a prayer that they'd make this trip without incident. That included nothing going wrong at the ranch, either.

Duncan said his goodbyes to Joelle and his daughter, and he quickly got them out of the house and into the cruiser parked at the foot of the porch steps. Sandra, Luca and Bree went in the back seat with Bree in the middle. Duncan took the wheel with Woodrow at shotgun.

"I asked Austin PD to go ahead and put out an APB for Tara," Duncan explained once they were on the road. "They'll check with her family and friends, too."

If the woman had truly gone on the run, she might not go to places where she'd readily be found. But what had spooked her? Had it simply been Bree's phone call, or had something else alerted her? Luca was hoping Manny might be able to provide some insight.

All five of them kept watch as Duncan made the short drive to the hospital where Carmen was indeed waiting for them, so Woodrow and Sandra got out. Then, Duncan continued up the street to the sheriff's office. They breathed a whole lot easier once they had made it to the private entrance outside Duncan's office.

The moment they stepped in, Luca saw the man in the small waiting area. When he immediately stood, Luca slid his hand over his gun until he got a good look at the guy's face and realized it was Manny. Luca recognized him from his driver's license photo and the background info he'd accessed.

Tall and with a lanky build, Manny was only thirty-three which made him the same age as Luca. He'd owned the Hush, Hush for seven years, since the death of his father. He didn't exactly look the part of a business owner though, more of a rocker with his blond hair that fell past his shoulders. His faded, ripped jeans and plain black tee had that rocker vibe as well.

There were two deputies in the squad room, Sonya Grover and Ronnie Bishop, and even though they were both on their computers, Luca could tell they were also keeping an eye on Manny.

"He's already gone through the metal detector," Ronnie volunteered. "And he consented to a search. He's not armed."

Good. Though it wouldn't have been very smart for Manny to come in here armed.

"I'm early," Manny muttered. He also seemed nervous and was rubbing his hands down the sides of his jeans. "Bree," he greeted. "Please tell me you've found Tara and the person who tried to kill us."

She muttered an "I'm sorry" and shook her head. Luca noticed her wince a little from the movement. She hadn't said anything about being in pain, but he figured the stitches had to hurt.

"This is Sheriff Holder and Deputy Vanetti," she explained. "They'll be conducting the interview."

"And you'll be there, too, right?" Manny asked.

"No—" she started.

"But I want you there," Manny insisted, glancing at Luca and Duncan to plead his case. "Bree's the only one who knows what I'm going through right now. Someone tried to kill us," he spelled out.

"Yes, but I'm not a cop," she reminded him.

"You're a lawyer," Manny argued. "And I can have a lawyer with me, right?"

Bree sighed. "I can't be your lawyer."

Because it would possibly be a conflict of interest, but she didn't spell that out. No need to make Manny defensive when they brought up the possibility that he could have faked his attack and could be the person responsible for this current nightmare. That was a long shot, but it was still on the radar.

Manny glanced around as if trying to figure out what to do. His nerves seemed to be building.

"Tell you what," Duncan said. "Why don't we talk here in my office for now and Bree can stay with us. I'll still Mirandize you," Duncan tacked onto that. "It's procedure," he said when Manny's eyes widened, and he started shaking his head. "When we catch the person who tried to run you off the road, we want to be able to use anything you say to help with the prosecution. If your statement's official, then it makes things easier."

That was all true, but Luca knew there was another reason for the Miranda. If Manny said anything incriminating, Duncan would be able to use it without Manny claiming he hadn't been read his rights.

Duncan waited for Manny to nod before he motioned for Manny to come into his office. When all four of them were inside and seated, Duncan shut the door and Mirandized him.

"I'm going to record this," Duncan continued, turning on the recorder and stating the time, date and attendees. "Now, Manny, I want you to tell us what happened yesterday when you were driving."

Manny glanced at Bree, and even though there was still plenty of uneasiness in his expression, he began. "Like I told Bree and the other cops, I was driving from my house into Austin so I could meet with a supplier. A big silver truck came up from behind and rammed into me. The driver tried to push me off the road. I think he was trying to kill me," Manny added in a hoarse mutter.

"And from what I understand, you didn't get the license plate?" Duncan asked.

Manny shook his head. "I didn't even think to do that. I was just so shocked. And I didn't think to try to follow the truck or anything."

"Who knew you'd be traveling on that road at that particular time?" Duncan pressed.

"Lots of people." Manny shrugged. "I live alone, but I had the appointment on my big wall calendar in my office, so anyone who came in there could have seen it."

"Tara would have known?" Luca asked.

Manny gave another nod, and the sigh that came from his throat was hoarse and filled with emotion. "You think she could have done this. You think that's why she disappeared. But why?" Manny asked.

"Why do you think she would have done that?" Luca countered.

"I don't know. But if she did it, it must have something to do with Bree since the same thing happened to her." Manny stopped again, groaned. "It's just hard for me to believe Tara would try to scare us. Or kill us. But if she did, it could be connected to the questions Bree was asking about that murdered woman. I can't remember her name," he said to Bree.

"Brighton Cooper," Bree supplied. "I found out Brighton had gone to the Hush, Hush shortly before she was killed—"

"Yes," Manny interrupted, and he reached into his pocket to take out a memory stick. "You wanted the old credit card receipts, and I finally got them from my finance guy. I didn't have your email address so I put them on this."

Bree didn't take the drive though. "Why don't we go ahead and enter this into evidence?" she suggested. "To preserve the chain of custody."

Duncan was already moving to do just that. He took out an evidence bag from his desk, dropped in the memory stick and then sealed and labeled it. Luca knew they'd soon be going through that.

"Did you look at the receipts?" Bree asked Manny.

"I glanced through them. You know, just to see if anything

jumped out at me. It didn't. We had a DJ in for the nights you asked about so business was good. Lots of customers, lots of credit card charges. The cash receipts are on there, too, but obviously there aren't names on those."

If Brighton's killer had been there that night—and that was a big *if*—it was possible one of the cash charges might belong to him or her. But Brighton's murder didn't seem planned so maybe her killer's name was indeed on those receipts.

"Look, is there any way to keep me out of all of this?" Manny asked. "I mean, I know it's important to find who did that to the woman, but I don't want to get mixed up in it. I want to be able to drive to work without someone trying to kill me."

Duncan gave a sigh of his own. "Your name's already connected to this," he said. "Of course, I won't advertise that you came in today for an interview, but someone might find out about it." He tipped his head to the bag. "Especially if there's anything on here to link to a killer."

Manny groaned and pressed his hands against the sides of his head. He stared down into his lap, muttering some profanity.

"Did you get the sense that anyone followed you here today?" Duncan asked.

"No," Manny said.

Duncan continued to press. "How about any unusual visitors at the bar?"

That got another "no" from Manny. "The cops said they could do patrols on the road near my house, but that won't stop a killer. Do you think I should hire a bodyguard?"

"If that'll make you feel safer, then do it," Duncan agreed. "It's probably a good idea not to put your appointments on your wall calendar for a while. Also, shake up your routines if possible. Do you have a security system for your house?"

Manny nodded, but then he glanced at the large window that looked out onto the squad room and reception. All of them did. Because the front door opened, and they saw a woman come in.

Tara.

Luca was sure of it, and she did indeed bear a striking resemblance to the sketch. She seemed just as nervous as Manny and was disheveled, too, in her wrinkled gray shirt and jeans. She'd scooped back her long brown hair into a ponytail, but there were just as many strands pulled back as were falling onto her shoulders.

Both Sonya and Ronnie were on their feet now, and Sonya started toward their visitor.

"Tara," Manny muttered. He walked toward her as well. Then, he stopped. Probably because he remembered Tara might have been the one who'd nearly run him off the road.

"Wait here, Manny," Duncan instructed, and he went into the squad room. So did Bree and Luca. "Tara Adler?" he asked.

She nodded. "I'm looking for Bree McCullough..." Her words trailed off when she saw Manny. "And you," she muttered. "Manny, I think someone's trying to kill me." With that, Tara broke into a sob.

Despite Duncan's warning for Manny to stay put, the bar owner came out into the squad room, but Duncan stepped in front of him. Just as Luca had done to Bree.

"Tara, I want you to go through the metal detector," Duncan instructed.

She looked more than a little startled at the request, but she complied. No alarms went off, and when Sonya searched Tara's purse, she didn't find anything.

"I'll call to have the APB dropped," Sonya said, returning to her desk.

Volleying glances at Bree and Manny, Tara made her way through the squad room toward Luca, Duncan, Manny and Bree. "Why are you here?" she asked Manny. "Did someone try to run you off the road again?"

He shook his head. "The sheriff wanted to talk to me... about you, among other things. Where the hell have you been?"

Duncan motioned for her to hold back on answering that, and as he'd done with Manny, he read Tara her rights.

"I'm a suspect?" Tara blurted once he was finished. She frantically shook her head. "I'm a victim. Someone followed my car this morning. Not a silver truck," she added. "This was a black one."

Duncan led her into his office. "Did you report it?"

"No." Tara suddenly seemed flustered. Or else she was pretending to be anyway. She sank down into a chair in Duncan's office. "I thought someone was following me," she clarified, "but I'm not sure. I'm hoping I'm wrong. Am I wrong?" she pleaded.

"I don't know," Duncan answered. "Now, tell me why you're here and where you've been for the past eighteen hours."

Tara certainly didn't launch into an explanation, but she handed Duncan her phone and pointed to a text from an unknown number. "I got this yesterday, right after Bree talked to Manny."

"'Talk and you die,'" he said, reading the text out loud.

"Did you report this?" Duncan repeated.

Tara shook her head. "I was terrified," she insisted. "And I panicked. My instincts were to run, to get away from the bar. I didn't want to end up like that dead woman Bree asked about, or have her killer track my phone, so I took out the SIM card."

That explained why the cops hadn't been able to find her, but most people wouldn't have thought to do something like that. Especially if they were in a panic as Tara had claimed.

"It's the woman's killer who wants us dead, right?" Tara asked. "He wants to silence us all for good."

Bree made a sound that could have meant anything. Obviously, she wasn't going to volunteer that to Tara.

"Sonya," Duncan called out to the deputy. "I need phone records for this number. See if you can find out who sent that text." He passed Tara's phone to Sonya and then turned his attention back to Tara. "We're looking into connections between the recent attacks and the murder of Brighton Cooper," Duncan said. "Did you know her?"

"No," Tara was quick to say. "I told Bree I didn't remember her, but after I got to thinking about it, I think I recall her coming into the bar. *Think*," she emphasized, "but I'm not positive."

Luca didn't read much into that. Witnesses often recalled things long after being questioned.

"And you didn't know Brighton either?" Duncan pressed, shifting his attention to Manny.

"No." Manny's response was equally fast.

Duncan drew in a breath as if that wasn't the response he wanted. "Well, we know Brighton was in the Hush, Hush shortly before her murder."

"And that's why her killer is coming after us," Tara concluded.

"Maybe," Duncan muttered. "Where did you go after you got that text?"

It took Tara a couple of seconds to shift gears in the conversation. "Home first. To my apartment. I packed a bag, grabbed the emergency cash I keep on hand and then went to a motel. I put the SIM card back in my phone this morning so I could call Manny and ask him what I should do," Tara went on. "It went straight to voicemail so I called the bar. Otto answered, and he said he heard Manny talking on the phone about coming to Saddle Ridge for an interview. So, I came here, too."

"Otto?" Duncan questioned.

"Otto Gunther," Manny supplied. "He's the janitor."

Luca immediately took out his phone to do a quick run on the man. The guy was seventy-three and had no criminal history. That didn't exclude him from being a killer though, so Luca requested a background check. While he was at it, he ordered that for all of the Hush, Hush employees.

"You can't think Otto would try to run someone off the road," Manny protested. "He's a good man. He'd give you the shirt off his back, which is why I've kept him on long after normal retirement age. He loves his job, and the rest of the staff love having him around."

"Manny's right," Tara piped in.

Duncan didn't address their comments. He opened a folder on his desk and took a printed copy of the drawing that the sketch artist had done. "This woman was seen driving the silver truck that was involved in the incidents with both Bree and you," he said to Manny.

Manny's eyes widened, and he turned to Tara. "That looks like you."

Tara fixed her gaze on the drawing, but she was also shaking her head. "It's not. There must be a mistake. I've never driven a silver truck, and I wouldn't try to run anyone off the road."

"Then why does that look so much like you?" Duncan asked, going full cop mode. The muscles in his face had tightened, and his eyes were narrowed.

"I don't know..." Her denial trailed off, and her gaze shot to Duncan. "Is it my sister, Shannon?"

The moment she asked the question, Luca started the background check on Tara's sister. He silently cursed when Shannon's DMV photo came up because while she wasn't Tara's twin, the two women did look a great deal alike.

Luca showed the photo to Duncan, and Luca was betting he did some silent cursing as well. They'd believed Tara was their suspect, but now that was in serious doubt.

"Where's your sister?" Duncan demanded.

"I'm not sure. We've lost contact," Tara said. She paused, then sighed. "Look, Shannon's a trouble magnet. Always getting involved with the wrong guy. Always in and out of messes. I washed my hands of her about a year ago. Last I heard, she was seeing some lowlife from Bulverde."

The burned-out cabin was near that particular small town.

"You know this lowlife's name?" Duncan pressed.

"No. I didn't want to know," she insisted. "Like I said, I'd washed my hands of her." She stopped again, and this time she groaned. "Oh, God. Is Shannon the one who sent me that text? Is she the one who tried to kill Manny and Bree?"

Luca figured that fell into the "to be determined" category. "Do you have your sister's phone number?" Luca asked.

Tara shook her head again. "She never had the money for a good phone so she always used cheap disposable ones."

Burners. Which would be next to impossible to trace.

But if Shannon was indeed behind this, then she probably hadn't been acting alone. Her low-life boyfriend would also need to be questioned.

"Where were you both yesterday morning starting at nine and going past noon?" Duncan asked, and Luca knew Duncan was trying to see if either had alibis for the incident with Bree and the shooting.

"I was home," Manny said. "Well, I was after I reported the silver truck to the cops. Why?"

Duncan ignored the question and turned to Tara. "And where were you?"

"At my apartment," Tara answered.

"Alone?" Duncan pressed, glancing at both of them.

Manny and Tara nodded.

"Did you see or speak to anyone during that time?" Duncan continued.

"No," Tara was the first to say, and then Manny repeated it. Manny also repeated his, "Why?"

Before Duncan could answer, there was a knock on the side door of the office. "It's me," Woodrow announced. "Sandra's appointment was quick so I brought her back here."

Duncan unlocked and opened the door. He got Sandra in as quickly as possible.

"The doctor did some blood tests," Sandra said. "And I should have the results soon." She stopped when she glanced at the others in the room. "Oh, I'm sorry, I'm interrupting—"

Sandra gasped when her attention landed on Manny.

"It's you," Sandra muttered, and the color drained from her face.

"You know Manny?" Duncan was quick to ask.

Sandra nodded. "He's the man who was having an affair with Brighton." She swallowed hard. "I think he might have been the one to kill her."

Chapter Eight

Bree certainly hadn't expected her mother to say what she had. And apparently neither had anyone else in Duncan's office.

Especially Manny.

He jumped to his feet, and for a moment Bree thought he might try to run, but Luca and Duncan prevented that. Duncan, by stepping in front of the side door, and Luca by blocking the path toward the squad room. Manny cursed and dropped back down into the chair.

"It's not what you think," he insisted, aiming that at Luca and Duncan. "I didn't kill Brighton. I've never killed anyone."

"But you had an affair with her?" Duncan asked. "And you lied about it during an official interview?"

Tara, who was now also standing, spoke before Manny could respond. "You had an affair with her?" She was clearly upset.

Jealous, maybe?

It was hard for Bree to tell, but it seemed to her that Manny wasn't the only one who'd lied.

"You said you didn't know Brighton either," Bree pointed out to Tara.

Tara opened her mouth, closed it and then huffed. "I didn't know her name. But when you asked about her, I went to

Manny to see if he knew her. He said he didn't," she practically spat out.

Oh, yes. Jealousy. And Duncan picked up on it. "I take it Manny and you had a personal relationship around this time?" he asked Tara.

Again, she hesitated, and it was Manny who answered. "Not a relationship," he insisted. "We had sex, and yes, I know that was stupid since I'm her boss."

"It was more than sex," Tara muttered, but then she seemed to freeze. Maybe because she'd realized she was spelling out a motive for killing Brighton. "Manny and I were together for about six months, and we agreed to end things."

"I broke things off with you," Manny corrected. "And it wasn't because I was having an affair with another woman," he was quick to add. "I ended things with Tara before I started seeing Brighton."

Duncan huffed, and glared at Manny. "I could charge you with lying to a police officer. And I still might do that if you don't tell me everything about Brighton and how her murder connects to what's going on now."

Manny got that panicked look again, and he dragged in some quick breaths. So quick that Bree thought he might hyperventilate. Duncan must have also thought that was a possibility because he got the man a bottle of water from the small fridge behind his desk.

"Talk," Duncan demanded after Manny had taken some long drinks. "Start with your affair with Brighton."

Manny nodded. "Like I said, I was having sex with Tara, but it was causing the other waitstaff to gossip. It was hurting morale so I ended things. About a week or so later, Brighton came into the bar, and we started talking. That led to us seeing each other. Not for long," he quickly tacked on to that. "And I don't think it was exclusive for her."

"Brighton was involved with someone else?" Luca pressed.

"I don't know for sure, but Brighton would get texts when we were out together, and I think the texts were from another man. It was just a feeling I got. She never confirmed it."

"How long were the two of you involved?" Duncan asked.

"Only about a month." Manny shut his eyes for a moment. "I'd made dinner reservations at a place in Austin, and Brighton didn't show. She didn't call or text so I figured she was ghosting me."

"And you didn't call or text her?" Duncan wanted to know.

He shook his head. "I just assumed she was done with me." Manny paused again. "Then, about two weeks later, I saw something online about her being murdered. The cops were asking anyone to come forward with information, but I didn't know anything."

"You should have let the cops decide that," Duncan snarled. "You should have let us know about the relationship."

"I didn't kill her," Manny snarled right back. "And I didn't want to get caught up in an investigation."

Bingo. That was the bottom line, and Bree had to wonder if he hadn't wanted to be involved because he'd killed Brighton and didn't want to be on the police's radar. But he'd come on their radar when she had spotted Brighton on the video outside the bar.

Manny looked at Sandra. "How'd you know I was involved with Brighton? Did she tell you or something?"

Sandra took in some deep breaths as well. "Brighton's mother and I were best friends, and after she died, I tried to keep an eye on Brighton. I was at her apartment and saw a photo of the two of you on her phone. I asked who you were, but she dodged the question. Why would she do that?"

"Well, it wasn't because she was afraid I was going to kill

her," Manny protested. "Maybe she just didn't want to talk to you about her personal life."

"Possibly," Sandra admitted. "During that visit with Brighton, she mentioned she'd been going to some interesting bars in Austin. Hush, Hush was one of them, but she named a couple of others. Then, a week or so later when I went to visit her, she was crying. Sobbing, really. And again, she wouldn't get into specifics, but I think she was having trouble with a man she'd been seeing."

"Again, it wasn't me," Manny insisted. "Brighton and I didn't have that kind of relationship. It was casual, barely more than friends with benefits."

Of course, they had no proof that was true. At least, Bree didn't have proof. Except...

"If it was so casual, then why would Brighton have a picture of the two of you on her phone?" Bree asked.

He leveled his gaze on her. "Who knows? Maybe she liked the way she looked in it, or, hell, maybe she was just in the mood for taking a picture and then didn't bother to delete it. There's all kinds of reasons for pictures to be on someone's phone."

True, but the photo could be an indicator that the relationship wasn't as casual as Manny was making it out to be.

Bree turned to her mother. "You went to the Hush, Hush shortly before Brighton was killed. Did you hear anything about her involvement with Manny then?"

"No," Sandra said. "And I didn't see Manny either. I went to try to figure out what was going on with Brighton, but then that fight started, and I got spooked. I left." Her mouth trembled. "If I'd stayed, I might have figured out who'd wanted to hurt her." She looked at Manny. "I didn't know who you were, so I couldn't give your name to the police during the investigation."

Manny jumped to his feet again. "This inquisition is over," he snarled to Duncan. "If you want to talk to me again, go through my lawyer. Am I free to go, or do you plan on arresting me right now?"

Duncan took his time, though Bree knew what his answer was likely to be. There wasn't enough evidence to arrest Manny. Yes, he'd lied, and Duncan could charge him with that, but it was probably best if Duncan used that for leverage to bring Manny back in if anything else did come to light.

"You can go," Duncan finally said. "For now," he immediately tacked onto that.

Manny stormed out, and Tara kept her eyes on him until he was out the door. "He wouldn't have killed Brighton," she muttered.

"You're certain of that?" Duncan challenged.

Tara didn't issue a quick, resounding yes. In fact, she didn't verify that at all. She merely shrugged. "What about me? What if someone wants me dead?" Her gaze drifted to the door again where Manny had just made his exit, and Bree wondered if the woman was actually thinking—what if Manny wants me dead?

"I can't provide police protection to you in Austin," Duncan explained. "But I can call Austin PD and explain the situation. If they feel it's warranted, they'll assign someone to watch you."

Bree figured the cops there wouldn't consider it warranted, not when the only threat had been the text from an unknown number. Still, that seemed to placate Tara because she nodded.

"Thank you," she muttered. "I'll need my phone back, too."

Duncan motioned for Sonya to bring it back in and the deputy did. "Did you get anything from it?" he asked Sonya.

She shook her head. "The text came from a burner."

That surprised absolutely no one, not even Tara who sighed and slipped the phone into her pocket.

"Manny and you had a relationship," he spelled out to Tara. She'd already started for the door, but she stopped. "He broke up with you and yet you still continued to work for him. Why?"

"Because I'm in love with him," Tara admitted. "Because I want to be near him. Manny wouldn't have killed that woman," she repeated as she walked out.

"You think Tara believes that because she's in love with Manny or because she was the one who murdered Brighton?" Luca asked, taking the question right out of Bree's mouth.

"She's definitely a suspect for all of it," Duncan concluded. "And not just for the murder but for the cover-up attempts that I think are going on now."

Yes, a cover-up. Bree thought that was what was happening as well. And if so, the cover-up had started with her mother's kidnapping.

"Tara bears a strong resemblance to the sketch, and both Manny and she have means, motive and opportunity," Duncan summarized, and then he looked up at Sonya. "Try to find out if either of them own a gun or have had firearms training. I also want their phone records to see if either made calls anywhere near Saddle Ridge yesterday."

Sonya nodded and went back to her desk in the squad room.

"If we can get their financials, we can check and see if either bought burners or supplies we can maybe match to those taken to the cabin where Sandra was being held," Luca suggested.

Duncan nodded and looked at Woodrow. "I can request

a warrant for that. Everything we've got is circumstantial, but it might be enough," Woodrow said.

"Go for it," Duncan agreed, and Woodrow stepped to the side to make a call.

Duncan picked up the evidence bag with the memory stick. "You two want to work on this back at the ranch?" he asked, directing the question to Bree and Luca.

They both nodded. Bree was eager to get started on that since it might give them a vital clue. Of course, it could take a lot of searching to find anything, but it'd be worth it if only to close off that particular investigative thread.

"I'll get this to the techs, then," Duncan said, "and I'll have them copy what's on it and forward it to you as a secure email attachment." He shifted his attention to Sandra. "I'd like for you to take a look at it, too, in case anything pops for you."

Sandra nodded and made a soft groan. "Am I responsible for what's happening? Are all of you in danger because I was digging into Brighton's murder?"

"I was digging into Brighton's murder, too," Bree assured her, and because she hated seeing those fresh tears in her mother's eyes, she went to her and pulled her into her arms. "We aren't responsible for what a killer's doing," she added, hoping that she would start to believe that as well. It certainly felt as if she'd set all of this in motion, especially since she'd been investigating Brighton's murder at the time her mother had been taken.

When Bree eased back from the hug, her mother attempted a smile. She failed miserably. So did Bree, but the moment still felt like some kind of turning point, and it was so very good to have her mother back.

"I love you," she whispered to her mom.

Now Sandra really did smile. "I love you, too."

Bree hadn't actually forgotten that they weren't alone, but

then she noticed Luca, Woodrow and Duncan were all looking at them. Not with impatience though she figured they had to be feeling some of that. The investigation had to take priority. Had to. But Bree was hoping they could all have a proper homecoming once the danger was over.

"I'll have Woodrow and Ronnie accompany all of you back to the ranch," Duncan explained, motioning for Ronnie to come out of the squad room and into the office. "I want to wait here until the techs have picked up the memory stick, and then I'll head home, too."

"Not alone," Sandra was quick to say.

"Not alone," Duncan assured her.

He walked with them to the side door, opened it and glanced around the parking lot. He must not have seen anyone suspicious because he stepped back to let them all out. The cruiser wasn't far, only about ten feet away, and Woodrow and Ronnie went out first. Bree and her mother followed with Luca behind them.

When they reached the cruiser, Bree caught the strong smell of gasoline. The scene barely had time to register in her head before there was a sharp sound, like someone blowing out a huge candle.

And the flames shot up around them.

THE MOMENT LUCA heard the sound, he hooked his arm around Bree and yanked her back from the cruiser. Thankfully, Woodrow did the same to Sandra, and they fell back on the ground.

Not a second too soon either.

Because the fire blazed over the cruiser and the pavement beneath it. And the flames were spreading, too.

Ronnie, who'd been the closest to the cruiser, had a harder

fall than the rest of them. The impact knocked him back, and Luca could hear his fellow deputy's sharp groan of pain.

"Get back," Duncan shouted from the doorway.

With his left arm still around Bree, Luca drew his gun and started to bolt toward the still open office door. He stopped though when he saw the fire snaking along a trail of gasoline that stopped there. It had barely had time to register in his mind when the flames shot up there, too, forcing Duncan back into his office.

Luca yanked Bree away from the door. Away from the cruiser and toward the front of the sheriff's office.

And into what he knew could be extreme danger.

He couldn't see who'd ignited the gasoline, but he knew the person could be nearby, ready to gun them down. That's why he moved in front of Bree. Woodrow did the same to Sandra, and he practically dragged the woman toward Luca. Once Woodrow had her there, Luca got to a crouching position.

"Wait here," Luca told Woodrow. "I'll get Ronnie."

Ronnie groaned in pain again, and Luca knew that moving might make his injuries worse. Still, it couldn't be helped. If he stayed out in the open like that, he'd be an easier target. Luca ran toward him, the heat from the fire stinging his face. He couldn't see any gasoline in this particular spot, but the liquid and the flames could easily spread.

Something they were already doing.

Luca had no idea how much gasoline had been spilled, maybe only a gallon or two, but it'd obviously been more than enough to create this blaze that could be a cover for another attack.

While he tried to keep watch around him, Luca hooked his left arm around Ronnie, helping the deputy to his feet. Not easily. Ronnie outsized Luca by a good thirty pounds, and Luca had to take the man's weight so he could get them started across the parking lot.

Each step felt as if it took an eternity, and it didn't help that everything inside Luca was telling him they could all be gunned down at any moment. Telling him, too, that Ronnie could have serious internal injuries from the fall.

Thick black smoke billowed up from the fire, cutting across his path to the building. For a few terrifying moments, Luca lost sight of Bree, and his mind immediately went into some worst-case scenarios. Maybe this wasn't a murder attempt but a kidnapping. The killer could be trying to take her.

That possibility gave Luca an extra shot of adrenaline, and he fought his way through the smoke and heat so he could reach the side of the building. He finally saw Bree. Saw the fear and worry that was there, and he cursed their attacker for putting them through this.

Whatever this was.

Bree reached out for him, taking hold of Luca's arm and pulling both Ronnie and him closer until they were all in a huddle.

"Tara or Manny could have done this," Bree muttered.

Yeah, they could have, and it wouldn't have been especially hard if they'd already had the gasoline with them. Manny and Tara had arrived separately and would have used this parking lot. If they'd parked on the other side of the cruiser, the side that wouldn't have been easily visible from the street, one of them could have poured the gasoline from the door while seated in their vehicles. That theory worked.

But there was a problem.

He didn't see either Manny or Tara, and their vehicles weren't in the lot right now. So, how had the flames ignited?

Luca soon came up with the answer.

There were clusters of trees and shrubs at the far back of the parking lot, and one or both of them could have poured the gasoline, driven away and parked somewhere up the street. They could have then made their way back to the trees and shrubs and waited. If the stream of gasoline was nearby, all it would have taken was lighting a match and tossing it. Then the person could have run away and taken up the vantage point to fire some shots.

"An ambulance and the fire department are on the way," Duncan called out.

Luca glanced at the front corner of the building and saw Duncan and Sonya. Both had their weapons drawn and were firing glances all around. Clearly, they'd braced for an attack, too.

"Try to get inside," Duncan instructed.

Since that wouldn't happen from the side door where the fire was still blazing, it meant going through the front. The sheriff's office was on Main Street and there were buildings on each side as well as across the street. Places for a gunman to hide and take aim. Still, it wasn't safe where they were either.

Woodrow hurried to the other side of Ronnie and, along with Luca, they hoisted up the deputy. "Stay against the side of the building," Luca told Bree and Sandra.

At least that way, a gunman would have to shoot through Woodrow, Ronnie and him to get to them. Maybe though the threat wouldn't come from a gunshot. Luca realized that when he looked at the fire shooting up the front of the cruiser.

Hell.

Luca knew it was rare for a vehicle to actually explode during a fire, but it was possible their attacker had added something to the mix. Like maybe some other chemical that could be toxic to breathe in.

"We need to evacuate the area," Luca shouted to Duncan, and he tipped his head to the cruiser to let him know what was going on.

Duncan cursed and made a frantic motion for them to move faster. They did, but it wasn't easy. Ronnie was unconscious now so Luca hefted him over his shoulder in a fireman's carry so he could put some distance between them and the cruiser.

Bree and Sandra thankfully stayed against the wall of the building, and they all moved together. All keeping watch as best they could, considering the slashes of smoke that kept coming their way.

It seemed to take a lifetime or two before they finally reached the door, and the moment they did, Duncan got Sandra and Bree inside. Luca moved to do the same to Ronnie, but he caught some movement from the corner of his eye and whipped around in that direction.

Luca caught just a glimpse of Tara running from the scene.

Chapter Nine

Bree just wanted to stop feeling as if she were about to jump out of her own skin. She wanted her heart rate to go back to normal. She wanted to stop being afraid for her precious little boy.

But none of that was likely to happen anytime soon.

She was back at the ranch with Luca, Woodrow and her mother. Away from the fire and smoke-filled parking lot. Away from immediate danger. But nothing felt safe right now.

Probably because it wasn't.

If their attacker could come at them in the parking lot of the sheriff's office, then he or she could come after them here. Luca obviously understood that was a possibility because the ranch was on high alert with the security system activated and ranch hands patrolling the grounds.

Bree watched the laptop screen as Duncan was finishing up his interview with Tara. Not at the sheriff's office. That entire area had been evacuated so when they'd seen Tara running from the fire, Duncan had gone after her, caught her and ultimately taken her to an office in city hall. He'd then set up a laptop to do a live feed of the interview so Luca, Woodrow, Joelle and Bree could watch from the ranch.

So far, Tara wasn't saying anything Bree wanted to hear.

"I didn't start that fire," Tara insisted for the umpteenth

time. "I told you that I was walking to my car that I'd parked up the street. I saw the fire and ran."

"We've requested the camera feed from the bank," Luca muttered to Bree while he stood right next to her. Right next to her had been his default position since they'd escaped the fire.

And Bree wasn't complaining.

As bad as her frayed nerves were right now, she knew they'd be even worse if Luca wasn't there. Ditto for Gabriel. Even though the baby was asleep, she was holding him because she wanted him as close as possible.

"The angle of the bank camera won't help with the parking lot," Luca added, knowing that Tara couldn't hear him, "but it might be able to confirm or disprove what Tara is saying."

Bree considered the location of the bank, which was more than a block away from the sheriff's office. It was the only security camera in the area. Still, they might get lucky and be able to see Tara's movements. If she had indeed parked up the street, then it wasn't likely she'd spilled that gasoline and ignited it. Well, not likely unless she'd spilled it before she'd ever parked on Main Street and then come into the sheriff's office. It was possible she'd done just that, but it might be hard to prove unless Tara had left behind some evidence that pointed to her guilt.

Bree continued to watch as Duncan pressed Tara, trying to trip her up with different versions of the same question. But Tara was staying steady, insisting she was innocent.

Luca's phone dinged with a text, and when he lifted it, she saw Sonya's name on the screen. Ronnie's conscious, the deputy texted. Doctor says no serious injuries but he'll be admitted for an overnight stay.

Bree latched on to the "no serious injuries" part. They'd

gotten lucky. With a fire of that size, all of them could have gotten burned, literally.

Luca texted back to thank Sonya for the update, but his phone dinged again before he could put it away.

"The tech picked up the memory stick and copied it," Luca explained. "He just emailed me the bar receipts."

Bree glanced at the laptop screen with the interview, then at Gabriel who was deep into his nap and would no doubt still be asleep for at least two hours. "Let me put him down in his crib, and maybe we can go over the receipts in the guest room." That way, they'd still be able to watch Gabriel while they worked.

Luca took one of the laptops scattered around the room and told the others what they were doing. Woodrow assured him if anything came up in the remainder of the interview with Tara that he'd let them know. They agreed to do the same if they found anything in the receipts.

Bree and Luca made their way up the stairs to the guest room, which was now empty since Coral had already gone home. Bree welcomed the quiet. For a couple of seconds anyway, and then the flashbacks came.

Mercy, did they.

There was a whirl of images of the attack on the road, the shooting into the barn and the fire, all mixed with the memories of her father. It was a volatile combo, and her hands were already starting to tremble when she crossed the room toward the crib.

Luca set the laptop aside and steadied her by slipping his hands beneath hers, and together, they eased the baby onto the mattress. Gabriel stirred just a little but stayed asleep.

"Thank you," Bree whispered. And it wasn't just gratitude for helping her with this but also for what he'd done during the fire. "You put yourself in front of me again. You shielded me."

"I'm a cop," he said as if that explained everything. Maybe in his mind it did. Maybe he would have done that for anyone. After all, he'd run out into the parking lot to rescue Ronnie.

It was a bad time for her to make direct eye contact with him, but Bree found herself doing it anyway. As usual, things passed between them. Unspoken but still intense. Things always seemed intense between Luca and her.

Yes, the eye contact was a mistake, but she made it much worse when she stepped toward him. And into his arms. Luca pulled her to him, brushing a kiss on the top of her head. A kiss of comfort. So was the hug when he tightened his embrace. It was wrong to take this from him, but Bree couldn't make herself back away.

She stayed there where it felt so safe. So right. The first part was the truth. The second, wasn't. Luca and she weren't together, and this was not only playing with fire, it was wrong. As if she were leading him on.

That gave her the steel to move back, and he eased his grip to let her do that. But it was another mistake. Because now they had the intense eye contact and the body-to-body touching. Definitely not good.

Bree felt the heat slide right through her. Of course, it did. There was always heat whenever she was around Luca. Heat and need. Another bad combo. Still, she stayed put, looking at him. Holding her breath.

Waiting.

Luca didn't stay put though. He lowered his head and brushed his mouth over hers. This was not a gesture of comfort. No. This was about the fiery attraction. And she felt it. Felt it not only on her mouth but in every inch of her.

He pulled back, looked at her, no doubt gauging her reaction, and he muttered some profanity. She didn't think his reaction was because he saw any objection on her face but because he probably saw the invitation she could feel her body sending out to him. An invitation that could complicate an already complicated situation.

Did that stop her?

No.

Bree moved in and kissed him. Really kissed him. Hard pressure of her mouth on his. Then, more. She was the one who deepened the kiss, the one who slid her hand around the back of his neck to pull him down to her.

Luca certainly didn't resist. Just the opposite. He made a sound that came from deep within his throat, and he snapped her to him. Not that she could get much closer, but instead of merely touching, they were now pressed against each other. Like lovers.

Her body knew just how to react to the feel of his chest against her breasts. Everything inside her went warm and soft. Then, hot. Everything inside her pushed her to take more, more, more. She had no doubts, none, that Luca would give her that more, but there was another sound.

Gabriel whimpering.

That sent Luca and her flying apart, and both of them whipped their attention to their son. Gabriel stirred, stretching and making a face before he sucked at a nonexistent bottle and went back to sleep.

Luca and she stood there. Breaths racing. Heartbeats, too. She knew that because she could see Luca's pulse on his neck. A neck she wished she could kiss. Heck, she wished she could do a lot of thing with Luca, but the timing was all off. Might always be off if she couldn't set aside the horrible flashbacks.

"Saved by a whimper," he muttered. Luca shook his head.

Then, he surprised Bree by smiling. "I'm not sure I want to thank Gabriel for the interruption."

He seemed to be waiting for her to agree. Which she did. That whole not being sure was front and center in her mind. But so was the heat. Since she didn't want to give in to that heat, which might lead them straight to the bed, Bree motioned toward the laptop instead.

"The receipts," she reminded him, keeping her voice at a whisper.

Luca nodded, sighed and picked up the computer. He took it to the small seating area in the corner, booted it up and set it on the table that was between the two chairs. The email was indeed there with the large attachment of the receipts. Bree's heart dropped a little when she realized it was well over a hundred pages, and each page had at least two dozen transactions.

"These are for the three weeks before Brighton's death," Luca pointed out.

So, Manny had been thorough. Or it appeared he had been on the surface anyway. If he was the person who'd murdered Brighton and was now responsible for the attacks, then he might have turned over the receipts only because he knew they wouldn't incriminate him.

"Neither Tara nor Manny have alibis for the attacks," Bree said, "but we didn't ask them where they were when Brighton was murdered."

Luca nodded. "I'm sure Duncan will do that. If anything pops in their background checks, he'll have cause to bring them back in for interviews. The same could happen if we get that warrant for their financials. If one of them held your mother captive for all these months, there could be a money trail."

True, and that was a trail they'd have to find since neither Tara nor Manny would likely confess to something like that. Kidnapping and imprisonment were serious crimes that would carry long jail sentences. Ditto for the attacks. Added to that, if the kidnapping and the attacks could be linked to Brighton's murder, then life with no parole could be doled out. Heck, even the death penalty.

First, they had to find evidence to prove their guilt or eliminate them as suspects. They probably weren't going to be able to do that based solely on the receipts, but it was something that needed to be investigated.

"Email me a copy of the list," she said, standing so she could get her laptop she'd had brought over from her house. "I'll start at the bottom. You can start at the top."

Luca pulled his computer onto his lap to send her the email. "Flag anything that seems suspicious," he muttered.

Bree made a sound of agreement and settled back in the chair to get busy. Since she had no idea what the usual daily revenue was for the bar, she flagged large charges, those over a thousand dollars, just in case Manny or Tara was using the Hush, Hush to launder money. Still, she supposed charges that high wouldn't necessarily be anything sinister but rather a single payment for large group.

"Your mom's on here," Luca said, snagging her attention.

She leaned over and looked at the charge. Less than five dollars, which meant it was likely water or club soda. The date matched Sandra's account of being at the Hush, Hush the night of the fight.

"And here's Brighton," Luca added a moment later.

"Clearly, you got the good end of the list," she muttered. "So far, I haven't recognized a single name on mine." And she leaned toward Luca's laptop for another look. "Twenty-three dollars, and this would have been the same night Mom was there."

"Does the bar serve food?" he asked.

"A few items. When I was researching it, I looked at the menu on the website. Typical bar stuff. Sliders, nachos, that sort of thing."

Of course, they had no way of knowing if Brighton's bill had been for food or drink. And maybe it didn't matter unless twenty-three dollars was to pay for her drink and that of a companion.

"Funny that Manny didn't give her the drinks or food on the house," Luca pointed out.

"Manny will probably say he'd broken things off with her by then. Tara might be able to say otherwise though." Unfortunately, Bree wasn't anywhere near certain they could believe what Tara would tell them.

"I'm going to flag the bar tabs paid around the same time Brighton paid hers," Luca said. "Then, we can maybe contact these people and see if they remember her."

"Good idea," she said and continued with her list. Finally, she got a hit. Maybe a huge one. "Another charge from Brighton, for eighteen dollars. And this was the night she was murdered."

That got Luca's attention, and he leaned over to take a look. "Definitely flag the other receipts within an hour of that."

Bree started doing that, using a highlighter function on the laptop, but her fingers froze when one name practically popped off the screen at her.

"What?" Luca questioned.

He'd obviously heard the sharp sound of surprise she'd made, and he leaned in again. Then he cursed. Because the customer's name was one they both recognized.

Nathan.

LUCA STOOD AT the window, waiting and watching. It definitely wasn't standard procedure to interview a suspect at the ranch, but with the CSIs and fire department clogging up the parking lot of the sheriff's office, Duncan had decided to hold the interview here. Luca didn't especially care where they questioned Nathan. He just wanted it to happen.

They needed answers. And this just might be the break they'd been looking for.

"Even if Nathan's guilty of murdering Brighton, he won't confess," Bree said. She was right next to Luca, keeping watch as well while Sandra was upstairs with Gabriel.

Luca agreed. But sometimes confessions weren't intentional. And it was possible that Nathan being at the bar had nothing to do with Brighton. The timing was suspicious though, and the receipts could put Brighton and Nathan together at the bar at the same time. Since they were from the same small town, they would have likely recognized each other. Yet, Nathan hadn't said a word about seeing Brighton mere hours before she'd been murdered.

And that gave Luca an idea.

He took out his phone. "I'm going to text Nathan's picture to Manny and Tara to see if they recognize him. I won't mention Brighton, but it's possible one of them remembers seeing him with her. If so, Nathan won't be able to deny knowing that Brighton was at the bar the same time he was."

Bree made a quick sound of agreement, and Luca sent off the first text to Manny. When the man would answer was anyone's guess. Manny might want everything to go through his lawyer. Ditto for Tara, but Luca sent her an identical message anyway.

The moments crawled by with no response, so Luca put his phone away and continued to keep watch for Nathan. While still standing right next to Bree. With their arms pressed against each other. It wasn't anywhere near the embrace they'd had upstairs, but any contact with Bree was a mental distraction for him.

So was the memory of that kiss.

Hard to forget that, and that sensation of heat and need. He'd been on the verge of losing control with Bree. Again. Apparently, he hadn't learned his lesson about that from eleven months ago. He'd surrendered to the kiss knowing full well that it was a bad idea, that there'd be a serious loss of focus. But that hadn't stopped it, and he had to figure out a way to make sure he kept this heat in check so he could keep Bree safe.

She looked up at him. Their gazes connecting. And he cursed. She muttered some profanity, too, so he knew they were on the same page here. A page that likely would have involved them talking about it if his phone hadn't sounded with a text.

"Manny," he said when he saw the screen.

Once again, Luca had to push aside thoughts of Bree and that amazing kiss and nail his attention to this investigation. Well, to this response anyway, which Luca knew could be Manny lashing out to demand to be left the hell alone.

But it wasn't.

Yeah, I've seen him before, Manny texted. He was in the bar with Brighton a couple of times.

Bingo. They now had the verification they needed in case Nathan lied to them. Of course, this was still just hearsay, but it'd be strong hearsay if Tara confirmed seeing Nathan as well.

Do you know if Brighton was dating him? Luca messaged back.

They were together, that's all I know. They weren't like having sex on the bar or anything like that, but I did see her kiss the guy. I figured she was doing that to try to make me jealous because I'd recently ended things with her. Why? Are you going to grill him the way you did me?

Luca definitely intended to do some grilling when it came to Nathan. For now though, he reread Manny's text. Bree was obviously doing the same thing.

"Interesting," Bree said.

It was indeed, and Luca could see one way this might have played out. "If Brighton was truly using Nathan to make Manny jealous and Nathan found out, Nathan wouldn't be happy about that. In fact, he could have been so angry that he attacked her."

Of course, there was no proof of that, not yet anyway. And it was equally possible that Manny was lying. The bar owner might say or do anything to point the finger at someone other than himself.

Thanks, Luca texted to Manny. Please let me know if you remember anything else about the guy in the picture.

He didn't get an immediate response from Manny, but Luca did see something else he'd been waiting for. Nathan's car as he pulled into the driveway. Duncan must have heard it because he, too, went to the window to stand behind Bree and Luca.

"I want you to do the interview," Duncan told Luca. "I figure if the doctor has any hot buttons, you'll be able to push them better than I could." He looked at Bree. "And I want you close to Luca while he's questioning him."

Bree's eyebrow lifted. "You want Luca and me to pretend to be together so that it'll rile Nathan?"

Duncan gave them a flat look. "Just sit close to each other. If Nathan's not an idiot, he'll pick up on the vibe between you two, and it could set him off."

Luca could tell Bree wanted to deny there was any *vibe*. She couldn't though because it was indeed there.

"I just got these texts from Manny," Luca said, passing his phone to Duncan. "I'm waiting to hear from Tara."

Duncan smiled when he read Manny's responses. "Definitely use this," he insisted.

When Nathan parked and got out of his car, the three of them stepped away from the window to go to the front door. Bree must have taken Duncan's advice to heart because she stood arm to arm with Luca while Duncan ushered in Nathan. Duncan also immediately riled the doctor by checking him for weapons and reciting the Miranda rights.

The annoyance was building on Nathan's face. Until he turned his attention to Bree. Then Luca saw the quick change. Worry and concern rather than anger.

"Are you all right?" Nathan asked Bree. Completely ignoring Luca, he went to her and laid his hand on her shoulder. "Are the stitches hurting?" He proceeded to examine them.

"I'm okay," Bree said, stepping back and aligning herself with Luca again.

And, yeah, Nathan noticed all right. It'd been a good call on Duncan's part to go with this ploy since it caused a spark of fresh anger to flare in Nathan's eyes,

"Good," Nathan muttered, but his tone indicated her actions were anything but. "I'm betting you'll be glad when you can get back to your own place," he said, speaking to Bree. "It can't be easy being cooped up here in a house that holds so many horrible memories for you."

Luca silently cursed because the remark had hit pay dirt. Bree flinched, but it was obvious to Luca that she was trying to suppress her reaction. Hard to do though when there were indeed bad memories here of her father's murder.

"Not all bad," Bree said. "I grew up here so there are plenty of good memories, too."

Bree's remark hit pay dirt as well because she coupled it by brushing her arm against Luca's. A subtle gesture, but it obviously packed an emotional punch for Nathan. He practically snapped to attention toward Duncan.

"So, where are we doing this interview?" Nathan asked him.

"Actually, Luca will be conducting it in the living room," Duncan was quick to say. "I've asked Bree to stay in the room as well as an observer." He'd no doubt added that to cover any legal bases. "Hope you don't have a problem with that," Duncan added like a challenge.

"No," Nathan muttered, his response in direct contrast to his expression. It was obvious he did have a problem, but Luca figured it wasn't because Bree would be there but rather that Luca would be the one doling out the questions.

They went into the living room where Duncan had already turned around the incident board and Slater was working on his laptop at a makeshift desk in the corner. Duncan motioned for Nathan to sit in one of the chairs that he'd obviously positioned like a hot seat directly across from the sofa and chair that Duncan, Bree and he would be using. Duncan revved up the tension some more by turning on the recorder and putting it on the coffee table only a couple of inches from Nathan.

For the record, Luca read in the date, time and those present, and he added, "Dr. Bagley has consented to Attorney Bree McCullough being present as an observer for this interview. Could you state your consent for the recording?" Luca added.

Nathan's teeth came together. "Bree can be here," he said.

Good. With that formality out of the way, Luca jumped

right to the heart of the matter. "Tell me about your relationship with Brighton Cooper."

Nathan seemed to do a mental double take. "Brighton?" He shook his head. "I was aware of who she was. She'd come into the hospital a couple of times, but there wasn't a..." He stopped, studying Bree's and Luca's expressions.

The doctor had been about to lie. Luca was certain of it. But Nathan must have sensed this could be a trap.

"Has that bar owner and bartender said something about me?" Nathan asked.

"You mean Manny Vickery and Tara Adler?" Luca prompted when Nathan didn't add anything.

Nathan nodded.

"How did you know we'd interviewed them?" Luca pressed.

Nathan's jaw went tight again. "Word about that sort of thing gets around. Did they say something about me?" Luca didn't respond. He just stared at Nathan until the doctor huffed. "Manny or Tara probably told you I occasionally went to the bar. You might even have proof of that if you looked over old credit card charges. Is that it? Is that why I'm here?"

Luca felt as if some of the wind had been taken out of his sails. He'd been hoping that Nathan would deny even being at the Hush, Hush, but if word had indeed gotten around about Manny and Tara being questioned, then Nathan might have realized it'd be stupid for him to lie.

That didn't mean the doctor was innocent though.

"And your relationship with Brighton?" Luca repeated.

Nathan huffed. "It was hardly a relationship. We didn't exactly travel in the same social circles or anything."

The man's snobbery was coming through so Luca gave that a nudge. "What do you mean by that?"

Nathan huffed again and looked at Bree. "I swear, I didn't

have anything to do with Brighton when I was seeing you. I didn't cheat on you."

Bree shook her head. "We dated, and that wasn't exclusive, so even if you were with Brighton or anyone else it wouldn't have been cheating."

Oh, Nathan didn't like that, but instead of doling out a verbal blast to Bree, he turned his frosty gaze on Luca. "All of this feels like a witch hunt and a gross violation of my privacy."

"Not a witch hunt," Luca said. "But interviews can definitely take pokes at privacy. Especially if the interviewee has something to hide. Did you want to hide your relationship with Brighton?"

"It wasn't a relationship," Nathan practically yelled, but the outburst was short-lived, and he made a visible effort to rein in his temper. "Brighton and I hooked up a few times, that was all. She wasn't my type, and she was six years younger than me."

"Hooked up?" Luca questioned. "Does that mean sex or just hanging out at the bar together?"

If looks could have killed, Nathan would have finished Luca off then and there. "Both. Briefly," he quickly tacked on to that. "I was only with her a couple of times and never when I was with Bree."

That was probably meant to give Luca a dig, to be a reminder that Bree and this jerk had once dated, but Luca didn't get the jolt of jealousy that Nathan was likely hoping for. Luca felt nothing but disgust over Nathan's behavior once Bree had ended things with him.

"Did you hook up with Brighton or hang out with her at the bar at the same time she was seeing Manny?" Luca asked.

Nathan did a double take, part flinch, part raised eyebrow.

"Maybe. I don't know when she was involved with Manny. I'd stopped seeing her long before she died. Months," he provided.

"Yet you were at the Hush, Hush at the same time the night she died," Luca pointed out.

"That could be true, but if so, she wasn't there with me," Nathan insisted.

Maybe. But Luca wished he had security footage of Brighton leaving the bar that night so he could see if she'd left with either Nathan or Manny. The camera footage hadn't been preserved since they hadn't known for weeks that Brighton had even been to a bar in Austin. By then, the security system had recorded over the old footage.

"I didn't have anything to do with Brighton's death," Nathan went on, talking to Bree now. "You know me. You know I'm not capable of violence."

Bree stared at him. "I know you're capable of stalking."

Nathan cursed. "That wasn't what was happening. I simply didn't understand why you said you didn't want to see me anymore. I thought maybe it was a misunderstanding and that if we just talked, you'd be able to see that I cared deeply for you. I still do," he added. "And that's why I'm so worried about you now."

Judging from Bree's stiff body language, she wasn't buying it. Caring deeply for someone didn't mesh with stalking.

"Where were you yesterday morning before you treated Bree at the hospital?" Luca asked.

Nathan pulled back his shoulders, obviously thrown off a little by the shift in subject. "I went on shift at seven, so I'd been there for a couple of hours before Bree arrived."

"Can anyone verify that?" Luca added.

"Plenty of people." Nathan had to answer that through

clenched teeth. "Nurses and other doctors. If you need names, you can ask for the duty roster."

"I'll do that," Slater volunteered, earning his own glare from Nathan.

"And what about after Bree left the hospital?" Luca went on. "Did you stay on duty or did you leave?"

Nathan opened his mouth as if ready to do that blast, but he reined in again. "I had nothing to do with the shooting at Bree's. I'm not a killer."

"Did you stay on duty at the hospital or did you leave?" Luca repeated.

"I stayed on duty until I heard about Bree's son being missing. I left then because I thought I could help look for him."

"So, you have no alibi for the time of the shooting," Luca concluded. "What about for earlier today when someone set the parking lot on fire?"

Nathan got up from the chair. "Enough. You clearly have it in for me."

Duncan stepped closer. "No one here has it in for you," he stated. "This is an interview with questions that should be relatively easy for you to answer. The fire was only a couple of hours ago so you shouldn't have any trouble recalling where you were."

"I was at the hospital," Nathan snarled. "You can check the duty roster for that, too."

Luca had no doubt that Nathan's name would be there, but that didn't mean he was innocent.

Duncan's phone rang, the sound slicing through the heavy silence that had fallen over the room. He took the call, moving away from them. Luca was about to continue the interview when he heard Duncan mutter some profanity.

Alarmed that there was more bad news, Luca went to

him. So did Bree and Slater, and they ended up huddled together in the corner.

Duncan put the caller on hold and looked at Slater, Luca and Bree. He cursed again before he said, "There's been a murder."

Chapter Ten

Bree watched from the window as Nathan drove away. She'd kept back because she hadn't wanted him to see her watching him and conclude that she was longing for him or anything like that. She just wanted to make sure he was gone and away from the house. She didn't want any of their suspects under the same roof as Gabriel.

"All right," she heard Duncan say after he'd finished his latest call. The third one he'd gotten since delivering the whispered bombshell.

There's been a murder.

Other than assuring Bree and the others that it wasn't a family member or one of the deputies, that was all Duncan had been able to tell them. He'd then dismissed Nathan, basically telling him to get the heck out of there, and then had started the calls. Luca and Slater had done the same, and even though Bree didn't know the specifics, it was obvious some things were happening in the investigation.

Duncan repeated his "all right" as if trying to gather his thoughts, and he slipped his phone back in his pocket. "About two hours ago, a hunter reported finding a dead body in the woods not too far from the burned-out cabin. Not on the grounds but about a quarter of a mile away. According to County Deputy Morales who arrived on scene, cause of death appears to be a single gunshot wound to the head."

That gave Bree a jolt. Even though that wasn't the exact way her father had been murdered, it still gave her the flash-backs.

"Any indications it could be a suicide?" Luca asked.

Duncan nodded. Then, shrugged. "Deputy Morales says it's set up to look that way. The gun is in her hand and po-sitioned more or less the correct way if the shot had been self-inflicted, but Morales believes the position of the body is off. He says it looks staged to him."

Staged would equal murder as far as Bree was concerned.

"The county sheriff's office had copies of the sketches done by the police artist," Duncan went on. "The ones that the two witnesses said were of the woman they saw driving the silver truck when Sandra would have been captive. Any-way, the responding deputy says he believes the dead woman is the one in the sketch. So, it could be Tara or her sister, Shannon. I've tried to call Tara, but she's not answering."

If the dead woman was indeed Shannon, then it was pos-sible she was the one who'd kidnapped Sandra. Sandra had said the woman who'd held her had had phone conversations with someone and appeared to be getting instructions. The person giving those instructions could have been Shannon's boss, and he or she might not want Shannon around to spill anything incriminating.

"She didn't respond to a text I sent her earlier," Luca pointed out.

Duncan scrubbed his hand over his face and seemed to consider that a moment. "Try to contact her again. If she still doesn't answer, I'll have the Austin cops go to her place and see if she's there. For now, call Manny and see if knows where she is. Find out, too, if he knows Shannon, and it's okay to tell him there's a body matching Shannon's descrip-tion."

Luca nodded, and he took out his phone, moving a few yards away into the adjacent formal dining room and motioning for Bree to join him. She did, and Luca put the call on Speaker when he tried to call Tara. Bree got a very uneasy feeling when it went straight to voicemail. Maybe Tara was just dodging them, but it was also possible she was dead.

"This is Deputy Vanetti," Luca said, leaving a message. "I need to speak to you right away." He paused a heartbeat. "It's about your sister."

That might prompt Tara to return the call. If she was in any position to do it, that is.

Luca pulled up Manny's number next and also put it on Speaker. "Didn't I make it clear that you'll have to go through my lawyer if you want to talk to me?" Manny greeted in a snarl.

"I'm looking for Tara," Luca said, clearly ignoring Manny's rant.

"I have no idea where she is. She's not at work, that's for sure." He paused. "Why are you looking for her? Did you find some kind of proof that she's the one who killed Brighton?"

"No," Luca answered. "I wanted to talk to her about her sister."

"Shannon?" Manny questioned.

"That's right. You know her?"

"Yeah, I've met Shannon a couple of times," Manny confirmed. "She's the spitting image of Tara, but they're nothing alike personality-wise. Or rather they were nothing alike. Tara used to be reliable. Shannon's a train wreck. She takes that whole bad girl attitude way too far."

"What do you mean Tara used to be reliable?" Luca asked. Bree knew he wasn't dropping the subject of Shannon, but that past tense could be a red flag if Manny knew Tara was dead. "Has something changed?"

"Damn right, things have changed. Tara's spooked out of her mind and believes this whole thing of someone wanting her dead. I'm the one who was nearly run off the road. I'm the one who was attacked, not her, but you'd think she was the only one at risk here. Hell, there's no indication other than her wild imagination that someone is after her."

Bree mentally repeated all of that, and there was something about it that didn't ring true. But she didn't know what part. If Manny was the mastermind behind what was happening, then he could be setting up Tara to take the fall. That didn't feel right either though.

"Truth is, I've told Tara that she should look for another job," Manny went on. "Now watch, she'll probably pull some 'hell has no fury like a woman scorned' deal and accuse me of all sorts of things."

"Like what?" Luca pressed, and Bree realized this was turning into the interview that they hadn't been able to finish with Manny when he'd been at the sheriff's office.

"Who the hell knows," Manny grumbled. "She'll probably accuse me of murder or something. She might even claim I'm the one after her." He paused. "Wait, is Tara working with Shannon to try to smear my name or something?"

"Not that I know of," Luca assured him. "Would Tara or Shannon do that?"

"Hell, yeah. Shannon would, anyway, and it wouldn't take much of a push for Tara to get Shannon to come after me for her version of payback."

"You think Shannon could be violent?" Luca went on.

Now, Manny wasn't so quick to answer. "Did Shannon do something? Does she want Tara to bail her out of jail again?"

"No," Luca said, but didn't add more to that. "Does Shannon have any identifying marks that Tara doesn't and vice versa? Like a birthmark or tat?"

Again, Manny hesitated. "Why are you asking that? Did something happen to Shannon or Tara?"

Luca dodged those questions. "We're looking into that. Tats or birthmarks?" Luca repeated.

Manny huffed. "Tara has a shamrock tat on her right ankle. As far as I know, Shannon's not into that sort of thing."

Bree hurried back to Duncan to let him know to have the cops on scene check for an ankle tat on the dead body. It didn't take Duncan long to make the call or for the cops to respond.

"No tat of any kind on her ankle," Duncan relayed.

So, this was Shannon. Bree didn't know whether to be relieved or not. The proximity of the body to the cabin and the eyewitness accounts of the woman driving the silver truck likely meant Shannon had been involved in not only her mother's kidnapping but perhaps everything else that'd happened.

But that didn't exclude Tara's involvement.

In fact, the conversations Sandra had overheard could have been Shannon talking with Tara. Tara might be the mastermind behind the kidnapping and the attacks. Why though, Bree still wasn't sure.

She went back to Luca to let him know that the dead woman didn't have a tat and found him in the middle of another Manny tirade. Manny was now demanding that Luca tell him what was going on, and the man was peppering the demand with plenty of profanity.

Bree mouthed the info about the tat. Luca nodded and interrupted Manny's rant. "A woman's been murdered, and it might be Shannon," he said.

That stopped Manny mid-sentence. "Murdered?" he questioned. "And you think I did it?"

"Did you?" Luca asked.

"Of course not." He paused again. "This is why you want

to talk to Tara," Manny concluded with a sigh. "Do you think she killed her sister?"

Luca frowned. "Why would you think that? Is Tara capable of killing Shannon?"

Manny did more cursing. "To hell if I know. A week ago, I would have said no, but I think Tara's had some kind of breakdown. There's no telling what she might do in this state of mind."

There it was again, the feeling that what he was saying just didn't ring true. Basically, Manny was throwing Tara under the bus. Maybe because he believed she was indeed capable of murder, but it felt to Bree as if Manny was trying to cover his own tracks by making them believe Tara was guilty.

"I really need to speak to Tara," Luca went on. "But she's not answering her phone. Any idea where she might be?"

"None whatsoever," he was quick to say, "but when you do talk to her, remember what I said. Don't believe anything she tells you about me. Or anything else for that matter," Manny added a split second before he ended the call.

Luca stared at his phone for a moment as if he might hit Redial, but something Duncan said must have caught his attention because he headed in that direction. Duncan was still talking to someone on the phone, but he finished his conversation just as they approached him.

"They ran the dead woman's fingerprints and got an immediate hit," Duncan explained. "It's Shannon."

Bree wasn't sure what to feel about that. With her death, she would no longer be a threat. But the threat was still out there, and if Shannon were alive, she might at least have been willing to spill the name of her accomplice. If she had an accomplice, that is. For now, all they could do was speculate as to what her part had been in Sandra's kidnapping and the attacks.

They knew from the witnesses' sketches that Shannon, or Tara, had been at the cabin and had driven the silver truck. So, one of them had held Sandra. It was too bad that Sandra had never seen her kidnapper's face or she might have been able to verify which one.

But the proximity of Shannon's body to the cabin pointed to it being her.

Shannon had that "trouble magnet" past, and she would have had an easier time getting to and from the cabin than Tara who, according to her work schedule, was putting in fifty-plus hours a week. That didn't totally exclude Tara, but at the moment the circumstantial evidence was skewed more to Shannon. She was almost certainly the one who had brought in groceries to Sandra.

"Deputy Morales will get the body to the ME and send the gun to the lab for analysis," Duncan explained. "Her address is listed as an apartment in Austin, so Austin PD will send someone out to take a look at the place."

Duncan was scowling. So were Luca and Slater. Probably because this had turned into a three-prong investigation with three different law enforcement agencies involved. That meant red tape and possible delays.

"I checked and Shannon Adler doesn't have a gun registered to her," Slater said a moment later. "Of course, that doesn't mean she didn't buy one illegally, but we still might be able to trace the gun to someone."

True. "How about our other suspects?" Bree asked. "Do they own guns?"

"Not Tara. Again, not legally anyway," Slater answered. "Manny has a permit to carry concealed, and he owns both a Glock and a SIG Sauer."

Those were normally cops' weapons, but plenty of civilians carried them as well. Manny could probably justify ownership of that kind of firepower though by saying he'd wanted protection for the bar. Added to that, if Manny was responsible for the attacks, he almost certainly wouldn't have used one of his own weapons. However, the concealed permit was an indicator that he knew how to shoot since he would have needed classes to get that.

"Did Morales say if the shot to Shannon's head was point-blank?" Luca asked.

"It was," Duncan verified. "There was stippling around the point of entry."

Bree knew that stippling was unburned gunpowder striking the skin, and it was an indicator that the shot had been fired less than two feet away. So, if this wasn't a suicide, it likely meant Shannon's killer had been someone she knew. Or at least someone who could get that close to her anyway.

"Morales thinks Shannon was actually killed in the spot where she was found," Duncan went on. "There were no drag marks, and there was an ample amount of blood to make him believe that's where she died."

"How far from the road?" Luca wanted to know.

"About fifty yards," Duncan answered. "It was a heavily treed area in between the cabin and the river. Morales said it was the very definition of *off the beaten path*."

"So, Shannon was meeting someone or was lured there," Luca concluded.

"This is all too pat for my liking," Slater said, reading through something on his laptop screen.

That got Bree's and everyone else's attention, and they turned to Slater, waiting for him to explain that.

"Shannon had a short stint in the army before she was dishonorably discharged," he said. "She would have gotten firearms training. She also had a record for drugs and B and E.

Everything I'm seeing in her background indicates she couldn't stay out of trouble and had issues with authority."

Bree figured she knew where he was going with this. "So, how could she have stayed on task for the eleven months Mom was held captive?"

"Exactly," Slater agreed. "She doesn't seem to fit the profile of someone who could have done this on her own. Yet, she also doesn't fit for someone taking orders either."

"I guess that could depend on whoever was giving the orders," Duncan suggested. "If it was someone she trusted... or loved, then maybe that allowed her to stay on task." He paused, shook his head. "And it's possible that Shannon is being used as a scapegoat in all of this."

Luca made a sound of agreement. "And if so, that points back to Tara."

It did indeed. But Bree knew they couldn't rule out Nathan or Manny. Especially Manny who'd admitted to knowing Shannon. That made Bree wonder if Nathan would admit to knowing the dead woman as well. She was on the verge of asking Luca, Slater and Duncan if they should ask Nathan that when Luca's phone rang.

"Tara," Luca said when he looked at the screen. The relief was in his voice, but the concern was still on his face. He took the call and immediately told Tara, "I've got the call on Speaker. Sheriff Holder, Deputy McCullough and Bree are here with me."

"What's so important?" Tara responded, the ice practically dripping off the question.

"I need to talk to you in person," Luca explained. "Can you come back to Saddle Ridge? If not, I can arrange—"

"I'm not going back there," Tara interrupted, "and I'm not talking to any Austin cops either. If you've got something to say to me, just say it fast because you've got exactly thirty seconds before I hang up and then block you."

Duncan nodded, giving Luca the okay to tell her about Shannon. Normally, this was something done in person, but it was obvious Tara wasn't going to consent to a visit with cops.

"Tara, I regret to inform you that your sister, Shannon, is dead," Luca stated.

There were a couple of seconds of silence, followed by a sharp gasp. "What?" she demanded but didn't wait for an answer. "You're lying. You're saying that so I'll meet with you."

"I'm saying it because it's true," Luca spelled out. "A positive ID was made of her body just minutes ago."

Tara muttered something Bree didn't catch. "Her body?" she repeated. "Shannon's dead."

"Yes," Luca verified but didn't add more. He was no doubt giving Tara some time to let it sink in.

"How did she die?" Tara asked a couple of moments later.

"We believe she was murdered," Luca said.

No gasp this time, but Tara's moan was plenty loud enough. There were some rustling sounds, and Bree thought maybe Tara was dropping down into a chair. "Who killed her?"

"We don't know yet. We were hoping you could help us with that," Luca explained.

More silence. "You'd better not be trying to pin this on me because I didn't kill my own sister."

The denial sounded adamant enough, but Bree knew that some people were top-notch liars. She had no idea though if Tara was one of them.

"Any idea who'd want Shannon dead?" Luca asked.

"No," Tara said, and her tone had softened some. "But you thought she was involved in what was going on with Manny and Bree, so maybe Shannon got mixed up with the wrong person. That wouldn't be a first," she added in a mutter. "I want to see her body. Where are you sending her?"

"To the county medical examiner. I don't have the number off the top of my head, but if you call the Saddle Ridge dispatcher, they can connect you. Then you can arrange a time to see your sister."

"Good," she said in a hoarse whisper, and she repeated it a couple of times as if using it to try to steady herself. "Please tell me you know who killed her because I want the SOB behind bars."

"I don't know, not yet, but there are a lot of cops investigating Shannon's murder. We're—"

"Did Manny kill her?" Tara blurted out.

That caused everyone in the room to freeze. "Why would you think that?" Luca asked.

"Because he's an SOB, that's why," Tara was quick to say. "He fired me, did you know that?" Again, she didn't wait for an answer. "Manny's a lying lowlife scum, and I wouldn't be surprised if he was using my sister. Used her and then killed her." A hoarse sob tore from her throat. "If he did kill Shannon, I will bury him."

"Tara," Luca warned, "you need to calm down. And you need to stay away from Manny. Leave this to the cops. Like I said, we're investigating several possibilities. Some cops are headed to Shannon's apartment in Austin now to see if there's anything there that'll point us in the direction of her killer."

"Her apartment in Austin?" Tara questioned. "She moved out of there close to a year ago."

Bree was certain Luca, Duncan and Slater didn't miss the timing of that. It meshed with when her mother had been kidnapped.

"Do you know where Shannon had been living?" Luca asked.

"The last time I saw her, she said she was staying in a travel trailer our grandparents left her. She had it parked on a lot she was renting... Hang on a sec," Tara muttered. "I put the address in my phone." A couple of seconds later, she read it off. "It's 116 Wilmer Cranston Road, Bulverde."

Slater immediately pulled up a map on his laptop and showed it to them. It was less than five miles from the burned-out cabin and where Shannon's body had been found.

"Get someone out there right now," Duncan told Slater, and Bree understood the urgency. Shannon's killer might intend to destroy the trailer if he or she hadn't done that already.

Slater stepped into the dining room to make a call while Luca continued with Tara. "Thanks for the address."

"I hope you find something there that tells you who killed her," Tara was quick to say. "And if it's Manny, then I think I can add a nail to his coffin."

"What do you mean by that?" Luca asked, obviously just as unnerved by the comment as Duncan and Bree were.

"I mean, I might have some proof that'll help you convict Manny of murder," Tara spelled out.

"What kind of proof?" Luca demanded.

But he was talking to the air because Tara had already ended the call.

Chapter Eleven

Luca, Bree, Duncan and Slater stood in the living room of the ranch, their attention pinned to Luca's phone. They watched as Woodrow, who had FaceTimed them, approached the travel trailer where Shannon had supposedly lived.

This was not the way Luca wanted to conduct a search. Especially a search that could finally give Bree and him answers as to who was trying to kill them. But Luca also hadn't wanted to leave Bree behind while he joined the search. Duncan had agreed, and that's why he'd sent Woodrow to accompany County Deputy Morales.

Thankfully, Beatrice and Joelle had agreed to stay upstairs with the babies. Both Izzie and Gabriel were way too young to know what was going on, but neither Luca nor Bree had wanted them in the room in case something god-awful was discovered in the search.

Like another body.

After all, Shannon might not be the only loose end a killer wanted to tie up.

Woodrow panned his phone the entire length of the trailer, and Luca could see it wasn't that large, but it seemed to be in good shape with no obvious damage to the sleek silver exterior. Woodrow then turned his camera back on Morales as he went up the narrow trio of steps. He already had his weapon drawn, and he knocked on the door.

"I'm Deputy Morales," he announced. "Anyone here?"

There was no response, which wasn't a surprise since there'd been no vehicles in the gravel driveway that led to the trailer. From what Luca had been able to see so far, this wasn't the sort of campground where people normally parked their RVs and such. There were no community buildings, no pristine trails. This was basically just a partially cleared area in the woods, with an old mailbox to indicate the address. It was secluded, and with no neighbors in sight, no one would have seen Shannon coming or going, which was probably why she'd chosen this particular location.

"Anyone here?" Morales called out again, and when he didn't get a response, he gloved up and tested the doorknob. The deputy frowned and glanced back at Woodrow when the knob turned. "It's not locked."

Even though Luca couldn't see Woodrow's right hand, he knew his fellow deputy already had his weapon drawn, and judging from the movement of the phone, Woodrow was adjusting his aim in case someone inside the trailer started shooting. Morales was doing the same.

Morales eased open the door and immediately stepped to the side. A classic cop move so he wouldn't be in the line of fire.

But no shots came.

In fact, nothing happened. There was only silence and darkness in the trailer.

Still staying to the side, Morales reached in with his gloved left hand and turned on the lights. He must have not heard or seen anything alarming because he stepped in with Woodrow right beside him. Woodrow set his phone aside for a couple of moments while he, too, put on some gloves.

When Woodrow resumed the call, Luca got confirmation that the camper was indeed small, with a kitchen on one side and a seating area on the other that had been let out into a bed. An unmade one. There were clothes strewn on the floor and take-out bags on the narrow strip of counter.

The bathroom door was open so Morales headed there while Woodrow focused on going through the pockets of the clothes at the foot of the bed and on the floor. "Nothing," he relayed, moving to the small table next to the bed.

There was a phone charger plugged in but no phone or laptop, though Luca saw a charger for that as well.

"I think someone's cleaned out the place," Morales relayed from the bathroom. "I can see where some things were, but the shelf and the trash can are empty in here."

That sent Woodrow to the cabinet under the sink where he, too, found an empty trash can. Considering the take-out bags were still there, it did appear that someone had almost certainly gone through it and removed anything incriminating.

And that someone was no doubt Shannon's killer.

"Any sign that the door had been jimmied open?" Luca asked, though he believed he already knew the answer.

"None," Woodrow confirmed while he checked behind the trash can. Nothing there. He moved on to checking the bags, stopping to check the receipt that was taped to one of them. "This was a pickup from this morning at eight, and it came from the diner in Saddle Ridge."

Slater and Duncan both cursed, and Luca figured Bree was mentally doing the same. This meant Shannon had likely been the one who'd set the fire in the parking lot, though it was beyond risky of her to order takeout from the diner since it was so close to the sheriff's office.

"She must have come back here after being in Saddle Ridge," Woodrow concluded, panning the camera around again. "But there's no blood. No signs that anything violent happened in here."

"No signs of that in the bathroom either," Morales added.

The deputy started going through the fridge while Woodrow went back to the bed. He lifted it and muttered, "What's this?"

The camera angle wasn't right for Luca to see what had caught Woodrow's attention, but it obviously got the other deputy's as well because Morales joined him and took Woodrow's phone so he could aim it at a piece of paper.

"It's a torn-off piece of a white delivery bag," Woodrow explained, "and there's some writing on it." He paused, did some cursing of his own. "It's Bree's address."

Luca heard the quick breath that Bree took in. Of course, Bree had known that Shannon was likely involved in the attempt to kidnap Gabriel, but it still had to feel like a punch to the gut.

"There's something else," Woodrow went on. "It's the name *Aubrey* with a circle drawn around it. There are some doodles, too."

Morales shifted the camera so they could see it, and it did indeed look as if someone, Shannon probably, had done some crude drawings of a rifle and a baby. Now it was Luca who felt the gut punch. Because one of the doodles was another name.

Manny.

The last letter of the name had a little heart dangling from it.

"Manny claimed he didn't know Shannon that well," Bree muttered.

Yeah, he had. "If we confront him with it, he'll probably just say he has no idea why Shannon wrote his name." Luca paused. "But Manny might own up to knowing who this other woman is."

"Aubrey," Slater repeated, and he hurried to his laptop.

"I've seen that name before." It took him nearly a minute before he finally got that *aha* gleam in his eye. "Aubrey Kincaid. She was arrested with Shannon about four years ago when they were caught doing a B and E. Aubrey didn't have a previous record so she got parole." He continued to type on his keyboard. "And Shannon and Aubrey were in the army together."

Bingo. That was a solid connection. "Contact information?" Luca asked, grabbing a notepad so he'd be ready. Slater rattled off an Austin address and a phone number.

"Slater, try to call her," Duncan instructed, "but block your number. If she sees a cop calling, she probably won't answer."

"True," Slater muttered, and he made the call and put it on Speaker. It was answered on the first ring.

"Shannon?" a woman immediately said. "Is that you?"

"Yes," Bree lied, making her voice a hoarse whisper.

"Where the hell are you?" the woman demanded. "We were supposed to leave for the McCullough ranch by now."

Hell. That was another gut punch. They'd planned to come here, and Luca figured that meant they'd planned another attack.

"Shannon?" the woman repeated. "Are you there?" She sounded suspicious.

It was that suspicious tone that no doubt had Slater responding the way he did. He cupped his hand over his mouth and muttered something that was indistinguishable.

"I can't hear you," the woman said, punctuating that with some raw profanity. "This is a bad connection. Where are you?" she repeated.

Slater did more of the muffled muttering.

"Hang up and call me back," Aubrey instructed. "And make

it fast. We're already running a half hour late, and we're not going to get paid if we screw this up."

Luca held his breath, hoping that Aubrey was about to say who was paying them. And for what? But she merely added. "Call me right back."

Slater hung up, hit Redial, and waited for Aubrey to answer. She did. "This better be a good connection. Are you still out there in the sticks?"

Slater repeated some muttering, causing Aubrey to curse some more.

"All right, just meet me at the ranch," Aubrey said. "We can…" She stopped, and a few moments crawled by. "Shannon?" she questioned. She paused again, doled out some more profanity, and Luca could hear her suspicions skyrocketing.

Not for long though.

Because Aubrey hung up.

Duncan whipped out his phone to call Austin PD. He didn't have to spell out that they had to stop an attack on the ranch. They needed to find Aubrey now.

BREE KNEW EVERYTHING possible was being done to find Aubrey, but that didn't help settle her nerves one bit. Aubrey's words kept racing through Bree's head. Words that tightened and twisted every muscle in her body.

We're already running a half hour late, and we're not going to get paid if we screw this up.

Aubrey had made it crystal clear that Shannon and she had plans to come here. Maybe to try to kill Luca and her. Maybe to try to kidnap Gabriel. It was possible Aubrey would carry through with it even if Shannon wasn't with her.

Bree had considered taking Gabriel and just leaving in a cruiser with Luca. But that could be a huge risk, too, since Aubrey could attack them on the road. At least here they had a security system. And now that they knew Aubrey was coming, they could watch for her.

That was the reason Bree had come back to the guest room so she could be with Gabriel and keep an eye out the upstairs window. Thankfully, Luca had come with her. Just having him nearby was a reminder that they were a united front there to keep their son safe.

Luca was on the phone, getting updates from Duncan, but he was practically whispering so Bree couldn't hear what he was saying. The low voice was no doubt so he wouldn't wake up Gabriel, who'd just been fed and was now asleep in Bree's arms. Since she very much wanted those updates, she eased him into his crib and went closer to Luca.

"I think we need to move another of the hands to the back part of the ranch near the pond," he said to whomever was on the other end of the line. "One is already patrolling that area now, but it's a weak spot. There's a trail there with easy access to the road."

There was. And it was a trail where Luca and she had parked and done some heavy making out when they'd been teenagers. It probably wouldn't be an easy place for a non-local like Aubrey to find, but the woman could and probably had researched such things.

Luca ended the call and slipped his phone into his pocket. "That was Slater. We're working out where to put the hands and the deputies who are keeping watch."

"Good," she muttered. And it was. Any and all security measures could keep Gabriel safe. But Bree knew there were plenty of weak spots where Aubrey could get through. "I read her background. She's had a lot of firearms training."

He made a sound of agreement. Then he sighed as he pulled her into his arms. "If she decides to do this mission solo, we have more than a dozen hands and deputies to spot her. It's my guess though that she's gone on the run. Or maybe run back to her boss because she was suspicious of the two calls she got from an unknown number."

"Yes," Bree said. She had to figure that Aubrey would at least contact her boss. Whoever that was. Perhaps Manny since Shannon had doodled the man's name along with Aubrey's. No matter who it was though, during that call Aubrey might learn Shannon was dead.

"Unless Aubrey was putting on a really good act, I didn't get the sense that she was the one who'd murdered Shannon," Bree added.

"Neither did I," he said.

Bree was certain that Luca had been through every one of the woman's words many times. For such a short one-way dialogue, they'd learned a lot. Shannon and Aubrey were basically hired guns, and they were supposed to have arrived at the ranch well over an hour ago. Added to that, Aubrey must have been accustomed to having Shannon call her on a burner with an unknown number since Aubrey didn't question that. She'd simply answered Slater's call and had assumed it was Shannon.

"If Aubrey goes to her boss, he or she could kill her, too," Bree pointed out, but she figured she was voicing what Luca already knew.

His nod confirmed that, and while neutralizing such a potential threat would be good for the here and now, it wouldn't be good in the long term. If they could make contact with Aubrey, they stood a chance of learning who'd hired her. If, like Shannon, she was killed, or simply vanished, the boss could just end up hiring other would-be killers to come after them.

At that thought, she had to close her eyes for a moment. Had to try to rein in the panic that was starting to slide through her. Luca helped with that.

By kissing her.

Since her eyes were closed, Bree hadn't seen it coming, but she certainly felt it. His mouth landed on hers for what he'd probably thought was a soothing gesture. And it soothed all right. It also gave her a jolt of pure, hot lust.

The heat came, skimming right over the panic and filling her with a need that she knew was a distraction. That didn't stop her from sinking right into the kiss. It didn't stop her from wrapping her arms around Luca and pulling him closer.

So many sensations hit her at once. The feel of his body against hers. His scent that was as familiar to her as her own. The taste of him. That had always revved up the heat, and this time was no different.

Bree wanted to just keep kissing him. To get lost for a moment in the hazy heat he was creating. She wanted to hold on to Luca and never let go. But this was the opposite of a security measure so with much regret, she eased back.

"Sorry," she muttered.

The corner of his mouth lifted in a dry smile. "I'm the one who started it." He paused, brushed a chaste kiss on her forehead. "When this is over—"

He stopped at the sound. Not Gabriel whimpering this time. This was a car engine, and it was approaching the house. Mercy. Was this Aubrey? Had she decided to go through with an attack?

Luca and she whirled toward the window and saw two armed ranch hands step in front of the dark blue car that was in the driveway. Both hands took aim at the driver, and a couple of seconds later, a woman stepped out.

Tara.

She lifted her hands high in the air, and even though she was saying something to the ranch hands, Bree couldn't make out what since she was so far away.

Luca's phone buzzed, and she saw Duncan's name on the screen just as Luca answered it. "I'm guessing you weren't expecting her," Duncan said.

"No," Luca verified. "I'll call her and see what she wants. The hands have instructions not to let her close to the house."

Luca ended the call with Duncan and made one to Tara. They watched as Tara said something else to the hands, and then she got back in her car. Seconds later, she answered.

"Deputy Vanetti," Tara said. "You need to tell your goons to let me through."

"They're ranch hands, not goons, and they're not letting any unscheduled visitors through," he snapped. "Why are you here, Tara?"

"Because of Manny," the woman was quick to say. "Because I want you to arrest him." Tara's voice trailed off into a sob. "I want him to pay for what he did to my sister."

"We're not certain Manny killed your sister," Luca pointed out just as there was a light tap at the door, and Duncan announced he was coming in. He did, and he headed straight to the window with Luca and her so he could hear the phone conversation.

"Well, I have something that'll help convince you," Tara argued. "Let me in, and I'll show it to you."

Luca huffed. Clearly, he wasn't convinced this wasn't some kind of ploy or maybe even a diversion so that Aubrey could get close to the house.

"What do you have, Tara?" Luca demanded.

"Something important. A video I recorded," she added when Luca only huffed again. "Trust me, you'll want to see it."

Bree certainly wanted to see it, and if it was indeed something that could lead to an arrest, then this could be the break in the case they'd been searching for. Then again, it could turn out to be nothing, so Bree tried to tamp down her hopes.

"Text me the video," Luca said.

"No, I want to show it to you," Tara insisted.

"I'm not letting you inside, Tara," Luca spelled out. "If you want me to see the video, then text it to me. If not, then hand your phone to one of the ranch hands, and he'll bring it to me."

Tara's next sob was even louder than her other one. "All right, I'll text it to you, but swear to me that you'll arrest Manny once you've seen it."

"I can't promise that," Luca said in a tone to indicate Tara was definitely testing his patience. "But I will view it and see if there's anything that could result in charges being filed."

That seemed to appease Tara because Bree saw the woman type in something on her phone. A few moments later, Luca got the text. Once the video loaded, Luca motioned for Bree to step to the side of the window. Probably because this could be some kind of ruse to distract them while a shooter got in place to try to gun them down.

Bree did move to the side but motioned for Luca and Duncan to do the same. They did, but both angled themselves so they could keep an eye on Tara.

The video finally came on the screen, and Bree immediately saw this wasn't some kind of security footage. It appeared to have been filmed from a camera phone, and the person holding it didn't exactly have a steady hand. There was also something obstructing the view, and it took her a moment to realize the person was likely recording this through an ajar door.

"Manny," Bree muttered when she saw him. He was in an office with a desk and bookshelves, and he wasn't alone. There was a woman with him, but Bree could only see the back of her head.

"I don't want you showing up at my apartment in the middle of the night," Brighton snarled. "I'm tired of going through this because it's over."

"It's not over until I say it is," Manny lashed out.

Just as Manny said that, the woman turned enough so that Bree could see her face. Yes, it was Brighton all right, and it was hard to tell with the shaky recording, but she seemed to be crying.

"If it was over, you wouldn't have called me," Manny continued. "You wouldn't have wanted to keep having sex with me."

"It was just sex," Brighton insisted, the anger coming off her voice. "And, trust me, I regret it. You think I enjoyed that scene you just made when you showed up at my place last night?"

"It wasn't a scene," Manny snapped. "I was merely talking to my replacement."

Replacement? So, Brighton had seemingly dumped Manny and moved on to someone else.

"You were causing a scene," Brighton said like a warning, "and I want it to stop. Don't contact me again. I love this bar, and I plan on coming here in the future, but I don't want to have to deal with you, understand?"

The camera stayed on Manny's face, and Bree had no trouble seeing the rage there. Yes, rage. Apparently, Manny wasn't ready to accept this breakup. And it also meant Manny had lied to them by omission.

"Check the date of the video," Tara insisted after the recording had ended.

Luca did. And cursed. Because this had been recorded just two days before Brighton's murder.

"Well, does that convince you that Manny killed Brighton?" Tara asked.

Luca didn't respond to that. Instead, he doled out a question of his own. "Do you know your sister's friend, Aubrey Kincaid?"

"A little," Tara said after a short pause. "Why?"

"Because we're trying to get in touch with her. Do you have any idea where she might be?"

Tara paused again. "No, but Manny might. Aubrey and he dated for a while."

Bingo. There was another red flag. Well, it was if Tara was telling the truth.

"So, are you going to arrest Manny?" Tara repeated with even more venom in her demand.

Duncan nodded, not responding to Tara but letting Luca and Bree know what he was about to do. "I'll get an arrest warrant started. Arrange to have Manny picked up right away."

Chapter Twelve

Luca kept watch as they made the drive into town to the sheriff's office. He was in the back seat with Bree who was firing glances around, too. Ditto for Woodrow and Duncan who were in the front. Luca figured Slater, Joelle and Carmen were doing the same back at the ranch, along with the hands and reserve deputies who were still patrolling the ground.

They had put a lot of security in place to keep Gabriel safe while they made this trip. There were now nine armed cops or ranch hands guarding him, and Luca had to hope that the small army would be enough. Had to hope, too, that maybe this journey wouldn't turn out to be a big mistake. But pretty much anything they did at this point could fall into the "big mistake" category.

That included doing nothing at all.

Yes, they'd likely be safer if they stayed put inside the ranch house. *Likely.* But if they'd done a correct interpretation of those notes in Shannon's trailer, then no place was truly safe. And they had to do something about that for Gabriel and everyone else who happened to be in the path of this killer.

That something meant Bree and him traveling into town to the sheriff's office to have a chat with Manny.

Manny hadn't resisted the warrant and had immediately

come in for an interview, but he had demanded to speak to Luca and Bree. Luca had considered refusing, or leaving Bree at the ranch, while he went to hear what Manny had to say. Hell, he'd considered a lot of things, but this was a murder investigation and at least some of the things had to be done by the book. That included holding the interview at the sheriff's office since that's where Manny had surrendered himself. It was also procedure for Manny to have his lawyer with him—which he did.

However, it wasn't the norm for a suspect to ask to speak with two of the people involved in the attacks. Still, Luca had reasoned that Manny might finally be ready to spill all. And spilling all could finally put an end to the danger to Gabriel.

During his visual sweep of their surroundings, Luca's gaze collided with Bree's. She was worried all right. And exhausted. Too bad he couldn't do squat about either of those things.

"A few days ago, our biggest concern was how we were going to co-parent Gabriel while being at odds with each other," she muttered.

For some stupid reason, that made him smile. "Yeah," he muttered.

They had much more serious concerns now, but Luca no longer felt the at-odds things. That was something good to come out of all of this. They were solidly on the same side. But would that last? Luca hoped it would but knew there were no guarantees that Bree would ever be able to look at him and not think of her murdered father.

When they reached the sheriff's office, Duncan was forced to park out front since the main parking lot was still being processed and cleaned. However, the fire chief, Elmore Dauber, was on scene, and he motioned that he needed to talk to them. Duncan indicated for the chief to meet them inside.

They hurried into the building, but the only people Luca saw inside were the two deputies, Sonya and Brandon Rooney. "Manny and his lawyer are already in the interview room," Brandon explained. "Sonya searched Manny and read him his rights again."

Duncan nodded and then shifted his attention to the fire chief when he came in. Elmore was a former deputy turned fireman, with over twenty years of experience under his belt, so Luca knew this part of the investigation was in capable hands.

"We're nearly finished up out there," Elmore explained, "and I'll be doing my report as soon as I'm back in my office. But I can give you the high points now." He drew in a long breath. "The accelerant was gasoline, and we found the empty can behind a tree at the back of the parking lot. It could have been there for hours. Maybe even days. There were some sticks lying around so it's possible they were used to cover the can."

So, this had been planned maybe well in advance. That didn't surprise Luca, but he wished someone had seen that can before it'd been turned into a weapon.

"A simple trigger device ignited the gasoline," Elmore went on. "We've got what's left of the device, and it'll be examined, but this is something anyone can learn to make from the internet."

"Was it on a timer?" Duncan asked.

Elmore shook his head. "It was set off with a remote control or maybe a phone. Again, not hard to do if you can read and follow instructions."

Luca considered that for a moment. "How close would the remote or phone have to be to ignite it?"

"Not especially close. We might be able to give you specifics on that once it's examined, but it's my guess the arsonist had line of sight of all of you when you exited the building and triggered it then."

That was Luca's guess as well. A timer would only be effective if the person had known the exact time they'd be leaving the sheriff's office.

"I figure we're looking for someone who was hanging around within a block of the building," Elmore added. He looked at Duncan. "You've requested footage from the camera at the bank?"

Duncan nodded. "The camera was working, but they're having trouble getting the footage off the server. The techs from the Rangers' crime lab are assisting, so we should have the recordings soon."

Luca was definitely hoping for that, and while he was at it, he was also hoping the arsonist didn't know about that particular camera and hadn't bothered to conceal his or her face. Of course, Manny and Tara would likely be on the feed since they'd been in the area for interviews. However, there would have been no valid reason for Shannon and/or Aubrey to be on scene. But it was possible that by the time of the fire, Shannon had already been dead.

"Go ahead and see what Manny wanted to tell Bree and you," Duncan instructed Luca. "I've got a few more questions for Elmore, and then I'll join you. Oh, and record everything Manny says. I don't want this to be an off-the-record kind of conversation just because Bree is there."

Luca was glad to hear that. He didn't want Manny trying to hide behind what he might consider to be private. As far as Luca was concerned, Manny's right to privacy was over.

"I'm a legal consultant for the Rangers," Bree pointed out. "Since the Rangers are assisting in this investigation, I can use that to be present during interviews of a suspect." She lifted her shoulder. "Well, I can as long as Manny's lawyer doesn't flat-out object and start some legal wrangling. I can wrangle right back, but I don't want to do anything to compromise an arrest."

Duncan stayed quiet a moment, obviously processing that and then nodded. "Get permission from Manny and the lawyer to be there," he agreed. "I haven't arrested Manny yet, but let's all hope he'll say something to the two of you that'll make that happen."

Yeah, that had to happen because if it didn't, there likely wouldn't be an arrest. There was no physical evidence to link Manny to Brighton's murder or any of the attacks. Of course, there was the recording that Tara had made, but it might or might not be able to be used as evidence. Even if it was, the video wasn't proof Manny had murdered Brighton.

Luca and Bree headed to the interview room, and the moment Luca opened the door, Manny practically jumped to his feet.

"I didn't murder anyone," Manny immediately volunteered.

Luca held up his hand in a gesture for Manny to wait, and he turned to Manny's lawyer. "I'm Deputy Vanetti, and this is legal consultant for the Rangers, Bree McCullough. Do either of you have any objections to her being here?"

"No," Manny snapped. "In fact, I want her here so I can make both of you understand that someone is setting me up."

Luca shifted his attention to the lawyer. "No objections at this time. I'm Corey Bennett," he said. He shook hands with both Luca and Bree, and Luca noted that the lawyer didn't seem anxious or ready to launch into a tirade about how they were treating his client.

"Someone is setting me up," Manny repeated, but once again, Luca gestured for him to hold off on that so he could start the recording and read in the time and those present.

"You believe someone is setting you up," Luca repeated. "Who and why?"

"I don't know." Manny groaned and dropped back into the chair. "But someone must be if there was a warrant for my arrest. Why the hell would your sheriff do that?"

Bree and Luca took the chairs across from Manny and the lawyer. "Because we recently got access to a recording of you having a very nasty argument with Brighton Cooper, a woman you claimed you didn't know well." Luca leaned in, spearing Manny with his narrowed gaze. "You knew her, and if you lie and say you didn't, then I'm arresting you on the spot."

Manny had already opened his mouth, but he closed it, huffed and leaned back in his seat. "A video," he repeated. "How did you get it and what's on it?"

"I'm not at liberty to disclose who gave it to us, but it's obvious from the recording that Brighton and you were lovers, and you were enraged when she ended things. Lie to me about that, and you're under arrest," Luca repeated.

Manny's lawyer started to speak, but Manny lay his hand on the man's arm. "Tara," Manny grumbled. "She recorded something and gave it to you. She's the one trying to set me up."

"Why would she do that?" Bree wanted to know.

Manny made a *duh* sound. "I've already told you that Tara's upset because I dumped her. She'd do anything to get back at me."

That was possible, but Luca didn't voice that to Manny. "Tara didn't make you lie to us about Shannon," Luca pointed out. "You did that on your own."

"I did," Manny admitted. "But lying about my sexual partners isn't the same as committing multiple felonies."

Maybe not. But it could be red flags.

"What about Aubrey Kincaid?" Luca pressed. "Is she a lover, too?"

Manny's forehead bunched up. "No. Why are you asking that? Did Tara claim I'd slept with Aubrey?"

Luca didn't respond to that either. He just sat quietly and stared at Manny until the man was practically squirming in his seat.

"I didn't sleep with Aubrey," Manny insisted. "I'll admit to having an affair with Brighton, and she did break up with me. But I didn't kill her, and there won't be anything on any video saying otherwise."

Luca gave that some thought. Manny could probably say something like that because perhaps he'd never come out and threatened Brighton with violence. The violence could have still happened though.

"I was in love with Brighton," Manny added, his voice lowering to a whisper. "I loved her, but she was seeing someone else."

"Who?" Bree immediately asked.

Manny shrugged. "It's all speculation. You're not the only one who investigated Brighton's murder," he said.

Luca and Bree exchanged glances. "What does that mean?" Bree pressed.

"After you called and asked me to give you those old receipts, I talked to some of the regular customers who were around back then. No one could confirm it," Manny explained, "but a few people recalled her having some conversations with that doctor."

Everything inside Luca went still. "What doctor?"

"Dr. Nathan Bagley," Manny spat out like profanity. "That snake oil quack who lives right here under your own nose."

Luca made a circling motion for Manny to continue just

as Duncan came in. Duncan announced himself for the re-cording and took a seat at the end of the table.

"Manny here was just telling us that he suspects that Brighton was seeing Dr. Bagley," Luca summarized.

Duncan's eyebrows rose, but he didn't get a chance to say anything because Manny continued. "I don't have proof of it so don't try to charge me for withholding evidence. And I only found out about this two days ago after Bree wanted the receipts."

"Why don't you just tell us what you do know about Brighton and the doctor?" Duncan prompted, not address-ing the withholding gripe.

"I knew Brighton was seeing someone else," Manny quickly confirmed, "and like I already told Luca and Bree, a couple of people I talked to said they recalled seeing her with Dr. Bagley."

Duncan pushed a notepad Manny's way. "Jot down the names of those people."

Manny huffed, but he wrote two names and passed the notepad back to Duncan. Luca glanced at the names but didn't recognize them. Bree shook her head, indicating that she didn't either.

"So, these two people saw Brighton with Nathan Bagley," Luca went on. "Did you know she was seeing the doctor?"

Manny wasn't so quick to respond this time. "No, but once she came in the bar sporting bruises on her arm. They were clearly marks left by fingers. It was obvious to me she'd got-ten them when someone manhandled her."

"Bruises?" Bree questioned. "When was this?"

"About a month or so before she died," Manny answered.

Luca had studied the photos of Brighton's lifeless body, and while there had been bruises on various parts of her torso and arms, there hadn't been any that resembled marks made by fingers. A month though would have been plenty of time for them to have healed.

Manny lifted his arm and clamped onto the fleshy part between his elbow and wrist. "There with the thumbprint underneath and the other four on top. I was furious that someone had hurt her like that, and I wanted her to come to my office so we could talk about it. She wouldn't. She said the bruises were nothing and that I should mind my own business, but then she admitted she was having trouble with someone she was seeing."

"Did she specifically say she was seeing Nathan Bagley?" Luca asked.

"No." Manny sighed. "But one of the bruises was bigger than the other, and when I pointed to it, she mumbled something about the guy wearing a class ring and that the stone in it was tilted to the side on his finger."

Luca tried to picture Nathan's hands, trying to recall if he had worn a ring with a stone, but he couldn't recall one. Apparently, neither did Bree because she shook her head again.

"I was trying to rein in my temper because I knew if I got mad, Brighton would just walk away," Manny went on, "so I tried to get her to tell me more about the bruise by saying it must have been a big ring. She said it was one of those chunky gold ones from Texas A&M."

Bree took out her phone, and Luca knew what she was doing. A couple of moments later, he got confirmation when she showed him the hospital information page with Nathan's bio. There it was.

He'd attended the Texas A&M School of Medicine.

Again, that was nowhere near proof that Nathan had murdered Brighton, but it was a connection that needed further investigation. They already knew from the receipts that Nathan had been at the bar the night Brighton was murdered, and if he had been involved in a volatile relationship with Brighton, then that would give him motive.

"Any reason you didn't tell us sooner about seeing those bruises on Brighton?" Duncan asked.

"Because I forgot about it. Hell, it's been five years, and I'd moved on with my life. Or rather I had moved on before you guys started trying to accuse me of things I didn't do."

"Then why didn't you tell the original investigating officer?" Duncan pressed. "You hear about a woman you claim to have loved had been murdered, and you know someone bruised her up just a month earlier, and you didn't think that was something the cops should know?"

Some of the color drained from Manny's face, and he shook his head. "Her death gutted me, and I wasn't thinking about anything but my own grief."

Duncan made a sound to indicate he wasn't totally convinced of that. Neither was Luca. Manny had had plenty of time to work out what to say so he didn't sound like a killer. And maybe he wasn't. But Luca wasn't taking him off the suspect list, and he doubted Duncan or Bree would either.

"I need to have a word with my client," the lawyer said.

Duncan nodded, stood, and Luca, Bree and he went back into the hall. "I want to get old work schedules for the hospital," Duncan said, keeping his voice low. "I need to see if Nathan was possibly on duty when Brighton was murdered. We know he was at the bar that night, but we don't have an exact time of death for her. I want to know where he was in the hours leading up to and after she was killed."

"Good idea," Bree muttered. "If he wasn't on the schedule, then he can't claim that as an alibi." She paused. "Nathan could have murdered her," she added. "Not premeditated but in the heat of the moment."

Luca turned to her so fast, he heard his neck pop. "You said Nathan never got violent with you."

"He didn't," she insisted, "but I thought maybe the potential was there because of his temper. It was always there, simmering just beneath the surface."

Luca had to rein in his own temper over hearing that. Not anger aimed at Bree but at the SOB Nathan. And anger wasn't going to help solve this investigation.

"Did you ever see Nathan wearing a Texas A&M ring?" Duncan asked her.

Bree shook her head. "And I think I would have noticed. Those class rings are usually big, and since I went to A&M's rival school, University of Texas, I probably would have made some kind of joke about it."

Luca considered that for a moment. "You dated Nathan long after Brighton had been murdered so maybe he quit wearing the ring after he killed her. He might have believed the ring had left a mark on her. Like the bruise on her arm."

Both Duncan and Bree made quick sounds of agreement. "Nathan might not have thrown the ring away," Bree added. "He could have just stopped wearing it." She looked at Duncan. "What are the chances of getting a search warrant to go through Nathan's house?"

"Nil on the evidence we have." Duncan groaned, shook his head. "Which as you know isn't much. Yes, he was in the bar the night Brighton was murdered, but with her estimated time of death, she wasn't killed until about four to six hours or so after she left Hush, Hush. Nathan could have been home. Or at work."

Bree groaned as well, not because she was disagreeing with Duncan, but because she knew all of this was true. It also wasn't a mark of guilt that two people had seen Nathan talking to Brighton. Neither was Manny's speculation that Nathan had put those bruises on her.

So, yeah, nil chances on the search warrant.

"We can't just ask Nathan if he has a ring like that," Luca spelled out, "because if he's guilty, he could toss it. If he hasn't already done it, that is."

They all went quiet, and Luca knew they were trying to figure out a way around this.

"I can pay Nathan a visit and try to have a discreet look around," Bree threw out there.

Luca gave her a flat look and was sure Duncan was doing the same. They both voiced a firm "no" together.

"I wouldn't take the ring if I spotted it," she went on. "I could leave it in place and then you could get a warrant. If the ring is still there, it could have Brighton's DNA on it since she was stabbed to death."

"No," Duncan repeated, and Luca shifted his flat look to a narrow-eyed stare.

"You're not going into the house of a potential killer," Luca insisted. "And even if he didn't murder Brighton, Nathan has a temper and a short fuse. You could be hurt. Or worse."

"I could have my phone on," she suggested. "And Duncan and you could be waiting nearby to run inside the house if anything goes wrong." She stopped and shut her eyes for a moment. "Look, I don't want to be around Nathan, but these attacks have got to stop, and this might be the way to do it."

"No," Duncan said for a third time.

Bree clearly didn't like that because she huffed. "Then, what? We can't just ask around to see if anyone recalls Nathan wearing a ring because it'd get back to him and he'd ditch it."

True, but an idea flashed into Luca's head. "We can search

through social media and look for any photos of Nathan that might have been posted of him wearing a ring. Coupled with Manny's statement, that might be enough to get a warrant."

Duncan didn't look convinced, but he nodded. "Let's do that." He took out his phone. "I can get Joelle started on it right now. She's been chomping at the bit to get more involved in the investigation."

Yes, she had, and when Bree and Luca got back to the ranch, they could search as well. Newspaper archives might have something as well.

At the sound of footsteps, they turned to see Brandon making his way to them, and the deputy had his attention on a laptop he was carrying.

"We just got back the footage from the bank camera," Brandon explained, turning the laptop toward them and hitting Play.

Luca watched as Main Street came into view. Not the sheriff's office since it was tucked just out of sight of the camera, but as the feed advanced, he saw the smoke billowing out of the parking lot.

He soon spotted the woman.

Luca instantly recognized her because he'd seen her driver's license photo. It was Aubrey. She was on the sidewalk, moving in the opposite direction of the sheriff's office and the fire, but she was glancing over her shoulder.

And she smiled.

Luca cursed. The woman was actually happy that she'd put them in danger like that.

"I want an arrest warrant for her," Duncan snarled.

"I'll make that happen," Brandon assured him. "For now, keep watching," he instructed, though he sounded just as angry at the smile as the rest of them were.

Someone had already zoomed in on Aubrey so they watched

as she lifted her phone that was already in her hand, and she made a call right before she walked out of camera range.

"The techs believe they can enhance the footage and get the number she called," Brandon said. "What do you bet she was calling her boss to let him or her know the job was done?"

There were no bets because that would have almost certainly been what she'd done.

"What are the odds they can get the number?" Duncan asked.

"Good," Brandon verified. "In a couple of hours, we might know the name of the killer."

Chapter Thirteen

Back at the ranch, Bree glanced around the living room and saw nothing but frustrated expressions. Her own expression fell into that category as well. For the past four hours while the nannies and Sandra had watched the babies, Luca, Jo-elle, Slater and she had been digging through social media and newspaper archives to try to find a photo of Nathan wearing the ring.

They'd all struck out.

There'd been plenty of pictures of Nathan, but so far, his hands hadn't been visible in any of them. So, Bree had moved on to a different approach. She was calling jewelers who specialized in making and selling rings for the A&M School of Medicine. So far, she wasn't having much luck with that either, even though she had introduced herself on the calls as legal counsel for the Texas Rangers and was looking for information pertinent to an investigation. The people she'd spoken to had all been cooperative, but none had a record of Nathan purchasing such a ring.

Duncan was clearly getting some frustrating news as well because he'd started pacing and muttering under his breath while he listened to the latest call he'd received. Bree seriously doubted he was hearing anything that would give them hope that this case would soon be solved.

And that's why she would have to push the visit to Nathan.

Duncan, Slater and Luca weren't just going to agree so she needed to come up with an angle to convince them. She considered that while she made a call to the next jeweler on her list. As with the other calls, it took her a couple of minutes to work her way through to speak to the manager, and then a perky-sounding woman who introduced herself as Laine Martinez came on the line. Bree went through her spiel again, and as she'd done with the others, she gave the woman three names to search. Nathan's and two others that Bree had plucked from A&M class rosters. That way, the person wouldn't solely home in on Nathan's name and try to contact him.

"The ring would have been purchased about eight or nine years ago," Bree explained. "But please check for a couple of years in either direction in case—"

"Nathan Bagley," Laine confirmed. "Yes, he did purchase a ring from us."

Bree practically sprang to her feet, and it got the attention of the others, except for Duncan who was still on the phone. Slater, Luca and Joelle, however, came closer.

"I'm putting you on Speaker," Bree informed the woman. "I have three police officers with me who'll want to hear this. You can verify that Nathan Bagley bought a ring from you?"

"He did. The ring had the Texas A&M School of Medicine logo and is fourteen-karat yellow gold with a full carat diamond in the center. A custom design," she went on. "And because of the design, it was priced higher than most class rings. He paid just under five thousand dollars for it."

Not a fortune but still expensive. Maybe so expensive that Nathan hadn't been able to part with it.

"Do you have a receipt for the purchase?" Bree asked.

"Not a paper one, but all the information is here in my computer files. Would you like me to send you a copy?"

"Yes," Bree couldn't say fast enough, and she gave the woman her email address. The moment Bree saw the info pop into her inbox, she thanked Laine, ended the call and pinned her attention to Luca.

"No, I don't want you going into Nathan's house to look for the ring," Luca snapped, and then he sighed, and his expression softened. "It's too dangerous."

"It is," Duncan verified, having obviously heard the gist of what Bree had learned. He put away his phone and joined them. "We'll get to the ring and Nathan, but first, I need to tell you about Aubrey. The tech's got the number she called, but it was made to a burner. The recipient of the call was in Saddle Ridge."

Bree wasn't sure whether to groan or curse so she did both. "All three of our suspects were in Saddle Ridge at the time of the call," she pointed out.

Duncan did some groaning and cursing of his own. "They were, which means the footage didn't help us narrow down anything. Well, nothing except Aubrey being responsible for the fire, and there's no sign of her."

Bree had to hope that would soon change since there was an APB out on the woman. Of course, Aubrey might have already fled.

"I went ahead and told Brandon to cut Manny loose," Duncan added. "His lawyer was squawking about no evidence to hold him, and he's right. So, I told Brandon to let him go with the warning that he not leave the state."

If he was truly guilty, Manny might run, but Bree figured he'd just stand his ground and fight any charges. Nathan would no doubt do the same, which was why they needed more proof. Or something they could use to exclude them as suspects.

Duncan took out his phone again. "I'm calling the hospital to see if Nathan is on duty." They waited, and like her calls to the jewelers, it took him several connections to get to someone who knew the answer. "He went home about an hour ago."

"I have an idea of how to deal with Nathan," Joelle said. She didn't continue until everyone faced her, and she kept her attention on her husband, maybe because she knew she'd have to convince him to go along with any sort of plan. "Since we now have proof that he bought a ring, I could go to his place with backup," she quickly added, "and ask him about it."

This time there were three negative responses. Luca, Slater and Duncan. Duncan's was the loudest.

"Hear me out," Joelle demanded, and Bree noticed her sister instantly switch to cop mode. "We aren't going to get a search warrant, not without alerting Nathan that we could be onto him being a killer. He'd just toss the ring before we got there and maybe say he lost it. But if I show up in an official capacity, with backup," she added again, "then I could question him about the ring. If he denies owning it, then you could use his lie to get a warrant and come straight over before he has the chance to dispose of it."

"And if he attacks you?" Duncan snarled. In contrast, he sounded more like a worried husband than a cop.

Joelle sighed. "He won't because Bree and Slater will be with me."

A hushed silence fell over the room. But it was short-lived. Then, the grumbles and complaints came.

"Nathan could be behind the attacks on Bree," Luca was quick to point out.

"Yes," Joelle admitted, "but he's also smitten with her. Mercy, what a word," she muttered. "But it's the truth. He'll be on his best behavior if Bree is there because he's trying to win her over."

"That's true," Bree said, earning sharp looks from Duncan, Slater and Luca. She went to Luca and ran her hand down the length of his arm while she met him eye to eye. "The attacks have to stop, and Aubrey is still at large. If I can do something to prevent Gabriel from being in danger, then I'll do it. And I'll go in armed," she said. "With Joelle and Slater."

Judging from the tight sets of their jaws, Luca and Duncan weren't convinced. Slater, however, seemed to be seeing the logic of this so Bree continued with the argument.

"The three of us can just show up at Nathan's," Bree spelled out. "Joelle or Slater could read him his rights, and I could hang back, looking sympathetic and acting as if he's being railroaded. That'll make him less defensive and more inclined to play nice. More inclined to lie, too, since he won't want to admit he has anything that can be linked to Brighton."

"I'll use my phone to record him," Joelle said, taking up the cause, "and if he lies, you get the warrant. Slater and I will detain him so he can't leave the room and toss the ring. If he admits he has the ring, then I'll ask him to let me take it into evidence for processing. If he refuses, get the warrant. This can work," she insisted.

Luca looked as if he wanted to curse a blue streak. Probably because he knew it could work as well. But he was also aware of something else.

"Yes, it's a risk," Bree admitted. "We could be attacked going to or from Nathan's house, but we could be attacked anywhere. Including here." Mercy, it twisted at her to voice that last part, but it was true.

"Maternity leave hasn't made me forget how to be a cop," Joelle pointed out to Duncan. "And I'm a good cop. I'll keep my eyes on Nathan the entire time, and if he tries to pull a gun, he'll have three people pulling theirs." She shifted to Luca. "I'm not going to let that scumbag lay one finger on Bree."

The silence came again, and the moments crawled by before Duncan sighed. Bree could tell from his expression that they had convinced him, but he turned to Luca, no doubt to get his take on the plan.

"I could go in with Bree and Joelle," Luca said, but then he immediately waved that off. "No, because Nathan would just get defensive. But I'm going to his house," he insisted. "I'll wait outside in the cruiser."

Bree would feel safer with Luca that close, but that left them with a big problem. "The babies have to be protected," she stated, though she was certain no one had forgotten that.

"I'll stay here," Duncan said, taking out his phone again. "And I'll have Woodrow and Sonya come and stay as backup. I'll have them drive by Nathan's place on the way here to make sure he's actually home." He made the call to get that started.

"You're okay with this plan?" Joelle asked, glancing first at Slater and then Luca before her attention settled on Bree.

Slater shrugged. "This could definitely shake things up. Maybe it'll shake in the right direction."

Luca settled for a nod, and Bree could practically see the nerves tightening in every part of his body. "Give us a minute," Bree said, taking hold of Luca's hand, and she led him out of the living room.

Since Sandra, the nannies and babies were using the family room and adjoining kitchen, she didn't head there. Instead, she took Luca to Duncan's home office, a room that had once been her father's. Yes, there were memories of him here, but at least it was private. She stepped inside with Luca and shut the door.

Then, she kissed him.

Bree hadn't actually intended to do that, but her body was calling the shots here so she kissed him long and deep. Kissed him until she felt some of those nerves start to settle. It worked for her, too, though she knew there'd be a price to pay for this. She could end up with a broken heart since she was falling for Luca all over again. For now, she just enjoyed the moment. The heat.

And Luca.

Definitely an enjoyment, and her body went a little slack in places. The man certainly had a calming effect on her. A surprise since at the same time, he could make her want him more than her next breath.

It had been like this that last time when they'd ended up in bed. The night she'd gotten pregnant with Gabriel. And it stunned her to consider they could easily end up in bed again. Things certainly seemed to be moving that way, and even though she'd been the one to initiate the kiss, Bree didn't think she was ready for that big of a step.

Especially now.

When their son was possibly still in danger.

She eased back, immediately feeling the loss of the heat, and she stared into his eyes. "I can apologize since I shouldn't have done that."

"No apology needed or wanted," Luca let her know. "Did you kiss me to distract me from this plan?" he asked.

"No. But maybe I did it to try to level myself out. I want to do this," she was quick to add. "I need to do this, but I know things can go wrong." He groaned, but she cut him off.

"Trust me when I say I'll do everything to stay safe. So will Joelle and Slater."

Luca stared at her for a couple of seconds and then let out a slow breath. "I do know it, but that doesn't stop me from worrying."

She nodded. "And I'll be worrying about you since you'll be parked outside Nathan's house. We'll both be worried about Gabriel," she added before she stepped back. "I need to go upstairs and get my gun." She'd put it on the top shelf of the closet when Slater had brought it over for her with some clothes and her toiletries.

"I'll check with Duncan to see if he wants to put any more security measures in place, and then I'll meet you in the cruiser," Luca said, and they headed off in different directions.

After Bree had gotten the gun and headed back downstairs, she saw Woodrow and Sonya pull to a stop in front of the house. It was showtime, and just as Sonya and Woodrow came inside, Joelle gave Duncan a quick kiss before Slater, Bree and she headed out to Duncan's cruiser. Bree took the back seat, and Slater got behind the wheel. Joelle was shotgun.

"Does Luca know you're in love with him?" Joelle asked.

Bree frowned at her sister. "Who says I am?"

"Me," Joelle and Slater said in unison.

Bree extended the frown to her brother, though he probably couldn't see her face since his focus was on keeping watch around them. "It's my guess you kissed Luca when you carted him off like that," Slater went on. "And it's also my guess that the two of you enjoyed that kiss way too much."

"Is there a point to this?" Bree asked, huffing.

Slater glanced back at her just long enough to flash her

one of his cocky smiles. "Yeah, the point is love, little sister, and that's what you're in when it comes to Luca."

Bree wanted to dispute that. Couldn't. Because, heck, Slater and Joelle could be right. But even if they were, she had no intentions of trying to work out her feelings right now.

"I'm looking for gunmen," she muttered, pinning her attention to their surroundings.

Thankfully, Joelle and Slater did the same. Also thankfully, Luca hurried out of the house and into the cruiser, and Bree hoped he wasn't picking up on the vibe that was still lingering around because of the short conversation she'd just had with her siblings. There was no need for Luca to be distracted with thoughts of how they felt or didn't feel about each other.

Slater immediately drove away, not exactly speeding but not dawdling either. They were all on edge. All bracing for the worst to happen. However, there were no signs of a gunman or any other vehicles for that matter.

They made it all the way into town before they encountered any traffic, and it was minimal. Slater took the turn off Main Street and drove the two blocks to come to a stop in front of Nathan's place. As the deputies had said, Nathan's car was in the driveway, indicating he was home.

The two-story white Victorian wasn't the biggest or most impressive in Saddle Ridge, but it did have an old money air about it, and Bree knew it was one of the first houses built in the area. At least one hundred and fifty years ago. And it'd been in Nathan's family the whole time. He'd inherited it from his parents after their deaths when Nathan had been in his twenties.

"See anyone hell-bent on trying to kill us?" Luca asked, his gaze combing both sides of the street.

Bree was about to say no, but then her attention landed on

the front window, and she saw Nathan standing there, staring out at them. Maybe he'd heard the sound of the cruiser approaching, but it didn't seem to Bree that he'd been expecting them.

Just the opposite.

He was scowling, possibly the cold, hard stare of someone who wanted them dead. Nathan moved away from the window, and a couple of seconds later, the front door opened.

"Let me phone Duncan so he can listen in," Joelle said, making the call, and when he answered, she reached for the door handle.

Bree reached for hers, too, but she also gave Luca a look. She didn't repeat that she'd be careful, and he held back on anything verbal. But both of those things passed between them, and then Bree got out to go to the house with Slater and Joelle.

"What's this about?" Nathan asked, clearly directing the question to Bree. "What happened?"

"May we come in?" Bree tried to keep any wariness and emotion out of her voice. She probably failed though because there was plenty of emotion since Nathan could indeed be a killer.

Nathan wasn't quick to agree to invite them in, but he finally stepped back. Not before shooting Luca a glare in the cruiser though. "What's this about?" he repeated.

"We have a few questions for you," Joelle said. She, too, had leveled her voice, and she was actually attempting a pleasant expression. "And we didn't want you to have to go into the sheriff's office." She took out her phone and lifted it to show him that it was connected to a call. "Sheriff Holder is listening."

Nathan eyed her with suspicion. "So, you brought the sheriff's office here to me, and that includes backup waiting in the cruiser," he grumbled, and he shifted his attention back to Bree. "Are you all right?"

There it was. That creepy concern that Bree in no way wanted from this man. "I'm holding up," she settled for saying.

He continued to study her. "I'm here for you," Nathan murmured. "You know that, right?"

His words made that icky feeling skyrocket, but Bree held back on saying anything. She didn't want Nathan on the defensive before they even got started.

"We don't want to take up too much of your time," Joelle interjected. "But since this is an official visit, I'm going to remind you of your rights." She didn't wait for Nathan to agree. Joelle just went ahead and recited the Miranda.

Nathan's eyes narrowed, and he whipped his gaze to Slater. "Have you come here to try to pin something on me?"

Again, it was Joelle who responded. "Actually, we were hoping you could help us clear up something. Something that could eliminate you as a possible suspect."

"I haven't done anything to make me a suspect," Nathan snapped. "What the hell is it you think I've done now?"

Bree's skin was practically crawling from being in the same space as Nathan, but she pushed that aside and went closer to him. Not too close but she wanted to do something to diffuse the anger she could see building inside him. She knew Joelle and Slater wouldn't be able to do that, but she could.

"We were hoping you'd help with the investigation," Bree said. "There's been some accusations, and while we're not at liberty to divulge specific information about the case, we need your help."

Nathan blinked, and just like that, the bulk of the anger

faded. Probably because he might think if he did help, then it might earn him some brownie points in her eyes.

"What kind of help?" he asked.

Bree waited until Joelle gave her a slight nod before she continued. "We need to know if you have a Texas A&M class ring."

Clearly, Nathan hadn't been expecting that because his eyes widened. "What does a ring have to do with the investigation?"

"Maybe nothing," she managed, "but it was just something that came up. Again, we can't spell out the specifics."

Nathan's gaze stayed pinned to her. "This has something to do with Brighton's murder? And with you being run off the road?"

"Possibly," Bree admitted. Then, she waited for what she was certain would be the denial.

The moments crawled by. Nathan's intense stare was making her stomach knot and twist. Her breathing and heart rate weren't faring much better either. But once he lied, she could stop the pretense of being nice to him—

"I have a Texas A&M ring," Nathan said.

Bree's heart dropped. This definitely wasn't what she'd expected him to say. They'd needed the lie to get the warrant.

Had Nathan figured that out?

Or was his admission simply the truth with no ulterior motive?

Bree didn't want to believe that, but she had to admit her personal feelings for Nathan were playing into this. She despised the man, and she'd maybe let that convince her that he was a killer.

"Uh, may we see the ring?" Bree managed to ask.

Again, Nathan didn't jump to agree, but he finally muttered some profanity. "I don't wear it often because it's bulky and could scratch a patient during an exam."

Or leave bruises on a woman. But Bree didn't voice that.

"I keep it in a safe in my bedroom." Nathan paused, continued to stare at Bree "Do you want to go upstairs with me while I get it?" he asked.

Bree figured that Duncan was silently yelling for her to say no, but she had no intentions of going anywhere alone with Nathan. Slater, however, quickly volunteered.

"I'll go," her brother said, causing Nathan's scowl to return in full force, but he didn't refuse.

Joelle and she paused in the foyer, watching as Nathan and Slater went up the stairs. Bree knew her brother was a good cop, but she felt the instant sense of worry and dread. She didn't want Slater alone with Nathan in case he tried to attack him and run.

"We'll come, too," Bree insisted.

That caused Nathan to stop, and he looked down at Joelle and her. Nathan wasn't doing a good job of covering up his anger, but there was also a touch of that ickiness, too, as if a small part of him was pleased that she'd be in his bedroom.

They all went up the steep stairs to a large bedroom at the front of a narrow hall. The door was open, and Bree could see the king-sized bed. Not antique. Nathan had gone for modern here, and nothing seemed out of place. Still, she continued to look around as Nathan went to a landscape painting on the wall and slid it to the side to reveal the safe.

While Nathan put in the combination, Bree looked around and knew that Slater and Joelle were both doing the same thing. They didn't have a search warrant and were not able to get one, but that didn't mean they couldn't spot something obvious that would link Nathan to Brighton and maybe the attacks. Of course, if there had been such a thing lying around, Nathan almost certainly wouldn't have invited them into the room.

The safe door made a clicking noise when Nathan opened it, and he took out a wooden box that he set on the foot of his bed. There was no lid so it was easy to see the contents. Assorted rings, watches and cuff links. Nathan plucked out the ring and tried to hand it to Bree. She looked at it but didn't touch it.

"May we take this into custody for a while?" Slater asked, pulling out a plastic evidence bag from his pocket.

"Custody?" Nathan challenged. The anger had risen again. "What the hell is this? Who said something about me and this ring that would make you want to take it?" He stopped, stared at Bree. "What do you think you'll find on this ring?"

"We're not at liberty to say," Joelle stated before Bree had to come up with a response.

Nathan did more staring, and then he cursed. For a moment, Bree thought he was going to refuse to give Slater the ring. He didn't though. He practically shoved it into Slater's waiting hand and then they all headed back downstairs.

"Was it Manny or Tara who lied to you?" Nathan came out and asked once they'd returned to the living room.

"What exactly would they lie about?" Joelle countered.

Nathan huffed. "Well, I'm guessing it's about the ring, and that's why you want to take it and send it to a lab. You're expecting to find something. Maybe DNA. Maybe gunshot residue." He leaned closer to Bree. "You won't. You won't find anything because I've done nothing wrong."

Both Manny and Tara had said pretty much the same thing about their innocence. And maybe they were innocent. Heck, maybe Nathan was as well, but someone was responsible for the nightmare that had been set in motion.

"I hope you're taking Manny's jewelry in for processing," Nathan went on. "Or arresting him. The man's a liar, and he's dangerous."

"How so?" Bree asked.

Nathan smirked. "How many lies has he told you? I'm betting a lot," he quickly tacked on to that. "Yet, he, or maybe Tara, convinced you that I had something to hide and that you'd find it on that ring. Don't you see what he's trying to do?" But he waved that off. "No, of course you don't. You have trouble seeing what's right in front of you."

Bree frowned. "What does that mean?"

He tipped his head to the front of his house. "Luca," he said and leaned toward her again. "Has it occurred to you that if you're dead, he gets custody of your son? Sole custody," he emphasized.

Bree had to bite back a whole lot of profanity, and she didn't take the bait he'd just tossed at her. Nathan could want her angry. Or scared. He could want her to say or do something that would compromise the investigation. Then again, maybe he was delusional enough to believe he could put a wedge between Luca and her.

He couldn't.

And as long as she knew that, there was no need for her to unleash some venom on him.

"Thank you for your cooperation," Bree said, using her lawyer's tone.

She glanced at Joelle and Slater to see if they had all they'd come for, and both gave her confirming nods. That was all Bree needed to turn and get the heck out of there. She didn't glance back to see Nathan's reaction. She just left out the front door with her siblings.

Luca had his gaze pinned to the house, but he was also on the phone with someone. One look at his face, and Bree knew that he was aware of what had happened in the house. Well, maybe not aware of that last part that Nathan had hurled toward her.

"Woodrow was listening to Duncan's phone," Luca explained as she slid into the back seat with him. "And he called me to tell me that Nathan fessed up to owning the ring."

She nodded, but that was all she managed to do because Luca's shoulders suddenly snapped back in reaction to something Woodrow had said. "Where?" Luca demanded.

That one-word question and his expression were more than enough to send a jolt of fear through her. The fear only intensified when Luca snapped, "Drive," to Slater. "One of the hands just spotted Aubrey near the ranch."

Chapter Fourteen

Luca tried to tamp down the panic. Tried not to think the worst could be happening. But it might be.

"Gotta go," Woodrow said, ending the call.

Luca wanted him to go, wanted him to do something to stop Aubrey from attacking them, but it meant Luca now had no way of knowing what was going on.

"Where was Aubrey spotted?" Bree asked, her voice already a tangle of nerves and adrenaline.

"By the back fence. A ranch hand using binoculars saw her, but then she ducked out of sight. He's sure it was Aubrey because Duncan had given all the hands photos of her so they'd recognize her if they saw her."

The back fence was about a quarter of a mile from the house, but a good marksman could hit a target from that distance. Luca didn't know if the target was the house—and those inside it—or if Aubrey had been getting herself into a position so she could shoot them.

"If Aubrey had the ranch under surveillance," Bree said, "she might have seen us leave and could be waiting for us to get back."

Yeah, that was a strong possibility. Well, it was if Bree and he were her intended victims. If Gabriel was, then Aubrey could be working her way to the house right now, and heaven knew how many people she'd shoot or kill to get to him.

Slater was already driving fast, probably too fast, considering the narrow country road, but Luca wished they could break speed records to get there. His son could be in danger. Everyone in the house and on the grounds could be, and he needed to be there to stop this woman.

Since it occurred to him that Aubrey could be some kind of decoy, Luca kept watch. He also gave Bree's hand a gentle squeeze. It wouldn't help. Nothing would at this point other than arriving at the ranch and finding everyone safe. But he needed the contact with her. Needed her touch to steady him some. Apparently though, she needed something from him as well because she looked at him with tear-filled eyes.

"We'll stop Aubrey," he swore to her. Luca didn't know how, but he would stop her. And her boss, too, once this threat had been neutralized.

But who exactly was her boss?

They still didn't know, and with Nathan volunteering to give them the ring, it might not be him. That left Tara and Manny. Hell, it might not be one of them either. It could be someone who wasn't even on their radar, but if so, they'd have to find that person. No way could Luca let Gabriel and Bree continue to be in danger like this.

Luca already had his gun drawn, but he readjusted his position when the ranch came into view. And his heart dropped. The two ranch hands who were guarding the driveway were still there, but they were on the ground behind their truck where they'd obviously taken cover.

Not merely a precaution, either.

Because Luca heard the crack of the gunshot.

The back fence wasn't anywhere near this spot, but if Aubrey had climbed into a tree, she could have fired pretty much anywhere on the ranch. Maybe she'd decided to take out the hands first, one by one, and from that range she could maybe manage to do it.

More shots came, tearing through the truck. Aubrey probably couldn't actually see the men on the ground, but the gunfire was keeping them pinned down. Preventing them from returning shots. The same might be happening to the other ranch hands as well.

"I'm going closer," Slater said. "It'll maybe draw the gunfire away from them."

Since the cruiser was bullet resistant, that was the right decision. However, that didn't mean shots couldn't get through to Bree. Luca wanted to ask her to get down, but she was already taking out her own gun.

"I need to protect Gabriel, too," she muttered. She met Luca's gaze, and he could see the fierce determination there. A determination he fully understood.

"If you get a shot, shoot to kill," he advised her, hoping it wouldn't come down to that. Right now, anything and everything was a possibility, including the fact that Aubrey might not be alone. Another hired gun could be with her.

Or her boss.

If so, Luca hoped he got to take a kill shot. Everything inside him was shouting for him to take out the SOB who'd put babies in danger like this.

Slater pulled up behind the hands' truck, and he motioned for them to move to the side of the cruiser where they'd be better protected. They did while the shots continued. The truck and the hands were no longer the target though.

The cruiser was.

A bullet slammed into the rear window, right where Bree was sitting, but thankfully the glass held. For now. It might not if shots continued to hit that same spot.

"Trade places with me," Luca said, not waiting for Bree to

agree to that. He wanted to be on that side in case the glass gave way. Because then he might be able to return fire and get Aubrey to back off.

"Should I open the door and let the hands in?" Bree asked.

"Not yet," Joelle said. "They're safer on the ground where they are. Besides, there could be a shooter waiting for you to open it."

Bree didn't gasp, didn't make any sharp sound of surprise, which meant those kind of scenarios had already occurred to her.

Slater's phone rang, the sound slicing through the noise of the stream of gunfire, and after he answered it, Luca heard Duncan's voice.

"Everyone inside the house is okay," Duncan was quick to say. "No shots have been fired at us. Lenny's spotted Aubrey though," he added, referring to one of the hands. "And she's no longer by the back fence. As you've probably guessed from the direction of the gunfire, she's taken up position near the back edge of the property by the road."

Luca immediately looked in that direction. And cursed. Because there was nothing but trees there. Thick clusters of them where Aubrey could be hiding.

"Lenny doesn't have a clear shot, but he can fire into the trees to distract her. I would suggest you just get yourself and the ranch hands to the house—" Duncan continued.

"No," Bree interrupted. "If we do that, she'll just try to shoot us there."

Duncan didn't dispute that. Couldn't. Because it was exactly what would happen.

"The hands here both have rifles," Luca said. "I might be able to take Aubrey out."

Bree was frantically shaking her head, but she stopped when Luca met her gaze again. This had to be done.

"I'll tell Lenny to fire those shots," Duncan said after a long sigh. "If it flushes her out, then put an end to her."

Luca gave Bree one last look, trying to reassure. Knowing he failed. Then, he moved back to the side with the hands just as he heard the new rounds of shots. From Lenny, no doubt.

"I need your rifle," Luca said, getting out of the cruiser. "Both of you get in the back seat."

The hands did as he'd instructed, and Luca took aim over the top of the cruiser. Not exactly the safest position, but he had to see if he could spot Aubrey. He didn't. Not at first anyway. But then, there was an exchange of gunfire, and Luca saw the movement in the trees. Aubrey was in one of the large oaks, and she was moving out onto a thick limb, probably so she could kill Lenny.

Luca didn't let that happen.

He took his own advice that he'd given to Bree. Shoot to kill. Even if that meant Aubrey wouldn't be able to tell them who'd hired her. He took aim. Fired.

And put two bullets in the woman trying to murder them.

BREE CONTINUED TO hold Gabriel even though the baby was asleep and had been for nearly a half hour. It was his bedtime, and she should have already put him in his crib for what would likely be a three- or four-hour stretch of sleep, but she needed to have him near her a few moments longer.

Those moments ended when Luca came into the guest room, and she could tell from his body language and expression that he needed to be near her as well. Along with that, he probably had updates on Aubrey. Updates she wanted to hear. So, she eased Gabriel into his crib, went to Luca and pulled him into her arms.

Bree hadn't planned to kiss him. But that's what she did, and the moment her mouth landed on his, she realized she needed this as much as he obviously did. Luca sank right into the kiss, stretching it out for several long moments before he ended it and pulled her close against him.

"There was nothing on Aubrey's body to indicate who hired her," Luca whispered. His voice was strained with fatigue, spent adrenaline and worry. "She had a burner phone, but she'd used that only to call another burner. We tried to call it, but no one answered."

Bree had expected that. Aubrey's boss likely would have demanded that she use a burner so Aubrey couldn't be linked back to him or her. But Aubrey's boss had almost certainly wanted her to kill or kidnap Gabriel, Luca or her, and the woman had failed. In fact, no one on the ranch had ended up getting shot except for Aubrey.

"Are you okay?" Bree asked him. She could only guess at the emotional toll this was taking on him.

He nodded, but she figured that was a lie. None of them were going to be okay until the killer was caught. The only thing they could do was make the ranch as safe as possible, but they all knew that might not be safe enough. Now that it was night, the killer could use the darkness to get close to the house. Bree tried to imagine which of their suspects could manage to do that. Maybe all of them.

Or none.

It was just as possible the killer would send another hired gun like Aubrey.

"I need a shower," Luca said, stepping back from her. "I, uh, have blood on my clothes. After the CSIs had photographed the scene, I helped them move the body into a bag," he explained.

Aubrey's blood. Bree hadn't seen for herself how that'd happened, but once she was secure in the house, Slater and he had gone to check the body, to make sure Aubrey was truly dead and no longer a threat.

Bree took Luca by the arm and led him into the bathroom. She left the door open to the bedroom so she could hear Gabriel and turned on the shower. When Luca just stood there, staring at her, she unbuckled his holster and laid it and his gun on the vanity.

He kept his gaze on her.

Bree didn't shy away from that. After she pulled off his shirt, her eyes locked with his—those incredible brown eyes that always seem to drown her in heat—and she considered her options. She could go back into the bedroom and let Luca have that shower. Or she could do something about those raw nerves. Not just his but her own.

She went with option two.

So did Luca.

He slid his arm around the back of her neck and kissed her. Not exactly a kiss of comfort either since it was long, deep and filled with need. Still, his mouth did the trick of firing enough heat through her that the raw nerves just melted. Heck, she melted, but then she always did when Luca kissed her.

Maybe because his jeans had blood on them, he moved his hands between them to undo his belt and unzip. The touching added to the flames, especially since Luca didn't break the kiss to do that. It took some maneuvering, some dipping down and moving to the side with him, but their mouths continued to pleasure each other while he rid himself of his jeans and boots.

Bree took full advantage of having a nearly naked Luca. She touched him, sliding her hands down his back over all those muscles. The man was certainly built. And even though she knew the feel of every one of those muscles, this moment, this now felt new, as if she'd never had him before. That was probably because her body was starved for him, and that's why Bree didn't hold anything back. She kissed and touched until Luca was cursing her.

Cursing her clothes, too.

That's when she realized that unlike him, she was fully dressed. Luca did something about that. He yanked off her top, immediately kissing the skin he'd just bared. Her neck. Then, the tops of her breasts. He stopped though. Just stopped, and his gaze fired to hers.

"Is it okay?" he asked, nearly stopping her heart because she thought he might, well, be stopping. "I mean, Gabriel's two months old."

Her heart revved up again. "Yes, it's more than okay." Except now, she had to pause. "Well, it is if you have a condom."

He pulled away from her, located his jeans and fumbled through his wallet until he came up with the foil wrapper. She'd known he usually carried one, but Bree had never been more thankful to see it.

Luca smiled, probably because of her obvious relief, and he launched back into another kiss. Not solely that, though. He was obviously a man on a mission, and that mission was to get her naked because he unzipped her jeans and push them down until they dropped around her feet. He lifted her, turning her so she was sitting on the vanity.

Then, he kissed her again.

This slam of heat was so hard and fast that she couldn't catch her breath. Soon, though, she didn't care if she ever caught it again because all she could think of was what Luca was doing to her. He was taking her on one wild ride all the while firing up the need until it became a throbbing ache in the center of her body.

Luca didn't ease away that ache but added to it when he

stepped between her legs and pressed them center to center. He was hard as stone and pushed against just the right spot to make the need skyrocket.

Bree wanted him naked, and she wanted it now so she went after his boxers. Luca went after her panties and bra, but he clearly wasn't in the frantic *now* mode. Not yet anyway. She did something about that by closing her fingers around his erection.

He cursed her, and the sound that rumbled in his chest was all male, all need. All now. Finally.

It was Bree who did some cursing when it seemed to take a couple of lifetimes to get the condom on, and she might have cursed, too, at the immense pleasure when he pushed into her. She didn't have breath to form words. The only thing she could do was feel, and she was having no trouble with that.

Luca and she had been lovers for a long time so she knew the familiarity of this rhythm they found. And because he knew every inch of her body, he knew how to draw out the pleasure. He knew how to take her to the peak, right to the edge and then bring her back down so it could last a little longer.

He kissed her again but then pulled back, spearing her gaze as he made those now frantic thrusts inside her. Bree couldn't have come down from the peak now even if he stopped. She was past the point of no return, and Luca knew it. That's why he gave her exactly what she needed to feel the climax slam through her.

Bree let herself shatter, let the sensations wrack her body and wash over her. And when it was Luca's turn to take that fall, she gathered him into her arms and held on.

Chapter Fifteen

Luca eased Gabriel back into his crib, and he hoped now that the baby was fed and dry he would sleep for another four-hour stretch. A stretch that might give Bree some rest and him as well.

They'd managed a couple of catnaps, but they needed more. Despite being revved from the incredible sex, Luca knew they were both exhausted. That's why he'd done the midnight feeding and diaper change.

Luca slid back into bed, and Bree made a sleepy sound of satisfaction and automatically snuggled against him. She was warm and naked, and he wished they didn't have the threat of danger hanging over their heads so they could truly enjoy every moment of this night. It was still amazing, but Luca figured this was just a short reprieve. Tomorrow, they'd need to dive back into the investigation, and maybe they'd finally get the break they desperately needed.

After that, after the killer was caught, well… Luca wasn't sure what would happen, but he sure as hell wanted the chance to have some time to try to work out things with Bree. Unfortunately, that working out might mean they still continued to be apart, but he thought this night was a good start in repairing their relationship.

"Thanks for giving Gabriel the bottle," she murmured.

He sighed because Bree obviously wasn't asleep as he'd thought. Of course, that only gave him an excuse to brush a kiss on her mouth. She brushed one right back, causing him to smile. A kiss from Bree was something to be savored despite everything else going on.

Luca didn't have a second condom or he might have pushed the kiss to something deeper, but the deeper didn't get a chance to happen. Bree and he both groaned when his phone vibrated. He'd turned off the ringer so it wouldn't wake Gabriel, but his phone was practically skittering across the surface of the nightstand, which meant it was making plenty of noise. Luca snatched it up and saw Slater's name on the screen.

Hell.

This couldn't be good. Not at this hour. The ranch should have been locked down for the night.

"What's wrong?" Luca answered in a whisper. He didn't put the call on Speaker, but Bree moved closer to him.

"Two of the ranch hands aren't responding," Slater quickly said. "We've been doing check-ins every hour, and they both missed the midnight one. I've tried to call them, but they aren't answering."

Luca mentally repeated his, *Hell*. "Where were they positioned?"

"Both by the back fence. One on the east corner, the other one the west. Yeah," Slater muttered when Luca groaned. If someone was going to try to sneak onto the ranch, those'd be the places to do it.

Luca got up and started dressing. Bree did the same. "I've got thermal imaging binoculars," Luca explained. He'd brought several back to the ranch from the sheriff's office, and Duncan had arranged for more to be delivered so the hands could use them. "Let me go to the window and see if I can spot anything."

"I've asked another of the hands, Mike Travers, to use his binoculars to see if he can locate them," Slater explained. "Mike's not at the best angle for that, but I don't want to pull him away from his area since he's guarding the spot near the road."

Luca made a quick sound of agreement. The road was a vulnerable part, too. Heck, there were lots of places that a killer could use to gain access to the house.

"The security system is on, right?" Luca asked, already knowing the answer, and Slater gave him instant confirmation.

"Woodrow's monitoring that," Slater explained. "He's trying to get some sleep, but he's got it set to alert him if there's any movement in or around the house."

The perimeter security and cameras were a new addition, put in just hours earlier. A series of motion-activated sensors had been staked into the ground around the entire house, and some had been positioned in the backyard.

"Good," Luca said, putting on the rest of his clothes and hurrying to the window that would give him a somewhat limited view of the east back corner of the pasture. Limited because of trees and the outbuildings.

Luca handed his phone to Bree who'd joined him at the window, and he looked out with the binoculars. He got a jolt when he saw the glowing eyes but then realized it was a deer. He picked up the livestock, too, and a couple of raccoons. What he didn't immediately see was a ranch hand or anyone else.

He shifted his view, panning the binoculars over the grounds, and he caught just a flash of a heat source. For a moment, he thought it was another animal, but then Luca realized the red blob was a torso. The person was on the ground, partially hidden by a tree, and he or she wasn't moving.

"I think someone's down," Luca relayed just as he saw another slash of red. He muttered a single word of profanity because he had no idea if this was one of the hands or a killer coming their way. "I'm pretty sure we've got a breach," he said, figuring the guy on the ground was indeed one of the hands.

Slater cursed, too, just as there was a knock on the bedroom door. Bree hurried to open it, and Duncan stuck in his head.

"The security camera has likely been compromised," Duncan immediately said. "Woodrow just told me he thinks the camera feed's on a loop."

Luca's stomach dropped because that was the same thing that'd happened to the baby monitor.

"I think we've got a hand down and someone already on the grounds," Luca explained, handing Duncan the binoculars so he could see for himself.

It took a couple of seconds with Duncan moving the binoculars around, but his muttered profanity told Luca plenty. "Someone's coming across the pasture, and I don't think it's one of the hands." His attention slashed to Bree. "Grab Gabriel because you need to take cover now."

THE FEAR AND adrenaline slammed through Bree. Oh, God. No. *Please not this again.*

She hurried across the room to scoop up Gabriel. She prayed this would turn out to be nothing, that her baby wasn't in danger yet again. But she had the sickening feeling that a killer was coming for them. And they still didn't know who was after them. Whoever it was, the person was relentless.

"Take Gabriel to the main bedroom," Duncan instructed. "Joelle and Sandra are there with Izzie. I want all of you in the bathroom. It's bigger than the one in here, and the shower stall is all tiled."

Tiled and therefore more resistant to bullets than a wall would be. Bree had to tamp down images of bullets slamming into the house, the way they had when they'd all been huddled in the barn. She had to tamp down a lot of things and focus on keeping Gabriel safe.

Bree glanced at Luca, and their gazes connected for just a second. He was checking his primary weapon and backup, obviously gearing up for a fight. One where he could be shot.

Or worse.

Yes, that was another image she had to shove to the side because she couldn't give in to the fear and panic. She had to do whatever it took to keep their baby safe.

Clutching Gabriel to her chest, Bree hurried down the hall. Unfortunately, the jerky movement woke him up, and he started to cry. She soon learned Izzie was doing the same thing as Joelle and her mother maneuvered them into the shower. The shower stall was plenty large enough, but her mother was trying to make it more comfortable by placing heaps of towels on the floor so they wouldn't have to sit on the tiles.

"I didn't grab Izzie's pacifier," Joelle muttered, handing off Izzie to their mother so she could run back into the bedroom.

Gabriel didn't use a pacifier, so Bree tried to rock him to soothe him. That wasn't working though, and she figured Gabriel had to be picking up on her racing breath and accelerated heartbeat. He was too young to understand the danger, but he likely sensed something was wrong.

When Joelle hurried back, she saw that her sister not only had the pacifier and a small stuffed animal but also her holster and gun. It was a reminder for Bree that she hadn't grabbed her gun from the closet. And she wanted it. If the killer managed to get into the house, she needed to be able to defend Gabriel and her family. Definitely not something she wanted to do because it would mean the killer had gotten way too close to them, but Bree didn't want to risk being unarmed.

Once Joelle had taken Izzie, Bree eased Gabriel into her mother's arms. "I'll be right back. I just want to get my gun and a bottle for Gabriel." He wouldn't be hungry, but a few sips might allow him to settle down enough to fall asleep.

As she'd done with Luca, Bree met her mother's gaze for a second. Of course, there was fear there. Plenty of it. But she also thankfully saw a resolve that Bree figured was in her own eyes and Joelle's. They weren't going to let a killer get near the babies.

Bree rushed back out into the hall and spotted Duncan and Luca on the stairs landing. Duncan went ahead down, but Luca stayed put while she made her way to him.

"What happened?" she asked because she could tell from his expression he'd gotten yet more bad news.

"Duncan's not sure how long the security system's been compromised," he said, the worry flaring in his eyes. "He checked the doors and windows, and they're all still locked, but he can't be sure someone didn't manage to get inside."

It felt as if someone had sucked all the air out of her body. She fired glances around as if someone might be ready to jump out at them. But she heard and saw no one other than Luca.

"I want to get my gun and a bottle for Gabriel," she managed to say.

Luca nodded. "Do that, and then go straight back into the bathroom. Lock both the bedroom and bathroom doors and turn off the lights. I don't want anyone watching the house to be able to pinpoint our locations."

She nodded and tried not to look ready to curse. But she was. It was heart crushing to know the danger could be so close to them.

Luca's phone vibrated, and when he took it from his pocket, she saw Woodrow's name on the screen. "Go ahead and get the gun and bottle. Duncan and I are going to do a room-by-room search downstairs and up here, but I won't do that until you're safe in the bathroom."

A horrible thought occurred to her, and Luca must have known what put the terror on her face. "The killer didn't sneak into our guest room or the main bedroom. If so, we would have heard it."

That restarted her breath because he was right. It was probably the same for her mother's room. That left the hall bathroom and the nursery. It was right next to the main bed-room and was empty since Duncan and Joelle had moved Izzie into their room.

Bree hurried into the guest room, grabbing a premade bottle of formula and the diaper bag since she wasn't sure how long they'd be stuck in the bathroom. She took her gun, shoved it into the back waist of her jeans and went back into the hall. Luca was still there, talking on the phone to Wood-row. He had his back to her and was peering down the stairs, no doubt looking for any signs of trouble. Judging from his body language, he wasn't seeing any.

Not until he turned toward her.

"Watch out!" Luca yelled.

Bree heard the sound of running footsteps behind her, and she whirled around to see the figure dressed all in black charging right at her. She dropped the diaper bag and bottle, reaching for her gun.

But it was too late.

She felt someone latch on to her, knocking away her gun

and dragging her hands behind her back. The person slapped plastic cuffs on her before pressing a gun to her head.

LUCA SHOUTED BREE'S NAME, but she didn't get the chance to run. Couldn't. That's because the person who'd run up behind her from the nursery hooked his left arm around her throat and put her in a choke hold. He pressed a gun directly to her temple.

Hell.

This had been exactly what they'd tried to avoid. What they'd been avoiding since the attacks had started. And now, the killer or one of his henchmen had Bree.

Her captor was probably a man, one several inches taller than Bree since he was hunching down behind her. He was dressed all in black, including a ski mask that covered everything but his eyes.

"What's going on?" Duncan shouted, and there were the sounds of movement at the bottom of the stairs.

Luca brought up his gun to take aim even though he wouldn't have a clean shot, but when the attacker turned his own gun in Luca's direction, Luca had no choice but to dive into the open door of the guest room. He landed hard on the floor, the fall knocking the breath out of him so he had to struggle just to get to his knees.

"Stay back," Bree yelled. "Everyone stay back." Which was no doubt what her captor had told her to say.

The man didn't come after Luca and follow up with what would have likely been a kill shot. But he did move. Luca heard the footsteps, heard the sounds of Bree struggling to get away.

And then she went quiet.

That got Luca hurrying to the doorway, ready to launch himself at her captor, but Bree was still alive and she shook her head.

"He says if I fight that he'll shoot into the bathroom," she muttered. There was terror in her eyes, and it came through in her voice. She reached in her pocket, pulled out her phone and dropped it on the floor. No doubt something else the man had instructed her to do.

"Who is he? Who has you?" Luca whispered.

"I'm not sure. He's using something to alter his voice. Probably because he was worried we'd recognize who he was."

Which meant this thug had come prepared. Of course, he had. He'd compromised the security system and then had gotten in and hidden until the time was right to launch this attack.

The masked thug leaned in closer to Bree's ear and said something, but Luca couldn't make out what.

"He wants you to stay put," she said, her voice cracking. "You, too, Duncan," she added, shifting her attention toward the stair landing. "I'm going with him."

"To hell you are," Luca snarled.

There was no telling what this SOB would do to Bree if he got her alone. But then something occurred to him. If he'd wanted Bree dead, he could have just killed her on the spot. So, he wanted her alive, maybe solely as a human shield.

Maybe for something else.

"Trade her for me," Luca bargained.

The guy laughed, and the sound was like a cartoon through the voice distorter. A sick sound that ate away at Luca like acid. Somehow, he had to stop this from happening. He couldn't lose Bree, but he also didn't want this armed snake so close to the bathroom where the babies were. He had to hope that Joelle had already locked the door and was ready to stop anyone who tried to get in.

Bullets could still get through.

And that was probably why Bree didn't put up any kind of struggle when the man started toward the stairs with her.

"Duncan, move back," Bree instructed.

The masked man turned, angling Bree so that she was not only in front of him but so he was pressed hard against her with his back against the wall. That would ensure no one would be able to get a clean shot, not with him plastered to her.

Staying low and prepared to dive again for cover, Luca came out of the guest room, his gun ready. He figured Duncan and maybe Slater and Woodrow were doing the same in the foyer.

"Duncan, he wants you to open the front door," Bree relayed.

Luca could see her glancing around, no doubt looking for a way out. He prayed she would find one. If she could just manage to drop down, he would be able to send this snake straight to hell.

There was more movement in the foyer, and Luca heard the front door opening. He crept forward, peering down the stairs just as Bree and the thug reached the last step. Lightning fast, the masked man turned his gun toward Luca.

And fired.

For a couple of heart-stopping seconds, Luca thought he'd been hit. But the bullet missed, smacking into the wall above his head.

"Stay back!" Bree shouted. "All of you please stay back," she added, her voice a strained plea.

Luca couldn't do that. He couldn't stay behind cover while she was in immediate danger, but he also had to time it so the masked man couldn't get off a shot inside the house. He inched forward again and saw the gunman and Bree had already reached the now open front door. Duncan, Woodrow and Slater were indeed all there. All had their weapons drawn and were peering out behind the arched opening that led into the family room.

The thug looked up at Luca, and even though he still couldn't see the guy's face, their eyes met for a moment. Luca couldn't tell for sure, but it seemed to him that the SOB was smirking. The rage knifed through Luca, but he didn't allow it to trigger him into doing something reckless. It definitely wouldn't help matters if he got shot. Or if he did something to cause Bree to be hurt.

The thug moved her onto the porch, and that got Luca hurrying down the stairs. Woodrow, Slater and Duncan all came out from cover, too.

And the sound of a gunshot blasted through the house.

It took Luca a moment to realize it hadn't come from the thug dragging out Bree but rather it'd come from the direction of the kitchen. Every muscle inside him turned to iron when he saw someone. Another person dressed all in black and wearing a ski mask. He or she had a gun and fired again.

This shot, too, missed, slamming into the wall and sending Woodrow, Slater and Duncan scurrying back. Luca didn't head back up the stairs. Instead, he bolted out through the front door and onto the porch.

He cursed when he realized he still didn't have a clean shot. And worse. The thug was dragging Bree toward one of the ranch hand's trucks that was parked behind a cruiser.

Luca could only watch as the man shoved Bree into the truck. Seconds later, he started the engine and sped away.

Chapter Sixteen

The moment her captor started driving away, Bree tried to figure out how to escape. She hadn't wanted to fight before now and risk him shooting into the house. Or shooting Luca, Woodrow, Slater or Duncan.

But someone inside the house had fired a shot.

Probably a hired gun, and she prayed that everyone had stayed out of the path of the bullet. Prayed, too, that she could figure a way out of this truck.

Her hands were cuffed, but her legs and feet were free, and she tried to swivel around in the seat and kick the driver in the face. She landed a blow on the steering wheel that caused the truck to jerk to the side, but before she could regroup, the driver landed a blow of his own. He bashed the gun against her head, the barrel cutting through her stitches. Had she been standing, the pain would have brought her to her knees.

She fell back on the seat, gasping for air, trying to tamp down the searing pain. But it was overwhelming, and her chest was so tight, she couldn't draw in a full breath.

"There are still people I can shoot," her captor snarled in that fake voice. "If you want them to live, stop fighting."

She immediately spotted two ranch hands running toward the truck as it reached the end of the driveway. They would indeed be easy shots, so she pulled back. Temporarily. She had to regroup. Had to push away the pain, so Bree waited until the truck was on the road before she geared up to try to land another kick.

"One wrong move, and your baby will pay," he snapped.

That got her attention all right, and she stopped again. Even though her head was pounding and making it next to impossible for her to think, she recalled the shooter inside the house.

Maybe more than one of them.

Maybe enough to overpower Luca, Duncan, Woodrow and Slater and get upstairs to the babies. Of course, an attacker would have to get through Joelle, but her sister could be gunned down. If so, Gabriel could be taken.

Or hurt.

Oh, God. That couldn't happen.

She couldn't lose Luca, her son and her family like this.

Bree cursed the tears that instantly burned in her eyes. Cursed that she didn't know what to do to save her little boy. Or even who had kidnapped her. She tried to pick through what she could see of him, but every inch of him was covered, and since he wasn't even using his real voice, she had no idea if this was Nathan or Manny. Or maybe neither. This could be another hired gun taking her to his boss.

"What do you want with me?" she demanded, hoping she'd be able to get answers that would help.

He didn't answer, but he was looking around for something. There were no other actual roads on this stretch, but he was still firing glances to his left. Maybe hunting for somewhere to stop. She had no idea though why he would want to do that.

The man continued to glance around, and this time he looked over his shoulder and ground out some harsh profanity. She soon saw why. There was a cruiser in pursuit. Somehow, Luca had managed to get away from that shooter in the house. He was coming after her.

That was both good and bad.

Because Bree very much wanted to be away from this killer, but she didn't want Luca or anyone else dying in the process. The odds were Luca would be able to catch up with them in the cruiser and follow them to wherever they were going. There could be a shoot-out, and she had no doubts that her captor would use her as a shield again so he could fire at Luca.

She turned back to her captor who was volleying glances ahead on the dark road and in the rearview mirror. And she thought of a ploy. Probably not a good one, but she tried it anyway.

"Are you taking me to Nathan?" she asked.

The driver's shoulders went stiff. Not a huge reaction. But she noticed it.

"Nathan wouldn't want you to hurt me," she tacked on to that.

He didn't respond, verbally or otherwise, but she thought maybe she'd hit a nerve. The man had recognized the name. Did that mean Nathan had hired him?

Maybe.

Or was this Nathan?

"If this is about Brighton's murder," she tried again, "then it's all for nothing. Silencing me won't stop the investigation."

He cursed again, maybe the sign of another raw nerve. But then, it could also be because the cruiser was quickly gaining ground. Bree saw in the side mirror as the driver pulled out into the lane next to the truck.

It was Luca, and Slater was with him.

Her captor saw them, too, because he belted out more of that profanity and jerked the steering wheel to the right.

There was the sound of metal slicing into metal, and the bottom part of the passenger's door started to cave in. Bree scrambled away from it so her foot wouldn't get trapped if the door collapsed.

"Finally," her captor muttered.

He twisted the steering wheel again, bashing into the cruiser. Bree watched in horror as the impact sent the cruiser into a ditch. She immediately geared up to try to kick her captor, but he must have seen it coming because he hit her with the gun again. Bree fell against the door, the back of her head hitting the window, and then she was immediately slung into the dash when he made a sharp turn onto a ranch trail.

Bree knew most of the trails in this area and was aware this one had gullies on each side caused by rain and erosion. She lunged across the seat and caught hold of the steering wheel to get them off the trail. The man cursed her and tried to knock her away with the gun, but Bree kept fighting. The truck finally veered off the narrow dirt path, and the front end plunged into the ditch.

The impact was like a collision, and Bree jolted forward. The airbags deployed, slamming into her captor and her and spewing a cloud of powder over the entire cab of the truck. Bree didn't waste a second. She dove toward the passenger's side door while the man tried to catch on to her. He had the disadvantage of being trapped behind the steering wheel by the airbag, but she had a huge disadvantage too. Since she was cuffed, she had to turn her back to the door to open it.

And her heart dropped when she realized it was jammed.

Pain shot through her shoulder and back, but she rammed against the door, all the while trying to kick her captor. When the door finally opened, she tumbled out onto the ground. She heard the man curse again, and he must have managed to bat down the airbag because he was there. Right behind her.

She kicked out again, somehow managing to get to her feet, and she started running toward the blue cruiser lights that were slicing through the darkness.

She didn't get far.

The man tackled her, both of them falling onto the ground, and he landed on top of her. She continued to fight. So did he. And in the struggle, the mask hiked up enough for her to see his chin and mouth. Even in the darkness, she recognized him.

Nathan.

LUCA RAN AS if his life depended on it. Bree's life certainly did, and he sprinted away from the cruiser and toward the trail where he'd seen the truck turn. He couldn't let the vehicle get out of sight.

He had to get to Bree in time to stop her from being driven off somewhere.

Slater was out of the cruiser, too, and running behind him, but he was also calling to get the status of the immediate backup they'd already requested. They needed a vehicle here now if he stood a chance of catching the SOB who'd taken Bree.

Still at a full sprint, Luca turned onto the trail and nearly skidded to a stop when he saw the truck.

And Bree.

She was running or rather she was trying to do that, but the thug tackled her, both of them dropping to the ground. Luca started running again, and when the thug pulled back his hand, Luca saw that he was trying to aim the gun at Bree.

The snake was going to shoot her.

"Stop!" Luca yelled, already bringing up his own gun. He didn't have a clean shot so he fired over the guy's head to get his attention.

It got it all right.

The man rolled to the side, dragging up Bree in front of him so he could cower behind her.

"Coward," Luca snarled plenty loud enough for her captor to hear him, and then he had to drop down into the ditch when the guy took aim at him.

He fired, too, and while the shot didn't come anywhere near Luca, he shouted for Slater to be careful. Luca definitely didn't want Slater to take a bullet meant for him. Hell, he didn't want anyone other than this thug dying tonight.

"It's Nathan," Bree managed to yell. "He's the one who took me."

Luca spat out the name like profanity, "Nathan." So, he was their attacker.

Nathan did some actual cursing, and he whipped off the mask and the voice alternator he had against his throat. He also latched on to Bree's hair and pulled her up so that his face was right against hers.

"It's too late for you to save her, *hero*," Nathan taunted. "Too late for Bree to choose the right man."

"You're not the right man," Bree snapped, and she tried to elbow Nathan in the gut.

Luca admired the fact that she wasn't giving up, but he didn't want her to fight right now. He didn't want Nathan to have any reason to kill her. At this point, though, her knowing his identity was probably the only motive Nathan needed to end her life. That's why Luca got down as low as he could and continued toward Bree. Maybe he'd get that clean shot he needed to take out this SOB.

"I've already told him if this is about Brighton, the investigation isn't going away," Bree said, straining against the grip he had on her hair.

"I don't need it to go away," Nathan was quick to say. "I just need the cops looking at someone else."

Luca mentally replayed the words while he glanced over his shoulder at the sound of the movement. Slater was in the ditch, crouched down and making his way toward Luca.

"You're going to set someone up for Brighton's murder?" Luca asked. "Another cowardly thing," he added in a mutter.

"I'm not going to jail for what happened to her," Nathan practically yelled. "It wasn't my fault." If he had any composure left, he seemed to be losing it fast. If he snapped, he just might start shooting before Luca could figure out a way to get Bree out of this alive.

"Are you saying it was an accident?" Luca asked.

Nathan jumped right on that. "Yes, an accident."

That didn't convince Luca one bit. Then again, there wasn't anything Nathan could say that would make Luca believe he was innocent. After all, he was holding Bree at gunpoint.

"Things just got out of hand," Nathan said, and then he made a hoarse sob as if he was about to break down and cry.

"Did things get out of hand with my mother, too?" Bree demanded. "Is that why you kidnapped her?"

"She was insurance, that's all," Nathan readily admitted. "Leverage. If the investigation had turned bad, then she would have been of use to lure out Bree. Or you."

"Me?" Luca questioned. "Why the hell would you want Bree or me?"

"Because Sandra had an alibi for the night of Brighton's murder. We didn't know that at first, but then we found a photo of her on Facebook that would have proved she couldn't have killed her. We couldn't set her up to take the blame."

Luca was surprised Nathan had admitted that since it also implicated him not only in Sandra's kidnapping but also Brighton's and Shannon's murders. So, why would he spill it? And why wasn't he just trying to get away with Bree?

Was Nathan waiting for a hired gun to show up?

Maybe the one at the ranch who'd fired those shots at Woodrow, Duncan and Slater?

When Luca and Slater had run out of the house to go in pursuit of Nathan, they'd left Woodrow and Duncan to deal with that. And Luca had to hope they had. It'd been two against one. Well, unless there had been others lurking around, but there'd been no choice about coming after Bree and trusting that Duncan and Woodrow would eliminate any threat at the ranch.

But maybe Nathan thought that person would escape and come to help him.

It wouldn't happen because Slater and he would hear an approaching vehicle and would prevent the person from getting to Nathan. Nathan should have realized that by now. He should be panicking and trying to run. Unless...

A thought flashed into Luca's head. A bad one. Nathan had turned onto this trail, and that might be because he knew help would be nearby.

Luca tried to pick through the darkness and look ahead on the trail. He couldn't see another vehicle, but that didn't mean one wasn't there. In fact, there almost certainly was since this particular trail fed out to a road.

"What? No questions for me?" Nathan shouted. "You don't want to know if I killed Bree's father? I didn't," he was quick to add.

Luca tuned him out because he was certain that Nathan was talking to try to distract him. It didn't work. Luca heard the sound of something or someone moving in the ditch on the other side of the trail. He pivoted in that direction and got just a glimpse of the man. Someone he instantly recognized.

Because it was Manny.

And Manny fired a shot at him.

BREE HEARD THE blast of a gun being fired, and for a heart-stopping moment, she thought Nathan had shot her. Or Luca.

But he hadn't.

The sound had come from her right, and she tried to turn in that direction. Nathan didn't let her. He tightened the chokehold, much harder this time, so she quit struggling so she could breath.

And pray.

That gunshot couldn't have hit Luca or her brother. And soon she got confirmation they were alive.

"Manny," Luca yelled, and she saw both Luca and Slater drop back down into the ditch.

"Manny?" she muttered.

What was he doing here? Had he come to help? Maybe he'd followed Nathan so he could try to clear his name.

But that wasn't it. If it had been, Nathan would have dropped flat on the ground with her, or he would have moved her so she'd be facing the direction of the shot. He didn't do either of those things.

"About time you got here," Nathan snarled.

"I was waiting up the trail where I was supposed to be," Manny snarled right back. "You're the one who messed up by wrecking the truck."

Bree heard every word they said, but it took her a couple of seconds to process it. Manny and Nathan were in this together. There hadn't been one killer but two.

"You tried to pin the blame on each other," Bree muttered.

"To muddy the waters of the investigation," Nathan readily admitted. "And now we've got to get out of here. Sorry, Bree, but you can't die here," he added in a mutter. "We haven't finished setting you up yet."

So, that's why they wanted her. Manny and Nathan were going to try to pin all of this on her. Unlike her mother, Bree didn't have an alibi, but that didn't mean anyone would be-lieve she would kill the woman and then launch into these attacks to cover it up.

"I had no motive to murder Brighton," Bree managed.

"There'll be the motive," Nathan said. "There will be texts to prove how much you loved me and how jealous you were of Brighton. They'll be an eyewitness who saw you go into Brighton's place that night. By the time we're done, even your darling Luca will have thought you did it."

Luca. Bree tried not to think of what he might be doing right now. He was no doubt trying to get into a position to save her. Slater, too. But what they wouldn't be doing was believing she'd had anything to do with Brighton's murder.

And that's why Nathan would try to kill them, too.

"Why are you helping him, Manny?" Bree asked. "Why are you doing this?"

Nathan chuckled. "Oh, Manny has just as much to lose as I do. Don't you, Manny?" He put his mouth to her ear as if telling a secret. "Because you see, Manny was there when Brighton died. In fact, he was the one who set all of this in motion."

Manny didn't address that other than to huff. "Nathan, we need to get out of here. More cops will be coming soon."

"You don't think I know that!" Nathan snapped. "I'm not an idiot. I know they called for backup, and they'll be here soon. Two minutes. If we haven't gotten the text by then, we both start shooting."

"What text?" Bree asked.

"More leverage. The best kind," he added with that de-spicable taunting in his voice.

Bree had to fight the panic. Had to fight the groan that was trying to claw its way past her throat. She couldn't handle worst-case scenario right now. She had to focus on getting Luca, Slater and her out of this alive.

"I thought you wanted me back," Bree said to Nathan. "I thought you cared about me."

"I despise you," he admitted through what had to be clenched teeth. "You took my love for you and threw it back in my face. It sickened me to act all moony-eyed around you, but I endured because I knew one day I'd make you pay."

In the distance, she heard the wail of sirens. A welcome sound for her, but it caused Nathan to curse and tense even more. He laughed though when his phone dinged with a text.

"Well, the payment you owe me is about to start," Nathan boasted.

Bree pushed aside any thoughts of what the text might be. Pushed aside everything but what she had to do. She gathered her strength and waited for Nathan to take out his phone so he could read the message.

Nathan kept his arm around her neck, kept the pressure so tight that she could barely breathe. But he finally lowered his hand, and therefore the gun, to his pocket. That's when she moved.

"Now!" she shouted to warn Luca and Slater, and she rammed her elbow into Nathan's stomach.

She didn't stop there. Bree scrambled away from him, landing on her back so she could kick him. She landed a hard blow to his face, and she heard the satisfying crunch of his nose breaking. Her satisfaction didn't last long though.

Cursing her, Nathan turned the gun toward her. Ready to kill her.

And the shot came.

The sound of it blasted through the air, and Bree waited for the pain. Waited for her own death.

But it didn't come.

Nathan stopped, his head or torso freezing while his arms dropped limply to his sides. The rest of him dropped, too, and that's when she saw the gunshot wound to the center of his head.

Bree snapped toward the ditch and spotted Luca. He still had his gun aimed at Nathan and had obviously been the one to shoot him.

"Stay down, Bree," Slater yelled.

"Manny," she muttered on a rise of breath. He was there, and he could finish the job that Nathan had started.

Before she could even look in Manny's direction, she heard the shots. Two back-to-backs that caused the fear to slam through her. Oh, God. Had Manny managed to shoot Luca and Slater?

Bree was terrified of what she might see, but she forced herself to look at Luca. He was still standing. So was Slater, and her brother had his gun on Manny. Or rather what was left of Manny anyway. Like Nathan, he was on the ground, and his lifeless eyes were staring up at the night sky.

The relief rushed through her so fast that Bree lost her breath again, but she still tried to get to her feet so she could go to Luca. He made it to her first though and pulled her into his arms.

"Are you all right?" he asked, fishing through his pocket to come up with a small knife. He used it to cut the plastic cuffs and then pulled her right back to him for another hug.

"I'm okay," she said. It was a lie. She was shaking and maybe in shock.

Because this wasn't over.

"The text," Bree managed to say. "We need to see what was in that text."

Luca was already steps ahead of her on that, too, and he

snatched out Nathan's phone. The screen was still lit with the message.

"Hell," Luca cursed. "Let's go." He took hold of Bree's hand and started running toward the road.

"What's wrong?" Slater asked, hurrying after them. "Who was that text from?"

"Tara," Luca blurted while he ran, the world of emotion in his voice. "She said she has Gabriel."

Chapter Seventeen

Tara.

The woman's name hammered through Bree's head as Luca, Slater and she ran. Tara had Gabriel. And that meant Tara had likely been the person who'd fired those shots inside the house at the ranch. She was in on this with Nathan and Manny.

All three had worked together to create this nightmare.

She didn't ask why Duncan, Joelle, her mother or Woodrow hadn't stopped Tara from taking Gabriel. Because Bree couldn't deal with the sickening dread that they were all now dead. If Tara had Gabriel, then she'd managed to neutralize them in some way.

No, she couldn't ask about that.

She could only focus on getting to the ranch so she could find Tara and get her son.

They ran out onto the road just as a cruiser braked to a loud stop next to them. Sonya was behind the wheel with Carmen in the passenger's seat.

"What the hell happened?" Sonya asked.

Luca didn't answer. He threw open the back door, and Slater, Bree and he all piled in. "Get to the ranch now," Luca demanded.

Sonya didn't hesitate. She gunned the engine, the tires

squealing against the asphalt, and she got them moving while Luca yanked out his phone. Bree saw that he was trying to call Duncan. If she'd had her phone, she would be trying to call Joelle or her mother.

Luca cursed when Duncan didn't answer, and Bree nearly lost it. She wanted to scream. She wanted to tear the world apart to get to her son, but losing it wouldn't help. They had to focus. They had to get to the ranch and find Gabriel.

Slater took out his phone, too, and he called Joelle. Since he put it on Speaker, Bree could hear the rings as she watched the scenery fly past the window. Her heart crushed with each unanswered ring.

And then Joelle answered.

"I'm a little busy here," Joelle said, sounding out of breath but very much alive. "Are you all okay? Did you get Bree?"

Bree didn't want to respond to those questions. Not when she only wanted to know one thing. "Gabriel," she blurted. "Did Tara take him?"

"She tried," Joelle confirmed. "But she didn't succeed."

Bree went limp with relief, and she sent up a thousand prayers. "But Tara sent a message saying she'd taken him."

"Sorry about that. The text was already composed on her phone, just waiting there, and during the scuffle to retain her, it was accidentally sent. We didn't know who the recipient was since it was being sent to a burner."

Bree was beyond thankful that was how things had played out. "Is Gabriel hurt?"

"No," Joelle was quick to assure her. "No one here is. Well, except for Tara. She's got some cuts and bruises from Duncan and Woodrow tackling her to get that gun and phone away from her. Duncan's cuffing her now." Joelle paused. "Please tell me Luca, Slater and you took care of Manny and Nathan."

So, her sister knew. "They're both dead." That prompted Carmen to make a call to dispatch to get someone out to the scene to secure the bodies.

"Good," Joelle murmured, and she repeated that as if trying to steady herself. "Tara's talking, and she said Nathan and Manny put this plan together."

Soon, Bree would want to hear all about that plan, but for now, she just needed to see her baby. Sonya was trying to make that happen. She was driving as fast as possible while Carmen continued her call to coordinate the efforts to secure the crime scene.

"They were all three in on this," Bree managed to say.

"Yeah." That was all Joelle said for a long time. "How far out are you?"

"Under a minute," Bree said after she glanced around. A minute that was already feeling like an eternity.

Joelle made what sounded to be a sigh of relief. "Mom's still in the bathroom with both babies, and Woodrow is there standing guard."

Bree didn't ask why he was doing that. She knew there could be other hired guns around.

"Some of the ranch hands are searching every inch of the house while others are going over the grounds," Joelle explained. "Every available deputy and reserve deputy will be here soon to help us make sure everything is secure."

"Thank you," Bree managed.

"You're more than welcome. Just get here," Joelle said. "I'm signing off so I can better aim my gun at Tara in case she thinks about trying to escape."

Her sister ended the call, and Bree turned to Luca. She hadn't allowed herself to really look at him because she'd known what an emotional punch it would be. And it was.

She couldn't fight back a sob any longer, and she practically tumbled into his arms.

"It'll be okay," he murmured, brushing a kiss on her head.

She winced a little because she realized she probably had some bruises there from being manhandled by Nathan. It felt as if she'd popped a couple of stitches as well. But that was minor stuff. They were all alive, and Gabriel was safe.

"I'm sorry," Luca said, and she got the feeling he wasn't apologizing because of the pain that had caused her to wince. No. Luca was putting all of this nightmare on his shoulders.

Bree eased back, caught onto his chin and kissed him. She made it long, hard and deep, and when she ended it, she looked him straight in the eyes.

"You did everything to put a stop to the danger," she told him. "You saved me."

Bree would have added more. So much more. But Sonya took the turn to the ranch, and both Luca and Bree readied themselves to jump out. That's what they did even before the cruiser was at a full stop, and they ran into the house.

Duncan and Joelle were indeed there, and Joelle had a gun aimed at Tara who was cuffed and belly-down on the floor. Duncan was in the process of bagging her phone and gun.

"I want a deal," Tara shouted when her attention landed on Bree. "Immunity for testifying against Nathan. He's the one who got me into this, and Nathan killed my sister."

"Manny and Nathan are both dead," Luca snarled, and he hurried up the stairs with Bree.

Tara continued to shout, but they ignored her and went to the bathroom door where Woodrow was indeed standing guard. He quickly let them in to the quiet room. Emphasis on *quiet*. Her mother was still in the shower stall with a baby in each arm, but both Gabriel and Izzie were sound asleep.

"Thank you," Bree told her mother and figured she'd be saying that a lot tonight.

Bree went to the shower and eased Gabriel into her arms. She immediately pressed against Luca so he could get in on kissing their son and making sure he was okay. There was so much relief in that moment. Relief that likely would have brought her to her knees had she not been leaning against Luca.

They both examined their little boy, making sure there were no injuries. Physically he was fine. And he thankfully wasn't showing any obvious signs of trauma because he continued to sleep.

Bree wanted to just stand there and hold him until some of the raw nerves had settled in her body, but there were still a few loose ends to wrap up. Added to that, she wasn't sure the hands had finished their search of the house.

"Just stay in here a little while longer," Bree told her mother and put Gabriel back in her arms. "As soon as Duncan gives us the all clear, we'll be back up to get you."

Her mother nodded, blinking away tears, but Bree thought they were definitely of relief. They'd all had a horrible scare tonight. A scare brought on by three people who'd joined forces to create a living hell.

Bree wanted Tara to pay for that.

Luca slipped his arm around Bree as they headed out of the bathroom and toward the stairs. He stopped on the landing, and even though they could hear Tara cursing and sobbing below, Luca still took a moment to kiss her. That helped with the nerves. Helped generate some heat, too, but she could practically feel the apology coming off him.

"Not your fault," she reminded him.

"I should have realized they were lying," he argued.

"You did realize it. You just didn't know what they were lying about. You need to request to be issued a crystal ball."

He gave her a flat look. "I needed to have been a better cop."

She could have reminded him that none of them had seen this unholy alliance between all of their suspects, but Bree figured a kiss was the way to go here. She kissed, and kissed and kissed until she finally felt some of the tension slide right off her. She might have continued but she heard Tara break into a sob. On heavy sighs, Luca and she went down to see what was going on.

"Manny's really dead?" Tara asked. Duncan had moved her to a sitting position, and both Carmen and Sonya were getting the cruiser ready to take her into custody.

"He is," Luca verified.

That brought on more sobbing from Tara. "He's dead," the woman said and she kept babbling it. "You didn't have to kill him."

"I beg to differ," Slater spoke up. "He was about to shoot Luca and me."

Tara sucked in a hard breath, nearly choking on it, and she shook her head while tears streamed down her cheeks. "This is all Nathan's fault. Manny and I wouldn't have gotten mixed up in this if it weren't for him."

"She's been Mirandized," Duncan informed them. "And she'd obviously decided not to remain silent."

"I want the world to know what Nathan did," Tara snarled. "All of this is his fault."

"How so?" Bree asked.

"Because he started up things with that woman. Brighton," she snapped out like profanity. "Nathan must have known that Manny was still sniffing around her, but that didn't stop him. So, Manny decided to go to Brighton's place to confront her. I followed him because, well, because."

"You were in love with him," Bree provided.

"Yes," Tara readily admitted, "and I was hoping once Manny saw Nathan and Brighton together that it would get her out of his system. It didn't." Her voice broke and she began to cry again. "Everything got messed up."

"How?" This time it was Luca who pressed for more details.

"A heated argument. Brighton said some horrible things about both Manny and Nathan." She paused. "Nathan slapped her, and Manny stepped in. A fight broke out, but then Brighton attacked Manny. She was punching, and I tried to stop her."

"Who actually killed her?" Bree asked.

"Nathan," she snapped but then shook her head. "Both Manny and Nathan. It was awful. Everything was out of control, and Brighton wouldn't hush. She just kept telling Nathan and Manny that they were pathetic losers. She said she was going to file charges against both of them for assault and stalking."

"Only one of them stabbed her to death," Duncan snapped.

Tara shook her head. "Both of them did. Manny lost it. He just lost it, and he grabbed a knife from her kitchen counter. It seemed to go on forever, and she didn't die. She just kept fighting and clawing at them. Then, Nathan shoved Manny aside and finished it."

So, Nathan was the killer. But Manny and Tara were accessories.

"Nathan said Manny and I would be charged with murder if we went to the cops," Tara went on. "He said as accomplices that we'd get the same sentence as if we'd actually killed her. I looked it up, and it's true."

Yes, it was. And while it likely wouldn't have been a capital murder charge had they reported it, they still would have ended up with life sentences.

"Nathan took Brighton's top because he said it would have all of our DNA on it," Tara added. "He said that was his assurance that we wouldn't try to save our own skins."

Bree shook her head. "So, you created a pact of silence. How did my mother fit into that? And my father?"

Tara's denial was fast and frantic. "We didn't kill your father. I swear. We were all stunned when it happened."

Maybe. But it was possible that Nathan was faking his reaction. Then again, he had denied killing her father when he'd been holding her at gunpoint.

"Your mother, well, we took her," Tara said. "Or rather Shannon and Aubrey did. Manny set that up, but he messed up by using Nathan's real name. Nathan was so mad and threatened Manny and me until Manny fixed it by linking it to some offshore account deal."

Manny had hidden those steps well. His business experience had likely helped with that.

"Your mother was continuing to dig and had made the connection between Brighton and the bar," Tara went on. "Manny and Nathan were worried she might learn the truth. So, we took her and thought we could somehow set her up for Brighton's murder, but we found out she had an iron-clad alibi."

Hearing that gave Bree a fresh slam of fury. "So, you what...just decided to hold her captive?"

Tara nodded. "Nathan knew you were digging, too, and he wanted to be able to use your mother as leverage." She swallowed hard. "Your son, too. He said you'd cooperate with anything if we had your son."

This time, it was more than fury. It was a whirl of sickening disgust at this trio who hadn't wanted to take responsibly for what they'd done.

"But Nathan wanted more than my cooperation," Bree pointed out. "He told me he was going to frame me for Brighton's murder."

Tara gave another nod. "It was all supposed to be over tonight. We'd have the baby to make you confess to the murder, and the investigation would all go away. We'd be in the clear." She shook her head. "But now they're both dead. Shannon, too. Manny killed her when she screwed up and let your mother escape."

So, Nathan and Manny had murdered at least two people, and they'd orchestrated a whole litany of other crimes.

"I didn't want to do any of this," Tara insisted. "But Nathan drew up the plan and said I'd go to jail if I didn't do everything he told me. Manny and I were to lie and point the finger at each other. Nathan said that way, it would mess with the investigation."

It had done that. All the lies. All the accusations. Peppered with attacks. In hindsight, those attacks hadn't been meant to kill her, but they could have. In fact, all of them could have been killed.

"You gave us that video of Manny," Luca reminded Tara.

Tara lowered her head. "Because I was so angry that Manny had killed Shannon. I thought, well, I wasn't thinking straight, but I couldn't come and say Manny had killed her so I'd hoped you'd arrest him for Brighton's murder. I figured Manny would accuse Nathan and me of helping him do that, but there wouldn't be any proof. Manny would end up paying."

"So, why'd you go through with the plan tonight?" Bree demanded.

"Because I was scared of Nathan. Of what he might do.

I'm not a killer like Manny and him. I'm not. I was supposed to kill the hands when we sneaked onto the ranch," Tara murmured. "I just couldn't. I used a stun gun on them instead, tied them up and took their keys so we could escape in their trucks. That counts for something, right? It counts that I didn't kill them?"

Disgusted, Bree only shook her head and stepped back. Luca was right there to take hold of her and walk with her into the dining room when Sonya and Carmen began to walk Tara out to the waiting cruiser.

"She'll spend the rest of her life behind bars, and that doesn't feel nearly enough," Bree muttered.

She felt the anger taking over, and she quickly shoved it aside. The anger was justified and would maybe always be there, but she didn't want this moment to be about that. Luca, their baby and she were all alive, and that's what she wanted to latch on to. Later, she'd deal with her feelings for Tara, but for now, she needed Luca.

Bree pulled Luca to her and dropped her head on his shoulder. Instant relief and comfort. Everything about it felt right.

Because it was.

Luca and she were right together.

Part of her had always known that, and it was why she'd found herself going back to him time and time again. It was why she wanted to be with him now.

"You know I'm in love with you," she admitted.

He eased back, lifted his eyebrow. "Really? You never said."

"Well, I'm saying it now. I'm in love with you, and I don't want to co-parent our son. I want the whole parent deal with you with us for, well, everything."

Now, he smiled and brushed his mouth over hers. "Good."

He kissed her. Really kissed her. And she felt the remnants of the anger and fear just vanish. The man could certainly work miracles. But he stopped the miracle kiss and stared down at her.

"You know I'm in love with you," he said, giving her back her own words.

She mimicked his gesture of a raised eyebrow. "Really?"

"Really," he verified, and he finished that off with exactly what she needed to hear. "And everything is exactly what I want with Gabriel and you, too."

* * * * *

Don't miss the stories in this mini series!

SADDLE RIDGE JUSTICE

Tracking Down The Lawman's Son
DELORES FOSSEN
December 2024

Child In Jeopardy
DELORES FOSSEN
January 2025

MILLS & BOON

Twin Jeopardy
Cindi Myers

MILLS & BOON

Cindi Myers is the author of more than seventy-five novels. When she's not plotting new romance storylines, she enjoys skiing, gardening, cooking, crafting and daydreaming. A lover of small-town life, she lives with her husband and two spoiled dogs in the Colorado mountains.

Books by Cindi Myers

Harlequin Intrigue

Eagle Mountain: Criminal History

Mile High Mystery
Twin Jeopardy

Eagle Mountain: Critical Response

Deception at Dixon Pass
Pursuit at Panther Point
Killer on Kestrel Trail
Secrets of Silverpeak Mine

Eagle Mountain Search and Rescue

Eagle Mountain Cliffhanger
Canyon Kidnapping
Mountain Terror
Close Call in Colorado

Eagle Mountain: Search for Suspects

Disappearance at Dakota Ridge
Conspiracy in the Rockies
Missing at Full Moon Mine
Grizzly Creek Standoff

Visit the Author Profile page at
millsandboon.com.au.

To Gini

CAST OF CHARACTERS

Tammy Patterson—The reporter for the *Eagle Mountain Examiner* knows what it's like to lose someone she loves. When she sets out to write a feature about the disappearance of a girl fifteen years before, she has no idea how personal the mystery will become for her.

Vince Shepherd—After seeing how hard volunteers worked to find his twin sister when she went missing when he was ten, Vince vowed to one day join search and rescue and help others. He also hopes the volunteer work will lead him to finding his sister someday.

Valerie Shepherd—Vince's twin disappeared on a camping trip in the mountains when the siblings were only ten. The mystery of what happened to her has haunted the family.

Mitch Patterson—Tammy's brother is a successful real estate agent and her closest confidant.

Elizabeth Rollins—Mitch Patterson's new girlfriend is everything Tammy is not—tall, gorgeous, poised and wealthy. But is Tammy's dislike of the woman all due to jealousy?

Bethany Ames—The newest search and rescue volunteer has taken a keen interest in Vince. She always seems to be around when disaster strikes.

Chapter One

"Look right down there in that gully. Just to the left of that tree branch that's sticking up out of the gravel. See that flash of white? I'm sure that's bones."

Eagle Mountain Search and Rescue volunteer Vince Shepherd moved in closer beside the couple who had summoned the team to this remote mountain trail above Galloway Basin. He squinted toward the spot the man had indicated. Yes, that definitely looked like a long bone. A femur, maybe? And was that a rib cage? His heart pounded with a mixture of hope and fear.

"They sure look human to me," the female half of the pair, a sturdy brunette who wore her hair in a long braid, said.

Search and rescue captain Danny Irwin lowered the binoculars he had focused on whatever was down there in the gully. "It's worth checking out," he said. "Thanks for calling it in."

"Looks like a pretty gnarly climb down there." The male hiker, red-haired and red-bearded, frowned into the gully. "Lots of downed trees and loose rock."

"We'll figure it out," Danny said. Tall and lanky, with shaggy brown hair and a laconic manner, in another context he might have been mistaken for a surfer instead of a registered nurse and search and rescue veteran. He looked past them to the gathered volunteers—only six responders, since this had been deemed a nonemergency call and not everyone was free on a Friday morning. "Three of us will make the hike down," he said. "The other three need to monitor the situation up top, in case any of us get into trouble."

"I'll go down with you." Vince stepped forward. He was one of the newer members of the group, but he had done a lot of hiking and climbing before he joined up, and he wanted to get a closer look at those bones. Part of him dreaded seeing them, but better to know the truth sooner rather than later. It was a long shot that those bones had anything to do with his sister, but what if they really did belong to her?

"I'll go too," Hannah Gwynn said. A paramedic, Hannah served as the team's current medical officer.

"If you hike down from the top end of the gulley, it's not that steep." Sheri Stevens, on summer vacation from her teaching position, looked up the mountainside. "You won't need to rope up or anything."

"Yeah, we just have to pick our way around the dead trees, boulders and loose gravel swept down by spring run-off," Danny said. He looked to Vince. "You ready to go?"

"Yeah."

They left Sheri, along with Grace Wilcox and Caleb Garrison, to monitor the situation up top. The hikers who had called in the find elected to head back down the mountain. Danny led the way, picking a path through the debris-choked gully. The July sun beat down, but at this high elevation the warmth was welcome. Wildflowers carpeted the meadows alongside the gully, and if it weren't for the reason for their presence here, it would have been an enjoyable outing. The climb wasn't physically challenging, but it was tedious and frustrating, requiring frequent backtracking and constant readjustments to the unsteady footing. "How did those bones ever end up down here?" Vince wondered out loud as he clambered over a fallen tree trunk, then skirted a large boulder.

"They might have washed down from farther up the mountain," Hannah said. She hopped over a mudhole, then pulled aside a fallen branch to clear a better path.

Danny stopped to gauge their progress, then pulled out his handheld radio. "How much farther do we have to go?" he asked.

"You've got about five hundred feet," Sheri replied. "You'll know you're close when you see that big branch sticking up. It's got most of the bark peeled off of it. The bones are just beyond that."

"I may need you to direct us when we get there," Danny said. "There's so much debris down here it's hard to distinguish details."

They squeezed through a tangle of tree limbs, then trudged across a section of mud, boots sinking with each step, before scaling a jumble of granite slabs. "Guess I'm getting my workout in for the day," Vince said, as he hauled himself to the top of what he hoped was the final slab. From here, he had a view down the gully. "I think that's the tree Sheri was talking about." He pointed toward a jagged branch, the bare wood shining white in the sun.

"I see a path through to there," Danny said. He hopped down from the slab and set out again, shoving aside knots of brush as he went. Hannah followed, with Vince bringing up the rear.

"You're almost there," Sheri radioed. "Look uphill."

A few minutes later, Danny stopped. "We're here," he said, and crouched down to examine something on the ground.

Vince hung back. "Is it human bones?" he called.

Hannah moved in closer and leaned over Danny's shoulder. "It's a skeleton, all right," she said. "Kind of small. Maybe a child?"

For a moment, Vince stopped breathing. Valerie had been ten when she disappeared from the family's campsite above

Galloway Basin. A four-foot dynamo with sandy-brown curls cut short, she had a dimple in her left cheek that matched Vince's own. He forced himself to move forward until he was standing beside Hannah, looking down on a small rib cage, and a heap of arm and leg bones.

Danny moved up the gully a few steps and began shifting a pile of rocks. After a few seconds, he stood once more. "It's not a human," he said. "It's a bear."

"What?" Hannah looked up from her scrutiny of the bones.

"The skull is right here." Danny pulled out something from among the rocks and held it up. The skull was oblong, with a prominent jaw, one oversize canine tooth jutting from one corner of the mouth.

"A bear?" Vince staggered a little. Not Valerie.

"Kind of a small one." Danny leaned over the skeleton once more. "See, if you look closer, you can tell the femur is too short to be human, and the shoulder blades are a lot wider."

"You're right," Hannah said. "I guess I was thinking 'human' because that's what the hikers called in, and at first glance it's similar."

"Maybe a cub that didn't make it through a hard winter," Danny said.

Vince was dimly aware of their conversation. A bear. Not a little girl. Not Valerie.

"It really did look like a human from a distance." Hannah hugged her elbows. "I can't say I'm sorry we don't have to try to transport a skeleton out of here."

Danny dropped the skull. "That's it, then. Let's get away from here." He pulled out his radio. "We're headed back up," he said. "The bones weren't human, but a bear's."

Hannah started to move past Vince but stopped. "Are you okay?" she asked. "You look like you don't feel so hot."

"I'll be okay." He ran his hand over his face. "I guess I was trying to prepare myself for the worst, and now..."

Hannah's eyes widened. She gripped his shoulder. "Oh my gosh, Vince. I didn't even think! You thought this was Valerie, didn't you?"

No sense lying about it. "I knew it probably wasn't," he said. "But our camp wasn't that far from here, and after all these years, we're still waiting for her to be found."

Danny had ended his radio transmission and joined them. "Is something wrong?" he asked.

Hannah squeezed Vince's arm. "I'm sorry," she said. "I should have remembered."

"No reason you should have," he said. "It was a long time ago." Fifteen years. Most of his life.

Danny was watching him, a puzzled look on his face. "Something I need to know about?" he asked.

"My sister." Vince cleared his throat and focused on pulling himself together. After this long, he hadn't expected to feel so emotional. "My twin sister. She disappeared on a family camping trip in the mountains the summer we were ten." He looked past Danny, toward the mountains rising around them. "Not that far from here. She was never found, so when I heard bones had been spotted up here, I couldn't help wondering..." His voice trailed away.

"That's rough," Danny said. "Do you have any idea what happened to her?"

"None. Maybe she fell or had some other kind of accident, but lots of people looked, for days, and we never found any sign of her."

"I was a little older than you, but I still remember the posters around town and people volunteering to help search," Hannah said. "It really is scary how someone can just vanish up here."

"Sometimes they get found years later," Danny said. "There

was that woman about ten years ago. She had disappeared skiing three years before, and her remains were found in a bunch of avalanche debris."

"You must think about Valerie every time you're up here," Hannah said.

"I do," Vince said. "And pretty much every time I'm up here, I look for her." Though that wasn't the sole reason he had joined search and rescue, it had been one consideration.

"I hope someone finds your sister one day," Hannah said. "I'm sorry it wasn't today."

"Really, I'm okay now. It was just kind of a shock." He shrugged, trying to appear steadier than he felt. "Like you said, now we don't have to haul a body bag up out of this gully." He didn't wait for them to answer, but turned and began retracing his steps. For a brief moment, when he had first looked down on those bones, a wave of dizziness washed over him, a mixture of profound relief that they would finally know Valerie's fate and gut-wrenching grief at proof that she really was gone. No matter how improbable it would be for her to still be alive after all this time, as long as they didn't have a body, they were able to cling to a sliver of hope that she was still walking around somewhere and maybe one day they would be reunited.

Finding out the bones weren't even human resulted in the kind of nausea-inducing whiplash experienced on roller coasters and bungee jumps. A few deep breaths and a little physical exertion, and he'd be all right again. Valerie was still gone. Probably dead. They would likely never know what happened to her. It was a reality he had grown used to, even if he had never fully accepted it.

"I HAVE AN idea for a series of articles I want to do." Tammy Patterson, the *Eagle Mountain Examiner*'s only full-time reporter, stood in front of editor Russ Saunders's desk, notepad in hand. Russ cast a jaundiced eye on anything he considered "too fluffy," so she would have to pitch this right.

Russ removed the cigar from the corner of his mouth—he never smoked the things, just chewed them. Tammy suspected he had adopted the habit when he first took helm of the paper when he was fresh out of college, thinking it made him appear more mature and even jaded. Now he actually was mature—north of fifty—and definitely jaded. "What's your idea?" he asked.

"This year is the twenty-fifth anniversary of the founding of Eagle Mountain Search and Rescue," she said. "I want to run a series of articles that looks back on some of their most dramatic callouts and daring rescues."

"Why would our readers care?" This was the question he always asked.

"People love reading about local heroism, not to mention danger, the outdoors and even unsolved mysteries."

"How is this going to contribute to our bottom line?" This was Russ's other favorite question, and one she had also anticipated.

"We'll ask local businesses to buy space for messages or special ads that celebrate Eagle Mountain Search and Rescue's anniversary. They get to advertise their business and support a favorite local organization."

He leaned forward, elbows on the desk. "How many articles are you talking about?" he asked.

"Six. One every other week for three months."

She could practically see him running through the calculations in his head. "When can you have the first article ready?" he asked.

"Two weeks. I want to start with the search for Valerie Shepherd." Before he could ask, she rushed on. "She was a ten-year-old girl who disappeared on a family camping trip in the mountains fifteen years ago. Never a trace of her seen again. Search and rescue was part of the largest wilderness search in local history. That search really ushered in a new era for the group, with a turn toward more professional training and organization."

"I remember," Russ said. "Local family. Wasn't she a twin?"

"Yes. Her brother, Vince, works for the county Road and Bridge Department. Her parents are in Junction."

"You'll talk to them for your article."

"Of course. And search and rescue has agreed to give me access to their archives. And there are lots of photos in our files we can use."

"Sounds good," Russ said. "But don't let this take precedence over your regular news coverage."

"When have I ever done that, Russ?"

He chomped down on the cigar once more and spoke around it. "You're not a slacker, I'll give you that."

Smiling to herself, Tammy moved back to her desk. Working for the only paper in town, which came out once a week, was a great way to feel like she always knew everything going on. But the sameness of reporting on the school board and county commissioner's meetings, as well as perennial wrangles over building codes or the budget amount to devote to promoting tourism, could get old. It was good to have something exciting and interesting to write about. The fifteen-year-old mystery of a missing girl definitely wasn't going to be boring.

Chapter Two

"You're Vince Shepherd, right?"

Vince accepted the beer from the bartender at Mo's Pub and turned to see who was addressing him. A young woman with a cascade of blond curls and a friendly smile eyed him through round wire-rimmed glasses. "I'm Vince," he said, wary. "Who are you?"

"I'm Tammy Patterson. I'm a reporter for the *Eagle Mountain Examiner*." She offered her hand, nails polished bright pink and a trio of rings on her fingers.

"Sure. I've read your stuff." He shook her hand. What did a reporter want with him?

"Do you have a minute to talk?" she asked.

He sipped the beer. "Talk about what?"

"I'm working on a series of stories about Eagle Mountain Search and Rescue, to celebrate their twenty-fifth anniversary. I have a few questions for you."

"Okay. Sure." He could talk about search and rescue.

"There's a spot over here where it's a little quieter." She led the way to a booth near the back of the crowded bar.

"I haven't been with the group that long," Vince said as he slid into the padded seat across from her.

"What group is that?" she asked. She was searching in an oversize black leather tote bag.

"Search and rescue. You said you were writing about them."

"Oh. I didn't know you were a member of SAR." She pulled out a notepad, a pen and a small recorder and laid them on the table in front of her. "That's even better."

He sipped more beer and frowned. "If you didn't know I was with SAR, why do you want to talk to me?"

"I want to talk to you about your sister. Valerie."

Valerie again. It wasn't that he never thought about his missing twin, but after fifteen years she wasn't on his mind every day. But today she had taken up a disproportionate space in his head, what with the callout about the bones that morning. And now this reporter was asking about her. "Why do you want to talk about Valerie?" he asked.

"I want to write about the search for her fifteen years ago. It was the largest wilderness search in county history, and as a result of that search, Eagle Mountain Search and Rescue instituted a lot of new policies and adopted a more professional approach to their operations."

"You know she was never found," he said. "It's not exactly a feel-good story."

"No, but it's an enduring mystery."

He braced himself for her to say that people were always interested in mysteries. That was true, but when it was your own family tragedy at the center of the mystery, it was tough to think of it as entertaining. But she gave him a direct look, her blue eyes showing no sign of guile. "It doesn't hurt to bring the case to the public's attention again. You never know when someone might have seen the one thing that could help you find out what happened that day."

"Do you really think there's a person out there who knows something they've never talked about?" he asked. "I'm pretty sure the sheriff's department—not to mention my parents—talked to everyone they could find."

"There was another camper in the area that day. No one ever found and talked to him."

"How do you know about him?"

"One of the news stories from the paper's archives mentioned law enforcement was looking for the man."

"He was backpacking, like us. It's not like he could have smuggled my sister out in his pack or anything. The general consensus was that Valerie fell or had some other accident. It's pretty rugged country, and there are a lot of places a little kid could get lost."

She glanced at her notes. "I plan to meet with the sheriff, and search and rescue has agreed to let me review their logs and other information in the archives about the search. And I want to speak with your parents."

"Let me call them first."

"That would be great." She smiled, and he felt the impact of the expression. How could someone put so much warmth into a smile? "I'll wait until I hear from you before I contact them. But it would help a lot if you could tell me about that day. I'd like to know more about Valerie and what she was like, and what your family was like before that day."

"I was only ten when it happened."

"She was your twin. You must have memories of her."

"I do."

She leaned toward him, her voice gentle. "I'm not trying to cause you pain, opening up old wounds. But Valerie is at the center of the story. I want to try to show my readers how her loss affected not just her family but also this town. I have a quote from the newspaper stories at the time. One of the volunteer searchers said that before Valerie disappeared, everyone thought of the wilderness as safe—not without risk, but a haven from the kinds of crimes that happen in cities and towns. That sense of security was taken along with her."

"We don't know that her disappearance was a crime."

"No. But because her body was never found—not a single trace—the possibility remains that someone took her. It's every family's worst nightmare, isn't it?"

"Yeah." A nightmare. One from which they had never completely awakened.

Fifteen Years Ago

"COME ON, VINCE. Race me to that big red rock up ahead." Valerie turned around and walked backward along the trail, thumbs hooked in the straps of her blue backpack, her legs like two pale sticks between the frayed hem of her denim shorts and the folded cuffs of the striped knit socks she wore with her green leather hiking boots. She had had what their mom deemed a growth spurt that summer, and was now three inches taller than Vince and all angles. Except for the corkscrew curls that stuck out from the green bandanna she had tied around her head.

"I don't want to race," he said. He didn't even want to be on this trip, lugging a heavy pack up into the middle of nowhere instead of hanging out with his friends at Trevor Richardson's birthday party, which was going to be a pool party at the rec center in Junction. Some of the boys—including Vince—had been invited to spend the night, with sleeping bags in the Richardsons' basement rec room, where they planned to stay up all night eating junk food and watching horror movies.

But Vince's parents had put an end to that prospect, insisting Vince needed to come on this trip. "We've been planning it for weeks, and family comes first," his mother said when Vince had protested.

So here he was, with the straps of his backpack digging into his shoulders and Valerie doing her best to be the kid who was *soooo* happy to be here. Instead of sympathizing with her twin, she was purposely making him look bad.

"How can anybody be such a grumpy-pants when we're surrounded by all this gorgeousness?" Valerie turned to face forward again and raised her arms in the air like she was auditioning for *The Sound of Music* or something.

No one answered her. Instead, their dad said, "I think there's a good spot to camp up ahead, off to the left in the shelter of that dike." He pointed toward a gray rock wall that stood out from the rest of the more eroded mountainside. An amateur geologist, Dad liked to use these trips to talk about various rock formations and how they had come to be. Usually, Vince found this interesting, but how could that stuff—much of which he had heard before—compare to the lost prospect of swimming, pizza, and a sleepover with unlimited junk food and horror movies?

"Awesome!" Valerie raced toward the campsite, pack bouncing. Vince brought up the rear of the group. When he got there, Valerie had already scaled a flat-topped chunk of granite. "There's another camper over there!" She pointed straight ahead. "Looks like a guy with a blue dome tent."

"Come down and help set up camp," their mother said. She was already pulling the rain fly and a bag of stakes from her pack while their father unpacked the folded tent. They each carried their own sleeping bags and pads, and the food for the weekend was divided among them.

"I'll help with the tent," Valerie said.

"Vince can help with that," their father said. "Why don't

you see if you can find firewood? I thought I spotted some dead trees on the other side of the trail."

Valerie raced off to gather wood while Vince reluctantly helped his dad assemble the tent. "There will be other parties," his father said.

"Not like this one." Vince pounded a tent stake into the hard ground. "And there will be lots of other camping trips."

"Maybe. But you and your sister are growing up fast. In a few years you'll have jobs, then you'll be going away to college. It won't be as easy for the four of us to get away. These trips are important, though you may not realize how important until you're older."

"Trevor's party was important to me."

His dad paused in the act of feeding one of the collapsible tent poles through the channel in the top of the tent. "I can understand that. And maybe insisting you come with us wasn't the fairest decision, but it's the one I made. It's too late to go back, so you might as well try to make the best of it. Maybe we'll do something for your birthday to make up for it. I can't promise a pool party, but you could invite your friends to spend the night and watch movies."

"Really?"

Dad smiled. "I don't see why not."

Vince grinned. Wait until the guys heard about this! Then his elation faded. "What about Valerie?" He and his twin always celebrated together, usually with a joint party, featuring games and cake and ice cream.

"The two of you are old enough for separate celebrations, I think. I'll talk to your mom."

"Thanks!" By the time they had finished with the tent, he was feeling better. He helped spread the pads and sleeping bags inside, then emerged to find the light already fading, the air cooling. He retrieved a fleece pullover from his pack. "Find your sister and tell her to come back to camp," his mother said.

He crossed the road and hadn't gone far before he met Valerie staggering toward him, arms full of dead tree branches. She was dropping more than she was transporting, and he hurried to take half the load from her.

"I met our neighbor," she said when both loads were balanced.

"Who?"

"The man who's camped over there." She nodded up the road. "He was looking for firewood too, but he said I could have this and he would look somewhere else."

"What's his name?"

"He didn't say. He just smiled and left. He had a nice smile." Her dimple deepened at the recollection.

"You're not supposed to talk to strangers," Vince said.

"I didn't say anything. He did all the talking."

"That's hard to believe. You never shut up."

She hip-checked him. He did the same to her. "You are such a dork!" she said.

"You're the champion dork."

"I'm number one!" she shouted, and ran ahead of him.

They raced into camp. Mom smiled at them. "As soon as the fire is going, I'll start supper," she said.

"What are we having?" Valerie asked.

"Sausage spaghetti."

"And s'mores for dessert?" Valerie asked.

"Yes."

"Yay!" Valerie shouted.

"Yay!" Vince echoed.

They ate all the spaghetti and the s'mores, then lay back by the campfire and watched for shooting stars. Vince counted five of them streaking across the sky in the space of half an hour. Valerie nudged him. "Admit it, you're glad you came," she said.

"I wish I could have done both—the party and this."

"Yeah. That would have been fun. But I'm glad you're here."

He fell asleep there on the ground, and his father woke him to go into the tent, where he burrowed into his sleeping bag beside Valerie. She lay curled on her side, the rhythm of her deep breathing lulling him to sleep.

He woke early the next morning when she crawled over him on her way to the door. "What are you doing?" he whispered, then glanced toward their parents, who slept side by side a few inches away.

"I'm going to get wood and start a fire." Valerie pulled on one green boot, then the other, then ducked out the tent flap and zipped it up again.

He lay down again and must have fallen back asleep. Next thing he knew, his mother was shaking him. "Vince, have you seen your sister?"

"Huh?" He raised up on his elbows and looked around. Valerie and his dad were both gone from the tent, and his mother was dressed in tan hiking shorts and a blue fleece, her brown hair pulled back in a ponytail.

"Valerie isn't here. Do you know where she went?" Mom asked.

"She got up early and said she was going to get firewood." He sat up. Bright sunlight showed through the open tent flap. "What time is it?"

"It's after eight. When did she get up?"

"I don't know. Really early, I think." He had that impression, anyway.

"Get up and get dressed. We need to look for her."

When he crawled out of the tent, he noticed the firepit was empty and cold. "Valerie!" his mother called.

"Valerie!" His dad echoed from the other side of the dike.

Vince climbed onto the granite slab and shaded his eyes, searching for movement or a flash of color. His father joined him. "Do you see anything?" Dad asked.

"No. Yesterday, she said there was a man camped over here, but I don't see anyone."

"Come on. We need to spread out and look farther away."

They searched for an hour. Vince peered into canyons and climbed atop rocks, but there was no sign of Valerie. "I'm going to hike back to the car and go for the sheriff," his father said. "You stay with your mother and keep looking."

His mother pulled him close. Her eyes were red and swollen from crying. "Where could she have gone?" she asked. "Did she say where she was going?"

"No. She just said she was going to get some wood."

"How can she have just vanished?"

But she had. None of them would ever see her again.

Chapter Three

Tammy met with Sheriff Travis Walker on Monday morning. When she had first moved to Eagle Mountain, the handsome dark-haired sheriff was considered one of the most eligible bachelors in town. Now the married father of twins, he had a reputation for being an honest, hardworking lawman who had run unopposed in the last election. Not long after Tammy had started work at the newspaper, she had been attacked by a pair of men who had been preying on women in the area. She had escaped unharmed, and Travis had been gentle, but firm, in digging out all the information she could remember about her attackers.

As she waited in his office, she studied the photo of his smiling wife, a baby in each arm. It probably wasn't easy being married to a man who had to face his share of danger, but Lacey Walker looked happy. Tammy felt a pinch of jealousy as she stared at the photo. She wanted that kind of happiness—that settledness of having a mate who loved you and children who were part of you. So far, that had eluded her.

"Hello, Tammy." She turned as Travis entered the office. He settled behind the desk, the chair creaking as he sat back. "Sorry to keep you waiting."

"I haven't been here long."

"I had a copy of the Valerie Shepherd file made for you.

There's not a lot of information here." He handed a single file folder across the desk.

"I spoke with Vince Shepherd Friday," she said. "He told me the consensus was that Valerie must have fallen and either been killed instantly or so injured she wasn't able to cry for help."

"By all accounts, she was an active, adventurous little girl," Travis said. "There are a lot of steep drop-offs, deep canyons and unstable rock formations in the area."

"But if that was the case, don't you think someone would have found her? According to the accounts I've read, there were literally hundreds of people searching for her for weeks. And yet not one item of clothing or any part of her remains has been found."

He shrugged. "If she ended up deep in a canyon, or in a cave or rock crevice, her remains might never be discovered."

"What about the other camper who was in the area? A single man."

"I can only tell you what's in the file, since I wasn't part of the force then. The notes you'll find in there indicate that while Valerie mentioned seeing a man camping a short distance away from the Shepherd family, no one else in the family actually saw him, and no one else we talked to saw him either."

"Do you think she was making him up? Was she like that?"

"I don't know. I'm mentioning it as one possibility."

She opened the file folder and began flipping through the notes and reports inside, scanning each page. She stopped at one report. "This says a deputy spoke to a couple of hikers who saw a man with a backpack in the area. He was alone, and they never saw him again."

"He might be the man Valerie saw, or he might be someone else," Travis said. "The department put out an appeal asking anyone who had been in the area that day to come forward, but no one ever did."

She closed the file and looked at him again. "Were there ever any suspects?"

"None," Travis said.

"What about the family? Could one of them have done something to Valerie and hidden it from the others? I know it's horrible to think about, but it does happen."

"There are copies of interviews with each family member, as well as background information from neighbors and teachers who knew them. Everyone agreed that Valerie was a loved, well-cared-for child. The parents and her brother were devastated by her loss."

"Whenever I write stories like this, I always hope someone will come forward with new information," she said. "We usually run a box at the end of the article that asks anyone who might have information to contact the sheriff's department."

"I'd be happy to hear from anyone who could shed more light on what happened that day, but I think it's doubtful that will happen."

"Probably not. Of course, the main point of the article is to highlight the efforts of search and rescue that day. Can I get a quote from you about that?"

"My understanding is that prior to Valerie's disappearance, the group was a loose-knit band of volunteers without the formal structure they have today. They worked with local law enforcement, but they weren't under the direction of the sheriff's department, as they are today. Today Eagle Mountain Search and Rescue is a professional, highly trained organization I would consider one of the best in the mountain west."

She scribbled the quote in her notebook. "That's great," she said. "Exactly what I'm looking for."

He flashed one of his rare smiles. "I'm glad I could help."

She left the sheriff's department and was walking back to the newspaper office when a voice hailed her. She turned and was surprised to see her younger brother, Mitch, striding toward her. Mitch had inherited their father's darker, straighter hair, which he wore long and pulled back in a ponytail. Dressed in fashionably cut jeans and a loose linen shirt, he looked ready to make a deal on Wall Street or—a more likely scenario—sell a luxurious vacation home to that Wall Street denizen.

"How's the real estate business?" she asked as Mitch drew even with her.

"I just came from a showing I hope will result in a sale of a ranch over near the county line," he said. "Now I have time to kill and thought I'd see if you wanted to grab lunch."

"I do if you're buying," she said. She nudged him with her elbow. "Seeing as you're about to earn a big commission and everything."

"It's not a done deal yet," he said. "But I can buy my sister lunch." He hugged her briefly. "How are you doing?"

"I'm doing okay."

"Not better than okay? Are you still upset about Darrell?"

"No, I am not upset about Darrell." Not anymore. Breaking things off with him had been the right decision, she knew. He wasn't interested in ever settling down and she was ready to look for something long term. "Ending things between us was sad," she said. "But I know it was the right thing to do."

"You'll find someone else," he said. "Maybe a handsome, wealthy, single, straight man looking to make his home in Eagle Mountain will walk into my office this afternoon and I'll introduce him to you."

"Please do," she said, and laughed.

"Where should we have lunch?" he asked.

"Let me drop this off at my office, then you can pick," she said, holding up the file folder.

He gestured at the file. "Something you're working on?"

"I'm writing about the search fifteen years ago for a little girl who went missing."

"How old was this girl?"

"Ten."

The lines across his forehead deepened. "Why are you writing about something that happened that long ago?"

She explained her planned series of articles focusing on Eagle Mountain Search and Rescue.

"And she was ten, huh?"

"Yeah, I know." The same age as their older brother, Adam, when he had been killed by a speeding car. "I interviewed the girl's twin brother Friday. When he talked about feeling lost after she was gone, I knew exactly what he was going through." She had been nine when Adam was killed, Mitch seven. Young enough to not fully comprehend how someone could suddenly be gone. Old enough to see the way their family changed forever on that day.

"Did you tell him about Adam?" Mitch asked.

"No. It's not something I talk about with anyone but you." Her mother, the only parent left now, had long ago stopped talking about her eldest son, the memories too painful.

"Yeah, me either."

She left the file on her desk; then she and Mitch walked over two blocks to the edge of the park and a food truck that sold tacos and other Mexican street food. She and Mitch had just settled at a picnic table with their purchases when Vince and two other men in the khaki uniform shirts of Eagle

Mountain Road and Bridge took their place in line. "Hey, Tammy," Vince said.

"Hi, Vince. How are you?"

"Can't complain." Then he was called to place his order, and he turned away.

"Who is that?" Mitch asked.

"Vince Shepherd. Valerie's brother."

"Is he single?"

"Why? Are you interested?"

He made a face. "I was thinking for you."

It was her turn to scowl at him.

"I'm just saying," he said. "The two of you seem to get along well."

She laughed. "Saying hello to each other doesn't tell you anything about how we'd get along."

He held up both hands in a defensive gesture. "Don't blame me for wanting you to be happy."

"I am happy," she said. Maybe not the level of happiness she craved, but life wasn't all bliss and she didn't expect it to be. She touched her brother's wrist. "I'm fine, Mitch. You don't have to worry about me."

"Just don't go stirring up trouble with this article."

"Oh, please. There's nothing about this article that could cause me trouble. I'm not an investigative reporter digging up dirt in a big city." Maybe in another life, she would have chosen a more exciting career, but being the sole reporter at a small-town paper suited her. It was comfortable and safe, and that's what she craved—most of the time, at least.

"I DIDN'T KNOW you knew Tammy Patterson," Vince's co-worker, Cavin, said when the three of them were seated at a table a short distance from where Tammy and her friend were eating.

"We've met." Vince poured salsa onto his tacos.

"I heard she split up with the guy she was dating," the third man at the table, Sandor, said.

Vince stared at him. "How do you know these things?"

"My wife works at the salon where Tammy gets her hair cut. She knows everything there is to know about half the female population in town. And then she comes home and tells me everything."

"The scary thing is, you remember it," Cavin said.

Sandor shrugged. "People are interesting."

"If you say so." Vince bit into his taco. He glanced over at Tammy. She was pretty, in a friendly, down-to-earth kind of way. All those soft curls. She was laughing with the guy she was with.

Cavin nudged him. "Caught you looking," he said.

Vince focused on his food once more. "She and that guy look pretty cozy, so I'd say she isn't available," he said.

"That's her brother," Sandor said. "He's a real estate agent over at Brown Realty. He helped us find the house we're in."

Vince couldn't help himself—he had to look at the pair again. Maybe a family resemblance was there. Tammy rested a hand on the man's forearm and smiled into his eyes. He felt a pang. What would it be like to have a lunch with a grown-up Valerie like that? To have someone besides your parents who had known you your whole life, who had seen life from a similar perspective and had the same frame of reference? He would never know.

Cavin shifted the conversation to a discussion of parts he needed to order for one of the county graders, and Vince turned his back on Tammy and her brother. Maybe he wasn't cut out for relationships. He didn't like getting too close to people. That was okay. Everybody was different, and he was happy enough. Most of the time.

"As we say goodbye to our friend Paul, it is with great sadness, as well as gratitude for having him in our lives. Though his physical body is gone from us, his memory endures, and we will hold him in our hearts forever." The black-suited man from the funeral home who had agreed to lead this graveside burial looked across the open grave at the trio of mourners. "Go in peace," he said. "And I'm sorry for your loss."

"Thank you." Valerie choked out the words, then cleared her throat, pulling herself together. Paul never liked it when she cried. It was the one thing she did that ever made him angry. She turned away, not wanting to see them shovel dirt onto the coffin.

"It's hard to believe he's gone."

She glanced at the speaker—Bill, who had played on the local softball team with Paul. "I guess so," she said. Though after staring at his dead body, slumped in his favorite chair in front of the TV, she hadn't any doubts that he had died. An asthma attack, the coroner had said.

"I mean, he was so young," Bill continued. "Only forty-five."

Thirty-nine, she silently corrected. But he told everyone he was older because of her. She hadn't realized herself until she had found papers with his real age on them one day when she was sixteen. It made sense, though. No one would have believed he was her father if they knew he was only fourteen years older. Not that it was anyone's business.

"I know there's not any formal wake or anything, but do you want to get coffee or something?"

She stopped walking. So did Bill. He shoved his hands in the pockets of his baggy suit and hunched his shoulders the way tall people sometimes did, as if trying to look smaller. He was thin and bony, and already losing his hair despite the fact that he was still in his twenties. He wasn't bad looking, but his cloying infatuation with her was grating. "No thank you," she said. "I don't feel like company."

"Well, sure. Of course." He took a step back. "Maybe another time."

She walked alone to her car and drove back to the house that had been home the past fifteen years, in a drab suburb of Omaha, Nebraska. She had been happy here while Paul was alive. Happy enough. Happy as a person could be who had been abandoned by the people who were supposed to take care of her. As Paul had often reminded her, she was lucky he had come along when he did, to look after her.

But now Paul was gone. She had no one.

She was alone now. Free to do whatever she wanted. Paul had left her a little money—several thousand in cash he kept in the safe in his bedroom closet, as well as the house and ample funds in the bank accounts they shared. She would take that money and spend some time making things right.

Chapter Four

Monday night, Vince called his parents. He had been putting the conversation off since he had talked to Tammy on Friday, but it was time he let them know. Though they had moved to Junction several years before, they still subscribed to the *Eagle Mountain Examiner*, and he didn't want them surprised by Tammy's request for an interview. Besides, she was waiting on him before she could finish the article.

His father answered the phone and put the call on Speaker right away. "Hello, Vince," he said. "Your mother is right here. How are you doing?"

"I'm okay, Dad. How are you and Mom?"

"We're fine," his mom answered. "A little tired. We played golf today—a full eighteen holes. With Barb and Ray Ferngil. Do you remember them? Ray used to work with your dad."

Vince had no idea who they were talking about. "You had beautiful weather for a game," he said.

"We did," his dad said. "I like living near a good course."

"Did you just call to chat, or did you need something?" his mom asked. "Not that we don't love to hear from you, but you don't usually call on a Monday night."

"A reporter here in Eagle Mountain is doing a series of articles on the local search and rescue organization," he said.

"One of the articles is going to be about the search for Valerie. I just wanted to warn you so it didn't come as a shock."

"Oh." One short, sad exhalation from his mom that made his chest tighten. He hoped she wasn't going to start crying. She hadn't done that in a long time, but it always unsettled him.

"Did this reporter talk to you about it?" his dad asked. "Is that how you know?"

"Yeah. She interviewed me. I think it's going to be a good story. Apparently, the search for Valerie was a catalyst that transformed the rescue group into a professional organization."

"Well, good. Good." He could picture his dad nodding in that thoughtful way he had—lips pursed, brow furrowed.

"She wants to talk to you and Mom too."

"Well…" Now he pictured his father looking at his mother, gauging her reaction to the request.

"Of course we'll talk to her," his mom said. "Maybe someone will come forward who remembers something about that day that got overlooked. Or the article will inspire people to look for her while they're hiking in that area."

"Maybe so, Mom. Though after such a long time, I don't think we can hope for much."

"You never know. Maybe…maybe Valerie will see the article and get in touch."

He winced. His parents—especially his mother—had never given up hope that Valerie hadn't died that day but that she had been taken, perhaps by the mysterious camper no one had ever identified. "I don't know about that, Mom," he said.

"I know you think I'm foolish, but it's not such a farfetched idea. There have been other missing children who were discovered as adults. And I still say if Valerie had died that day, someone would have found her. You may not remember, but they literally had people spaced two feet apart in long lines, searching every inch of the area around our campsite for miles. How could they have not found her if she was still there?"

"I didn't mean to upset you," Vince said. "I just wanted you to know."

"We appreciate that," his dad said. Gone was the cheerfulness with which he had started the call. Now he sounded tired. Old.

"I'll let you know if I hear anything else," Vince said. "I'd better go now."

"Goodbye, son." This from his dad. In the background, he heard a sound he thought might have been his mother, crying.

He ended the call and leaned against the sofa, head back, eyes closed. For years, his mom had sworn that if Valerie was dead, she would know it. "She's my daughter," she said. "That's a bond that doesn't break."

Once, years ago, she had pressed Vince to admit that he still felt his sister was alive too. "She's your twin," Mom said. "You're halves of the same whole."

"We're not identical twins, Mom."

"Oh, you know what I mean."

"I'm sorry, Mom, I don't."

"You don't feel Valerie is still alive somewhere?"

"I don't know, Mom."

Her face crumpled, but she pulled herself together. "Do you feel like she's gone, then?" she asked.

"I don't know, Mom."

When he thought of his sister, he didn't feel anything. Just…empty. Not a wrenching loss or a sense that she was just away for a while. There was a void where his sister was supposed to be, and he didn't expect anything would ever fill it.

AT THE THURSDAY-evening meeting of Eagle Mountain Search and Rescue volunteers. Vince settled on one end of the sofa in the hangar-like building that served as search and rescue headquarters, next to newlyweds Jake and Hannah Gwynn. When he wasn't volunteering with SAR, Jake was a deputy with the Rayford County Sheriff's Department, which put him on the scene for many of the accidents SAR responded to. After seeing the volunteers in action, he had decided to join their ranks. And it had been one way to guarantee he would see more of Hannah.

"All right, everyone. Let's go ahead and get started." Danny, clipboard in hand, walked to the front of the room, and conversation among the volunteers died down. "First up, I want to introduce our newest volunteer, Bethany Ames."

A slender young woman with a mass of dark curls stood and waved. She had a heart-shaped face and an upturned nose, and a dimple in her cheek when she smiled. "Bethany is new to the area and works at Peak Jeep and Snowmobile Rentals," Danny continued. "Everyone, introduce yourselves later." Bethany sat, and Danny consulted his clipboard again. "Next, most of you already know that this summer marks the twenty-fifth anniversary of the founding of Eagle Mountain Search and Rescue."

"Happy birthday to us!" Ryan Welch called out while several others responded with whistles or clapping.

"Will there be a cake?" someone else asked.

"Cake is always welcome," Danny agreed. "We'll see what we can do. In the meantime, the *Eagle Mountain Examiner* is planning a series of articles about the organization, focusing on several of our missions over the years, as well as sharing how the group has grown and changed."

Murmurs of approval greeted this news.

"The first article is going to run next week. Most of you

know Tammy Patterson, the paper's reporter. She's starting the series with a feature about the search for Valerie Shepherd fifteen years ago."

A number of people turned to look at Vince. "Are you okay with this?" Jake asked.

"I already spoke with Tammy," Vince said. "It's fine."

"Valerie was never found," Tony Meisner, the volunteer who had been with the group longest—over twenty years—said. "Why start with that mission?"

"Because that search—and the failure of anyone to find Valerie—changed the way the group organized and trained," Danny said. "After that, we formally operated under the direction of the sheriff, we required more training, restructured the command system with new roles, and sought accreditation with the Colorado Search and Rescue Association."

Tony sat back. "Okay, that makes sense. Still seems a bummer to start with such a sad case." He looked over at the sofa. "No offense, Vince. I always felt bad we didn't find your sister."

"It's okay," Vince said. "I know everyone tried their best." He didn't remember that much about the actual search for Valerie. His parents had kept him home, perhaps fearful that he might wander off and come to harm. But he had seen the appeals for people to help with the search, and photographs in the paper showing lines of volunteers marching across the area where they had camped.

"This series is going to be great publicity for the group," Danny said. "We want to take advantage of that by stepping up our fundraising."

Groans rose up around the room. "I know, I know," Danny said. "Nobody likes begging for money. But the work we do is expensive—equipment constantly needs replacing and supplies replenishing. Training costs money, and then there are the everyday expenses, like gas for vehicles and utility bills for this building and the occasional meal to keep you people from resigning. We rely on donations for the bulk of our funds."

"I guess when people read this article and think about how great and wonderful we are, we might as well be there with our hands out," Ryan said.

Many in the group laughed. Danny smiled. "The paper has agreed to print a coupon people can use to mail in a donation, as well as information about how they can donate online. We're also going to have our usual booth at the community Fourth of July celebration," he said. He held up the clipboard. "I've got the sign-up sheet here. We've also been asked to participate in something the city is calling First Responders Fun Fair."

"What is that?" Sheri asked.

"The Elks Club is hosting their usual carnival games, but this time they're asking fire, sheriff's, EMS and SAR personnel to man the various games, with all the proceeds from ticket sales split among the four groups. Last year they took in almost five thousand dollars in proceeds, so it's a significant addition to our coffers."

"Sure, we can do that," Eldon Ramsey said.

"I have a sign-up sheet for the carnival as well. Everyone needs to come up and choose your time slots." He set the clipboard aside. "No training tonight, but we do need to pull out and inspect all the climbing gear and reorganize and replenish first aid supplies. Sheri and Tony are in charge of the climbing gear, while Hannah and I will oversee the first aid supplies. We each need people to help, so spread out and let's get to work."

Vince was trying to decide who to work with when Bethany approached. "Hi," she said. "Have you been with search and rescue long?"

"About six months," he said. "So I'm still a rookie too."

"It's a little intimidating being around so many experienced volunteers." She scanned the room. "I don't have any special skills, but Danny said I didn't need them, just a willingness to work and follow direction."

"You'll do fine," Vince said. "Everyone here pitches in to help the newbies learn the ropes."

Her expression sobered. "I was sorry to hear about your sister."

"Um, thanks." She was looking at him with those big, dark eyes, her expression a familiar one—mixed curiosity and pity. He never knew how to respond to that, so he was relieved when Tony approached. "Come help with the climbing gear," he said. He glanced at Bethany. "I know Hannah could use another hand with the medical supplies."

"Sure. Thanks." Bethany touched his arm. "It was nice talking with you, Vince," she said, and hurried away.

Vince and Tony moved to the closet that held the ropes and hardware used in climbing. The steep canyons and high peaks of the terrain around Eagle Mountain meant that many of their rescue operations involved climbing or rappelling, and a significant part of volunteer training focused on the skills needed for these activities. Sheri and Tony began laying out ropes, and she explained how to inspect the colored braided strands for damage and excessive wear.

Vince accepted a coil of rope from Tony. He realized the veteran was the only one here tonight who'd been part of the search when Valerie disappeared. "Did you help look for my sister?" he asked.

"I did." The lines around his blue eyes deepened. Lean and muscular, Tony had the weathered complexion of a man who spent a lot of time outdoors, his neat beard and blond hair beginning to show streaks of gray. "We went out every day for a week."

"What was that like?" Vince asked. "I mean, what about it led to so many changes for the group?"

Tony considered the question for a long moment, then said, "It wasn't that we were disorganized, but we hadn't had any formal training. We knew some basic principles, but the training we get nowadays teaches us about the psychology of searches. People who are lost have patterns of behavior. Most people tend to stick to trails or roads, even animal trails. In the mountains, they tend to move up, to try to get a better view of terrain. They may believe no one is looking for them and they have to walk out of a situation to be found, which may lead them to keep moving, even if they're disoriented and have no idea where they are. Today we use mapping techniques and even mathematical formulas to determine the most likely area a person will be located, and focus the search on these areas first. We didn't have any of that kind of data fifteen years ago—we just tried to search as wide an area as possible, with no precision."

"Does it seem odd to you that no trace of her was ever discovered?" Vince asked. "Not a piece of clothing or a bone or anything?"

"One thing I know now that I didn't know then was that children will sometimes hide from searchers or refuse to answer when people, even family members, call for them," he said. "They're afraid of getting into trouble. We might have walked right by your sister and not known she was there if she didn't respond to our calls. Then too, there's a lot of country up there, much of it rough and pretty inaccessible. Most people who die in the back country are found eventually, but not everyone. I'm sorry."

"We always wondered if she was taken."

"That happens too," Tony said. "But who took her? There was no one else up there."

"Valerie said there was a man camped near us. None of us ever saw him, but we didn't look. And she wasn't one to make things up."

"Then maybe that's what happened. If it is, I'm sorry about that too."

Vince knew the statistics. Children who were taken were almost always killed unless they were kidnapped by a relative, and he was pretty sure that hadn't happened to Valerie. He didn't like to think of his sister ending up that way, any more than he wanted to believe she had fallen into a crevice in the mountains and been killed. He had long believed she had died, but he wanted to know how. Wasn't that human nature—to not like unanswered questions?

IN THE FOUR years Tammy had been reporting for the *Eagle Mountain Examiner*, she had written feel-good pieces about local citizens; straightforward accounts of town council and school board meetings; reports of burglaries, fires and murder. She had even written a first-person report of her own escape from a pair of serial killers who had terrorized the area one winter. While some of these stories had been tougher to write than others, none had affected her as much as her recounting of the disappearance of Valerie Shepherd.

More than one volunteer had teared up as they spoke of the search for the little girl. "She used to come into my store with her mom," said the owner of the local meat market. "Such a grin on her face. She was an impish kind of kid— always up to something. Her twin brother was quieter, following her lead. We couldn't believe she would just vanish the way she did."

"It hit me hard," another volunteer admitted. "I wouldn't let my own kids out of my sight for a long time after that. To think of anything like that happening here, where we always felt safe. It was hard to believe things could change that suddenly—one minute she was there, the next she was gone."

But Tammy knew how suddenly life could change. The day Adam had been killed, the three of them—Adam, Mitch and her—had been playing in the front yard, kicking a soccer ball back and forth, when the ball had rolled into the street. "I'll get it!" Adam called, and ran after it.

He didn't see the car race around the curve. And the driver didn't see Adam until it was too late. One minute he had been there with them, laughing and playing. The next moment he was gone. A hole was torn in their family that could never be repaired. They had done their best to heal, but they all carried the wound inside them.

She had seen the same kind of damage in Vince Shepherd when she had interviewed him. He knew what it was like to walk through life with an empty space in your heart or your soul that could never be filled. Tammy coped by avoiding thinking about Adam and what had happened that day. But talking to Vince and to the volunteer searchers had forced her to feel all those feelings again—grief and anger and confusion. How could something like that happen? How could a person who was practically part of you suddenly not be there?

She had wanted to ask Vince if he was like her—if he coped with the loss by avoiding thinking about it. She had apologized for bringing him and his family any pain, but was an apology enough?

That was why she turned up outside Vince's condo at eight thirty on a Wednesday night, a fresh copy of the latest issue of the *Examiner* in her hand. She rang the bell to his unit and shifted from foot to foot, jittery with nerves. What if he hated what she had written?

Footsteps sounded on the other side of the door, and then Vince stood on the threshold, a wary expression on his handsome face. His hair was damp, curling around his ears. The T-shirt that clung to his chest and abs was damp too, as if he had pulled it on hastily, along with the jeans. His feet were bare. "I didn't mean to disturb you," she blurted, feeling her face heat. "I just wanted to give you this." She thrust the paper at him. "Everyone else will see it in the morning, but I wanted you to read it first."

He unfolded the paper and scanned the headlines, stopping at the story that filled the front page below the fold. "'Search for Missing Girl Shaped EMSAR Future.'"

Tammy bit her lower lip and forced herself to remain still as he read. She had rewritten the lede so many times she had memorized it. *When ten-year-old Valerie Shepherd vanished from the mountains above Galloway Basin on a sunny summer Saturday, she changed the family who loved her forever. But she also changed the community of Eagle Mountain. And her disappearance spurred the transformation of Eagle Mountain Search and Rescue from a group of dedicated amateurs to the highly trained professional-quality organization they are today.*

Vince glanced up from the paper. He didn't look upset, which was a relief. "Come on in," he said, and took a step back.

"Okay. Sure." She moved past him, the scent of his soap—something herbal—distracting her, not to mention the realization that mere inches separated her from his seriously ripped body. How had she not noticed this the other night? He hadn't been wearing a clinging, wet T-shirt, but still, how had she missed those shoulders?

She pushed the thought away and moved into a small living room furnished with a sofa, matching chair, coffee table and a large wall-mounted television. He slipped past her, picked up the remote and switched off the TV. "Have a seat," he said.

She settled on one end of the sofa. He took the other, the newspaper spread out on his lap. "Thanks for bringing this by," he said.

"I figured people might mention the article to you, and you'd want to know what's in it."

He nodded and looked down, reading again. She gripped both knees and pretended to study the room, but she was almost entirely focused on Vince, attuned to any reaction he might have to her words.

He was a fast reader. Or maybe he was skimming. Not many seconds passed before he looked up again. "It's good," he said. "All the stuff about search and rescue is interesting. I didn't realize all the emphasis on training was relatively new."

"Part of that is because there's a lot more training courses available now."

He glanced back down at the paper. "I didn't know so many people still think about Valerie. I always figured my mom and dad and me were the only ones who remembered her."

"I didn't have to remind anyone about what happened," Tammy said. "As soon as I said her name, they remembered. And everyone asked if I knew anything more about what happened to her."

"I guess no one came up with any new information? I mean, the article doesn't mention anything."

"There's nothing new. I'm sorry."

"I guess it would be surprising to think anything else would come to light after all this time."

"Will you share that with your parents?" She tapped the

paper. "I should have brought a copy for them too. I wasn't thinking."

"It's okay. They have a subscription. They're looking forward to the article. Dad said they enjoyed talking to you."

"I enjoyed talking with them." Though, in some ways, it had been uncomfortably like talking with her own mother—the familiar sad and wistful expressions, along with the way they second-guessed every action that day. If they had done this instead of that, maybe they could have prevented what had happened.

"My dad said you were empathetic. I guess that's an important quality for a writer."

She looked away, then forced her gaze back to him. No reason not to tell him. "I had a brother, Adam. He died when he was ten. I was nine. We were playing in the front yard of our house—me and Adam and our brother, Mitch—and our soccer ball rolled into the street. Adam ran after it and was hit by a car."

"Then you know what it's like," he said. "Everything is fine, and the next second, nothing will ever be the same again."

"Yeah." The lump in her throat startled and embarrassed her. After all this time, she didn't cry about Adam. What good would that do? But her eyes stung and her chest tightened. She clenched her fists, digging her nails into her palms. "What happened to Adam was terrible," she said. "But at least we know what happened to him." There was a grave her mother visited, though Tammy never did. The Shepherds didn't even have that.

"That was your brother with you at lunch the other day, right?" Vince asked.

"Yes. Mitch."

"It's nice that he's here in town. I always wondered if it

would have been a little easier if I had had a sibling. Some- one else for my parents to focus on. Someone else who had the same story I did."

"It was comforting having Mitch, especially right after Adam died, when my parents were struggling. He and I made sure to look after each other."

"I would have liked that, but I got used to being on my own. And my folks pulled themselves together after a while."

"They seem like great people."

"What about your parents?" he asked. "Do they live near here?"

"My dad died five years ago. But my mom is here. She and I share a house, actually."

"I don't think I could live with my parents again."

"My mom is a pretty good roommate."

Silence. He was looking down at the newspaper again, and she started to feel awkward. She stood. "I won't keep you. I just wanted to drop that off."

He set aside the paper and rose also. "Thanks."

He followed her to the door. When he had first invited her inside, hope had flickered that maybe they could connect on another level. As friends. Maybe even potential dates. Not that she was eager to rush into anything, but Vince was sin- gle, good-looking and close to her age. She couldn't deny a certain attraction, and while lost siblings maybe wasn't the most solid foundation on which to build a relationship, it did give them something in common.

Now all she wanted to do was get out of his condo. Every- thing felt too awkward and forced. She shouldn't have told him about Adam. It was too personal. Too close to home. She hoped he hadn't thought she was using her tragedy to get close to him. The idea made her queasy. "Good night," she said, and reached for the doorknob.

He put his hand over hers. He had big hands, and calluses on his fingers, the roughness registering against her skin, making her hyperaware of his physical presence. He wasn't an overly large man, but he was muscular and fit—so *male*. She would never write that in an article. The only reason she was even thinking it now was because he had her stirred up and confused. He looked into her eyes, and though she didn't move, she felt knocked off-balance. Such an intense look. Staggering. "Thanks for telling me about Adam," he said.

"I don't talk about him much," she said. "But I thought you'd understand."

"Yeah, I do." His gaze flickered to her lips, and she wondered if he was thinking about kissing her. Entirely inappropriate, and yet she fought to keep from leaning toward him, inviting his touch. *Okaaay.* She needed to get a grip.

"Good night," she said again. "I'll, uh, see you around."

She did turn the doorknob then, and he moved his hand away and stepped back. "Good night."

She managed to walk all the way to her car without breaking into a run or melting into a puddle. In her car, she sat and took deep breaths. What the heck had just happened in there? She had gone to Vince's condo to give him a copy of the newspaper, not to bare her soul or fall madly in lust. If he had felt even half of what she had, he was probably thinking she was the most unprofessional reporter he had ever met. Or worse, did he think she was chasing after him? She closed her eyes and rested her forehead against the steering wheel. Please, no, not that. She was not desperate, and she wanted nothing to do with a man who thought she was.

As for telling him about Adam, that hadn't been a bid for sympathy. She had wanted him to know she sympathized with that special brand of grief they shared. She was just being friendly, but too many times that kind of thing got misinterpreted. It had happened to her before. Once, when an intern at the paper arrived in town after a long day of travel, clearly exhausted and famished, she had invited him to dinner at her place. He had misinterpreted this as an attempt at seduction, which had embarrassed them both and made for an awkward six months as they worked side by side. Vince's father was right—she was an empathetic person. Too empathetic.

She straightened and started the car. Maybe she had embarrassed herself again tonight, but she would get over it. She had survived worse—what was one more injury to her dignity?

Chapter Five

All day Thursday, people stopped Vince to comment on the article in that day's paper. People expressed sympathy over the loss of his sister. Many wanted to hear Vince's take on what had happened that day, or hoped to glean details that hadn't been revealed in the article. "I never knew you had a sister," Sandor said as he and Vince made repairs to a guardrail that afternoon.

"It's not something I talk about." Vince shoved on the guardrail support to bring it into line. "Tighten that bolt there."

Sandor began tightening the bolt. "I wonder what happened to her. I mean, you think after all this time, they would have found something."

"You'd think. Okay, shove rocks up against this post to keep it upright. Then we'll pack the dirt down around it."

"I wonder if it was, like, aliens or something."

Vince stared. "Aliens."

"Yeah. I mean, what if she was abducted by aliens?"

"I don't believe in aliens."

Sandor frowned. "You don't? But there are a lot of stories…"

Vince shook his head. "Finish setting that post. I'm going to check the other side of the bridge."

No one else mentioned aliens, but several felt compelled

to share their theories, most involving kidnapping, or maybe, they said, Valerie had run away. Vince listened to them all, then found somewhere else he needed to be. It wasn't as if he hadn't already thought of all these things over the years— except the aliens. But without proof, he would never know what happened to his sister.

He arrived at his condo a little after five, ready to take a shower, have dinner and a drink, and binge TV. He was walking up to his door when a neighbor called out to him. He braced himself for sympathy or speculation as he waited for Tasha Brueger to reach him. "Hi, Vince," she said. "I just wanted to tell you there was a young woman here about an hour ago. She was asking about you."

"Who was she?"

"She didn't tell me her name. She just stopped me and asked if I knew when you'd be home. She was standing here at your front door. I guess she'd been ringing the bell and not getting an answer. I told her you usually got home a little after five."

He couldn't imagine who would be looking for him. Another reporter, maybe? "What did she look like?"

Tasha—who was a foot shorter than Vince's six feet and had to tilt her head back to look up at him—tugged on one long brown curl and pursed her lips, deep dimples forming on either side of her round cheeks. "She was just sort of average, you know? Dark hair, pulled back in a ponytail. Not too tall, not too short. Not fat or skinny. She wore sunglasses. I had to go pick Sammy up from practice, so we didn't talk long."

"Thanks." He turned back to his door, and Tasha hurried away. Could the woman looking for him have been Tammy Patterson? The description didn't really fit her, and if Tammy wanted to talk to him, why not call or text?

He let himself in and dropped his backpack by the door.

He wasn't sure if Tammy would ever want to see him again. Last night had ended awkwardly between them. That was all on him—he'd been caught so off guard by the intensity of his attraction to her that he had frozen. He considered himself a pro at keeping things casual when it came to women. His default setting for relationships might be summed up as "don't bother getting too close." But Tammy, with her warm smile and earnest expression—as well as the revelation about her brother's death—had cut through his carefully manufactured defenses with breathtaking ease. He didn't have to explain his feelings to her because she had experienced them herself.

Whether it was that understanding or her soft curves and cloud of blond curls, he had been bowled over by the desire to touch her. To kiss her. To discover what it would be like to be close to her. He thought she might be feeling a little of the same, but he couldn't be sure. If he had actually done any of the things his mind insisted on picturing, she might have slugged him. He knew plenty of women, but he couldn't say he knew *about* them. Would things be different if he had a sister to ask?

He shed his clothing as he walked down the hall and hit the shower. He closed his eyes and let the hot water beat down and willed himself not to think about anything for just a few minutes.

Half an hour later, he was in the kitchen, staring into the open refrigerator and trying to decide what to make for dinner, when his phone rang. It was a local number, so he answered. "Hi, Vince. It's Tammy." She sounded out of breath. Anxious.

"Hey. What's up?" Did he sound cool or just not too bright?

"Would it be okay if I came by your place for a few minutes? I have something I need to show you."

"Is everything okay? You sound upset." Or at least, less

than thrilled by the prospect of yet another awkward visit with him.

"I'm just…confused. Anyway, I think you need to see this."

"What is it?"

"I'd rather show you than talk about it."

"Okay. Sure. Come on by."

"I'll be right over."

He ended the call and closed the refrigerator, then leaned back against it, no longer hungry. Tammy had sounded rattled. He hadn't known her long, but she had struck him as a calm person. Someone who didn't panic easily.

He rubbed his jaw, and the scratch of whiskers made him wonder if he should shave. Would she think he was trying too hard?

He didn't have much time to wonder. Five minutes later, his doorbell rang. He opened it to Tammy. She was a little pale and a lot agitated. "Sorry to bother you again," she said as she rushed past him into the condo.

"No problem. Did you stop by earlier, before I got home?"

"What? No. No, I just left the office."

"Okay. What is it you need me to see?"

She looked around the room. "Can we sit down?" Without waiting for an answer, she started for the sofa.

"Do you want a drink or something?" he asked.

"Not now. Maybe after." She sat, then took an envelope from her purse and set the purse on the floor beside her. "Someone put this through the mail slot beside the door of the newspaper office this afternoon," she said, and tapped the envelope. "No one even uses that slot anymore—it's a relic from when the building was occupied by the electric company and people used the slot to leave their payments. But every once in while we get a Letter to the Editor dropped off that way. When I came in about five o'clock and saw the envelope, that's what I thought this was. A complaint or something like that."

He sat beside her, angled toward her, their knees almost touching. "Whatever it is has you upset," he said. "Is it a threat or something?"

She thrust the letter toward him. "Read it," she said.

He took the envelope. It was a blank, white business-sized envelope, unsealed. He opened it and slid out a single sheet of white paper. The message on it was typewritten.

Nice article about the search for Valerie Shepherd. But you got a few things wrong about that day. More than a few things, actually. I don't blame you. You were sold a bunch of lies. I think people lie more than they tell the truth, especially when the lies make them look better. Maybe one day we'll meet and I'll tell you what really happened.

He scanned the brief message. This was what had Tammy so upset? This rambling from a person who couldn't possibly know what had happened? He glanced up from the sheet. "It's just someone babbling about lies," he said.

"Look at the bottom of the page," she said. "At the signature."

He let his gaze travel to the bottom of the sheet of paper, to a cursive scrawl in black ink. The hair on the back of his neck rose as he stared, and he had trouble breathing. No. He was letting his imagination run away from him. It didn't really say what he thought it said.

"It's signed *V*," Tammy said. "*V* for *Valerie*?"

"IT CAN'T BE VALERIE." Vince looked and sounded calmer than Tammy felt. She wasn't one to overreact, but those chilling words about lies—and the single *V* at the bottom—had combined to set her heart racing and her adrenaline flooding. She had been alone in the newspaper office, with no one to offer a different perspective, so she had called the one person she was sure would know the truth. Except, now that she was here, she felt more foolish than frightened.

Vince dropped his gaze to the letter again, his eyes tracking the words across the page. Then he set the sheet of paper aside on the coffee table in front of them. "No one lied that day," he said. "At least, my parents didn't lie, and I didn't."

"Maybe the letter writer means someone else." Tammy wet her dry lips and glanced at the letter as if it was a spider she needed to keep an eye on in case it came any closer. "Maybe there's someone who saw what happened to Valerie and never spoke up."

"Then why not come forward and tell us what happened?" His voice rose on the last words, anger edging out the calm she suspected must have been an act. Of course he was upset. Having someone impersonate his sister must have been a horrible jolt.

"I'm sorry," she said. "I should have realized it was a fake. I didn't mean to upset you."

"It's okay." He blew out a breath. "You didn't expect this, but I should have. Every time any new publicity about Valerie's disappearance comes out, people like that come out of nowhere." He nodded at the letter. "I don't know if they're mentally ill or running a scam, or maybe both. I can't tell you how many times my parents have dealt with this kind of thing."

"How horrible for you all."

"It was. For months after she first went missing, they would get calls from people who promised to find Valerie— for a price. So-called psychics and private detectives. My parents spent a lot of money paying off various people. They wanted so badly to believe it was Valerie that they lost all common sense. I'm betting this is more of the same."

"That makes me sick," she said. "What is wrong with people?"

"You're a reporter and you ask that?"

She let out a shaky laugh. "I guess I don't let people like that take up any more headspace than necessary." She glanced at the letter again. "Should I throw it away?"

"File it. Just in case this person decides to cause trouble." His expression grew troubled again. "I wonder if they were trying to shake me down too."

"What do you mean?"

"When I got home today, my neighbor told me a woman had stopped by looking for me. I thought it might have been you, but you said you hadn't been by. Now I wonder if it was the person who wrote the letter."

"You would know if the person was Valerie?"

"I hope I would. Though after fifteen years, who knows? Anyway, a scammer would claim to know Valerie or to be her 'representative'—a friend, or a lawyer."

"You do know how these things work, don't you?"

"Unfortunately, I do." He stood. "I wouldn't worry about that letter, though. If you ignore these people, they move on and look for an easier victim."

She tucked the letter back into the envelope and returned it to her purse. "Sorry to disturb your evening."

"No. That's okay. I didn't have any plans." He shoved his hands in the pockets of his jeans. "I was getting ready to make dinner. You want to stay and eat with me?"

"Oh, uh…"

"Sorry, you probably have plans."

"No. I'd be happy to stay. I can help too."

"Then come into the kitchen, and let's see what we've got to work with."

Together, they assembled a meal of pasta, chicken and vegetables. As they worked, they talked about everything but Valerie—his love of climbing, her passion for gardening, his experience with search and rescue, and her volunteer position working with high school journalism students.

"Are you seeing anyone?" she asked when the conversation lulled. Maybe the question was a bit forward, but she was dying to know. And she hadn't seen any sign of a romantic interest around his place.

He didn't look up from draining the pasta. "No. Are you?"

"No. I broke up with a guy a few months ago."

He dumped the pasta in a bowl and carried the bowl to the table. "Is that good? Bad?"

"A little sad." She sat in the chair across from him at the table. "We'd been together awhile. But it wasn't working out." They had fallen into a pattern of fighting more than they got along. "Breaking up was the right thing to do."

"But lonely when you're used to having someone around," he said.

Was that the voice of experience speaking or just someone who was very empathetic? "I've managed to avoid long-term relationships," he continued. "I'm not the easiest guy to get along with."

"You haven't thrown up any red flags for me." Her cheeks warmed. She hadn't meant that to sound like she was sizing him up for potential-mate material. "I mean, I haven't noticed any upsetting tendencies—a bad temper or substance abuse, or narcissism."

He laughed. "According to several exes, I don't trust people, I don't confide in people and I don't care enough about people."

"Harsh."

"Yeah, well, who's to say they haven't been right? Not everyone has to be part of a couple."

"You're absolutely right." She raised her wineglass. "To being happy with yourself."

"To being happy with yourself." He smiled, and his gaze met hers, and something lurched inside her, an internal shift that signaled she might be even happier with a certain untrusting, unconfiding but definitely not uncaring man.

Chapter Six

Elisabeth couldn't believe how great it felt to be in the mountains again. Was it possible she had been missing this without even realizing it? Amid all this bare rock and immense sky, anything seemed possible, as if the world truly had no limits. She continued up the trail, climbing higher and higher, thighs burning, lungs straining for breath. Obviously, she needed more time to acclimate to the altitude, but she was in pretty good shape, considering she hadn't spent much time on athletic pursuits.

She stopped and assessed her surroundings. There was a flat-sided dike jutting up from the adjacent rock like a jagged tooth. And there was a big boulder, lichen spattering the surface in green and white and orange. She climbed the rock, scrambling a little for purchase, and stood atop it. She stared at the clump of pinions below, in a kind of trance for a long moment.

She snapped out of it and turned to face the dike. She pulled out her phone and took a few pictures to document the scene; then she headed back down the trail. She met only a few people on the way down—a couple and a larger group of friends. No little kids. Did families not come backpacking up here anymore?

Back in town, she grabbed a decent veggie wrap from

the coffee shop at the Gold Nugget Hotel, then walked down the street to a real estate office she had spotted earlier. She stopped on the sidewalk outside Brown Realty to study the flyers tacked to the window, all for overpriced vacation homes, luxury condos and one huge ranch that was listed for over a billion dollars. Did people really pay those kinds of prices to live here? If that was the case, she might stick around a little longer and meet some of those wealthy people.

A chime announced her arrival as she pushed open the door. A man who was the sole occupant of the place looked up from behind the desk and smiled. "Hi," he said. "Can I help you?"

He was maybe a little older than her, his long dark hair pulled back in a ponytail. He wore a tailored white shirt, sleeves rolled up to reveal strong forearms, and dark jeans that definitely hadn't come from the nearest discount store. Paul would approve of this man's style. "I'm looking for a place to rent in town," she said. "Just for a couple of months. A house or condo. Something nice."

"We have several beautiful vacation properties available for short-term rentals." The man stood and extended his hand. "I'm Mitch."

"I'm Elisabeth." His fingers were cool against hers, his grip firm but not crushing. And he looked her in the eye with a direct gaze. A sizzle of attraction raced through her. No ring on his finger.

"Have a seat, Elisabeth, and I'll show you what we have available." He sat also, and swiveled the computer monitor so they both could see it. "Do you have a particular location in mind?"

"There's a condo complex by the river. Riverside. Do you have anything there?"

"We do have a few units available in that property," Mitch said. "Though they require a six-month lease."

"If they're vacant, maybe we can negotiate something shorter."

"I can't promise anything, but why don't we take a look?"

He bent over the keyboard, typing with two fingers, but rapidly. She studied him, feeling the sizzle of awareness again. Maybe there were advantages to sticking around town that she hadn't yet considered.

"Here are some interior shots of one of the units," he said. "It's a top floor, corner unit, so a little more privacy. As you can see, it has updated appliances and a modern, airy interior. You'd be close to the river and the hiking and biking trails, and just a few minutes from town. Another few minutes to the highway and access to both Junction, an hour to the north, and the miles of trails in the backcountry. Hiking and jeeping in the summer, rock and ice climbing, winter skiing. Fly-fishing, photography, camping—we offer everything in the way of outdoor adventure."

He spoke with a natural enthusiasm that helped negate the salesman's spiel. "I like the condo," she said. "Could we drive over there and take a look?"

"Of course. Do you want to see any others before we go?"

"No. That's the one I want."

"What about the six-month lease?" he asked.

"I'm sure we can work something out." She could always agree to the lease, then leave whenever she wanted without paying the rest of the rent. She knew how to disappear so that they would never find her to sue for the rest of the money.

"Let me forward the phones and lock up here, and I'll be set," he said.

She waited by the entrance while he took care of these tasks, then followed him out the door. After he had locked up, she moved closer and slipped her arm through his. "After we see the condo, maybe you can show me around town," she said. "Then I'd love to buy you a drink."

Extra heat sparked in his smile, and he covered her hand with his own and squeezed it. "That sounds like a great idea, Elisabeth."

"I'm full of great ideas." So many, and so few people to truly appreciate her greatness. But she had learned to never sell herself short. Other people had failed her, but that was no reason to ever fail herself.

SUMMER SATURDAYS WERE busy days on the backroads and trails around Eagle Mountain, which meant they were also busy for search and rescue volunteers. The first call that day came in just before 11:00 a.m. A young man had fallen from the rocks above Rocky Falls. "The family member who called in the accident says the young man—fifteen—is responsive but in pain," Danny told the volunteers who assembled at search and rescue headquarters. "He thinks the boy—his nephew—might have broken bones."

"How did he happen to fall, do we know?" volunteer Chris Mercer asked. An artist who wore blue streaks in her dark hair, Chris had several years' experience with SAR but wasn't an elite climber or a medical professional. She was simply dedicated and hardworking, willing to do the mundane driving, fetching, carrying and following orders that made up the bulk of a volunteer's efforts.

Danny grimaced. "He climbed up onto the rocks to pose for a picture and slipped."

"The rocks behind the sign that says 'Danger: Do Not Climb on Rocks'?" Harper Stevens asked.

"Yep." Danny raised his voice to address them all. "Let's hustle, everyone."

As they were loading their gear, Bethany slipped in next to Vince. "Hi." She flashed a smile, her eyes not meeting his. "This is the first call I've been on. I'm a little nervous."

"That's natural," Vince said. "Just do what you're told and pitch in whenever you can." He handed her a plastic bin full of climbing helmets. "Find a place to stow these in the Beast there." He pointed to the specially outfitted Jeep used for rescue operations. "I'm going to get more supplies."

"I think you have an admirer," Ryan said when Vince returned to the supply closet for another load. "I saw the new girl, Bethany, making eyes at you."

"'Making eyes'? Seriously, what does that even mean?" Vince slung a coil of rope over one shoulder.

"Bet she'd go out with you if you asked her," Ryan said. "Just saying."

He glanced back and saw Bethany standing where he had left her, still watching him. He quickly turned around. "Not interested," he said. Bethany was cute and probably really sweet, but there was no spark there. Not like when he looked at Tammy. "Come on," he said. "Let's get this stuff loaded so we can head out."

The young man who had fallen got off lucky, with a broken leg and some cracked ribs. The search and rescue team climbed the trail to the top of the falls and identified a point from which Hannah and Ryan Welch could be lowered on ropes to the teen, Lance. At first, he denied climbing on the rocks, though eventually he admitted to ignoring the signs and boosting himself up on the boulder for a selfie with the waterfall in the background. "Am I going to be, like, disabled or something?" he asked, his expression stricken.

"You should heal just fine," Hannah said as she fitted his leg with a splint. Once the leg was stabilized, she and

Ryan fitted him with neck and back braces and a helmet, then helped him into a litter and wrapped him up warmly.

Meanwhile, up on the trail, Vince worked with Eldon, Tony and Sheri to rig a rope-and-pulley system for getting their patient back onto the trail. Once they had lifted him safely out of the canyon, another group of volunteers took over to transport him to the waiting ambulance. The family—his mom, dad, uncle and sister—followed the litter team down.

As the remaining volunteers disassembled the rigging and packed up to return to headquarters, Vince paused to look over at the sign that cautioned people against climbing on the rocks. "I feel like someone should write in 'We really mean it' underneath there," he said.

"It wouldn't work," Eldon said. He stuffed a brake bar into a carrying bag. "Kids that age think they're invincible. I did."

Unlike many of his peers, Vince had never known that feeling of invulnerability. What happened to Valerie had made him too aware of all the ways things could go wrong.

The group returned to SAR headquarters and were unloading gear when a second call came in. "Hikers with a medical emergency," Danny relayed after speaking with the emergency dispatcher. "Mount Wilson trail. A man with chest pains and a woman who's collapsed."

The words were like a shot of adrenaline through the group. They hurried to reload the search and rescue Jeep, as well as several personal vehicles, with equipment and personnel for an urgent ride to the Mount Wilson trailhead. "They're within a mile of the top," Danny directed as they unloaded the vehicles and distributed gear for the trek up the slope. "A thirty-eight-year-old woman and a forty-six-year-old man. No history of heart trouble, but he's reporting chest pain and dizziness and disorientation."

"What about the woman?" Hannah asked.

"The report on her is that she's unable to continue hiking."

"I don't like the sound of either of those," Hannah said.

A solemn team started up the mountain. Tony and Sheri elected to jog ahead with an AED and first aid supplies. Caleb Garrison was next with a canister of oxygen, while the others followed as quickly as they could, spread out along the steep trail to one of the most popular peaks in the region. Other hikers on their way down squeezed over to the side to let them pass when they recognized the blue windbreakers with *Search and Rescue* emblazoned on the front and back. "Good luck!" some called after them.

It took two hours of hard hiking to reach the couple, who were stretched out to one side of the trail, a few concerned onlookers gathered around. Sheri, Tony, Caleb and Hannah were arranged around them, the man receiving oxygen while Sheri spoke with the woman. Vince slipped off his pack, which contained another canister of oxygen and various first aid supplies, and fished out his water bottle.

"What's the story?" he asked Harper, who had arrived ahead of him.

"Hannah doesn't think he's having a heart attack, but he'll need to be checked out at the hospital to be sure," Harper said. "Mostly I think they weren't well prepared for a hike like this and they overdid it. They don't have hats or sunscreen or enough water. They're sunburned and dehydrated and dealing with the altitude and exhaustion."

The couple did look miserable. They were sipping water and listening as Sheri and Danny addressed them each in turn. They were probably hearing about how most of their problems could have been prevented with simple precautions like sunscreen, water and an easier pace. But that didn't help them now. For that, they would get a free ride down the mountain in litters carried by Vince and his fellow volunteers, and a checkup at the hospital to ensure they truly were all right.

The trip down the trail was equally as solemn as the hike up, but without the urgency. Even a small adult was a heavy, awkward burden to carry. After consultation, Danny declared that the woman would walk down—with Bethany and Harper on either side to steady her, if need be—and her husband would be transported on the litter. His chest pains had subsided, but no one wanted to chance their return. The litter was fitted with a large wheel to support part of the weight and help it roll along the ground, but it still required a volunteer at each corner to help steady and balance it. The position was awkward and uncomfortable, and volunteers switched off every half mile.

Meanwhile, the woman moaned and complained the whole way down. Vince decided that as much as maneuvering the litter made his back and knees ache, he preferred that duty.

The sun was sinking behind the mountains by the time they made it to the trailhead. The couple headed off in an ambulance, and the volunteers reloaded their gear. Some of the group announced they were going out for beer and pizza.

"Are you going out?" Bethany asked as Vince was shouldering his pack to head to his car.

"Not tonight," he said. All he wanted was a hot shower and to stretch out on the sofa, where he would likely fall asleep. "But you should go, if you want. It'll be a great way to get to know people."

She looked over toward the group—Ryan and Eldon, Caleb, and a few others. "I don't know."

"Suit yourself." He shrugged on the pack and headed out. He drove to his condo, parked, and collected his mail before he walked to his door and unlocked it. Inside, he shed his shoes, pack and SAR windbreaker, then stood sorting through the mail. Mostly junk, but a colorful postcard caught his eye. A larger-than-life cartoon Viking stood beside an impossibly buxom and equally cartoonish female Viking. *Welcome to Williams's Valhalla-Land!* proclaimed large green letters above them.

Vince stared, heart pounding. He and Valerie and their parents had stopped at this roadside attraction, somewhere in Minnesota or Michigan, on a road trip to visit his dad's brother and his family on the Upper Peninsula the summer before Valerie disappeared. Somewhere, pasted into an album tucked into his parents' bookshelf, was a photograph his mother had snapped of him and Valerie, posing with these same cartoon Vikings.

He flipped the card over and read the message, in loopy cursive handwriting: *Hello, Vince the Viking. I bet you're surprised to hear from me. V.*

Chapter Seven

"Slow down, Mitch. I can hardly understand you, you're talking so fast." Tammy juggled her phone and the salad she had been carrying to her kitchen table when her brother called Saturday evening.

"I met this great girl—*woman*. Her name is Elisabeth. She came into my office looking for a rental, and we hit it off. We had drinks afterwards, and we're going to have dinner tomorrow night."

Tammy sat at the table. Her brother wasn't normally this effusive. In fact, he rarely talked about the women he dated. "Wow, she must be special," she said.

"I think so." She could hear the smile in his voice. "I hope you'll meet her soon."

"You said she was looking for a rental. Is she new in town?"

"She's here for several months, but I'm hoping to talk her into staying longer."

"Where is she from?"

"Somewhere in the Midwest, I think. We didn't talk about that."

"What *did* you talk about?"

He laughed. "She asked a lot about me, and about Eagle Mountain. But she told me a few things about herself. She said her father just died and left her some money, so she's taking the opportunity to see more of the country. And she likes to hike—we talked about checking out a few of the local trails while she's here."

"It sounds like the two of you really clicked."

"We did. I've never met anyone who is so easy to talk to. I tried to talk her into having dinner with me tonight too, but she said she had things she needed to do. I thought at first maybe I had come on too strong, but then she said she'd love to go out with me tomorrow night, so that was a relief."

"I'll look forward to meeting her." She took a bite of salad and chewed, angling away from the phone as Mitch told her more about the wonderful Elisabeth.

Her phone beeped, and she checked the screen. "I have to go, Mitch," she said. "I have another call coming in, and I need to take it."

"A breaking news story for the paper?" he asked.

"Someone connected with an article that I need to talk to." Not a complete lie.

"All right, then. I'll talk to you later."

"Have fun tomorrow night." She ended the call and answered the incoming one. "Hey, Vince," she said.

"Do you still have that note that was supposedly from Valerie?" he asked.

"I think so. Why?"

"Because I got a postcard today." His voice broke, and the silence that followed made her think he was struggling to pull himself together.

"Vince, are you all right?" she asked.

"The postcard—it had something on it only Valerie, or someone who knew us, would know about," he said.

She sat up straighter. "Do you think Valerie sent my note and your postcard?"

"I don't know what to think. I mean, if she is alive, why not just pick up the phone and call? Or come to see me in person?"

"Have your parents heard anything? It seems like she would want to contact them too."

"If they have, they haven't told me about it. And I'm too afraid to call and upset them. What if this is just another scam?"

"Maybe you should contact the sheriff's office," she said.

"Maybe. Before I do that, could you come over, and bring the note you received? Or I could come there. I thought we could compare the signature and decide if it's the same person."

"The note is at the newspaper office," she said. "Why don't you meet me there?"

"Great. I'll see you in a few minutes."

She ended the call, then sat for a moment, her salad untouched. The reporter side of her was intrigued by the turn this story was taking. But she hadn't missed the pain in Vince's voice. She wanted to protect her friend while still getting to the bottom of what could be major news.

VINCE WAITED ON the sidewalk outside the newspaper office. A few people passed on their way to the pizza place at the end of the block, but otherwise this part of town was quiet. The sun had set, but it wasn't yet full dark. The silhouettes of the mountains above town stood out against the gray sky. The tops of those peaks were miles away, yet they looked almost close enough to touch.

He slipped off his backpack and felt in the side pocket, where he had tucked the postcard. His sister couldn't have sent it, could she? Why now, after so many years? And why be so vague?

A blue Subaru zipped around the corner and pulled to the curb in front of Vince. Tammy got out. She looked harried, her cheeks flushed, her blouse half-untucked and her hair a little mussed. "I hope you haven't been waiting long," she said.

"Not long." He waited behind her while she unlocked the door, then tapped a code into the alarm keypad beside it.

"Come on back here to my desk." She moved through the office, flipping light switches as she went, until she reached a large desk crowded with a desktop computer and stacks of notebooks and loose sheets of paper. "The letter is in the file here," she said, and pulled open a bottom desk drawer. She rummaged among the contents of the drawer, then stood, waving a piece of paper. "I never throw anything away," she said. "As you can tell by the state of my desk."

She sank into the desk chair, and Vince sat in a straight-backed wooden chair across from her. She set the letter on the desk between them and smoothed out the folds. "Could I see the postcard you received?" she asked.

He opened the backpack and handed the card to her. She smiled as she studied the cartoon on the front, then turned it over to read the message on the back. "'Vince the Viking'?" she asked.

He grimaced. "The summer before Valerie disappeared—when we were both nine—we took a family trip to the Upper Peninsula to visit my dad's brother, Ricky. On the way, we stopped at every tourist attraction my dad could find—windmills and arrowhead collections and little museums." He nodded to the postcard. "And Valhalla-Land."

Tammy's smile vanished and her eyebrows drew together. "It would be a wild coincidence for someone who didn't know about that trip to send this to you out of the blue."

"I think so," he said. "And it's not just Valhalla-Land.

After the trip, Valerie and I called each other 'Vince the Viking' and 'Valerie the Viking' for weeks afterwards. No one else would know that. I mean, my mom and dad would, if they even remember. And maybe Uncle Ricky. But they wouldn't pretend to be Valerie."

Tammy turned the postcard over. "This is postmarked in Junction, but it could have been mailed here in town. All our mail is routed through the Junction office. But that's a long way from Valhalla-Land."

"Whoever sent it must have brought it with them," he said.

"Could you order something like this online?" Tammy asked.

"Even if you could, you would have to know its significance to me and Valerie." He sat back, legs stretched out in front of him. "I'd forgotten all about that little pit stop on a long-ago vacation until I saw that card."

She laid the card beside the letter on the desk and leaned over to study it more closely. "It's signed the same way as my note—just the single V," she said.

"I thought so too. But if it's Valerie, why not sign her whole name?"

"Do you think your parents still have a sample of her handwriting?"

"Probably. But she was ten. A person's handwriting changes as they get older, doesn't it?"

"I don't know." She sat back. "Do you think you should contact your parents? I'm sure if we go to the sheriff's department with these notes, they'll want to talk to your parents as well."

Vince blew out a breath. "I don't want to upset them, but better me than a call from a sheriff's deputy." He took out his phone.

His mother answered on the second ring. "Hello, Vince," she said, cheerful. Glad to hear from him.

"Hi, Mom. I'm not interrupting anything, am I?"

"No, I'm just sitting here trying to read this book that isn't all that interesting. It's for my book club, and it's supposed to be a big bestseller, but I must not be the intended audience."

"Is Dad there?"

"No, he had a meeting. Do you want me to ask him to call you tomorrow, or can I help you with something?"

He took a deep breath. He saw no way to ease into the subject. "Have you gotten any letters from someone claiming to be Valerie?" he asked.

"You mean recently?"

"Yes."

"No, dear. Years ago we received a couple of letters that were vague and rambling. We showed them to someone from the Center for Missing and Exploited Children. They told us they were almost certainly a scam. Other parents had received similar letters."

"I didn't know," he said.

"You were still young. We didn't see any reason to involve you. Why are you asking about this now?"

He glanced across the desk at Tammy. She was watching him intently. "I got a postcard from someone who sounded like they could be Valerie," he said. "It was just signed with the letter V."

"Oh my. I'm sure it's because of the article in the paper. It was a good article, of course, but this kind of attention seems to bring out the worst in people. What did the postcard say?"

He picked up the card. "Do you remember that summer we went to Uncle Ricky's place?"

"The summer you were nine. That was a fun trip."

"We stopped at a place called Valhalla-Land. With a bunch of Viking stuff."

"Oh my, yes. So kitschy. But you kids loved it."

"Valerie and I called each other Vikings for weeks after that."

His mom laughed. "I'd forgotten about that, but you did. Vince the Viking and Valerie the Viking. But what made you remember that?"

"This postcard has a picture of Valhalla-Land. And on the back, it says 'Hello to Vince the Viking.'"

His mother drew in her breath sharply but said nothing.

"Mom! Are you okay?"

"I'm... I'm fine. Just a little surprised. It's such an odd thing to write. And how would anyone know about that?"

"I don't know. The reporter who wrote the story for the paper, Tammy Patterson, received a note too. Hers was more generic. All about how she got things wrong in her story and 'You were sold a bunch of lies.' She and I think we should show these to the sheriff, just in case someone is trying to scam us. But I wanted to talk to you first."

"Yes, you should show them to the sheriff," she said. "Not that it will do any good. No one ever caught any of the other people who tried to swindle us. There are some evil people in this world who will take advantage of a family's grief."

"Tomorrow we'll talk to Sheriff Walker or one of his deputies," Vince said. "I'll let you know what they say."

"I'll tell your father when he gets in. It's odd. And upsetting. What if this really is Valerie, reaching out to us after all these years?"

"Why send teasing notes?" he asked. "Why not just show up and say, 'Here I am'?"

"I don't know. Maybe it's a kind of game. Valerie did always like games and teasing. The day she disappeared, we thought she was hiding from us, playing a joke."

"If she's alive, she's twenty-five," Vince said. "Too old for silly games."

"I don't know what to think," his mom said.

"I'll let you know what the sheriff says."

They said good-night, and he ended the call. He felt worse than ever.

"Do you want me to go with you to the sheriff's department tomorrow?" Tammy asked.

"They'll want to talk to you too." He looked around the room, at the silent computers and framed front pages of past issues of the *Eagle Mountain Examiner*. "Are you going to write about this for the paper?"

He couldn't read her expression. Was that hurt in her eyes? "Not unless something comes of it that's newsworthy," she said.

"What would that be?"

"I don't know. If they catch someone trying to scam you."

"Or if Valerie actually is alive and well."

"People do show up sometimes," Tammy said. "There was a case last year where a woman had been living in Europe with her kidnapper for years. I'm not trying to get your hopes up," she hastened to add. "I'm just saying that's one possibility."

"Yeah. I guess we'll find out." He stood. "Thanks for meeting with me. I'll let you know in the morning when I can go with you to the sheriff. I need to check my work schedule."

He left the building. She followed, locking up behind them. "Do you want to go for a drink?" she asked. "Or coffee?"

"No. I need to go home."

"All right. I'll see you tomorrow." She hesitated, then patted his arm. "I'm sorry my article pulled this person—whoever they are—out of the woodwork. Especially if it's someone who wants to hurt you."

"It's not your fault. And maybe it *is* Valerie." He didn't believe that, but it was something positive to cling to, at least for a little while. Over the years, he had thought about what it might be like to see his sister again, but after so long it was hard to picture her as anything but the rambunctious ten-year-old she had been. A grown Valerie would be a stranger to him. She would still be his sister—his twin. But they would have lost so much of their shared history. Would she even be someone he liked? Worse—would she like him, or what he had become in her absence?

Ten years ago

"I LEFT DINNER for you in the refrigerator. Leave the plate covered and heat it in the microwave for three minutes." Mom fussed about the kitchen, wiping down the counter and putting stray glasses and silverware in the dishwasher as she talked. "If you need anything, call the Wilsons next door for help. Don't open the door to strangers. And don't stay up too late watching TV. You know you have school tomorrow."

"Mom, I know how to look after myself. I'm not some little kid," Vince protested. At fifteen, he towered over his five-foot, two-inch mom, and was the same height as his dad. Any day now, he'd probably start shaving.

"I know, dear." His mom stilled, looking as if she wasn't happy about this news. "I just want you to be careful. I couldn't cope if anything happened to you."

Inwardly, Vince cringed, though he tried not to show how much he resented statements like this. He got it—his parents had lost one child and were terrified of losing another. They were hyperprotective of him, so much so that even leaving him alone for a few hours while they enjoyed a rare evening out with friends was a big deal. But none of his friends had as many rules and curfews as he did. It wasn't fair. But the one time he had tried to point this out, his mother had gotten all teary and said it wasn't fair that Valerie disappeared and they never knew what happened to her. After that, he gave up trying to reason with his parents and settled for breaking their rules whenever he could. Tonight, for instance, his friend Jackson Greenway was coming over. Their plan was to smoke a joint and watch a porn video Jackson had stolen from his older brother Parker, who was nineteen and had his own condo. They were going to order pizza and maybe call these sisters Jackson had met. His parents would be horrified if they knew any of this, which was kind of the point.

He hugged his mom. "Don't worry," he said. "I'll be safe here. You and Dad have a good time."

She gave him a wobbly smile and patted his back. "You're a fine son," she said. "Your father and I are so proud of you. You know that, don't you?"

He had done a lot to make his parents proud. He made good grades and was a top player on a regional youth lacrosse team. When he did break the rules, he made sure not to get caught, and he had never gotten into serious trouble. It didn't make up for Valerie being gone, but it was something.

He waved from the front door as they pulled out of the driveway, then slipped out his phone and called Jackson to tell him the coast was clear.

Twenty minutes later, Jackson's mother's Camry eased down the street, the throbbing bass from the stereo rattling the windows. Six months older than Vince, Jackson had his driver's license, and his parents let him borrow his mother's car whenever he wanted, as long as he topped off the gas tank.

Jackson—taller even than Vince, with long, thin arms and legs and blond hair past his shoulders—parked at the curb, then exited the car with the pizza box in one hand and a DVD and a bag of weed in the other. "Are we ready to party?" he asked.

"Ready." Vince held the door open wide. "We have the place to ourselves for at least four hours."

"Sweet!" Jackson breezed in and set the pizza on the bar that separated the kitchen from the living room. "And look what I got to go with our pizza." He fished in the pockets of his baggy cargo shorts and pulled out two cans of beer. "I snagged them from the garage refrigerator on my way out. My dad will never miss them."

"Let me grab some plates for the pizza," Vince said. "I'm starving."

They had popped the tops on the beer and were digging into their first slices of pizza when the Shepherd's house phone rang.

"Don't answer it," Jackson said. "It's probably just some phone solicitor or a politician asking for your vote."

"I have to answer it," Vince said. "It might be my mom, with some last-minute instruction about dinner or something." He moved to the phone on the kitchen wall and picked up the receiver. "Hello?"

"Hello? Vince, is that you?"

A cold shiver raced up his spine. "Hello?" he said. "Who is this?" His mind played tricks on him sometimes. He would be in a crowded hallway at school and would think he'd heard Valerie's voice, only to turn around and discover it was someone else. Once, after a lacrosse game, he had followed a teenage girl all the way to the parking lot because something about how she looked from the back was so familiar. Then she had turned around and spotted him, and he had to pretend he was merely retrieving something from his car.

"It's Valerie. Don't you remember me?" The person on the

other end of the line began to sob. "I need you to help me, Vince."

"Where are you?" he asked. Then: "Who are you, really?"

The line went dead. Vince stared at the receiver in his hand.

"Dude, your face went all white," Jackson said. "You're not going to faint, are you?"

"How do you call back the last number you talked to?" he asked.

"Star-six-nine." Jackson's chair scraped loudly against the floor as he shoved it back and stood. "What's going on? Who was that on the phone?"

"I don't know." He punched in *69 and waited while the phone rang. And rang. And rang. After ten rings, he hung up.

Jackson was standing beside him now. "You don't look so hot," he said. "Who was that calling?"

"She said she was Valerie."

Jackson's eyes widened. "Your dead sister?"

"We don't know for sure she's dead, but yeah. She knew my name, and she said she was Valerie."

"Did it sound like her? What you remember?"

"It did." But was that because it was her, or because he wanted it to be her? "I think you'd better go," he said. "I need to call my parents."

He thought Jackson would argue, but instead, he patted Vince's back. "I can stay here if you want. You can tell your folks you called me for moral support. We'll hide the beer and stuff before they get home."

"Thanks, but I'll be okay by myself."

Jackson gathered up the beer and pizza, the pot and the DVD, and said goodbye. When he was gone, Vince braced himself and called his dad's cell phone. "I had a call just now," he said. "From someone claiming to be Valerie. She said she needed help, and she started crying. It sounded real." A sob broke free on the last word. He couldn't help it.

"We'll be right there," his dad said.

His parents came home right away. Vince had pulled himself together by the time they arrived, but he could tell his mom had been crying. Her eyes were red and puffy, and when she hugged him, she held on too tightly, for a little too long.

He told them about the call, and they contacted the local police and the FBI agent who had worked with them when Valerie first went missing. The cops arrived, then two FBI agents. They matched the number from the call to a pay phone in Nebraska, then said the pay phone had been vandalized, probably before that call was made, though they couldn't be sure.

They never heard from the caller again, and everyone agreed it had likely been a scam. But for months afterward, Vince replayed the call in his head. Valerie's voice, begging him to help her.

Chapter Eight

"We can take this into evidence, but without more context, there's not a lot we can do." Sheriff Walker faced Tammy and Vince across his neat desk Sunday morning, the letter and postcard side by side on the almost-empty expanse of oak. "Unfortunately, it's not unusual for twisted people to prey on the families of crime victims this way."

"We don't know that Valerie's disappearance was a crime." Vince flushed when Travis turned to look at him.

"That's true," Travis said. "But it's a crime to pretend to be someone else for the purpose of extorting money or other compensation."

"The letter writer hasn't asked for anything," Tammy said.

"Not yet." Travis considered the letters once more. "If you receive any other correspondence like this, handle it as little as possible. We might be able to recover prints or DNA."

They promised to keep the sheriff informed of any developments and left his office. Outside, on the sidewalk, Vince pulled out his keys. "I have to go," he said. "I promised my parents I'd have lunch with them."

"Before you go, there's something I need to say." Tammy had been rehearsing this little speech all morning, and she needed to get it out before she lost nerve.

He stopped and turned to face her, expression wary.

"You asked me last night if I'm going to write about this," she said.

"Have you changed your mind?"

"No." She shook her head. "Not unless you want me to. If you think it will help us find who did this, I will."

"No. The last thing I want right now is more publicity. It draws out the scammers."

"I'm your friend, Vince," she said. "First. Reporter, second. I want to make sure you understand that. I want you to feel free to talk to me without fear of what you say ending up in the paper." Having him believe anything other than that hurt more than she wanted to admit.

"Thanks," he said. "I appreciate it."

"Good. I wanted to make sure you knew that."

Embarrassed now, she turned and led the way down the sidewalk toward the lot where they had parked their vehicles. They hadn't gone far before she spotted a familiar figure. "Hey, Mitch." She waved.

Her brother stopped and waited for her to catch up. She turned back to Vince. "Vince, this is my brother, Mitch. Mitch, this is Vince Shepherd."

The two men shook hands. "How's it going?" Vince asked.

"I'm headed over to Riverside Condos." Mitch glanced at Tammy. "Elisabeth signed a lease on an empty unit there, and I want to make sure there's no problem with the paperwork."

"Vince lives at Riverside," Tammy said.

Mitch grinned. "Then you'll see me around. At least, I hope you will."

"Mitch is so gone on his new client," Tammy said.

"Elisabeth is a special person," Mitch said. He checked his watch. "Gotta run. Nice to meet you, Vince."

Mitch loped away. They were at their cars now; Tammy

turned to Vince. "Let me know if anything else happens," she said. "Because I'm your friend. Not because I'm a reporter."

He took a step back, hands in his pockets. "Thanks. Um, maybe we could have dinner later."

She fought back a grin. "I'd like that."

"Just…as friends," he added.

"Sure." It wasn't all she wanted, but it would do. For now.

As a rookie with just a few months of search and rescue experience under his belt, Vince saw every call as a new challenge. Though veterans might approach another auto accident or fallen hiker as the type of incident they had competently dealt with dozens of times before, Vince's mind raced with a review of everything he had learned about the protocol for this type of emergency, and the awareness that one misstep could potentially jeopardize someone's life.

No one was looking at their mission Tuesday evening as routine, however. Rescuers lined the road above Carson Canyon and followed the beam of a handheld spotlight until it came to rest on a pickup truck snagged in an almost-vertical position on the sharply sloping canyon wall. The truck's front end was smashed, the windshield shattered, the back bumper and half the rear-cargo area extending out into the darkness beyond—a canyon that was easily a hundred yards deep. "It looks like the front axle is snagged over that boulder." Danny lowered the binoculars he had been using to survey the scene and handed them to Tony. "See what you think."

"I don't see anything to secure chains to," Ryan said. "How are we going to stabilize the wreck enough to make it safe for us to go down there?"

"Shine that light into the cab," Tony said.

Grace, who was holding the light, shifted the beam to illuminate the cab.

"Looks like at least two people in the vehicle," Tony said. "Still secured by seat belts. They're not moving, so they're either dead or unconscious."

"We need to get a wrecker out here," Caleb said. "They could hook onto the frame with chains and it wouldn't go anywhere."

"One of us will have to climb down and hook it up," Eldon said. "We've done it before."

"We've done it before," Ryan said, "but not to a vehicle in that kind of precarious position."

"And not in the dark."

"Let's get some lights out here," Danny said. He took out his phone. "I'm going to call for a wrecker. But I want you to start rigging for the rescue. Approach it as if we don't have a wrecker available. You need to secure the vehicle, get the rescuers down safely, and lift out the driver and passenger."

"See if a helicopter is available," Sheri said. "It might be easier to lift the victims out by air than to try to drag them up this steep slope."

Danny acknowledged this and spoke into his phone. Ryan turned to Vince. "Come help us with the rigging."

"Could I help?" Bethany spoke up.

"Have you done any climbing training yet?" Ryan asked. "Not yet."

"Then it's probably better that you help with setting up the portable work lights. Everything will make more sense to you after you've got a little more training under your belt."

"Oh, uh, sure." She gave a wobbly smile and hurried away.

Ryan smirked. "Don't say anything," Vince warned. He wasn't in the mood for teasing—no matter how good natured—over the new girl's infatuation with him.

Ryan held up his hands. "I didn't say a thing."

Ryan, Vince and several others set to work constructing

the intricate series of ropes, chains, anchors, pulleys, knots, brake bars, carabiners and other hardware to construct a spiderweb of lines that would enable volunteers to travel safely up and down the steep slope.

Two trucks from the highway department pulled up with a bank of work lights that did a better job of illuminating the accident scene. Close on their heels, Bud O'Brien arrived with his largest wrecker, which featured a long boom that could extend over the canyon. A portly man in his late fifties with a wad of chewing tobacco puffing out one cheek, Bud peered over the edge at the smashed truck. "I can get it out of there," he said. "But one of you will have to hook it up."

Danny delegated Ryan and Eldon to make the initial climb down. Once the vehicle was secure, Tony and Sheri would follow, with Caleb and Vince on standby if they needed more assistance. "We'll need to package the victims for transport on the helicopter flying in from Delta. The chopper will set them down in the road, and we'll transfer to an ambulance."

"Any response from the truck?" Vince asked.

"Nothing," Danny said. "I tried hailing them and got no reply. I thought I saw movement earlier, but it's difficult from this distance to be sure." He looked past Vince. "I think Bud has the wrecker in place now." He raised his voice. "All right, everybody. Let's do this!"

Vince positioned himself across from Caleb to monitor the rigging as first Ryan, then Eldon descended. He found himself holding his breath as Ryan neared the vehicle. One false move might send the truck plummeting the rest of the way into the canyon. From here, he couldn't see the people inside. Maybe it was a good thing they were unconscious, since that made it less likely they would move about and possibly dislodge the vehicle.

With Ryan in place just above and behind the truck, Eldon

started his descent. Vince watched carefully, trying to absorb everything. Maybe one day he would be the one setting the rigging or even making the descent. He had a little experience climbing, though nowhere near the training Sherri, Ryan and some of the others had completed in high-angle rescue.

When Eldon had almost reached Ryan, Danny signaled to Bud, who began lowering the heavy cable and hook from the boom, which was extended out over the canyon. Eldon snagged the hook, then prepared to crawl beneath the truck.

Bud radioed down. "Be sure to attach that to the frame, not the axle."

"Understood," Eldon said. "That truck better not slip and take me with it."

"We've got you," Caleb called over the radio. Eldon and Ryan were both attached to safety lines tethered to anchors at the top of the cliff.

A cheer rose up when Eldon emerged from beneath the truck, thumbs up. Then he and Ryan approached the truck's cab, one on either side. They had to hold on to the vehicle in order to balance on the narrow ledge. Ryan cleared away broken glass and leaned into the driver's side of the vehicle. A moment later he leaned out again. "A driver and one passenger. The driver is unconscious, lacerations on his head and face. The passenger is female. No pulse. We're going to need the Jaws down here to get them out."

The mood among the volunteers sobered at the news that the passenger was dead, but they set to work securing the hydraulic extractor, more commonly known as the Jaws of Life, for cutting into the truck to make it easier to free the driver and passenger. They attached the tool to a line, and Tony and Sheri took it down when they descended.

"This is the scariest thing I've seen," Bethany said as she

and Vince watched their fellow volunteers work on cutting the truck cab apart. "One slip and the whole truck might go over, and everyone down there with it."

"Part of me is glad I'm not down there," Vince said. "But it's hard to be up here too, wishing I could do more to help."

"Somebody has to be up here, making sure nothing goes wrong with the rigging," she said.

"You're right." He glanced below again as Tony and Eldon eased the driver from the truck cab onto a backboard. "I'll be glad when everyone is up top safely."

"I hear you."

Someone called to Bethany, and she moved away. Vince relaxed a little. Bethany was nice, but her obvious interest in him made him uncomfortable. She hadn't said or done anything out of line, but every time he turned around, she was either standing next to him or watching from across the room. Others besides Ryan had noticed. He didn't want to be rude to her, but he wished she would back off a little.

He focused again on the scene below. The volunteers fitted the driver with a helmet, neck brace and an oxygen mask and strapped him into a litter. They had a radio conversation with Danny, who, in addition to being the search and rescue captain, was also a registered nurse.

A heavy throb signaled the arrival of the rescue helicopter. The beam from its searchlight had them shielding their eyes from the glare. The chopper swept in, then hovered over the crash site and lowered a cable. The team below had affixed lines to the litter and attached these to the cable from the helicopter. At a signal from Tony, the helicopter rose and ferried the injured man to the middle of the closed road, where another team of volunteers helped lower the litter to the ground, unfastened it from the cable and carried it to a waiting ambulance.

The helicopter headed for the canyon again, this time to retrieve the black bag containing the body of the passenger. This second transfer accomplished, the volunteers collected their gear and ascended, one at a time, up the canyon walls. Vince, Caleb and Chris monitored the climbers. As soon as everyone was up top and out of their climbing harnesses, they began the tedious chore of disassembling all the rigging and putting everything neatly away, ready to be used in the next emergency.

"How did the passenger die?" Caleb asked Tony as they disconnected various pieces of hardware from the climbing ropes they had used to assemble the rigging.

"Can't say for sure," Tony said. "But maybe a broken neck. The driver had a head injury. I think he may have banged his head into the window. Everything in the vehicle was thrown around. I think it was a pretty violent descent."

Vince shuddered, imagining. This was the first call where the real threat of danger had superseded the adrenaline rush of helping someone out under challenging conditions. Today, there had been a real threat of harm to everyone involved. His worries over a couple of annoying notes seem petty in contrast.

THE PASS WAS closed by the time Tammy arrived. She had to park half a mile from the accident scene and hike up the road in the dark, past the line of cars waiting to get over the pass when it reopened, then past parked vehicles belonging to search and rescue volunteers, highway department employees and local law enforcement.

The accident site was lit up like a movie set, halogen lights on tall stands ringing a section of roadside and shining down into the canyon. Tammy stopped to take a picture, struck by the contrast of the bright lights and the shadowy cliffs. She was tucking her camera away when someone brushed past her. A slim, dark figure was running down the mountain, away from the accident. Tammy stared after the woman—she was sure it was a woman, though she had seen the figure for only a few seconds. Nothing about her was familiar, though.

She moved closer. Deputy Shane Ellis, who was standing beside his patrol vehicle, watching the search and rescue team work, waved in greeting. Tammy took out her camera once more and moved closer, in time to get a shot of volunteer Ryan Welch begin his descent into the canyon. She took a few more photographs of other volunteers. She didn't see Vince, but he would be easy to miss in the crowd with so many people milling around in the darkness.

She joined Shane by the sheriff's department SUV. Shane—a former professional baseball player who had surprised everyone by becoming a sheriff's deputy—nodded at her. "Good to see the local press reporting the latest news," he said.

She took out a notebook and pen. "What happened here?" she asked.

"It looks like a pickup truck came around that curve with too much speed." He pointed ahead of them, to a sharp curve on the highway. "He slid on loose gravel and went over the edge. The canyon walls are really steep in this section, and he must have had quite a ride. But he got lucky. The undercarriage of the vehicle hung up on a boulder."

"The driver was a male."

"We don't know for sure. And there appears to be at least one passenger. But until search and rescue takes a look, I don't have any more information."

She scribbled notes she hoped she would be able to read when she sat down tomorrow to write the story. "I saw Ryan Welch descending into the canyon," she said.

"He and Eldon Ramsey are going down to stabilize the

vehicle so rescuers can free the people inside the truck and assess their injuries," Shane said. "Bud O'Brien has his biggest wrecker out for the job."

The boom wrecker, lit up by the spotlights, would make an excellent shot for the paper. And Bud might like to have one to hang in his office. She started to move closer to take more photographs when Shane's next words stopped her. "I heard you got a note that was supposedly from Vince Shepherd's long-lost sister."

"I turned it into the sheriff," she said. "Do you know if he's learned anything more about whoever wrote it?"

"I don't think so," Shane said.

"Then I don't know any more than you do." She pushed away from the side of the SUV. "I'm going to get more photographs and talk to some of the rescuers."

She fired off a dozen more pictures, then climbed onto a boulder, which gave her a birds-eye view into the canyon. A couple of scraggly trees partially blocked her view of the wrecked truck, but she could see enough to feel a little queasy at the prospect of anyone trying to work around the smashed-up vehicle.

The loud chop of helicopter rotors drowned out the rumble of the wrecker's engine and the conversation of the volunteers. The rescue helicopter swept in and hovered on the edge of the canyon, the backwash from the rotors flinging loose gravel at onlookers and whipping back their hair. People tried to shield their eyes, but none of them looked away as a cable slowly lowered from the belly of the chopper. A few tense minutes later, the cable rose again, a litter bearing the figure of a person, wrapped like a mummy. A cheer rose from the crowd when the litter was safely inside.

Moments later, the cable lowered again. This time the trip was faster, as was the return journey. Another litter rose, but this one carried no securely wrapped figure—only a black plastic bag. The body bag meant one of the occupants of the truck hadn't made it.

Tammy moved in to speak with SAR Captain Danny Irwin. "Was there just the one fatality?" she asked.

"Yes. The passenger," Danny said "But the driver—a man—has a good chance of making it."

"Do we know who they are?" she asked.

Danny met her gaze. "We checked for ID, but I can't reveal that until their families are notified."

"Just tell me if they're locals," she said.

"They are not," he said.

Some of the tension that had been building since she had gotten the call about the accident lessened. The fatality was a tragedy, but not as wrenching as if it had been someone she knew. "What can you tell me about the rescue efforts?" she asked.

Danny straightened. "This was a highly technical rescue that put our training to the test," he said. "The truck was in a dangerous position, and our volunteers risked their lives to stabilize the vehicle and free the driver and passenger from the wreckage. This rescue involved everyone on-site, from those doing the climbing and rendering medical aid, to the volunteers who monitored the rigging, to those who provided backup support. This was an example of the teamwork Eagle Mountain Search and Rescue is known for."

"I got some great photos," Tammy said. "Everyone who lives here already knows how lucky we are to have such a great search and rescue group, but this kind of thing reminds them how awesome you all are."

"We're not doing it for the glory," Danny said. "But all that training and equipment isn't free. Anything that might net a few more donations is welcome."

Laughter from a group just beyond them distracted her. She looked past him. Was that Vince?

"Looking for someone?" Danny asked.

"Vince Shepherd. Is he here tonight?"

Danny looked around. "Vince is here somewhere."

"I'm sure I'll find him." She hurried away before Danny could ask why she wanted to speak with Vince. Even she wasn't completely sure of the answer to that question, except that she liked Vince a lot. She wanted to know him better. And she wanted him to like her.

She hadn't seen him since they had parted company after their interview with the sheriff Sunday morning. He hadn't followed up on his dinner invitation. She had picked up the phone to text him half a dozen times but had stopped herself from following through on the impulse. She wasn't going to chase a man who wasn't interested in her. Whatever happened between them would have to happen in its own time. If it didn't, well, maybe it wasn't meant to happen at all. Was that the coward in her, making excuses? Maybe so, but she was reluctant to let go of the notion that a real love should be strong enough to overcome the obstacles life put in its way. If it wasn't, what was the point? Life was so fragile and fleeting, why risk grabbing hold of something that was even more unreliable?

VINCE SHOVED THE last duffel of supplies into the back of the search and rescue vehicle known as the Beast. Six volunteers had snagged a ride to the scene in the specially outfitted Jeep, but he wasn't one of them. Instead, he and the rest of the crew had driven their personal vehicles. He had left his truck parked down the road from the accident site.

"I'm parked right behind you." Grace Wilcox fell into step beside him. Grace had been with the team a few months longer than he had, but he didn't know much about her, except that she was an environmental scientist and she was dating a new deputy with the sheriff's department.

"That was an amazing rescue tonight," he said.

"I'm in awe of people like Sheri and Ryan, who make those dangerous climbs," Grace said. "And in the dark. I'm literally just learning the ropes, and I don't ever think I'll be that skilled and confident."

"How did you get involved with search and rescue?" he asked.

"I like helping others and making a difference." She flashed a smile. "And it gets me out of my own head. I could easily turn into a hermit if I didn't force myself to get out and be part of the community. This is a good way to do that. And I'm learning new skills, getting into shape—I love it. Even when the rescues are hard or dangerous. It's all important, and how often do any of us get to do something that's really important?"

"I guess you're right." He had joined search and rescue because he remembered how hard they had worked to help find Valerie. Even though they hadn't succeeded, the memory of those dedicated volunteers had stuck with him. And though he had never mentioned this when he applied to be a volunteer, he had hoped that time spent in remote locations in the mountains might lead to him uncovering a clue about what had happened to Valerie. He had imagined that would mean finding her body, or at least something that had belonged to her. That hadn't happened, but until the mystery of her disappearance was solved, he would never let go of the hope of finding a solution.

"The new girl seems really nice," Grace said.

"Bethany? Yeah, she's nice."

"She's shy, like me, but I can tell she's trying to come out of her shell."

"I guess so." Maybe he was reading too much into her attention to him. Some people were just friendly.

"Hey, what is that all over your truck?"

Grace's steps faltered, then stopped. Vince stopped also, and stared at his truck. The moon had risen, and even in that silvery light, he could tell something was wrong with the paint job on the truck. It was too splotchy. He broke into a run and stopped when his boots crunched on broken glass. Every window in the truck was shattered. The windshield was still holding together, though a spiderweb of cracks spread out from a spot centered over the driver's side.

"Is that red paint?" Grace spoke from beside him.

Vince crunched toward the truck until he could touch the dark stain across the hood. His finger came away red and sticky. He stared, realizing something was scrawled amid the broken lines of the windshield glass—messy words in the same red paint.

YOU THOUGHT I WAS DEAD, DIDN'T YOU?

"What's that at the bottom?" Caleb had joined Vince and Grace. "It looks like a check mark."

"It's not a check mark," Vince said. He stared at the two slashes of paint meeting at the bottom. "It's a *V.*" *V* for *Valerie.*

Chapter Nine

Tammy headed back down the hill toward her car. She searched groups of people she passed, hoping to spot Vince. She would say hello, and they could make small talk about the accident. Maybe they could firm up dinner plans.

A crowd had gathered on the side of the road up ahead. Curious, Tammy pushed through the clot of people and was startled to see Vince standing in front of his truck. Several people were shining flashlights on the vehicle, revealing a broken window and splashes of red paint. Tammy stared at the message on the windshield: YOU THOUGHT I WAS DEAD, DIDN'T YOU? V.

Deputy Shane Ellis, along with Colorado State Patrol Officer Ryder Stewart, moved in alongside Vince and began talking to him. Tammy snapped off a few photographs of the scene, then joined them. "Hello, Vince," she said during a lull in the conversation.

"Hey, Tammy." He resumed staring at his truck. "I can't believe this happened."

Tammy turned to Shane. "Who did this?" she asked.

"We haven't found anyone who saw anything," Shane said.

"Everyone was focused on the accident, and it was dark," Ryder said. "The road was closed, and there weren't a lot of people along this stretch where the volunteers parked their cars. We've got a shoe impression where a person stepped in the paint. It may have been the perpetrator, or maybe someone who was trying to get a closer look." He studied Tammy's tennis shoes. "The print is about your size."

"No paint on me or my shoes." She extended her leg so he could examine the sole of first one shoe, then the other. "So you think a woman did this?"

"It's a possibility," Ryder said. "But only *one* possibility."

"Someone could have parked on the other side of the closure and hiked up the road like I did," she said. "If they waited until everyone was up at the accident site, maybe when the helicopter arrived and was making a lot of noise and attracting everyone's attention. Then they smashed the windows, wrote the message and tossed the paint, and left before anyone saw them."

"That could be how it happened," Ryder said. "Do you know something about it?"

"I got to the accident site a few minutes before the helicopter arrived," she said. "While I was walking up the road, a woman ran past me. I didn't get a good look, but I'm pretty sure it was a woman—slender and not too tall, dressed in dark clothing. I noticed her because she was running—and away from the accident, not toward it like everyone else."

Vince was focused on her now. "What color hair did she have? Did you get a look at her face?"

"No. I was focused on getting to the accident scene. And she was moving pretty fast."

"Did you see where she went?" Shane asked.

"No, I didn't," she admitted.

"The message is signed *V*," Vince said.

"Do you think it's Valerie?" Tammy asked.

"I don't know what to think," he admitted.

"Both of you need to come down to the department and

give a statement," Shane said. "Meanwhile, we'll go over the truck for evidence."

"I can give you a ride to town," Tammy said.

Vince looked glum. "Why would anyone go after my truck? And why the cryptic message?"

"I don't know," Tammy said. "Maybe the sheriff can figure something out." She didn't believe that. Whoever was pretending to be Valerie, she hadn't provided them with evidence of her motive, other than to harass Vince. "Do you have an ex who is angry with you? If she knows about Valerie, she might be hiding behind the name as a way of unsettling you."

"It's unsettling, all right. But no, I don't have any exes, angry or otherwise. I told you, I'm not the best at relationships."

She wanted to reassure him that he was just fine, that no one was an expert at these things, but what did she know? Better to focus on being his friend. If something more developed, that would be good, but better not to force it.

VINCE SLID INTO the passenger seat of Tammy's Subaru, the image of his vandalized truck still fixed in his mind. *You thought I was dead, didn't you?* Of course he thought Valerie was dead. Hundreds of people had searched for her immediately after she went missing, and they hadn't found one clue as to what happened to her. No one had heard from her in fifteen years. She had disappeared in the high mountains, where people died in accidents every year. One wrong step or a slip could send a person plummeting off a cliff or into a deep fissure in the rocks, and no one would ever see them again.

Whoever was doing this couldn't be Valerie. She would have no reason to taunt him this way. The real Valerie would be happy to see him again.

But a scammer would demand money, and that hadn't happened yet.

Which left someone who was doing this in order to torture Vince and his family. A person who enjoyed making other people suffer. Was it someone he knew or a stranger who had read the article in the *Examiner* and decided to focus on him? "Has anyone contacted the paper about the article you wrote?" he asked Tammy.

"What do you mean by *contact*?" she asked. "A few people complimented me on the article. And some people asked what else I had planned for the series."

"I'm thinking maybe someone saw the article and fixated on it as a way to harass me," he said. "I've heard of people who enjoy psychologically torturing others. Some of the calls my parents received soon after Valerie disappeared were made by people like that. They would say things like 'Your daughter is being tortured, and you'll never see her again.'"

"That's so cruel," she said.

"It is. I'm trying to figure out if the person who sent that postcard and vandalized my car is like that. They've decided for whatever reason to target me, and Valerie's story is a convenient one to hide behind." The idea made sense—more sense than the possibility that Valerie had suddenly shown up again after all these years.

"You should tell the sheriff that," she said. "There might even be someone who contacted your parents before who has resurfaced."

At the sheriff's department, Tammy left with Shane to give her statement while Jake Gwynn escorted Vince to an interview room. They had scarcely settled into chairs across from each other when Travis entered. "I might have a few questions after you've given your statement to Jake about what happened tonight."

Vince took him through the events of the evening, from when he had first parked his truck on the side of the closed highway to his arrival back there two hours later, and the vandalism he had seen. "You're sure the note was signed *V*?" Jake asked. "It couldn't have been some random paint drip?"

Vince thought back to the message on the windshield. "I'm pretty sure it was *V*," he said.

"Do you know who *V* might be?" Jake asked.

"I think it's someone who is trying to make me think the message was written by my sister, Valerie." Vince looked to Travis. "Maybe the same person who sent that postcard."

"You don't believe this really is Valerie?" Travis asked.

"How could it be? If she's still alive, why haven't we heard anything for fifteen years? And if she was kidnapped and suddenly escaped, you'd think she'd be thrilled to see us again. She wouldn't hide and try to frighten us."

Travis scooted his chair closer and looked Vince in the eye. "Did you have anything to do with your sister's disappearance?"

"What? No!"

"Is it possible Valerie might have thought you had something to do with the accident or whatever happened that day?" Travis continued. "Maybe you were playing and she slipped and fell, and you were too afraid to tell anyone. Or you dared her to do something and she took the dare and was hurt."

"No! I was in the tent, asleep, when she disappeared. I saw her leave the tent, then fell back asleep. By the time I woke up, my parents were already searching."

Travis's expression gave nothing away. Vince glared at him. "Do you think this is Valerie? And that she's exacting revenge for something I did to her?"

"I think it's always a good idea to look at every possibility," Travis said.

"If this is my sister, where has she been all this time? And why couldn't hundreds of people searching for her find any trace after that day?"

"I don't know," Travis said. "But I'm doing my best to find out. Is there anything else about tonight, or about the postcard or the message left on your truck, that makes you think of anything or anyone?"

"No. I've gone over and over it in my head, and I can't think of anything, except that this is another scammer or one of those people who likes to torture others. My parents got calls like that after Valerie disappeared. Is it possible this is one of those people and the article in the *Examiner* shifted their focus to me?"

"Do you know the names of any of those people?" Travis asked.

"I don't think so, but I'll ask my parents." Although that would mean involving them in this, and he had been hoping to avoid that. "Maybe you have something in your files on the case," he said.

"I haven't found anything, but I promise I'll take a look." Travis stood. "Jake will print your statement and you can sign it, then you're free to go. Call us in a day or two, and we'll let you know when you can have your truck."

"I hate to think how much it's going to cost to restore the truck," he said.

Travis didn't comment on this, merely said good-night and left the room. Vince waited for the printout of his statement, read over it and then dashed off his signature. It wasn't until he was walking down the hall that he wondered how he was going to get to his condo. But when he stepped into the lobby, Tammy rose from a chair by the door. "I waited to give you a ride home," she said.

"Thanks."

He didn't say anything else until they were seated in her car. "Are you going to write about my truck being vandalized for the paper?" he asked.

"I don't know," she said. "I have to work on the story about the truck accident and the rescue." She glanced at him, then back at the road. "Why?"

"I'd rather you didn't," he said. "I don't want to upset my parents, but most of all, I don't want to give whoever this is more attention."

"If we do run anything, it's most likely to be a line item in the sheriff's report. But it isn't my decision to make. That would be up to my editor."

"You don't have to give him the photos you took," he said.

"No, I don't." She fell silent, and he worried he had hurt her feelings.

"I'm not trying to tell you how to do your job," he added. "And I'm grateful for all the help you've given me. I'm just trying to sort out how to handle all of this."

"I know." She turned into the parking area for his condo and pulled into an empty space. She unfastened her seat belt but kept the engine running. "I'm sorry about your truck," she said. "That has to feel like a personal attack."

"It does," he agreed. "That message—'You thought I was dead, didn't you?' As if I betrayed my sister by believing she was no longer alive."

"Even though a lot of people share that assumption."

"I'm angry that I'm letting some sick person get to me this way," he said.

"Don't beat yourself up for being human." She reached over and took his hand. Her skin was cool and smooth, her touch firm and comforting. "I wish I could do more to help."

"You're doing a lot just being here." He turned toward

her, and she surprised him by leaning over and pressing her lips to his.

He leaned into the kiss, pulled by attraction and need. Then, just as suddenly, she pulled away. The kiss was brief, but the impression of it lingered. She gave a nervous laugh and didn't meet his gaze. "Call me if you need anything else," she said, and fastened her seat belt.

That seemed the definite signal for him to leave. "I will," he said. "And thanks for everything."

He got out of the car and forced himself to walk up to his condo without looking back. He was relieved to find no nasty notes on his door. He sank onto the couch and leaned forward, elbows on knees and head in his hand. His lips still tingled from that kiss. He liked Tammy. He liked being with her. He was attracted to her, and it would be fun to explore that attraction. But was now the time to get involved with anyone, with everything stirred up over Valerie?

Though, when he looked at his life closely, he recognized that Valerie had been his excuse for not getting serious about anyone all his life. Since his twin had vanished all those years ago, he had grown used to being alone. Valerie wasn't half of him, but she was part of him. She was part of his life even though she was no longer in it, and he didn't know how to explain that to someone else. Valerie wasn't dead, but she would never be truly gone either. He had always wondered if finding her body would make it easier to finally lay her to rest.

Instead, he was grappling with someone who claimed his sister was still alive and wasn't happy with him. Valerie was still taking up too much room in his head and his life to make it possible to be there for someone else.

Chapter Ten

Wednesday morning, Tammy sat at her desk in the office of the *Eagle Mountain Examiner*, reviewing the photos she had taken the night before. She was supposed to be selecting the image from the rescue to run with the story she had already turned in. But her attention kept returning to the shots she had taken of Vince's vandalized car. *You thought I was dead, didn't you?* And that slash of a *V* beneath. If it was possible for a painted message to look angry, this one did.

She replayed those few seconds when the figure had run past her in the dark—slender body, long hair—and something about the way they moved had made Tammy certain it was a woman. Who would be running away from the accident, unless it was the person who had vandalized Vince's car?

Tammy had arrived at the scene after all the rescue personnel were in place. Law enforcement was either stationed at the highway barricade or near the accident site. Could one of them have seen the same fleeing woman?

She stood and walked to the open door of Russ's office. He was hunched over his desk, frowning at his computer monitor, but looked up at her approach. "What?" he asked.

"I'm going out to do background interviews for a story I'm working on," she said.

"Go." He waved her away and returned to scowling at the monitor.

She slung her handbag over one shoulder and headed on foot to the sheriff's department. It was the kind of perfect summer day that made tourists congratulate themselves on having chosen such an idyllic spot for a vacation—sunny but not hot, with cloudless turquoise skies and blooming flowers everywhere you looked.

The atmosphere was less sunny in the lobby of the sheriff's department. Office Manager Adelaide Kinkaid looked up from her command center at the front desk, her expression stern. "What can I do for you, Ms. Patterson?" she asked.

"I'd like to speak to the sheriff," Tammy said.

"Sheriff Walker does not have time to speak with the press," Adelaide said, her response to every request Tammy had ever made to speak with the sheriff.

"Then I need to speak with one of the deputies who responded to the accident at Carson Canyon last night."

Adelaide's eyes narrowed. "What do you need to know?"

"I need to clarify a couple of facts for the article I wrote." Pause, and an earnest expression. "I would hate to get anything wrong."

Adelaide's frown tightened, but after a few seconds, she picked up the phone and asked a deputy to come to the lobby to speak with "the reporter from the *Examiner*." As if everyone in town didn't already know Tammy was the sole reporter—well, except for the high school student who covered school sports each year, and Russ, who did write his share of news stories.

Deputy Jamie Douglas smiled when she saw Tammy. Tammy returned the smile. She and Jamie were friends, and she didn't have to worry about her friend being evasive. Jamie glanced at Adelaide. "Come on back, and we'll talk at my desk," she said.

As they walked down the hallway to the crowded bullpen where Jamie shared a desk with other deputies, the two friends exchanged the usual pleasantries. "How is Olivia?" Tammy asked.

"We think she's going to start crawling any minute now," Jamie said of her three-month old daughter. "And she's growing like crazy. Nate says she's going to be tall like him, but I think it's too soon to tell." They arrived at Jamie's desk. "Adelaide said you had some questions about the accident last night?"

"Yes. I wanted to know who was working the barricade where they closed the highway."

"I was."

"Did anyone try to get past you? On foot, maybe?"

"No. You and the rescue personnel are the only people we let through."

Maybe the woman she had seen had slipped through before the barricade went up. "Did you see anyone leaving the area?" Tammy asked. "Anyone you didn't recognize, or who wasn't authorized to be there?"

"No. Why?"

She explained about the running woman who had passed her as she hiked up the hill.

"I didn't see anyone like that," Jamie said. She looked over Tammy's shoulder. "Dwight, come here a minute."

Deputy Dwight Preston joined them. "Hi, Tammy."

"Dwight, did you see anyone come or go past the barricade last night who you didn't know? Anyone who wasn't with search and rescue or highway patrol?"

"There was the other reporter," he said.

"What other reporter?" Tammy asked.

"With the *Junction Sentinel*. She said the couple in the truck were from Junction, and she was covering the story." Tammy's heart raced. "What did she look like?"

"About your height. Slender. She was wearing dark jeans and a dark shirt and a baseball cap. I couldn't see her hair."

"Did she give a name?" Jamie asked.

"No. She just said she was a reporter with the *Sentinel.* She had a camera and a notebook, so I let her through."

"Were the couple in the truck from Junction?" Tammy asked.

Jamie and Dwight looked at each other. "I'll check," Jamie said, and turned to her computer.

"Is something wrong?" Dwight asked.

Tammy explained about the running woman. "It sounds like it could have been the same woman," Dwight said. "Maybe she was in a hurry to get back to town and file her story."

Jamie looked up. "The couple was from North Carolina," she said.

Tammy thanked them and hurried back to the newspaper office. From there, she telephoned the Junction paper and asked for her friend, Tyler Frazier. "Hey, Tammy!" he greeted her. "This is a nice surprise."

"Hey, Tyler. I'm trying to locate a reporter there at the paper. She was here in Eagle Mountain last night, covering an accident we had where a couple's truck went off the road and over a cliff."

"Sounds like a wild story, but I don't think we would have sent a reporter to cover it," he said. "That's pretty far out of our coverage area."

"Would you mind checking for me?"

"Okay. Hold on a second."

He put her on Hold. A song that was popular when her parents were teenagers came on, and Tammy hummed along as she studied the photos of the vandalized truck once more. She had taken one of the red footprint, left when someone—

the vandal?—had stepped in the red paint. Red like blood. She shivered at the thought.

Tyler came back on the line. "No one here went down to Eagle Mountain yesterday to cover an accident or anything else," he said. "What did this reporter look like?"

"Female, young, slender, about my height. Maybe with long hair." The woman who had run past her had had long hair.

"That doesn't sound like anyone we have on staff," Tyler said. "Sorry I can't help you."

She hung up. Someone had posed as a reporter in order to get past the highway barrier. Had she done so specifically to get to Vince's truck? But why? Why target him?

The phone rang, the screen showing a familiar name. "Hello, Mitch," she said.

"Come have lunch with me," Mitch said.

She started to tell him she was too busy. Truthfully, she wasn't in the mood to socialize, even with Mitch.

"Please. Elisabeth will be there, and I want you to meet her."

"All right." She couldn't pass up the chance to meet the woman who had captivated her brother.

"Meet us at the Rib Shack at twelve thirty."

When she arrived at the barbecue stand near the river, she spotted Mitch already in line. Next to him was a slender, dark-haired woman about her height, whom he introduced as Elisabeth. The woman's smile was warm, her handshake firm. "It's nice to meet you," she said.

"It's good to meet you too," Tammy said. "And welcome to Eagle Mountain. Mitch tells me you're new in town."

"Yes. He's been helping me get settled." She gave Mitch an adoring smile, which he returned. Tammy had never seen her brother this besotted. Why was that unsettling?

"What brought you to Eagle Mountain?" Tammy asked. "We're not exactly on the beaten path."

"I had a friend who used to live here," she said. "She raved about how beautiful it is, and I can't say she was wrong."

It was their turn to order. When they had collected their food, they carried it to a picnic table in the shade of a towering blue spruce. Elisabeth and Mitch settled across from Tammy, sitting so close their shoulders touched.

"Elisabeth, where are you from?" Tammy asked.

"Nebraska."

"Oh, do you have family there?"

Elisabeth's expression saddened. Something about her was familiar to Tammy, but she couldn't place her. "Not anymore. My father passed away recently, and I'm all alone."

"I'm sorry to hear that. You don't have other family?"

"No one close, no." She glanced at Mitch. "Not everyone is lucky enough to have a close sibling."

"Are you in Eagle Mountain for long?" Tammy asked.

"I hope so." She beamed at Mitch, and he beamed back. Why did this set Tammy's teeth on edge? Was she jealous that Mitch was happy and she wasn't? No. She wasn't like that. And Elisabeth seemed perfectly nice.

"Mitch tells me you're a reporter," Elisabeth said, her attention on Tammy once more. "That must be such interesting work."

"It is."

"What are some of the stories you've covered?" She propped her chin on her hand, eyes laser-focused on Tammy.

Tammy shifted, uncomfortable under that intense gaze. "Last night I covered an accident. A truck went off the road and plunged over a cliff, but it was caught halfway down on a boulder. Search and rescue had to make a dangerous climb down to stabilize the truck and retrieve the accident victims."

"That certainly sounds dramatic," Elisabeth said.

"It was." She studied the other woman more closely. "You weren't up there near the accident scene last night, were you?"

"Who, me?" Elisabeth looked amused. "Why would you think that?"

"I thought I saw you up there." Tammy couldn't be sure, but Elisabeth might have been the figure who ran by her.

Elisabeth chuckled. "It wasn't me." She leaned into Mitch. "I was otherwise occupied."

"Elisabeth was with me last night," Mitch said. He put his arm around her shoulders.

"It must have been someone else, then." Tammy focused on her lunch, though she scarcely tasted the spicy barbecue.

"You wrote that article about the little girl who disappeared, didn't you?" Elisabeth said.

"Yes."

Elisabeth glanced at Mitch. "I read it when I first got to town. It's hard to believe anyone could just vanish that way."

"It happens more often than you would think," Mitch said. "There's a lot of hazardous country. It's easy to get lost or have an accident."

"I would think parents of a child would keep a closer eye on them." Elisabeth popped a french fry into her mouth.

"Apparently, Valerie slipped out of the tent early in the morning, before the rest of the family was awake," Tammy said.

"Well, the parents would say that if they wanted to cover up their own guilt, wouldn't they?"

Before Tammy could question this odd assertion, another local real estate agent stopped by their table to say hello. Mitch introduced Elisabeth, who smiled warmly and leaned closer to Mitch.

When the other man left, Tammy gathered up the remains of her lunch. "I'd better get back to work," she said. "It was nice meeting you, Elisabeth."

"You too." Elisabeth linked her arm with Mitch's. "I'm sure we're going to be seeing a lot more of each other."

Tammy took the longest route back to the newspaper office, trying to walk off her mixed emotions about her brother's newest girlfriend. Was it the swiftness with which the relationship had progressed that unsettled her? She clearly wasn't the woman who had impersonated a reporter from Junction last night, or the person who had run past Tammy and maybe vandalized Vince's car. Tammy hadn't dared press for more details, but her brother's smug expression seemed to imply that he and Elisabeth had spent the entire night together.

Back at the office, she got to work on an article summarizing the most recent town council meeting and rewriting a press release from a local charitable organization.

Hours later, she was gathering her things to leave when the receptionist, Micki, a high school student who worked from one to six most afternoons, came over to her desk. "Someone just put this through the mail slot," she said. "It's addressed to you."

Tammy accepted the envelope and stared at her name in crooked block print across the front. The printing looked familiar. She worked her thumb beneath the flap and teased it open. The message inside was typed.

Dear Tammy
As a reporter, I'm sure you're interested in the truth. I read the article you wrote about the disappearance of Valerie Shepherd and feel the need to set a few things straight.

   Despite what the Shepherds have told everyone for years, Valerie did not simply wander off. Her parents— and her brother, Vince—deliberately left her in those mountains to die. That was the whole reason they even went into the mountains that weekend. The family had other things to do that weekend, but Mr. Shepherd insisted they had to go. He couldn't wait to get rid of the difficult child in the family. I guess he thought life would be easier with only Vince, his perfect son, to contend with. If not for the kindness of a stranger who found her, Valerie would have perished. The truth is, her family didn't want her anymore. Fortunately, she ended up with someone who did want her.

   This is the truth you need to let the public know about.

V.

Chapter Eleven

Vince read the letter through twice, heart hammering wildly. "It's not true," he said. "My parents and I didn't abandon Valerie. My parents were crushed by her disappearance. We've never stopped hoping she would be found."

"Why would anyone write these accusations?" Sheriff Walker tapped the corner of the letter, which was laid out on the table in the interview room at the sheriff's department. After Tammy had telephoned to tell him about the note, Vince had agreed to meet her at the sheriff's office, a place that was becoming all-too familiar to him after his recent visits. Travis sat on one side of the table, his brother, Sergeant Gage Walker, standing behind him. Vince and Tammy sat side by side across from him, not touching, but close enough that he could sense the rise and fall of her breath. This note had clearly unnerved her, and seeing her so upset had shaken him.

He forced his attention back to the sheriff's question. "I don't know." He stared at the single *V* typed at the bottom of the letter.

"It sounds to me like someone's pretending to be Valerie," Tammy said.

"It's signed the same way as the message left on my truck's windshield," Vince said.

"Did your sister sign her name that way?" Travis asked. "A single *V*?"

"No. But we were only ten when she disappeared." He tried to think but drew a blank. "I can't say I'd ever seen her sign anything."

"The letter writer refers to Valerie in the third person," Tammy said. "She doesn't say 'I did not simply wander off,' but '*Valerie* did not simply wander off.'" She shrugged. "I don't know if that's significant. It's just an observation."

"Maybe she likes to refer to herself in the third person," Travis said.

"Or maybe this isn't Valerie." Vince shook his head. "Of course it isn't Valerie."

Gage spoke for the first time. "Why do you say that?"

"Because even if Valerie is alive, she has no reason to want to hurt me. We were twins." He looked down at the table and swallowed past a lump in his throat. "Losing her was like losing part of myself."

"She's been gone a long time," Gage said. "Maybe she thinks you didn't do enough to find her. Or she blames you for whatever happened to her."

"But what could have happened to her?" Vince asked.

Gage and Travis exchanged a glance, though he couldn't read the meaning behind that look. It was the kind of coded expression couples or siblings shared—the kind of communication he and Valerie had once enjoyed. "At the time your sister disappeared, both you and your parents mentioned another camper in the area," Travis said.

"Valerie said there was a man camped near us," Vince said. "I never saw him, and when we searched the area for him, we never saw any sign of him."

"Was it like her to make things up?" Travis asked.

"No. I believed there was a camper and he left early."

"Maybe he took Valerie with him when he left," Gage said.

"I know my parents thought so," Vince said. "They urged law enforcement to look for the man, and I believe they tried to find him. But no one else reported seeing him, and we didn't have much to go on—just a man with a blue tent."

Tammy leaned forward, her expression eager. "Do you think Valerie was kidnapped by this man and, after fifteen years, managed to escape and come looking for her family?" she asked.

"It's one possibility," Travis said. "Though that's not to go any further than this room."

Tammy shrank back at his stern look. "Yes, sir," she said.

Travis slid the letter into an evidence bag. "Or maybe this is a hoax." He regarded Vince for a long moment. Vince tried to remain still, to not reveal how unsettled the sheriff's scrutiny made him. "Are you sure you can't think of anyone who might want to harass you?" Travis asked. "An ex–romantic partner or someone you worked with? A former neighbor or classmate? Maybe another family member?"

"No one," Vince said.

"You can't think of anyone who has any reason to be unhappy with you?" Gage asked.

Vince shrugged. "No. I guess I'm not the kind of guy to upset people." The truth was, he seldom got close enough to anyone to upset them—or to make much of an impression at all. He had friends. He had dated several women. But he couldn't say any of those relationships had the depth he thought was required to end up with someone wanting to wreck his truck—or his life.

Travis stood and Gage moved away from the wall. "Those are all my questions for now," the sheriff said.

Vince followed Tammy out of the interview room, down the hall and onto the sidewalk. She stopped at the corner and hugged her arms across her chest. "That was frustrating," she said. "I was hoping the sheriff would have more answers."

"Do you think Valerie could be the one doing this?" he asked. "Sending those notes and vandalizing my truck? Has she been alive all these years and we didn't know?"

Tammy angled toward him, her expression soft with concern. "There have been other cases, of children who were abducted and turned up alive years later," she said.

"Then why not just contact me and tell me the truth?" Frustration made knots in his gut. "Why attack my truck and accuse me of helping to get rid of her?"

"It does feel like there's a lot of animosity in those letters—and what was done to your truck…" Tammy rubbed her hands up and down her arms as if she was cold.

It did. The idea that his sister—his twin whom he had loved without even having to think about it—would *hate* him this way felt dark and ugly.

They resumed walking, he assumed back toward the newspaper office. This time of day, the sidewalks were full of tourists and locals, running errands or visiting the shops and restaurants. He and Tammy had to walk close together, shoulders bumping frequently, in order to have a conversation. "What was Valerie like as a girl?" Tammy asked. "I mean, her temperament and attitudes? Was she like you or the opposite? Or somewhere in-between?"

He considered the question. Valerie had been such an essential part of his life that he had taken for granted she would always be there—until she wasn't. And at ten years old, he hadn't spent much time thinking about how other people felt or how they were different from him. But he had had a lot of time since then to examine everything he knew about his sister. "Valerie was more outgoing than I was," he said. "More daring. She would talk to strangers in public or wander off on her own when we were in the park or out shopping."

"Then she wouldn't have been afraid, necessarily, of a stranger who approached her?" Tammy asked.

"No. I mean, our parents and teachers had talked to us about stranger danger. Valerie was smart. I don't think she would have gotten into a car with someone she didn't know. But if a person struck up a conversation with her, she would have been friendly. And she liked attention. I guess she was kind of a show-off."

"Did that bother you when you were a boy? That she tried to get attention?"

"No. I didn't care. I wasn't interested in having people pay attention to me."

"Did she have a temper? Was she quick to anger or to take offense?"

"Oh yeah." He remembered. "She would get so mad sometimes. Her face would turn red, and she would stomp her foot." He almost smiled, picturing her rage over not being allowed to do something she wanted to do. "It's not fair!" she had howled, furious about not getting her way.

"But she could be sweet too," he said. "That weekend of the camping trip, I was upset about missing a friend's birthday party. Valerie tried to make me feel better. She even told my dad she thought I should be allowed to go to the party. And though she teased me about being afraid of things she wasn't—spiders and steep mountain bike tracks and things like that—she was never too hard on me."

"The two of you were close, then?"

He shrugged. "We were twins. And we didn't have any other siblings or cousins who lived nearby. The two of us were kind of a team."

"It must have been hard for you when she disappeared."

"For a long time, it didn't feel real," he said. "I kept thinking the door would open and she would be there, laughing and telling us all it had been a joke, that she had merely been hiding."

"Cruel joke," Tammy said. "Would she have done something like that?"

"Maybe," he said. "It would have been better than the truth—that we never knew what happened to her."

But what if the person who was harassing him now did turn out to be Valerie? Would that be worse than believing she had died? He couldn't wrap his head around the answer. "I'd like to know what happened to her," he said. "And I want whoever is sending these letters and whoever attacked my truck to be found and stopped."

"I want that too," Tammy said. She rested her hand on his shoulder. "And I'll do everything I can to help you."

It was the kind of thing any person might say, but he could sense the sincerity behind her words. She cared. The idea touched him—and unsettled him too. He had spent years keeping his distance from people. If you didn't get too close to people, you wouldn't be too hurt when they left you. He understood that not everyone wanted to live that way, but it had worked for him so far. Why should he change now just because one curly-haired reporter was getting under his skin?

Fifteen years ago

"It's my turn to hide. You have to find me!" Before Vince could protest, Valerie slapped his shoulder and ran away.

Annoyed, he closed his eyes and began to count. "One, two, three…"

He hated when it was his turn to find Valerie. She never failed to choose the best hiding spots. Impossible spots, like the gap between the cushions and the underside of their hide-a-bed sofa in the den, or in the rafters of the garage. He could spend hours searching for her with no luck, except he often gave up long before then.

Not that it was better when it was his turn to hide. She always found him, usually within ten minutes. Then she would crow about how terrible he was at this game. Which was why he never wanted to play. But today he had made the mistake of promising to play whatever Valerie wanted, never thinking she would choose hide-and-seek on such a hot afternoon. It had to be near ninety degrees out, and the sun was beating down. Maybe that wasn't hot to people like his aunt and uncle from Texas, but here in the mountains, with no air-conditioning in their house, ninety degrees was sweltering.

He reached fifty and decided that was enough. He was supposed to count to one hundred, but with Valerie, he needed any advantage he could grab. He opened his eyes and looked around, searching for any clue as to which direction she had run. He didn't see any footprints in the rocks and grass that made up the empty lot behind their house where they were playing. No flash of the bright red T-shirt she was wearing. The shed door wasn't ajar. Would she hide inside one of the parked cars?

He hurried to his mom's Chevy and opened the rear door. A blast of heat pushed him back. Valerie had better not be in there. She'd roast. He forced himself to stick his head inside and look around, but no Valerie.

No Valerie in the shed either, or behind any of the trees or bigger boulders that ringed the lot. Their rule was that they had to stay within the lot, which was bordered on two sides by wooden fencing. The back side gave way to a steep drop-off. Vince approached this and looked over. It would be just like Valerie to slide down there, thinking it would be a stealthy hiding place, and not be able to get back up. But there was nothing in the gully below but more trees and rocks.

He turned around and faced the house. He hadn't heard a door open or close, but Valerie might have managed to slip inside if she had been quiet. She was good at stealth. Better than he was. He was going through another growth spurt, and everything he did was clumsy. Squinting in the bright sunlight, he moved toward the house. He approached the back door, then looked under the steps. There was a shadowed hollow there where Vince had hidden once. It had taken Valerie over fifteen minutes to find him that time. She had even said it was a good hiding place.

But she hadn't decided to use it this time. He moved along the house, looking behind the lilac bushes, their blooms spent brown twigs now.

Something scrabbled in the loose mulch behind him, and he whirled, heart pounding. He stared at the ground beneath the lilacs. What was down there? He didn't see anything, but something had made that noise. "Valerie?" he asked, tentative.

Fingers gripped his ankle, hard, and yanked. Vince screamed and staggered back, arms flailing. Raucous laughter brought him up short.

Valerie, cobwebs draped across her hair like old lace and a smudge of dirt across one cheek, crawled out from beneath the porch. "Oh my gosh, that was great!" she shrieked, doubled over with laughter. "You screamed like a little girl!"

"You're supposed to be hiding, not attacking me!" he yelled.

"You walked right past me!" she said. "I couldn't resist. Your ankle was right there!"

He stared at the gap in the foundation she had squeezed into. "You have spiderwebs in your hair," he said.

She swept her fingers through her wavy locks, and the sticky webbing clung to them. "There are spiders under there too," she said.

He shuddered. "That's disgusting."

"No it's not. I'm not afraid of a few bugs." She lifted her chin. "I'm not afraid of anything."

Vince envied his sister's fearlessness. He was afraid of so many things—spiders and falling, not catching a fly ball in Little League, failing a math test and being stuck in fourth grade forever. "I bet you're afraid of dying," he said. "Everyone is afraid of that. Even adults."

Valerie shrugged. "I'm not."

"Liar."

She leaned forward and slapped his shoulder. "Your turn to hide. And pick a good place." Then she closed her eyes and started counting out loud. "One, two, three…"

Vince ran. He thought about leaving the yard and heading down the street to his friend Brett's house. That would make Valerie mad, but she'd either tell their mom—in which case, Vince would end up grounded—or she wouldn't tell anyone, but would exact her own revenge, like putting ants in his underwear drawer or putting dog poop in his bed. She had done both of those things before, and Vince had ended up punished when his mother found out. "Valerie wouldn't do something like that," she had said.

And Valerie had played the innocent like a pro, looking at him with wide, hurt eyes. Later, she had sidled up to Vince in the hallway, after his mother had sentenced him to spend an hour every day after school pulling weeds in the flower beds, and whispered, "That'll teach you to try to get the better of me."

Vince ran to the shed and hid behind the lawn mower and paint cans. It wasn't the best hiding place, but it was a good

enough spot to sit and think in the moments before Valerie
came to find him. He would think about all the things he
could do to get back at Valerie, but wouldn't. If she hadn't
been his sister, he would have admired her daring instead of
being jealous of it. And when it came down to it, he would
rather have her on his side than angry with him.

Chapter Twelve

Thursday afternoon, Tammy sat at her desk in the *Examiner* office and paged through the folder of information she had assembled about Valerie Shepherd's disappearance. She had all the original newspaper articles and notes from search and rescue about their role in the hunt for the missing girl, as well as the copy of the sheriff's department file that Travis had given her.

She stopped and reread the initial interview with Victor and Susan Shepherd, then took out a highlighter and ran it over the section where they talked about the camper Valerie claimed to have seen. "Right after we got to camp, Valerie climbed up onto a boulder and said she could see another camper nearby. Someone with a blue dome tent," Susan said. Her husband hadn't even heard this remark. The most information came from Vince, who said Valerie told him she met the man when she went to collect firewood. He had given her wood he had gathered and smiled at her. "She said he had a nice smile," Vince had said.

The sheriff's deputies had asked every person in the area that day if they had seen a lone male camper or backpacker, or one with a little girl who matched Valerie's description. No one had seen him. Appeals to the public who might have seen such a man had yielded nothing.

A man with a nice smile. Had the smile won Valerie over enough that she had gone with him? But where? Vince and his parents swore they had never seen the man, who, if he had been real, had seemingly vanished without a trace. Valerie had risen before the rest of the family and gone out to search for more wood. Had she encountered the man again and he had spirited her away in those early hours before anyone else was on the trail? It was possible, but if that was the case, where had they gone?

She continued reading through the file and came upon a single paragraph from a statement taken from a woman and her boyfriend six months after Valerie's disappearance. They had seen a man with a backpack on a trail near the one the Shepherds had taken, on the day before the Shepherds' camping trip. They described him as medium height and build, brown hair, early to mid-twenties. He wore jeans and a black T-shirt and hiking boots, and had a blue backpack. They hadn't spoken to him and had only come forward after seeing repeated appeals for information about a lone male hiker. "But it was the day before the little girl disappeared, and on a different trail," the woman—Jennifer—had said.

A handwritten note at the bottom of the page stated they were unable to obtain any further information about this man. A second note, in a different colored ink and different handwriting, contained just two words: *probably unrelated.*

That was the last entry in the slim file. Tammy closed the folder and stared into space, hoping for inspiration but finding none. Her stomach growled, and she decided maybe she would think better after lunch.

She walked down the street and was waiting in line for a booth at Kate's Café when a voice behind her said, "Tammy Shepherd? That is you, isn't it?"

She turned to find Elisabeth slipping in behind her.

Tammy glanced past her, expecting to see Mitch. Elisabeth laughed. "Mitch is showing a big ranch over near Delta," she said. "I'm on my own. And it looks like you are too."

The pause after these words was so weighted Tammy felt it pushing against her. "We should have lunch together," she said.

"I'd love that." Elisabeth linked her arm with Tammy's. "It will give us a chance to get to know each other better."

The server arrived to escort them to a booth along the side, and Tammy focused on the menu. But after a few moments, she became aware of Elisabeth studying her. She looked up. "You don't look like Mitch, do you?" Elisabeth said.

"He takes after my dad," Tammy said. "I look more like my mom. Though people say there's a resemblance."

Elisabeth shook her head. "I don't see it. Though maybe some family traits run stronger than that. For instance, my brother and I looked just alike. People thought we were twins."

"Oh. How many siblings do you have?" It seemed a safe enough topic of conversation.

"None. At least, not anymore. He died. My whole family is dead." She smiled, the expression so at odds with her words that Tammy was taken aback.

The server arrived to take their orders, providing a reprieve. Tammy tried to gather her thoughts. When they were alone again, she asked, "Have you been enjoying your time in Eagle Mountain?"

"I have. This morning I went shopping. There's a boutique in the Gold Nugget Hotel. Lucky Strike—do you know it?"

Tammy knew of the boutique, though its prices were beyond what she could manage on her reporter's salary. The styles displayed in the boutique's front windows were more upscale than what she usually wore. She dressed for comfort, ready to race out to the scene of an accident or to interview someone at a construction site or mine. Elisabeth, in her short skirt and heels, looked straight out of a magazine spread. There was no missing the way heads turned to follow her when she crossed a room.

"You're the first newspaper reporter I've ever met," Elisabeth said. "I thought that was one of those jobs that didn't exist anymore."

"People are still interested in the news," Tammy said.

"On television and online, maybe. I thought printed news was going the way of the dinosaurs."

This wasn't the first time Tammy had heard similar statements. "Not our paper," she said. "There's no other source for local news."

"Then you enjoy your job," Elisabeth said.

"Yes." The hours were long and the pay wasn't the best, but reporting was what she had always wanted to do. "The work offers a lot of variety," she said. "And I end up knowing about everything going on."

"What interesting things are going on in Eagle Mountain?"

"Everyone's gearing up for the Fourth of July. It's a big holiday here, for the locals and the tourists. There's a festival and a parade and fireworks."

"It sounds charming."

Tammy couldn't tell if *charming* was a positive or a negative to Elisabeth. "Do they do anything special for the Fourth where you're from?" she asked.

"Different places have fireworks." Elisabeth unrolled her napkin and spread it across her lap. "Mitch told me the two of you have a sibling who died. That's too bad, isn't it?"

Was that a question or an observation? Tammy was saved from having to reply by the arrival of the server with their food. She focused on the food, pondering a way to take the conversation in a less personal direction.

"Do you have a boyfriend?" Elisabeth asked.

Tammy had just taken a large bite of her sandwich and almost choked. She chewed and tried to think of an answer that wouldn't beg elaboration when Elisabeth added, "I saw you with a cute guy outside the sheriff's department. Tall, dark and handsome."

Tammy's face warmed. "That was just a friend."

"Uh-huh." Elisabeth gave her a knowing look. "Does your *friend* have a name?"

"Vince."

Elisabeth poked at her salad with her fork. "What's he like?"

"He's a great guy."

"And you like him a lot. I can tell."

"I do." There was relief in admitting this out loud, an easing of pressure. "But I'm not sure how he feels about me."

"Hmm. Then maybe you should ask him."

Tammy made a face. "I don't want to put him on the spot." And risk scaring him off.

"Okay. Then why not try a little experiment?"

"What do you mean?"

"Turn up the heat and see how he responds."

Tammy flashed back to the one kiss she and Vince had shared. There had been plenty of heat there, but nothing had happened since. "I don't know..."

"Oh, come on," Elisabeth said. "Just try a little seduction. If he goes for it, you'll at least know he's attracted to you physically. That's a place to start."

"Thanks for the suggestion, but that's not my style. Say, how long are you going to be in town? Mitch mentioned you weren't sure when you first moved here."

"I'm still not certain, though this place is growing on me.

And I like your brother. He and I have really clicked." The way she said the words—and the smile that accompanied them—left no doubt that Mitch had responded well to any seduction Elisabeth had directed at him.

But Tammy could have guessed that, seeing how besotted her brother was with this gorgeous woman.

Her phone buzzed, and she slipped it out of her pocket and checked the screen. Where are you? Russ had texted. She imagined the irritation behind the words. The editor wasn't known for his patience. "I have to get back to work," she said. She took out her wallet.

"Oh no." Elisabeth raised a hand. "This is my treat."

"Oh. Thanks. At least let me get the tip."

"It's all taken care of." She pulled out a sleek black credit card.

"Thanks. And I'll, uh, see you soon," she said, and made her exit. No one, she was sure, watched her as she hurried away.

Lunch had been…unsettling. Elisabeth had been friendly and the two women had gotten along, but Tammy realized she still didn't know anything about her brother's new girlfriend—except that startling revelation about a dead brother and two dead parents. Though she had mentioned when they first met that her father had recently died. Elisabeth had deflected any questions about herself, each time turning the conversation back to Tammy.

Maybe Elisabeth was a private person who didn't like to talk about herself. Tammy could respect that. But she wished she and her brother's girlfriend had connected better. Mitch liked her so much that Tammy wanted to like her too.

Some people take longer to warm up to than others, she reminded herself. If Elisabeth did decide to remain in Eagle Mountain, the two of them would have plenty of opportunities to get to know each other better.

VINCE WAS JUST stepping out of the shower Saturday morning when his phone alarmed with an Amber Alert for a missing teen. He was reading through the description of a fifteen-year-old male who had walked out of his family's home the night before when he received the call-out for search and rescue.

Fifteen minutes later, he gathered with other volunteers at search and rescue headquarters. "We're looking for Nicholas Gruber," Danny told the assembled rescuers. "Five feet nine inches tall. Blue eyes. Brown hair. Last seen wearing jeans and a black T-shirt and black running shoes." He lowered the phone from which he had been reading the description. "Apparently, Nicholas had a fight with his mom and dad last night and stormed out. He has done this before, and he always returns in the morning after he's had time to cool off. When he didn't show up this morning, they contacted all his friends, but no one has seen him."

"They must be worried sick," Carrie Andrews said. Vince remembered that she had two children of her own.

"The Grubers live on County Road 7, near Coal Canyon," Danny said. "Nicholas left the house on foot about nine o'clock last night. The sheriff wants to get Anna and her search dog, Jacquie, out there first to see if the dog can pick up the trail. We're on standby to assist in a ground search if they don't find him."

Everyone shifted to look at volunteer Anna Trent and the black standard poodle at her side. The dog, Jacquie, wore a blue vest with *Search Dog* in large white letters on the side. "We're ready," Anna said.

"You and Jacquie can ride with me," Deputy Jake Gwynn said.

He, Anna and the dog left, and the others moved in closer to Danny and Deputy Ryker Vernon. Bethany was there, standing next to Harper, across from Vince. She caught his eye and he nodded, then quickly looked away. He really didn't want to encourage her attention. "We've established a staging area for search volunteers at the lumber mill about a mile from the Grubers' home," Ryker said. "If you'll make your way there, you'll be handy if we need you to help search or if we find Nicholas and he's injured."

While several volunteers piled into the Beast, Vince opted to drive his own vehicle to the lumber mill. Or rather, the car his mother had insisted on lending him when she learned of the damage to his truck. The white Ford Escape was newer and more luxurious than Vince's truck, but he missed his own vehicle, which was still at the sheriff's department impound yard, awaiting the completion of their investigation. Vince wasn't pressuring them to give it back because he doubted he had the funds to pay for the work the truck would need to restore it.

Set back off the road in a stand of tall Douglas fir, the small mill specialized in deck railings, rustic benches and other rough-cut lumber projects. Though the saws were silent today, the smell of fresh sawdust hung in the air. Vince parked beside Ryan Welch's pickup and opened the driver's-side door to let in the scented breeze.

Ryan came over to stand beside Vince and was soon joined by Caleb and Eldon. "I hope Anna and her dog find the kid," Eldon said.

"He's probably just hiding out somewhere," Ryan said. "I did the same thing a couple of times when I was his age—blew up at my parents, then just had to get away for a while."

"Yeah, I guess I did too," Eldon said. "But I'd go stay with my aunt—my dad's younger sister. And she would call my dad and let him know where I was."

"I would go and stay at a friend's house for a couple of days," Caleb said.

The others looked at Vince, who shifted uncomfortably. "I guess I was lucky," he said. "I never fought with my parents." Even if he had, after what had happened with Valerie, he wouldn't have walked out on his mom and dad. It would have worried them too much not to know where he was, even for a few hours.

A loud whistle split the air, and they all turned toward the sound. Danny was standing in the bed of a pickup, motioning for everyone to gather.

"Anna and Jacquie found Nicholas," Danny said when everyone was assembled around the truck. "Apparently, he got disoriented in the darkness and slipped or fell into the canyon. He's okay, except he thinks he broke or sprained his ankle. We're going to have to get him out."

Relief that Nicholas was alive and not in imminent danger energized the group. They gathered equipment and set out to hike to the spot where the teen had fallen. A middle-aged man and woman, both with short hair in shades of brown, were already there. The man lay on his stomach, his attention focused on the boy sprawled fifty yards below. The woman sat beside the man. They both looked up as the rescuers approached. "We're Nicholas's parents," the woman said.

"We're with Eagle Mountain Search and Rescue." Danny introduced himself and shook hands with each of them. "If you could wait back there, away from the edge, we'll have your son with you in no time."

"All right." Mr. Gruber glanced down into the canyon. "He's barely hanging on down there. Are you sure you can get to him without him falling?"

"We'll take care of him." Danny put a hand on the man's shoulder and gently urged him farther back.

The rescuers moved in, the challenge of what they needed to do quickly apparent. The soil along the edge of the canyon was loose, crumbling and raining down onto the boy below repeatedly as they worked. "How are you doing, Nicholas?" Danny called down.

"I'm worried I'm going to fall," came the thin, strained reply. "My ankle's hurt, and every time I try to move, more rock falls."

"Stay still and hang on," Danny instructed. "We need to get things set up here, then we're going to come down to get you."

"Okay. But hurry." Nicholas's voice trembled with fear, but Vince thought he heard determination too.

They were forced to establish an anchor on a tree across the road and ended up using a shovel to dig to more compacted soil before Eldon began the initial descent. Vince helped with the rigging, monitoring the ropes and pulleys and passing whatever equipment Ryan requested as he helped first Eldon, then Danny to descend. Vince found himself holding his breath as the men searched for solid hand- and footholds, the descent slowed by the need to continually reroute to more stable ground. No wonder the kid had fallen.

"I wonder if I'll ever be able to do anything so dangerous."

Vince looked back and found Bethany standing there. She was focused on the scene unfolding below. Then her gaze shifted to him, and the brief, shy smile he had come to associate with her flashed across her face. "I've been doing a little climbing in Caspar Canyon. Sheri and Hannah and some of the others held a kind of clinic for female volunteers."

"That's good," he said.

"At least I know the names of everything now so I can help with the gear."

"You'll get more comfortable the more time you have in." Vince remembered his early days with the group, when he had been overwhelmed by the magnitude of the job they did and uncertain where he fit in with the team.

Bethany was focused on the rescue efforts again, which gave Vince time to study her. She had her dark brown curls pulled back in a low ponytail, and exertion or the breeze in the canyon had reddened her cheeks. She wasn't beautiful, exactly, but cute, in a girl-next-door kind of way. Valerie had been like that. In fact, she and Bethany had the same hair and the same dimple in one cheek. His heart stumbled in its rhythm at the thought, and he stared harder, waiting for some spark of recognition. But nothing happened.

He cleared his throat, and Bethany shifted her attention to him once more. "How long have you been in Eagle Mountain?" he asked.

"Two months."

"Do you have family here? Friends?"

"No. I came for the job at Peak Jeep." She shrugged. "I was ready for a fresh start."

"Why search and rescue?"

"I was looking for a way to get to know more people. And I wanted to do something that would make a difference. Oh, look. They've reached the boy."

Nicholas had been huddled against the ground, one hand over his head to shield him from the worst of the debris that rained down, though more than one fist-sized rock struck his back and many smaller pebbles or dirt clods peppered him.

But now the two rescuers reached him and established themselves on either side of him, and he slumped between them. Eldon fitted the boy with a helmet and harness while Danny assessed his physical condition. "I'm going to fit the ankle with an air boot and give him something for the discomfort," Danny radioed up to Sheri, who was serving as incident commander. "I can't find any other injuries, though he's a little dehydrated from being out here all night. We'll give him some water, and the paramedics can take charge once he's up top."

They sent down more lines, and with a volunteer on either side, Nicholas began the slow ascent. Once he slipped and cried out, but the safety gear arrested his fall, as it was designed to do, and the trio started up again.

Mr. and Mrs. Gruber had gradually moved closer and closer to the edge of the drop-off and were waiting to embrace their wayward son as soon as he stood, somewhat shakily, before them. "I'm sorry," Nicholas said. "I didn't mean to scare you."

His mother wiped at the tears streaming down her son's face, then dashed away her own. "You must have been frightened too, falling in the dark and spending the night not knowing where you were," she said.

"I was worried I'd never get to see you again," Nicholas said, and fought back a sob.

Paramedic Merrily Rayford approached. "We need to get you to the hospital to take care of that ankle," she said. "Mom and Dad can follow in their car."

Vince moved in to help with the ropes while Bethany cleared a path to the waiting ambulance. "That was pretty intense," Vince told Eldon as his fellow volunteer stepped out of his harness.

"Good ending, though," Eldon said.

"Bet he won't be so quick to storm out of the house next time," Ryan said.

"Or maybe his folks will pay a little more attention to how he's feeling," Caleb said.

Vince helped load the equipment, then headed for his car and drove back to his condo. He parked and looked up to find a familiar shapely figure standing in the glow of the light over his front door.

Chapter Thirteen

Vince's heart beat faster as he made his way to the front door. Tammy waved and held up the pizza box she was carrying. "Hey," he said as he drew closer.

"I heard about the rescue," she said. "I thought you might be hungry."

The aroma of pepperoni and cheese made his mouth water. "Thanks," he said, and fished out his keys. "Come on in."

He unlocked the door and she followed him inside. "I hope you don't mind me stopping by," she said.

"Of course not. It's always good to see you."

"I didn't know if you had other plans. After all, it's Saturday night."

"No plans," he said. "Just let me put away this gear."

"I'll meet you in the kitchen."

When he reached the kitchen, she was bent over, sliding the pizza into the oven. She glanced over her shoulder at his approach. "I thought I'd warm it up a little."

"Good idea." She was a little more dressed up than usual, in a pink top that showed a hint of cleavage and a bit of lace. She smelled good too. He wanted to nuzzle her neck and inhale deeply.

He slipped past her and turned away so she wouldn't see the erection this thought had aroused. "How did you hear about the rescue?" he asked as he took plates from the cupboard.

"I have an emergency scanner. It's handy for news stories."

"I'm surprised you weren't there, covering this one."

"Russ lives two houses down, so he volunteered to take it. Didn't you see him there?"

"I wasn't paying attention. I was focused on the rescue."

"Of course. How is the kid who fell?"

"He's going to be fine. And maybe less quick to run away the next time he and his parents don't see eye to eye."

"That's what happened? He ran away?"

"He probably just wanted to take a walk and let off steam, but he got disoriented in the dark and ended up falling into the canyon. The road is pretty narrow, and the soil on the edge was crumbling. It kept collapsing as we were working, trying to set up the rigging to bring him up."

"Sounds like it was a happy ending, though."

"Yeah."

She took the pizza from the oven and carried it to the table. Vince helped himself to a couple of slices. "What happened today made me think about Valerie," he said.

"Oh?"

"This kid was a few hundred yards from his house. When he first fell, he must have shouted for help, but those trees and the dirt and everything absorbs sound. Apparently, no one heard him. And though his parents said they searched for him, they couldn't see him where he was and couldn't hear him. I wonder if something like that happened with Valerie."

"I guess it could have happened that way," she said. "Though you would think, with so many people searching for her, they would have found something."

"Not if she ended up in a deep crevice or a long way from where she fell."

"That's terrible to think about."

It was, but he had tortured himself for years with speculation about his sister's fate. No need to pull Tammy into that. "Did you ever get into fights with your parents and leave the house to cool off when you were a teen?" he asked, thinking about his conversation with his fellow volunteers.

She plucked a piece of pepperoni from the pizza and popped it into her mouth. "I wanted to a few times," she said. "But I never did. My parents had lost one kid. They were terrified of losing another. It made them overprotective, and I chafed against that. But at the same time, I didn't want to hurt them. At least, not any more than they had already been hurt."

"Yeah. It was like that for me too," he said.

She set aside a pizza crust. "I can hardly remember anymore what Mom and Dad were like before my brother died," she said. "Their pain was part of them, like my mom's curly hair or my dad's cleft chin."

"Yeah. I guess you never get over something like that."

"Were your parents overprotective too?"

"Not exactly." It made sense that having lost one child, a parent would hold even more tightly to the offspring left behind. But it hadn't been like that in his house. How to explain it to her without making his parents sound like terrible people? "Losing Valerie was such a blow they kind of, I don't know, checked out for a while," he said. "They couldn't cope. I knew they loved me—and they tried, they really did. But it was like they were in so much pain they didn't have more of themselves to give. I was kind of on my own."

"Oh, Vince."

He winced at the sympathy in her voice. "It was okay. Most of the time, anyway. Birthdays were hard."

"Because it was her birthday too."

"Yeah. When we took that camping trip, my dad tried to make up for me missing my friend's party by saying that when it was my birthday, I could have a sleepover. Not a joint party with Valerie, the way it usually was, but a celebration just for me and my friends. But that never happened."

"Did they not celebrate your birthday at all?" Tammy asked.

"There were always presents and a cake. But there was too much sadness. It was like a weight, pressing us down." He shrugged. "I don't celebrate my birthday anymore. I can't." That day could never be only about him anymore.

"I'm sorry," she said. "But I get it. I always felt like I didn't just lose my brother when Adam died. Our whole family lost itself. We couldn't be the same family we were before, and we never figured out how to completely put ourselves back together."

"You can't," he said. "That one piece is always missing."

They ate in silence for a while, but it wasn't uncomfortable. Tammy was the only person he had ever known who truly understood what growing up had been like for him. And he knew what things had been like for her too. He felt closer to her right now than he had to anyone.

"You look nice tonight," he said.

She smiled, and her cheeks blushed a little pinker. "Thanks." She glanced down at the pink shirt. "I had lunch Thursday with my brother's new girlfriend, Elisabeth. She's always perfectly put together. I guess she inspired me to make a little more effort with my appearance."

"You always look good," he said.

Their eyes met, and in that moment he felt so...whole. As if he didn't need anything else but to be here, right now, with this woman.

They finished eating and carried their dishes in the sink. She started to turn on the water, but he put his hand on her arm. "Don't worry about those now," he said. "Let's go into the living room and talk."

They sat side by side on the sofa, but instead of saying anything, she leaned over and kissed him. Her lips were soft, their gentle pressure making him aware of every sensation firing in his body at her touch. She pressed her palm to his chest, over his heart, every hard beat reverberating through them both.

He pulled her close, clinging to her like a drowning man, a wave of longing almost pulling him under. He kissed her hard, then drew back a little to look at her. She stared back. Was he reading her true feelings in that look or his own emotional turmoil reflected back at him? "I really, really like you," he said.

She looked amused, and slid her hand down his chest to the waistband of his jeans. "I really like you too."

Words failed him as she traced the top of his waistband with one finger. "I want you, Vince," she said.

"Yes." He smothered any reply she might have made with another kiss, and followed eagerly as she lay back and pulled him down with her. He slid one hand beneath her shirt, gliding over the satiny skin of her stomach and up to cup one full breast. He fought the urge to tear at her clothing, wanting to see and feel all of her at once. Only now did he realize how much he had been holding back. "That first day we met, I was attracted to you," he said, nuzzling her neck. "Your perfume drove me wild."

"I don't wear perfume," she said.

"Maybe it's something else, but you smell amazing." He inhaled deeply and smiled. Vanilla, floral and definitely sexy. "Maybe it's just you."

"Mmm." She wrapped both legs around him, pulling him

even closer, and for a long while, conversation ceased as they lost themselves in playful discovery.

Finally, flushed and a little out of breath, she pushed against him. "Why don't we go into the bedroom?" she suggested.

He levered up on his elbows. He must have been crushing her. "Good idea," he said.

"Oh, I'm full of good ideas." The knowing smile that accompanied the words sent a fresh jolt of heat through him. Wanting something this much was exhilarating. And a little terrifying. *You've done this before*, he reminded himself as he took her hand and pulled her toward his bedroom.

That was true, but he wasn't sure getting it right had ever mattered so much.

TAMMY WASN'T A WEEPER. Sappy commercials and sad novels didn't make her tear up the way they did many of her friends. But lying here in Vince's bed had her blinking against a stinging in her eyes. Vince cared so much. He cared about her and how she felt. "Is that good?" he asked as he moved down her naked body. "Do you like that?"

"Everywhere you touch me feels good," she said. "Just keep doing what you're doing. I'll let you know if there's anything I don't like."

But there wasn't anything about him she didn't like—from the sculpted muscles of his arms and shoulders to the strong curve of his thighs, to the smile that pulled at his lips as he traced the lines of her body with his mouth, proof that he liked what he was discovering.

He had taken out a condom without her having to ask, and when they came together, he was gentle, holding back. She stroked his shoulders. "It's okay," she said. "You can't hurt me."

"I don't want to be too rough," he said, his voice ragged.

"You won't be."

He was less careful then, and she was soon caught up in the intensity. There was something erotic about seeing him like this, on the edge of control, and knowing she had brought him to this point. She had never been this aware of her partner's desire in the midst of her own, and that knowledge acted like a multiplier, heightening every sensation. They found a rhythm, hard and deep, and she gave herself up to it, riding the waves of sensation, not even minding as tears slipped out of the corners of her eyes as she reached her climax.

He trembled in her arms, and she held him tightly as he found his own release. They lay together for a long moment, not speaking, his weight heavy but still feeling good.

Finally, he levered off her. "I must be crushing you," he said, and moved to lie beside her.

"No, it was wonderful." She idly stroked his hair. "You're wonderful."

He didn't say *You're wonderful too*, or any clichéd response. Instead, he rested his head in the hollow of her shoulder and his hand across her stomach, cradling her as if she was so precious he couldn't find the words.

"I wish we could stay here like this all day," Vince said the next morning after he and Tammy had made love again. They lay in a tangle of sheets, sunlight pouring through the thin sheers over the bedroom window.

"We'd have to send out for food," she said. "And coffee."

He sat up. "I'll make coffee," he said. "And breakfast. But then I have to leave. I promised my dad I'd play golf with him today, and he likes to get an early tee time."

"My mom is making Sunday dinner for my brother and his girlfriend," Tammy said. "I need to be there too."

Vince pulled on his jeans, then looked over his shoulder at her. "I'd rather be with you."

That look—a little possessive, a lot lustful—sent a tremor through her. "I'd rather be with you too," she said. "But family is important."

"Of course it is." He opened a dresser drawer and pulled out a shirt. She began dressing also. Even if he had never put it into words, she figured he felt the same obligation she did. It wasn't enough that they be their parents' children. They had to try to make up for their missing sibling, impossible as that might be.

They parted at his front door with a passionate kiss. "See you later?" he asked.

"For sure."

She had texted her mother the night before to let her know she was spending the night "with a friend" and expected a full interrogation, and maybe a lecture, when she walked in. Instead, the only thing her mother said was, "I need you to set the table while I finish the rolls. Use the wedding china."

Tammy set down her bag and followed her mother into the kitchen. "This is just a casual dinner," she said. "You don't need to use the wedding china." The service for twelve had been a wedding gift from Tammy's great-grandmother, and was only used on holidays and special occasions. The rest of the time, it was displayed in a large buffet on one side of the dining room, dutifully removed and hand-washed each quarter to prevent a buildup of dust.

"This is the first time Mitchell has brought anyone home for dinner." Her mother began shaping dough into rolls and arranging them in a buttered pan. "I want everything to be special."

"You don't have to worry about impressing her, Mom," Tammy said. "She should be worried about impressing you."

"Just looking at Elisabeth, you can tell she comes from money." Mom plopped another roll in the pan. "She's used to fancy things."

"Did Mitch tell you that—that she comes from money?"

She paused in the act of shaping another roll. "No, but it's obvious. Those clothes she wears didn't come from the discount store, and I'm sure her haircut cost at least a hundred dollars."

"If Elisabeth likes Mitch, it's not because he has money," Tammy said, trying to quell her annoyance. "It shouldn't matter what kind of plates we serve dinner on."

"Still, I want to make a good impression."

Tammy went to the buffet and began removing four plates. "If I'd known this was going to be such a big deal, I would have invited a friend," she called back to her mother.

"You can invite your friend some other time," her mother said. "Today, I think the focus should be on Mitch and Elisabeth."

The excitement in her mother's voice set off alarm bells. Tammy returned to the kitchen. "What's going on?" she asked. "Is something happening I should know about?"

Her mother smiled—something she did so seldom the transformation of her features shocked Tammy. "I don't know for sure, but Mitch hinted around that he's serious about this young woman. I think he might propose soon. She could be part of our family before long, and I want her to feel welcomed."

"He's only known her a couple of weeks," Tammy said. "She hasn't even said if she's going to stay in town."

"If they marry, of course she'll stay in Eagle Mountain," her mother said.

Tammy returned to the dining room and tried to process this turn of events as she set the table. Her mother could be wrong. She might be reading more into the relationship than was there.

Then again, Elisabeth's eagerness to have lunch with Tammy last week could have been a way of reaching out to someone she saw as a future sister-in-law. A shudder went through her at the thought; then she immediately felt terrible. If her brother loved Elisabeth, Tammy would learn to love her too.

By the time Mitch and Elisabeth arrived, the table was set with the wedding china and fresh flowers, and the aromas of the Sunday roast and fresh-baked rolls perfumed the air. Elisabeth wore a sleeveless summer sheath in cherry-pink linen, with matching high-heeled sandals. Tammy, dressed in jeans and a T-shirt advertising a defunct local band, reminded herself she had nothing to be defensive about. "It's good to see you," she said.

"Everything looks lovely, Mrs. Patterson," Elisabeth said.

"Not as lovely as you, dear," Mrs. Patterson said. She had changed into slacks and a gauzy top Tammy had never seen before.

"Elisabeth always looks great," Mitch said, and pulled her closer. She smiled up at him, a pleased-with-herself look. Though maybe that was Tammy projecting. She was beginning to realize this wasn't going to be their usual laid-back Sunday meal.

For the next hour, Tammy's mother and brother remained focused on Elisabeth, showering her with compliments and asking her about herself. But while she revealed the same details Tammy already knew—she was from Nebraska and her family had all died—that was all they got. "What kind of work do you do?" Mrs. Patterson asked.

"Oh, I've done a lot of different things," Elisabeth said. "I helped my father manage his investments."

"Do you mean, trading stocks and bonds?" Tammy asked. "Or real estate?"

"Something like that." Elisabeth turned to Mitch. "Mitch had an exciting week. He thinks he's found a buyer for a big ranch near Delta."

Mitch looked pleased. "The deal isn't final yet," he said. "But it's looking promising."

"It would be the largest commission you're earned yet, wouldn't it?" Elisabeth said.

"Yes, it would."

"I could steer you toward some sound investments, if you're interested," Elisabeth said.

Was she legit, or was this some kind of scam? Tammy wondered, then immediately hated herself for thinking it. Her brother was smart enough to see through a scam, even through the rosy lenses of infatuation. And Elisabeth was allowed to be beautiful, charming and good with money.

"What about you, Tammy?" Elisabeth asked. "Did you report on anything particularly interesting this week?"

"The county commissioners agreed to buy a new grader for the road crew," Tammy said. "And the Elks Club has sold almost all of the tickets for the Fourth of July Jeep raffle."

Even Elisabeth's laugh sounded delicate and feminine. "You have to love what passes for news in a small town, don't you?"

"It's reassuring to know there's very little serious crime around here," Mitch said.

"I suppose so," Elisabeth demurred. "Though personally, I never minded a little more excitement."

"Then we'll have to make our own excitement," Mitch said.

Elisabeth smiled at him. "That's an excellent idea."

When the meal ended, Tammy offered to do the dishes.

Better to work off her bad attitude scraping plates than risk taking her annoyance out on her brother's girlfriend.

She was loading the dishwasher when Elisabeth came into the kitchen, a stack of dessert plates in hand. "These were overlooked on the side board," she said, and set them in the sink.

"Thanks," Tammy said.

"Let me help," Elisabeth said.

"No. Go back in with Mitch and Mom. I wouldn't want you to risk getting that beautiful dress dirty."

But Elisabeth made no move to leave. "How's it going with your friend—Vince?" she asked.

Tammy cursed her inability to hold back a blush. "It's going well."

"Did you do what I suggested? Turn up the heat a little?"

Tammy nodded.

"Didn't I tell you?" Elisabeth grinned, and Tammy couldn't help but grin back.

"What are you two plotting in here?" Mitch came in. He stood between them, one arm around each of them. "It's good to see my two favorite women getting along."

"Don't let Mom hear that," Tammy said. "She might feel snubbed."

"My two favorite young women, then." He released his hold on Tammy but took Elisabeth's hand. "Did Elisabeth tell you she's decided to stay in Eagle Mountain?"

"No. That's good news?"

"Of course it's good news," Mitch said. He turned to Elisabeth. "You were asking about my childhood. Mom pulled out her photo albums. You're going to get a laugh out of some of these shots."

They left, still holding hands, and Tammy returned her attention to the dishes. Whatever it was about Elisabeth that set her teeth on edge, she needed to let it go. She was a pleasant woman who had gone out of her way just now to be friendly. Tammy would return the favor. She wanted Mitch to be happy, and if Elisabeth was the one who made him happy, Tammy needed to find a way to tolerate her, even if she doubted she could truly love her.

Chapter Fourteen

Once every couple of months, Vince's dad invited Vince to play golf. He didn't have his father's love for the game, but he enjoyed the time they spent, just the two of them, walking the course and talking. Most of the conversations were superficial, but he still relished these moments with the man he admired most in the world.

"When do you think you'll get your truck back?" Dad asked after they had teed off that Sunday afternoon.

"I don't know. The sheriff's department hasn't completed its investigation." He hooked the shot, and the ball went sailing into the rough. "Do you and Mom need your car back? I could borrow one from a friend."

"No, you keep it as long as you like." They trudged toward Vince's wayward ball. "I was just wondering. Do they have any idea who did it?"

Vince lined up his shot and took it, hitting the ball back onto the fairway. "No. The sheriff asked if I thought it could be Valerie."

He expected his dad to be shocked or to protest that that wasn't possible. Instead, he looked thoughtful. "I've often wondered if she is still alive somewhere."

"Why do you think that?"

"Take your shot, son."

Vince's heart wasn't in the next strokes, but he managed to keep the ball on the fairway and eventually in the hole.

His dad led the way to the next tee box. "Why do you think Valerie is still alive?" Vince asked again. Had his dad been keeping something secret from him all this time?

"I suppose because we never found her," he said. "And because she's my daughter. It's a fanciful idea, I guess, but if she's dead, wouldn't I feel it? I know your mother feels the same way."

What did Vince feel? Valerie was his twin, yet he had long ago accepted she was dead. But what if she wasn't?

He waited until his dad had taken his shot before he spoke again. "If Valerie is alive, why not contact us?" he asked. "Why write cryptic notes or mess up my truck?"

"Maybe she's under someone else's control and this is her only way to communicate." He swung and connected with the ball, sending it straight up the fairway. He was so calm that Vince realized he must have spent a lot of time thinking about this possibility.

"Dad, she'd be twenty-five years old now. How could she be under someone else's control?"

"Someone could be threatening her, forcing her to do these things."

"But why? No one has asked for money. No one has tried to physically harm us. It's just…annoying." He took his stroke and sliced the ball to the right.

"And a little frightening." Dad put his hand on Vince's shoulder, a rare moment of physical closeness from his normally undemonstrative father.

"Yeah, it is frightening," Vince admitted. "I keep wondering what's going to happen next."

"If they want something, you'll find out," his dad said.

"Scammers are experts at the long game, reeling people in slowly."

"Is that what happened with you and that guy who claimed to be ex–special forces? The one you and Mom paid all that money to?" That had been a particularly elaborate scam, and a costly one. The man claimed Valerie was being held prisoner in a Mexican brothel, and that, with funds for their expenses, he and some other former military friends could rescue her.

His dad looked rueful. "I thought I was smart enough to see through all the liars by that time. Valerie had been missing five years, and I thought I had heard it all. But this man was a pro. He presented just the right image. I resisted him for a long time, but then he sent pictures—photographs of a young woman he claimed was Valerie. We could only see her from the back—that should have been my first clue this wasn't legit. But she had the same hair, and we could see the resemblance. He said if we paid for him and a team to fly down there, they promised to get her back. We wanted so much to believe, and he counted on that."

Vince's chest hurt, listening to this sad tale, even though he had known the basic outline for a long time. "I think anyone would have done the same in your shoes," he said.

They played through the next hole, the heaviness of their memories wrapped around them. After Vince's next shot, his dad said, "I never told your mother this, but I thought I saw Valerie once."

Vince's breath caught, and he stared. "Where? When?"

"Seven years ago. I had a work meeting outside of Omaha, Nebraska. A group of us visited a casino on the Missouri river one evening. There was this cocktail waitress—pretty, young, very friendly. I noticed her, but I wasn't paying any particular attention to her. Then one of the guys nudged me and told me she obviously liked me because she kept star-ing at me. I looked over, and she caught my eye and smiled. And—I recognized her. It was Valerie."

"In a casino in Omaha? Dad, why did you think it was Valerie?"

"Her eyes, and the way she looked at me. I hurried toward her, but she darted away. I spent the rest of the night search-ing for her. I even went back the following day and asked the manager about her. He said they didn't have any employees that fit the description I gave them. But I know what I saw."

"What did you do?" Vince asked.

"I took an extra day after the conference. I went back to the casino, then spent hours driving around the area. I guess I thought I might spot her again, but if she didn't want to be seen, there were a million places she could hide. I finally convinced myself that I must have been mistaken. I went back home and tried to forget about her. But I've always wondered."

"If Valerie is alive, I have to think she would want to see us," Vince said. "We're her family."

"I like to think that too, son. But we don't know what she's been through in the time she's been apart from us."

She isn't alive, he wanted to say but didn't. If it made his father feel better to believe his daughter wasn't dead, Vince wasn't going to dissuade him. But that kind of hope felt to Vince like a chain holding them all back. Valerie was dead. Until they accepted that, they could never move on.

MONDAY, TAMMY TRIED to focus on work, but her mind con-tinually drifted to thoughts of Vince, replaying the two amaz-ing evenings they had spent together. She thought she had been head over heels for a man before. The giddy sensation of wanting to be with someone every minute wasn't new.

But things with Vince were different. More intense, yet less stressful. They connected in a way she hadn't known was possible, and didn't feel any pressure to hide the "weird" side of herself from him. She hadn't realized how much she was holding back in other relationships until she got close to Vince.

"What are you grinning about?" Russ asked as he passed her desk that afternoon.

She immediately assumed a sober expression. "Nothing," she said.

"What are you working on?" he asked.

She glanced at her computer screen, the cursor blinking on the beginning of an unwritten paragraph—the same position it had been in for the last half hour. She started to repeat *Nothing* but thought better of it. "I'm writing that piece about the women's club rummage sale," she said. "And I'm finishing up my next piece about search and rescue."

"Don't forget the planning commission meeting at six."

She groaned. "Nothing ever happens at those meetings."

"Then why are they having a meeting?" he asked.

"So they can table making a decision on land-use codes— the same thing they've done the last three meetings."

"They can't table a decision forever," Russ said. "And when they reach a conclusion, our readers will want to know what it is."

She sighed. Russ was right, of course. And she did have the meeting on her calendar. It was just that she would 100 percent have preferred to spend the evening with Vince.

But the meeting did give her an excuse to text him. Though they hadn't made definite plans for tonight, she sensed that spending every night together was becoming a habit neither was in a hurry to break.

Can't get together tonight, she typed. I've got to cover the planning commission meeting.

She pressed Send and waited, not exactly holding her breath but unable to look away from the screen.

The phone vibrated, and a small thrill raced through her as she read his reply. Too bad. Guess I'll have to sit at home alone and think about my plans for next time we get together.

She started to type a reply asking for more specifics about what he had in mind but became aware of Russ watching her. "You're grinning again," he said.

She frowned and turned the phone so the screen was definitely out of Russ's line of sight. Looking forward to seeing you again, she typed. TTYL.

The meeting that evening proved as boring as she had anticipated, though the commission did spring for pizza from Mo's to feed themselves, Tammy and the two locals who showed up. At least she didn't have to listen to them debate the exact definition of *agricultural use* on an empty stomach.

By nine o'clock everyone in the room seemed to have had enough. The committee had agreed on some definitions and tabled other decisions until the following month. Tammy gathered her belongings and drove home. She debated dropping by to see Vince but decided instead to call him when she got in.

Her mind played out possible avenues for such a conversation as she climbed out of her car and headed up the walkway to her house.

Then something—or rather, someone—hit her with such force she was knocked off her feet. She didn't even have time to scream before her attacker landed on top of her and began pummeling her.

Chapter Fifteen

For a moment Tammy couldn't fight back or even breathe. She forced her eyes open, trying to see who was hitting her, but could make out only the shadowy outline of a figure dressed in dark clothing. Her attacker grabbed her hair and forced her head back, then rammed it into the dirt.

Pain rocketed through her and freed her from her momentary paralysis. She shoved against her assailant, then brought her knee up, hard, between the other person's legs. The reaction wasn't the one she had expected. Her attacker grunted, then laughed.

Whoever this was, Tammy realized they weren't much bigger than her. Another shove pushed them off her. She kicked out again, this time connecting with the other person's shin. She grabbed for any hold she could find and wrapped her hand around an ear and pulled hard.

This time her attacker screamed—a high-pitched wail of rage. They staggered up and began kicking at Tammy, who rolled away, then shoved to her knees.

By the time she got to her feet, whoever had assaulted her was running away, feet pounding hard on the pavement. Tammy stood, staggering a little as a wave of dizziness rocked her. The front door creaked open. "Tammy? Is that you?" her mother's voice asked.

The words forced her into action. She hurried to the door and gently urged her mother back inside. "Let's go in, Mom." She followed her mom into the front hall and locked the door behind them.

Mrs. Patterson stared at her daughter. "You're bleeding!" she said. "What happened?"

Tammy turned to the mirror by the door. Blood trickled from her swollen lip, and her hair was sticky with clotting blood. One eye was starting to swell, and her shirt was torn. "Someone attacked me right in our driveway," she said.

"We need to call the sheriff." Her mother looked around, as if searching for a phone.

"Yes. You'd better do that."

While her mother dialed 911 and talked to the operator, Tammy went to one of the front windows and peered out. Hers was the only vehicle visible near the house, and she could see no sign of her attacker, though the darkness past the circle of light from the porch was so intense she could scarcely make out anything.

"They're sending a deputy right away." Her mother came to stand beside her. "Let me clean up that cut," she said.

"No, thanks. I'll be okay until after the deputy gets here. They may want to take pictures or something." Was that only in cases of rape? Had that been the attacker's intent? This felt like violence for the sake of violence. Someone wanted to hurt her.

Deputy Declan Owen knocked on the door approximately ten minutes later. The handsome dark-haired deputy was relatively new to the Rayford County Sheriff's Department, but he had impressed Tammy as smart and professional. He studied her battered face for a moment when she opened the door, then said, "Why don't we sit down somewhere, and you can tell me what happened."

She led him to the living room, where they sat on either end of the sofa. Her mother took the armchair nearest Tammy and perched on the edge of the seat, hands knotted together. "I drove home from the planning-commission meeting, parked my car and started up the walkway," Tammy said. "Then someone attacked me. I hit the ground hard, my attacker on top of me, pummeling me. We wrestled for a few minutes, then I managed to fight them off and they ran away."

"Did you see your attacker?" Declan asked. "Can you describe them?"

She shook her head. "It was dark, and I think they were wearing dark clothing. I think they even had something covering their face, like a balaclava."

"How big a person? Did they say anything? Could you tell if it was a man or a woman?"

"Not much bigger than me," she said. "I think that's why I was able to shove them off. And I think... I don't think it was a man. They felt—softer. Like a woman. And...and I kicked them hard between the legs, and while they didn't like it, it didn't exactly disable them."

Declan made more notes on the pad in his hand. "Did they say anything?"

"Not a word."

"Do you have any idea who this was?"

"No. I don't know why anyone would attack me. Especially another woman."

"Anyone who might be upset by an article you've written lately?"

"No. I haven't written anything controversial lately. And when people get upset by an article, they write angry letters to the editor. Or they tell me to my face what I did wrong. This person just started hitting me without saying anything."

"Could it be a jealous girlfriend or wife who thinks you're involved with their husband or boyfriend?"

"No. I haven't been dating anyone." She blushed. "Well, I'm sort of seeing Vince Shepherd. But he doesn't have a girlfriend, or a wife." Not that she knew of, anyway.

Declan turned to Tammy's mom. "Did you see anything unusual this evening before Tammy came home?" he asked. "A strange car in the neighborhood, maybe someone who stopped by the house, looking for her?"

"No. I didn't know anything was going on until I heard a scream. I went to the door to see if Tammy had fallen in the dark or something."

"Did you get a glimpse of her attacker?" Declan asked.

"I'm sorry, no." Her mother frowned at Tammy. "I didn't know you were dating anyone."

"Vince and I are taking things slow," she said. She turned to Declan. "Have there been any other attacks like this?"

"No," Declan said. "Is there anything else you can tell us about the person who attacked you? Did they have long or short hair, or anything that stood out to you?"

"I think they had their hair covered, perhaps by the balaclava. I didn't feel any hair. Whoever it was, they were strong—and angry." She touched her swollen lip. "I need to clean up and get some ice on my face."

Declan stood. "I'll talk to your neighbors and see if any of them noticed anyone hanging around who shouldn't be in the area. Let us know if you think of anything else."

Tammy walked with him to the door. As soon as he was gone, her mother started fussing. "We should go to the hospital," she said. "You might need stitches."

"I'll be okay, Mom. I'm going to take a shower, then go to bed." The fight had left her exhausted, and in no mood to talk to anyone. Not even Vince.

"I'm going to call Mitch and ask him to come over."

"Mom, no. He's probably with Elisabeth."

"I don't care. I'll feel a lot safer with him here. She can come with him, if she likes."

Tammy studied her mother's placid expression. "You like her, don't you?"

"I like that she makes your brother happy. That's what I want most for both of you children."

"Do you worry that she's not right for him?"

"The most unlikely couples can make a good match," her mother said. "As long as each partner has an equal stake in making things work. Otherwise, there's going to be trouble ahead."

Tammy retreated to her bathroom. If she let herself, those terrifying moments on the ground with her assailant would replay themselves over and over and in her mind. Instead, she thought about Vince. The two of them seemed equally matched. And they were both equally hesitant to be hurt. Did that bode well for their future or mean they were condemned to never get close enough to last?

THE SEARCH AND rescue training Tuesday evening was mandatory for rookies like Vince, who were preparing for their SARTech II certification test. He took a seat at the end of a table, next to Grace Wilcox. Bethany turned to smile at him. "Hi, Vince," she said.

"Hey." The intensity with which she studied him unnerved him. He didn't want to be unfriendly, but he didn't want to encourage her attention either.

"Don't you have anything better to do on a Tuesday night?" Grace Wilcox asked as Eldon slipped past them to settle on her other side.

"It never hurts to refresh my memory," Eldon said. He

picked up a pencil and slotted it behind one ear. "Plus, May is out of town at an art show, and there's nothing good on TV. I might as well be here."

Danny moved to the front of the room. "Let's get started, everyone. Somebody dim the lights." He hit the button for the first slide. "We're going to start with some definitions."

A loud creak from the door interrupted him. Everyone in the room turned to see Tammy slip inside. "Sorry I'm late," she said, and took a seat at the back of the room. She had her head down, hair falling over one eye. Vince sat up straighter and tried to get a better look. Normally, he expected her to smile and maybe search the room for him, but she wasn't doing that. Was something wrong?

"It's okay," Danny said. "Let's get started with the first section."

They took a break after the first hour, and Vince made his way toward Tammy. He stopped short when she turned to look at him. One eye was swollen shut, and her lips were puffy. "What happened to you?" he asked. At the sound of his voice, everyone who hadn't already been looking their way turned toward them.

Tammy's face reddened. "Somebody jumped me outside my house last night when I got home from the meeting," she said. She put a hand on his arm. "I'm okay. Really."

"Who was it?" Eldon asked.

"I don't know," she said. "It was dark and I didn't see a lot, and they never said anything. I fought them off, and they ran away. Apparently, none of the neighbors saw anyone suspicious in the area." She put a hand to her face. "I know I look terrible."

"You look fine." Vince hesitated, then put an arm around her. "But I hate that you were hurt." He leaned closer and spoke more softly into her ear. "Why didn't you tell me?"

"I didn't want to upset you," she said. "You've got enough on your mind right now."

"Not too much to care about what happens to you," he said.

This made her smile, though she immediately winced, probably because her lip hurt.

"Are you thinking of joining search and rescue?" Bethany asked. She had moved up on Vince's other side and was studying Tammy with that piercing way of hers.

Tammy looked grateful for the change of subject. "No. I told Danny I wanted to write more about the training you guys undergo, and he suggested I attend the class tonight."

"It's an overview of the general knowledge we need to have," Danny said. "Though there's a lot more that goes into wilderness rescues."

"So I'm learning," she said.

"Is that your next article, about training?" Caleb asked.

"No. I'm going to write about the Denise Darling case."

A buzz arose as several people asked about Denise Darling, and others rushed to explain. Danny, being the most senior volunteer present, gained the floor. "She was a thirteen-year-old girl who disappeared during a youth hiking trip seven years ago," he said. "She became separated from her group and got lost. She was found eight days later, almost ten miles from the place she had last been seen."

"Was she alive?" Bethany asked.

"She was alive." Vince hadn't realized he had spoken loudly enough to be heard until everyone turned to him. "I remember the story," he added. "It was all anyone talked about for a while." And he remembered it because of Valerie. When Denise Darling had been found, his mother had burst into sobs. Not because she wasn't glad that a girl had been restored to her family, but because the same thing had never happened to them. Why wasn't Valerie ever found?

"I wonder what became of her," Danny said. "She did an amazing job of taking care of herself—better than most adults under similar circumstances."

"I'm still trying to locate her for an interview," Tammy said. "If I do, I'll let you know."

Danny checked his watch. "We'd better get back to work, or we'll be here all night."

Vince tried to focus on the material, but he kept looking back at Tammy's battered face. Who would hurt her that way?

He hoped the notes he was taking would help him cram for the SARTech test, because he had been too distracted to absorb much information tonight. As soon as Danny turned the lights up, he was out of his chair and headed for Tammy. She smiled at his approach. "Don't look so worried," she said. "I really am all right."

"Where did this happen?" he asked.

"Right in front of my house. I think the person might have been waiting for me. Either that or they followed me home from the planning-commission meeting."

"You're not making me less worried," he said.

She took both his hands in hers and squeezed. "Mitch is staying at the house for a while," she said. "I guess it does feel safer having him there."

"You're welcome to stay with me whenever you like."

"I like that idea." She rose on tiptoe and pressed her lips to his. He wrapped his arms around her and turned it into a proper kiss.

A shrill whistle sounded. "Hey, get a room!" someone shouted, followed by raucous laughter.

They pulled apart. "Why don't I follow you home?" she

said, and reached for her car door. She immediately recoiled, and let out a moan.

"What is it?" Vince took her arm. "What's wrong?"

She pointed, and now he saw that something red was smeared across the car door and windshield. He leaned around to examine the windshield and went cold all over when he read the message scrawled in the same red across the glass: *Next time you won't be so lucky. V.*

Chapter Sixteen

"It's not blood." Paramedic Hannah Gwynn cleaned the red goo from Tammy's hand. A crowd had gathered around the Subaru, and someone said the sheriff's department was on the way. Another volunteer had switched on the outdoor spotlights on the side of the building, flooding the gravel parking area with yellow-tinged light.

"I think it's stage blood." Jake Gwynn leaned closer to the car to study the smears of red. "It smells sweet, like corn syrup."

"Why would someone leave you a message like that?" Eldon asked.

"It's because of me," Vince said. His face was pale, the muscles along his jaw tight, as if he was grinding his teeth. He had both hands shoved in the pockets of his jeans and kept sneaking looks at Tammy, though he wouldn't directly meet her gaze.

Her hands clean, she moved to his side and took his arm. "This isn't your fault," she said.

"This was done by the same person who trashed my truck," he said. "It's probably the same person who attacked you last night."

"You can't know that," she said.

"The signature is the same." He pointed to the message on the side window.

She read the threatening words again, freezing when she came to the single *V*, like a check mark near the driver's-side windshield wiper. "I didn't notice the V before," she said.

"The message does seem to be referring to your previous assault," Jake said. "And I'm no expert on graffiti, but this looks similar to the writing on Vince's truck."

"At least they didn't smash my windows." She was trying to make a joke, but the effect was spoiled when her voice broke on the final words.

The crunch of tires on gravel signaled the arrival of a sheriff's department SUV. Sergeant Gage Walker exited the vehicle and strode toward them. Tammy had interviewed Gage many times for cases she had reported. Though similar in appearance to his brother, the sheriff, Gage was more easygoing and less intimidating. He nodded to Tammy, then studied the red-smeared car and the sinister message. Then he turned to the crowd. "I'll talk to the rest of you in a bit. Meanwhile, give us some room, will you?"

The others moved away, herded by Jake. Gage turned back to Tammy. "Tough way to end the night," he said.

"It sure is."

"Any ideas who's behind this and the attack on you last night?" he asked.

"None."

"I think it's the same person who trashed my truck," Vince said. "The same person who sent those notes about Valerie."

"*V*," Gage said. He stepped back and took a few photos of the car, then turned to Tammy. "Why threaten you?" he asked.

She glanced at Vince. Their relationship wasn't exactly a secret, but she also wasn't sure where they stood. "Tammy and I are friends," he said. "Good friends. If this 'V' has been watching me, they've seen us together. Maybe they think hurting Tammy is a way to get back at me."

"I read the report on your assault," Gage said. "You told Declan you thought your assailant was a woman?"

"Yes." Vince frowned at her. Something else she hadn't told him. But again, she hadn't wanted him to worry. If V and her attacker were the same person, did that mean it was Valerie? Or someone pretending to be her?

"Why would V want to get back at you?" Gage asked.

"I'm not sure whoever this is has a reason," she said. "Or at least, not one that would make sense to us."

"In some of the communications, V seems to be assuming the role of Valerie," Vince said.

"Any chance this is your sister?" Gage asked.

"The sheriff asked me that too," Vince said. "I don't know. Valerie disappeared fifteen years ago. Why appear out of nowhere now, and why try to hurt me?"

"When you came here tonight, did you see anyone or anything out of the ordinary?" Gage asked.

"No. And I was looking. After what happened last night, I was spooked."

Gage took her through her steps that evening, from the time she left the newspaper office until she drove to search and rescue headquarters, and verified that she was the last person to arrive at the meeting.

"No one arrived or left after you?" Gage asked.

"No one," she said.

"I didn't see anyone come or go," Vince said.

"All right. We'll process the scene and see if we come up with anything," Gage said. "You'll need to leave your car here. Do you have someplace safe to stay tonight? And what about your mother? Is she home alone?"

"My brother is with her. He's moved in temporarily."

"I'll see that Tammy gets somewhere safe," Vince said. He straightened and took his hands from his pockets. "Do you need anything else?"

"Not right now," Gage said. "I may have more questions later."

"I have a backpack in the car I'd like to grab," she said.

Gage slipped on a glove and opened the back door of the vehicle, and waited while she leaned in and took out the backpack. "Check to verify nothing is missing," he said.

She did so, pawing through the notebooks, extra camera battery, tape recorder and other tools of her trade. "Everything looks okay."

"You're free to go, then."

Vince led her a little ways to the white Ford Escape he was driving these days. "It's my mother's," he said by way of explanation.

Tammy stashed her pack in the back seat, then slid into the passenger seat. Vince drove without speaking, not to her home but to his condo. "I'd feel better if you stayed here tonight," he said. "You can call your mother and brother to let them know you're okay."

"I'd like that." Spending the night alone, even with her brother and mother in other parts of the house, would be too uncomfortable. Even though Vince might be right and the attacks on her might be because V was targeting him, she felt safer with him beside her. If V came around again, it would be two against one.

He carried her pack into the house. Once inside, he pulled her close. "I felt awful when I saw you tonight, hurt." He brushed his lips across her swollen eye, then barely touched her wounded lip. "When I think I could have lost you—" His voice broke.

"You didn't lose me. I'm okay and I'm right here." She

kissed him. It didn't hurt. Instead it felt good, the way his strong arms around her felt good. The kiss ended, and she looked into his eyes, trying to judge what he was feeling. "I'm sorry I didn't tell you about the attack right away. It was just...a lot to process. I wanted time to think."

"You think it was a woman?" he asked.

"I think so. She wasn't much bigger than me, and she didn't feel like a man."

He loosened his hold on her a little. "What do you want to do now?" he asked.

"I can think of a few things." She smiled. "But first, I want to take a shower." Her hand was still slightly sticky from the fake blood, and she wanted to wash away the whole experience.

"Let's take one together," he said.

"Mmm." A pleasant heat washed through her at the thought. "Let me call my mom first so she doesn't worry."

She was surprised when her brother answered the phone. "Mitch, why are you answering Mom's phone?"

"She's in the bathroom and I saw the call was from you. What's up?"

Maybe it was better not to have to explain everything to her mother. "I'm staying with a friend tonight," she said.

"Do you mean, Vince Shepherd?"

"How do you know about Vince?"

"Elisabeth told me you and he had something going on. I'm cool with that, as long as he treats you right."

"I don't need your permission to date someone," she said.

"I'm just saying I think Vince is okay. Don't be so touchy."

"Is Elisabeth there with you?"

"No. She said she had something else to do tonight. To tell you the truth, I think she was uncomfortable with the idea of being here with you and Mom. She thinks the two of you don't like her."

"That's not true," Tammy said. "We hardly know her."

"Yeah, well, it's okay. I'll see her tomorrow."

"And I'll see you tomorrow," she said. "Make sure Mom knows I'm okay."

"Have a good night."

She ended the call and pocketed her phone. "Everything okay?" Vince asked.

"It's fine." She moved closer. She didn't want to talk about her brother or Elisabeth or anything outside the safety of these four walls. She wrapped her arms around him. "What about that shower?"

VINCE LAY AWAKE after Tammy had fallen asleep. He might never think about his shower the same way after tonight. Something about steam and soap and slick skin... It had been just what he needed after the shock of seeing her battered face, then reading the sinister message written in what he was sure was supposed to resemble blood on her car.

His phone vibrated, then the first notes of the ringtone sounded. He lunged for it, silencing it before it could wake Tammy. Then he sat on the side of the bed and checked the screen as the phone continued to vibrate in his hand. Unknown number. Which usually meant spam, but he'd better check in case it was a search and rescue call from one of the team members.

He spoke softly. "Hello?"

"Vin, Vin, Vinnie, Vince."

The singsong chant sent a cold shock through him. "Who is this?" he snapped.

"'Vince and Tammy sitting in a tree, *k-i-s-s-i-n-g*.'"

"Who is this?"

"You know who this is. Or have you forgotten your sister so soon? The twin Mommy and Daddy gave away. You thought you would all be happier without me. But I can't let that happen, can I?"

"Valerie?" He choked on the name as fear and disgust—that someone would stoop to impersonating his sister—warred with hope that she was alive. "Is that you? Where are you?"

"Closer than you think. But I'll never tell."

"Valerie, I—" The phone went dead. He stared at the screen, then hit the recall button. Nothing happened.

"What is it?"

He glanced back to find that Tammy had rolled onto her back and was looking at him. "Crank call," he said, and set the phone aside.

"You said, 'Valerie.'" She sat up now and put a hand on his arm. "Tell me."

He told her about the call. The whole experience had been surreal, but talking about it solidified the details in his mind. He hadn't dreamed it. "Did it sound like Valerie?" she asked.

"I don't remember what she sounds like. It was so long ago. But she used to sing that rhyme, about kissing in a tree."

"I used to sing that rhyme. It's something kids do."

"She started out the call saying 'Vin, Vin, Vinnie, Vincent.' She used to do that too, when she was trying to annoy me."

She leaned against him, soft and warm against his back. "We should call the sheriff."

"What are they going to do? Add this to their growing file of harassment?" He lay back down and pulled her close. "I don't want to deal with them now. Do you?"

"No." She laid her head on his shoulder.

"I had another call from Valerie once," he said. "Or someone claiming to be her. I was fifteen and home with a friend. My parents were out, and when I answered the phone, the person on the other end said she was Valerie and needed me to help her. Then she hung up. It sounded just like her."

"Oh, Vince, what did you do?"

"I told my parents and they called the police. They traced the call to a broken pay phone somewhere in another state. I remember being angry at Valerie for teasing me that way. My parents finally persuaded me that it had to be a cruel joke. This was probably the same thing."

"Whatever it is, it's horrible," she said. "But we'll get through it. Together."

"Yeah." He tightened his arm around her. As if that was all it took to protect them both. "I'm scared," he said. "Then it feels silly to be scared of someone who writes vague notes and makes prank calls."

"It's like being harassed by a ghost," she said. "That's pretty scary."

"I don't believe in ghosts," he said. "Whoever is doing this is a real person."

"I don't know what to tell you, except that I'm here for you."

"As long as you don't get hurt again. You should think about keeping your distance from me, at least for a while." He had to force the words out, but keeping her safe was more important than his own feelings.

"No way." She squeezed him tighter. "I'm sticking with you."

"I'm that irresistible, am I?"

"You are."

"I'm never going to be able to sleep now," he said.

"Me neither. What should we do instead?"

"We could play cards," he said, his voice teasing.

Her arm snaked around his waist. "I have a better idea."

"Tell me about it."

"I'd rather show you. After all, they say actions speak louder than words."

He rolled forward and pressed his body against hers. "Then I'm ready to hear everything you have to say."

ON WEDNESDAY, Gage Walker stopped by the *Eagle Mountain Examiner* office. Tammy's stomach gave a nervous shimmy when she spotted him standing in the doorway in his neat khaki uniform. "Hello, Gage," she said. "Can I help you?"

"I'm dropping off the weekly sheriff's report." He held up a single sheet of paper. The report—a summary of the number and types of calls made by the department during the previous week—was one of the paper's most popular features. People seemed to delight in reading about calls to chase bears out of people's gardens or put cows back into pastures. They speculated on who might be behind the more serious entries, from drunk driving arrests to domestic violence calls. But the report was usually delivered by a civilian clerk or a duty officer, not the force's second-in-command.

Gage approached Tammy's desk and handed over the report. "Any more word from V?" he asked.

"No. She hasn't contacted me." It seemed easier to refer to V as female since that was how she thought of her since the attack.

"What about Vince? Has he heard anything?"

"I don't think so." She had never been a proficient liar, and she was sure Gage would see through the falsehood. She had tried to persuade Vince to tell the sheriff's department about the late-night call from someone pretending to be Valerie, but he had refused, convinced they wouldn't be able to do anything.

"Did you find any fingerprints or DNA on my car?" she asked, hoping to divert Gage's attention.

"No. Not on Vince's truck either." He held up a finger. "But that's not for the paper."

"I know, Gage. I'm not writing about either incident."

"I just want to be clear. Tell Vince to get in touch if he hears anything else from V."

"I will." She stood and walked with him to the door. "I guess I'll see you at the Fourth of July festivities tomorrow?"

"I'm on duty in the morning," he said. "In the afternoon, I'm working the Elks' Fun Fair."

"I'll stop and say hello. Maybe get a picture for the paper."

When she was sure he was gone, she went into the back room, where old issues of the paper were stored, and pulled out her phone. When Vince answered, she said, "Gage was just here. He was asking if I had heard anything from V."

"What did you tell him?"

"I told him no. That wasn't exactly a lie, since she didn't call me. But then he asked if you had heard from her. I lied about that too."

"It doesn't matter. It was just a prank call. We haven't heard from her again."

"You're working the Fun Fair tomorrow, right? So is Gage. He'll probably ask you about V."

"My parents will be with me. I'll tell him I don't want to talk about any of this with them there. He'll respect that."

"Okay. I'll see you later, then."

"I'm making fajitas for dinner."

"Then I won't be late."

Though it wasn't official, she had all but moved into Vince's condo. Her mother hadn't even objected when she stopped by the house to get her clothes. "I feel better knowing you have a man to protect you," she said.

The feminist in Tammy resented the implication she couldn't look after herself, but the realist admitted having a strong, fit man who had made it clear he would do anything to protect her did make her feel safer. What neither of them admitted out loud was that they wouldn't be able to truly relax until V was identified and stopped. That didn't seem likely to happen anytime soon, so better for the two of them to stick together.

Chapter Seventeen

The next day, Tammy and Vince headed to the town park together. "How are you feeling?" he asked when they met, He studied her face. "The swelling is almost all gone and the bruises aren't as noticeable."

She resisted the urge to touch the worst of the bruises, which she had attempted to cover with makeup. "I'm fine. Really."

"Glad to hear it." He kept his arm around her on the walk to the park, but once there, they parted ways. Tammy was taking photographs of the parade while Vince helped set up the search and rescue booth. Later, she would take pictures of the Fun Fair while he fulfilled his duties at the SAR booth and the first responders' part in the festivities. He was also meeting his parents to spend time with them. The plan was for her to join them as soon as she was free. Later that evening, they would enjoy the fireworks.

The Eagle Mountain Fourth of July Parade was everything a small-town parade should be, from the high school marching band to dignitaries waving from fire trucks to clusters of kids pedaling red, white and blue-bedecked bicycles. Members of the historical society, dressed in turn-of-the-last-century garb, threw candy from a float decorated with papier-mâché rocks and old mining implements, while a trio of miniature horses and one full-size camel from a local hobby ranch enchanted onlookers.

The mayor's six-year-old son brought up the rear of the parade, riding a donkey with a placard attached to its backside that read *Follow My Ass to the First Responders Fun Fair*.

After a detour to photograph the historical society members handing out lemonade and brownies in front of the town museum, Tammy headed for the park, where the Fun Fair was in full swing. At the search and rescue booth, which was festooned with colorful T-shirts for sale and photographs from past rescues, she learned that Vince had just completed his shift. She took a photo to possibly run with her article, then hurried across the park, where she found Gage Walker supervising a pillow fight between two boys who straddled a sawhorse and flailed at each other until one slid to the sawdust below.

"Have you seen Vince?" she asked Gage after he had helped the children to their feet and sent them on their way.

"I think he's over at the dunking booth." Gage grinned. "He's probably pretty wet by now."

She had to stop and ask two people for directions to the dunking booth, but she arrived in time to see Vince, in swim trunks and nothing else, climb onto the narrow perch over a tank of water. "Just remember, that water's really cold," Deputy Shane Ellis teased Vince, egging on the crowd. "Five dollars for three throws," he said, holding up a baseball. "All the money goes to local first responders. Who wants to throw out the first pitch?"

"Why don't you show us how it's done, Shane?" someone called from the crowd.

"That wouldn't be fair, would it?" Shane demurred. He was a former big-league pitcher. Though an injury had ended his career, he was still feared on the local softball field.

"I'll go first." Ryan Welch stepped forward and handed over a five-dollar bill. His first pitch went wild, banging hard against the wood to the left of the target.

"A little more finesse there," Shane advised.

The second throw came closer but still failed to hit the bull's-eye.

"Come on," Vince taunted. "I'm getting hot up here."

Ryan clenched his jaw and palmed the ball, then hurled it, striking the bull's-eye dead center and sending Vince plunging into the tank.

He came up sputtering and laughing as the crowd cheered. Tammy snapped a series of photos; then he returned to his perch and Shane called for someone else to take a turn.

"Hey, Tammy."

She turned to see Mitch and Elisabeth working their way to her through the crowd. "So, that's Vince!" Elisabeth waggled her eyebrows at Tammy.

Mitch looked toward the dunk tank. "Looks like he's all wet," he said.

"Even better, huh?" She nudged Tammy.

"Anyone else want to take a try?" Shane called.

"I'll do it." Mitch raised his hand and pushed forward.

Elisabeth moved in closer to Tammy. "I didn't know Mitch was an athlete," she said.

"He's not." Tammy winced as her brother's first ball sailed past the dunk tank altogether. A trio of children chased after it.

"Steady there, Rocket," Shane said, and handed him another ball. "Go a little easier."

Mitch nodded and launched the second ball, which bounced harmlessly off the side of the tank.

Elisabeth cupped her hands around her mouth. "Go, Mitch!" she shouted.

Mitch waved back at her, then turned and fired the third ball toward the target. It glanced off the edge, but without enough force to trip the trigger. The crowd groaned.

"Let me have a try!" Elisabeth called, and waved her hand.

Applause greeted her arrival. To the delight of the crowd, she dusted off the ball with her shirt, then leaned forward like a pitcher waiting for a sign. Then she straightened and let the ball fly. It landed harmlessly in the grass, just shy of the target.

"Put a little more behind it this time," Shane advised, and handed her a second ball.

This one struck to the left of the target. Vince clapped his hands together. "You can do better than that!" he shouted.

Elisabeth glared at him and accepted the third ball. This time she stared not at the target, but at Vince, until he looked away. She wound up, then let the ball fly. It hit the center of the target, and Vince went down with a shout. The crowd roared its approval.

"Way to go, babe," Mitch said as Elisabeth rejoined him. He hugged her close. She accepted congratulations from those around her.

"That was fun," she said. "What should we do now?"

"I don't know," Mitch said. "Do you want—"

But before he could finish the sentence, Elisabeth was moving away. "I just saw someone I need to talk to," she called over her shoulder, and was gone.

"What was that about?" Tammy asked.

"I don't know." Mitch stared after her. She was weaving through the crowd, already a quarter of the way across the park. "I'd better go after her," he said, and left.

"It's Tammy, isn't it?" An older couple squeezed in beside her. The woman smiled. "I'm Vince's mom. I thought I recognized you from your picture in the paper."

"It's good to meet you." She nodded to Mr. Shepherd.

"Have you been here long?" Mrs. Shepherd asked.

"Long enough to see Vince get dunked twice," Tammy said.

"Us too." Mr. Shepherd smiled, fine lines deepening at the corners of his eyes. "He looks like he's having fun up there."

A loud creak and a cheer from the crowd signaled that Vince had once again been dunked. "Three strikes and you're out," Shane announced. "Give us a few minutes, folks, and we'll have your next victim—I mean, volunteer—up."

He handed Vince a towel as he emerged from the tank. "Let's go see if he's ready for lunch," Mrs. Shepherd said.

The three of them met Vince as he was pulling on a T-shirt. "Give me a second to change into dry pants, and we'll get some food," he said.

"It's good to see you," Mrs. Shepherd said to Tammy. "Are you working on anything interesting right now?"

"I'm doing another piece about the search and rescue team," she said.

"Vince has told us about some of the rescues he's been on," Mrs. Shepherd said. "We're so proud of him for volunteering, though I worry about the dangerous situations he gets into."

"One thing I've learned in researching my articles is that the search and rescue team trains a lot, and they always put safety first. They've never lost a rescuer."

"That's reassuring."

Vince joined them. He put one arm around Tammy. "Can you join us for lunch?" he asked. "Or do you have to work?"

"I might try to get a few shots of the fireworks tonight, but I'm free for the rest of the afternoon."

"Great. Let's hit the food booths. I'm starved."

They followed the scent of barbecue ribs and roasted corn to a parking lot filled with food trucks and refreshment booths. Tammy ordered shrimp tempura from one truck, while Vince and his dad opted for the ribs, and Mrs. Shepherd chose a hot dog. "That looks delicious," she said, nodding to Tammy's tempura. "But I guess I'm a traditionalist."

"We always grilled hot dogs and brats on the Fourth when the kids were little," Mr. Shepherd said.

Someone who wasn't watching closely would have missed the sadness that fleetingly shadowed Vince's mother's face. Though she had acted cheerful all morning, now that she was closer, Tammy could read the strain in the dark circles beneath her eyes and the slight tremor in her hand as she poked a straw into her drink. When she noticed Tammy watching her, she leaned closer. "You haven't heard anything more from V, have you?" she asked softly.

"No." Vince had told her he had decided not to tell his parents about the attack on her, the message on her car or the late-night phone call. "Hearing all that would just upset and worry them," he had said. She had agreed. As much as she hated the harassment V had aimed at her and Vince, at least she hadn't targeted these two older people, who had suffered so much.

They finished lunch and spent another hour walking around the park, visiting the various vendors and stopping to listen to a woman who played "America the Beautiful" on a hammered dulcimer.

"I'm walked out," Mrs. Shepherd said as they approached the food court again.

"Time for us to head home," Mr. Shepherd said.

"You're not staying for the fireworks?" Tammy asked.

"We can see great fireworks from our backyard in Junction," Mrs. Shepherd said. "Maybe not as spectacular as here in the mountains, but when they're done, we can go right to bed." She laughed. "I can see the idea is appalling to you, but when you get to be our age, it's a plus."

They each hugged Vince goodbye, then surprised Tammy by embracing her too. "Your parents are such nice people," Tammy said when they were gone.

"They are." He slipped his arm around her shoulders. "But it's good to be alone with you too."

"Was the water in the dunk tank cold?" she asked.

"Icy." He grimaced.

"It was for a good cause." She patted his chest. "And you looked good up there."

"That was your brother who tried to take me down toward the end, wasn't it?"

"Yes, that was Mitch. And the woman who got you afterwards is his girlfriend, Elisabeth."

"Elisabeth who?"

She frowned. "I don't remember." She or Mitch must have said, but the name escaped her. "She's from Nebraska, I think. Though I guess she's decided to stay here."

"Where in Nebraska?"

"I don't remember. Why?"

"She looked familiar."

"You've probably seen her around town. She's the kind of woman men notice."

"Nah. Not my type." He grinned. "I prefer curly-haired blondes."

They spotted Gage and Travis Walker, and Vince waved. The two law enforcement officers joined them. "I saw you at the dunking booth," Gage said. "You got soaked."

"Next year, I'm going to lobby for them to fill the tank with warm water," Vince said.

"It wouldn't be nearly as fun then."

"You can both pick your vehicles up from our impound

lot tomorrow," Travis said. "We weren't able to get a great deal of information off of them, unfortunately."

"I'll have to call a wrecker to haul mine away," Vince said. "I wish you could find who did that and make them pay for the repairs."

"No more love letters from V?" Gage asked.

"None," Vince said. Which wasn't a lie, Tammy reminded herself. Gage hadn't asked about phone calls.

She waited until the lawmen were some distance away before she asked, "Have you had any more phone calls?"

"No. I'm hoping we're done with all that. Whoever it was has moved on to bothering someone else."

She slipped her hand in his and they walked on, their lighter mood from earlier subdued. But they had a whole afternoon to regain that lighter feeling. And fireworks tonight, which never failed to lift her spirits.

"I need to stop here for a minute," she said when she spotted the restrooms. She slipped away to the ladies' room, leaving him waiting outside. When she emerged a few minutes later, Vince was talking to a dark-haired woman—one of the other search and rescue volunteers, Tammy remembered.

At Tammy's approach, the woman looked up, then hurried away. Tammy stared after her. "Who was that?" she asked.

"Bethany Ames. She's with search and rescue."

"Why did she run away when she saw me?"

Vince made a face. "I think she was embarrassed. She asked if I wanted to watch the fireworks with her tonight. I told her I was going with you. She stammered an apology and left."

Amused, she slipped her hand in his. "I didn't realize I had competition."

"No competition. Bethany isn't my type."

"She's cute."

"Yeah, but…she's a little too intense, you know? Something about her puts me off."

"How long have you known her?" Tammy asked.

"Not long. She just moved to town and joined the group."

Was it a coincidence that this woman had moved to town and taken an interest in Vince at the same time someone had started harassing him?

"What is it?" Vince asked.

"Nothing?"

"Are you sure? You look worried."

"It's nothing." No sense worrying Vince. She would do a little digging on her own to see what she could find out about Bethany Ames before she said anything. "Let's go back to the music stage," she urged. "There's supposed to be a bluegrass band there at four. I've heard good things about them."

The band deserved the praise she had heard, and she and Vince were soon tapping their toes and nodding their heads in time to the lively music. She was so engrossed that she didn't realize Vince had received a phone call until he moved away. One look at his expression set her heart racing, and she hurried to his side.

His eyes met hers, stricken. "It's my dad," he told her, then spoke into the phone again. "Are you and Mom okay? All right. I'll be there as soon as I can."

He ended the call, then pulled Tammy away from the crowd that had gathered to listen to the music. "My parents got home, and there were fire trucks lining their street. The fire was at their house."

Chapter Eighteen

"I'm coming with you to your parents'," Tammy said. It wasn't a question.

"You don't have to do that." He dug his keys out from his jeans pocket. Was there anything else he needed to do before he left?

"I want to come," she said.

"What about the fireworks photos?"

"Russ can take them. I want to be with you. And your parents."

He grabbed her hand and squeezed it. "Thanks. That means a lot."

He thought she understood what he was saying. After Valerie had disappeared, Vince had been left alone, his parents distracted by grief. It became a point of pride to get through things alone. Not having to do that anymore was a special gift.

They started walking toward his car. "Dad said the fire is out and most of the damage is to one upstairs bedroom," he said. "The rest of the house is okay except for smoke damage. He and Mom are waiting for the fire department to give them the green light to go inside."

"Do they have any idea what started it?" Tammy asked.

"Dad didn't say. The house is at least as old as I am. Maybe there was a fault in the electrical wiring?"

They didn't say much on the drive to Junction. Vince gripped the steering wheel and forced himself to keep within ten miles of the speed limit, willing the time to pass more quickly. His dad had said there wasn't a lot of damage, but what did that mean? Would his parents be able to remain in the house, or did they need somewhere else to stay? Was the fire an accident or deliberate? And why was all this happening now?

A lone fire truck sat at the curb when they arrived. A firefighter and a Junction police officer met them at the end of the drive, where Vince's parents also waited. "We're confident the fire is out," the firefighter said. "But call if you see any more smoke or flames."

"I don't understand," Mr. Shepherd said. "How did the fire start?"

The police officer introduced himself as Sergeant Fisk. "Where were you today, Mr. Shepherd?" he asked.

"We were in Eagle Mountain, visiting our son and attending the Fourth of July celebration," Dad said.

"Does anyone else live in the house besides you and your wife?"

"No."

"Do you know of anyone who might want to harm you and your wife or your home?"

"No. What are you talking about? Are you saying the fire was deliberately set?"

"The blaze started in the upstairs back bedroom," Fisk said. "Whose bedroom is that?"

"No one's," Dad said.

"That was our daughter, Valerie's, room," Mom said, her voice strained.

"Where is your daughter now?" Sergeant Fisk asked.

Her face crumpled and tears slid down her cheeks. Dad

pulled her close. "Our daughter disappeared fifteen years ago," he said. "We don't know where she is."

Fisk looked back toward the house. From this angle, it appeared undamaged. "Did someone set the fire intentionally?" Vince asked.

"It looks that way," Fisk said. He turned back to Vince. "You're the son?"

"Yes. I'm Vince Shepherd."

The officer turned to Tammy. "And you are?"

"Tammy Patterson. I'm Vince's friend."

"You two were in Eagle Mountain this morning also?"

"Yes," Vince said. "Tammy was taking photographs for the paper, and I worked a fundraising booth for the local search and rescue group. How did the fire start?"

The firefighter spoke. "Someone piled a bunch of papers—pages torn from books, from the looks of things—and set the fire in the middle of the bed. The neighbor whose backyard adjoins this one saw the smoke and called 911." He turned to Mr. and Mrs. Shepherd. "You can return to the house, but don't go into that bedroom. You'll need to have a restoration company see about cleaning it up. There's a lot of smoke damage, and we can't be sure there isn't structural damage from the flames."

Mom moaned, and Dad tightened his arm around her. "Did anyone see somebody near the house this morning?" he asked.

"We spoke with the neighbors," Fisk said. "No one remembers anything unusual. Have any of you noticed anything out of the ordinary recently?"

"No," Dad said. Mom shook her head.

Vince felt Tammy tense beside him, but he said nothing.

They waited until the firefighter and Sergeant Fisk had left before they went into the house. Vince smelled smoke when they entered, but the scent wasn't as strong as he had expected. He followed his mother and father up the stairs, Tammy behind him. The closer they walked to the bedroom, the more intense the odor of smoke.

They halted outside the bedroom. His dad pushed open the door to reveal the smoke and soot-blackened remains of a little girl's bedroom. Parts of the pink comforter on the bed were still intact, though the center was a black hole. Half a dozen books lay scattered at the foot of the bed, some splayed with spines showing, others with charred pages. Black outlines showed where flames had charred the walls, and everything was sodden.

Mom turned away, sobbing, and fled past them down the hall. Vince started to go after her, but his dad took hold of his arm. "Let her go," he said. "She needs a little time alone." He closed the door, and the three of them returned to the living room.

"Why didn't you tell the police about the notes Vince and I have received, and the messages left on Vince's and my vehicles?" Tammy asked.

"Those things happened in Eagle Mountain," Dad said. "We don't know that they have anything to do with us."

"Except the person who wrote the notes signed them with a V and implied they were Valerie." Tammy's voice was gentle but insistent.

Dad sat heavily on the sofa. "Why would Valerie destroy her own room?" he asked. "And those notes—why would she blame any of us for what happened to her?"

Vince sat in an armchair facing the sofa. Tammy perched on the arm of the chair. "Why didn't you and Mom ever have Valerie declared dead?" he asked. He had never voiced the question before, not wanting to cause his parents more pain. But he wondered if they knew something he didn't.

"We considered it," Dad said. "But we didn't want to give up hope."

"Did anything happen to give you hope?" Tammy asked.

He didn't answer. Vince cleared his throat. "You mentioned seeing a young woman in a casino who looked like Valerie."

Dad sighed, his gaze focused on the rug. "There were two phone calls, years apart. Once, the person—a female—just said, 'Help.' Another time all she said was 'Dad?' and then hung up before I could answer. I'm sure they were just people being cruel, but we always wondered, what if they really were Valerie?"

Vince's stomach rolled, and he feared he might be sick. Rescue work had schooled him to be strong when faced with others' pain, but broken limbs and gashed heads were nothing compared to seeing his father tortured this way.

"You must have tried to find her over the years," Tammy said.

"We did. We hired private detectives twice, but they never came up with anything. They tried to find the camper that was in the mountains the day we were but never found a trace of him either."

"I didn't know that," Vince said. "About the detectives, I mean."

Dad glanced at him. "You had your own life to lead," he said. "We didn't want to burden you with our concerns."

"What will you do now?" Tammy asked.

"We'll get someone in to fix the house." He looked at Vince again. "And before you ask, no, we won't move. Your mother, especially, would never leave this place."

"Because Valerie might come home." Tammy's voice was scarcely above a whisper, but it was loud in the still room.

"Yes. When you have children of your own one day, you'll

understand. We can never give up hope. No matter how much it hurts."

When would the hurting stop? Vince wondered. Sure, the pain of grief and the memory of a smiling little girl who had once been part of their lives would always be part of them. But this new pain, of a wound constantly reopened, when would that end? How could he make it end?

Fifteen years ago.

"WE'RE GOING TO need to give you a new name."

She looked up at the man who stood over her. The man with the friendly smile who had brought her to this place—a place she didn't know. The smile frightened her now, though she didn't know why. He hadn't done anything to hurt her. "Can you think of a name you would like to go by now?" he asked.

"Why do I have to have a new name?" she asked. "Why can't I go home?"

The man—he had told her his name was Paul—squatted down so he could look at her directly. He had dark eyes. They looked all black, like a cartoon character's. They had frightened her at first, but she was getting used to them. "I explained this already," he said. "Your mom and dad didn't want you anymore. They were going to leave you up there in the mountains to die, until I agreed to take you instead."

"Why didn't they want me?" Her heart beat so fast it hurt at the idea. "They said they loved me."

"They were liars." He shrugged. "People are, sometimes. You'll learn that as you get older. They thought they'd be happier with just one kid, and they decided to keep your brother because he's a boy. Some people feel that way. But I don't." He reached out and gently stroked her head. "I always wanted a little girl like you."

She began to cry. He let her. They sat like that for a long time, him stroking her hair. "It's going to be all right," he said. "You can help me with my work."

She sniffed and tried to control her tears. She didn't like the way crying felt. If she helped him, maybe he would let her talk to her parents. If she talked to them, she could get them to take her back. Whatever she had done to upset them, she could make up for it. She just had to convince Paul to let her see them again. "What kind of work?" she asked.

"People give me money to invest," he said. "You'll be good at persuading them to give me the money. You're a pretty child, and people will like you. Sometimes I'll ask you to talk to people while I take things they don't need anymore. Things we can use. You're smart. I could tell that just by watching you there at the camp."

"I got all As on my last report card," she said.

"I knew you were smart," he said. "I'm good at reading people. I'll teach you how to read them too. The two of us will make a fine team." He stood at last. "We'll be good together. You'll see. After a while you won't even think about your old family anymore."

I'll never forget my family, she thought. And that had turned out to be true. But over the years, she saw them differently. She saw them the way Paul saw them. It was an ugly view, but then, much of life was ugly. Paul had taught her that. She had learned a great deal from him. She had learned that a smart, daring person could get whatever she wanted from people who weren't as smart—money, admiration, sex.

Revenge.

Chapter Nineteen

"Should we tell the sheriff we think the fire at your parents' home might have been started by V?" Tammy asked as she and Vince made the drive back to Eagle Mountain.

"We don't have any proof at all that V started the fire," he said.

"Except that the fire was in Valerie's room, and V has connected herself with Valerie."

"That isn't proof, though, is it? And Junction isn't in Travis's jurisdiction. Not even close. Plus, my dad refuses to say anything to the Junction police about our troubles with V. He doesn't want to believe they're connected."

"Then what are we going to do?"

"I don't think we can do anything but wait for her to make another move. Travis has already admitted whoever this is hasn't left much evidence for them to trace."

Goose bumps rose on Tammy's arms, and she hugged herself, trying to fend off the sudden chill. "It feels like she's getting more dangerous—that attack on me and now this fire."

"The attack on you was terrible," he said. "And the fire was frightening and destructive, but she didn't try to burn down the whole house."

"If that neighbor hadn't seen the smoke and called 911, the whole house might have burned."

"I'm worried she might hurt my parents," Vince said. "But they won't move out of the house, even temporarily."

"They can't believe Valerie would hurt them."

"But someone pretending to be Valerie might. I tried to tell Dad that, but he won't listen."

"My mom never listens to me either," she said. "We're still kids to them, and they're still our parents. The police in Junction are still investigating the arson. Maybe they'll get lucky and find a witness or something else that leads them to V. In the meantime, you and I will have to keep our eyes open."

"It's not like either of us have the skills or the time to investigate this full-time," he said. "And I don't have money to hire a private investigator." He pounded his fist against the steering wheel. "It's so frustrating."

"It is," she agreed. "But we'll get through this. I have an idea we can try. I'll have to talk to Russ and see if he will agree, but I think he will."

"What's that?"

"I'm thinking I could do another story for the paper, about Valerie. V's version of what happened that day is so different from what actually happened, a new story might draw her out again."

"'Draw her out,' how? What if she tries to kill someone? What if she tries to kill you?"

Her stomach knotted with fear. "I'll be careful," she said. "I won't go anywhere alone. And it will be worth it if we can draw her out."

"But how are we going to catch her? What if your article just results in another taunting letter or phone call, or a sneak attack?"

Tammy chewed on her thumbnail, thinking. "We'll have to set a trap," she said. She sat up straight. "I know! We can say there's going to be a memorial to honor Valerie and keep awareness of her alive. In the park. The public is invited. She'll be sure to come. We can alert the sheriff, and they can have a deputy there. We can watch for anyone behaving suspiciously."

"It might work," Vince said. "Do you think the sheriff will agree?"

"We can ask. And the memorial itself will be news enough that I won't have any trouble getting Russ to run a small piece."

"If it's a memorial, we'll need to tell my parents. They'll want to come."

"They can come. But don't tell them it's a trap for V. Just say it's something you wanted to do to honor your sister. Tell them it was my idea, if that helps."

"Are people going to think it's strange we're doing this now, when we haven't done anything for fifteen years?"

"I don't think there's any timeline for these things," she said. "It might even help your parents to have a public ceremony like this. There will be other people who attend who remember Valerie, teachers and others who knew her. They'll know they're not alone in their grief."

"Like the funeral we never had." He nodded. "I think it will be a good thing—and if it helps stop V from harassing us, even better."

"You can talk to your parents tomorrow. I'll check with the sheriff and find out if we need a permit to hold the memorial in the park."

"It feels right to be doing something," Vince said. "Instead of sitting back, waiting for the next bad thing to happen."

VINCE WAS SURE his parents would resist the idea of a memorial for Valerie. He would have to work to persuade them, or even go through with the plan without their blessing. But once again, they surprised him. Instead of bursting into tears, as he had expected, his mother had responded with enthusiasm. "I have some wonderful pictures we can display at the memorial," she said. "And there's a poem I came across, not long after she went missing, that I found meaningful. I don't think I could read it out loud in front of people, but perhaps you could. Or maybe Tammy?"

"That sounds great, Mom. Tammy's arranging things with the city for us to be allowed to hold the memorial in the park."

"I used to think about doing something like this in the mountains, at the place we saw her last," his mom said. "But I suppose the park is more practical. Much easier for people to get to. Thank you for doing this."

"It wasn't my idea. It was Tammy's."

"She's a lovely young woman." His mother fixed him with the look that made him feel like a boy being quizzed on whether or not he had completed his homework. "Are things serious between you two?" she asked.

"We don't want to rush things," he said. Though the truth was, they were as good as living together, with Tammy spending every night at his place and most of her belongings there. He thought soon he would formally ask her to move in full-time, with a change of address and everything. The idea made his heart race a little, but not in a bad way.

After getting his parents on board, the next step was a meeting with the sheriff. He and Tammy went to Travis's office and laid out their proposal for catching V. "She associates so strongly with Valerie, I don't think she'll be able to stay away from the service," Tammy said. "Eagle Mountain is a small enough community we ought to able to spot someone new or out of place."

"I can't arrest someone for being a stranger," Travis said.

"And grief can make people behave in odd ways. That's not a crime either."

"But you can watch them, and if they do cause trouble, you can have a deputy there to put a stop to it," she said.

"All right," Travis agreed. "But you have to promise to let us handle any incidents. You focus on the memorial."

"I promise," Tammy said, and Vince agreed.

Travis sat back in his chair. "I understand there was a fire at your parents' house," he said. "In your sister's old bedroom."

"How did you hear about that?" Vince asked, unable to hide his alarm.

"I have friends with the Junction police. They called to verify that you and your parents were in Eagle Mountain the day of the fire."

"They were checking our alibis?" Vince's voice rose.

"It's routine in an arson investigation. They don't have any leads as to who set the fire. Do you think it was V?"

"It could have been," Vince admitted. "It's one reason we planned this memorial. I don't like her getting close to my parents. She's already hurt Tammy. I don't want her to hurt anyone else."

Travis turned to Tammy. "What do you plan to say in your article for the paper?"

"I'm just going to announce the memorial, say anyone who remembers Valerie is invited and give a brief outline of the circumstances of her disappearance."

"Play up the loving family who never stopped searching for her," Travis said. "That contradicts V's story that Valerie's disappearance was somehow orchestrated by the family. She may feel she has to show up to refute that."

"I thought we could have a portion of the memorial service where people can stand up and offer their memories of Valerie," she said. "Maybe V will have something to say."

"We could get lucky." Travis stood. "I'll have a couple of deputies at the service," he said. "Let me know if you need anything else."

THE DAY OF Valerie's memorial was hot and sunny. Vince's parents had insisted on a large flower arrangement, and a couple of Valerie's former teachers and a family friend had also ordered arrangements, which Tammy grouped around a series of enlarged photos of the little girl. Though she and Vince were not identical twins, the resemblance was definitely there, and one photo Mrs. Shepherd had provided showed the children together, arms around each other, grinning for the camera with such happiness it made Tammy's heart hurt.

"There are more people here than I thought there would be," Mrs. Shepherd said as they watched people fill the folding chairs they had set out. Latecomers stood around the chairs, all facing the small platform with the flowers and photographs. Tammy scanned the gathering, hoping to spot anyone who seemed out of place or who was behaving strangely. But no one stood out.

At two o'clock sharp, Tammy moved to the microphone set up in front of the platform. "On behalf of the Shepherd family, I want to thank you all for coming this afternoon," she said. "We are gathered to honor a beloved daughter, sister and friend. Valerie Shepherd vanished from our lives fifteen years ago, but she has never been forgotten. And the family has never stopped looking for her."

She looked out over the crowd and faltered for a moment when she recognized Mitch and Elisabeth, seated on the back row of chairs. She had mentioned she was planning this event for the family, and this show of support touched her. It wasn't the kind of thing Mitch would ever have done on his own, so it must be Elisabeth's influence. She would be sure to thank her later.

She looked down at her notes. "To start, I want to read a poem at the request of Valerie's mother." She read the poem, a sentimental piece about the joy a little girl brings to the family. By the time she was done, Mrs. Shepherd was wiping away tears, as were many others in the crowd.

"Now we'll have an opportunity for anyone who would like to share their memories of Valerie. Her brother, Vince, will start."

Vince, dressed in dark slacks and a blue dress shirt, sleeves rolled up and collar open, moved to the microphone. Tammy spotted a number of his fellow search and rescue volunteers in the crowd, some of whom must have been involved in the original search for Valerie. Bethany Ames was there. Did that mean she was Valerie?

Vince glanced at a note card in his hand, then cleared his throat and spoke: "When I think of my sister, Valerie, I think of her courage. We were twins, but she got most of the bravery in the family. She truly wasn't afraid of anything—spiders, heights, deep water, going fast on a mountain bike—all the things that made me nervous never fazed her.

"I remember once, we were riding our bikes in the woods behind our house. Our usual route took us over a ditch, where someone had laid down a couple of boards to make it possible to ride over. But on this day, spring snowmelt had the water in the ditch raging, and had washed the boards downstream. I told Valerie we would have to turn around and go back home the long way, but she insisted we could jump our bikes over the water.

"I looked at that rushing water and my other big fear—of drowning—had me almost paralyzed. I told Valerie I couldn't do it, but she insisted I could. She backed her bike up a hill, then pedaled furiously down it, gaining speed. When she reached the edge of the ditch, she yanked up on the handlebars and sailed over the gap with room to spare. She wheeled around, shouting in triumph, and told me it was my turn.

"I could have turned around and ridden home alone, but I would have had to live with the shame—and the constant taunts from her—that she had beat me. So I backed my bike up the hill, pedaled with everything I had and held my breath as my bike cleared that gap. Valerie was thrilled, congratulating me and telling me she had known all along that I could do it. I was just relieved that I had survived unscathed.

"After she was gone, I realized how much I had relied on her to lead the way. It was a hard lesson to learn, but I'm a better man for it. I learned that I needed to be brave enough for both of us."

Tammy watched the faces of those in the crowd as he spoke. Many people were smiling, some nodding their heads. But no one looked angry or upset by the story. Deputies Jamie Douglas and Dwight Prentice stood on either side of the crowd, assessing the attendees but not reacting as if they had spotted anything concerning.

Vince left the microphone and returned to his seat on the front row between his mother and Tammy. Others took turns speaking—two different teachers spoke about how smart Valerie was. Her former soccer coach spoke about her talent for the sport and cheerful attitude. Mr. and Mrs. Shepherd each shared memories of their little girl, their voices breaking as they painted a picture of a cheerful and loved child.

And then it was over. Members of the crowd moved forward to speak with the family while others drifted away. Tammy looked for Mitch and Elisabeth, but they had already left. It didn't matter. She could thank them later for being there.

Jamie came to stand beside her. "Did you see anyone out of place?" she asked.

"No," Tammy admitted. "Did you?"

"No. Everyone was quiet and respectful. I didn't see anything off."

Dwight Prentice walked up. "Everything seems okay," he said.

"I guess our plan didn't work," Vince said.

"It was still a beautiful memorial," Jamie said. "I didn't know your sister, but it sounds like she was a great kid."

"She was." Vince took a deep breath and blew it out. "I'm glad we did this, even if we didn't catch V. We should have done it years ago."

Tammy slipped her arm in his. "I'm glad we did it too. It helped me to know Valerie and your family better."

They helped his parents load the flowers and pictures to take back to their home in Junction, which Mr. Shepherd reported was already in the process of being repaired.

Tammy and Vince were walking across the park toward the lot where they had left the Escape when Vince's text alert sounded. He pulled out his phone. "It's a search and rescue call," he said, and scrolled through the message. "Hikers reported an injured man at the base of the cliffs north of Dixon Pass." He met her eyes. "I should go."

"Do you need to change clothes and grab your gear?" she asked.

"I keep a change of clothes and a gear bag in the car," he said.

"Then go."

"I can drop you off at the condo," he said.

"I want to walk over and visit my mother," she said. "I'll get her to drive me to your condo."

"You should start thinking of it as *our* condo," he said. "You're spending all your time there."

"I am, but I don't want to presume."

He took her by the shoulders. "I like having you live with me. I think you should go ahead and move in. Permanently."

She grinned, a little numb and a lot excited. "Yes. Let's do it."

"We'll iron out the details later." He kissed her on the lips. "Right now, I need to go." He started to open the car, then stopped. "Be careful. V is still out there somewhere."

"It'll be fine," she said. "It's broad daylight, and there are tons of people around. When I get to the condo I'll lock myself in. I promise. And you be careful too. Don't fall off a cliff or anything."

"I won't."

She waved goodbye and walked the three blocks to her mother's house. But her mother wasn't home. Neither was Mitch. Disappointed but undeterred, Tammy pulled her bicycle from the garage and set off toward the condo by the river.

Chapter Twenty

"It's a miracle anyone spotted this guy down there," SAR volunteer Harper Stanick said as she and a dozen other volunteers stood on the narrow shoulder of the highway, staring down into the canyon below.

"If those two guys hadn't decided to climb the cliff today, no telling how long he would have lain down there," Tony Meissner said. He looked around. "Where are they, anyway?"

"I sent them on their way," Deputy Ryker Vernon said. "We've got their names and contact info. They're locals, so they shouldn't be hard to get hold of if we need to talk to them later."

"They were pretty shook up," Deputy Declan Owen said. "They said they have no idea who the guy is. I think they were being truthful."

Danny lowered the binoculars he had been using to study the figure of the man below. "I can't tell if he's breathing or not," he said. "And there's a lot of blood. We need to get down there, ASAP."

"The descent is straightforward enough," Tony said. "But bringing him out is going to be pretty technical."

"Sheri, you and Tony go down first," Danny said. "Hannah, you're the medical on scene. Caleb, you and Vince up for following them down?"

"Sure thing," Caleb said.

"Of course," Vince answered. He had trained half a dozen times on similar climbs. He had never had any trouble and was anxious to try his skills in a real rescue situation.

Danny assigned other volunteers to help with the ropes and provide backup as needed. Ryker and Declan had already closed the road to traffic. Now they set about establishing a landing zone for a medical helicopter, should one be needed.

"Any idea how he ended up down there?" Vince asked as he and Caleb gathered their equipment.

"Solo climbing?" Caleb suggested. "Not a good idea, but people do it."

"There aren't any ropes, or even anchors at the top," Ryan said.

"Maybe he set an anchor and it pulled out." Eldon made a face. "If that happened, he's done for."

"No sense speculating," Tony said. "We'll find out when we get there."

The quartet carried their gear to the edge of the canyon above where the body lay. Tony and Sheri decided on the best place to set anchors, then directed the others in laying out the ropes, carabiners, brake bars and other equipment they would use to lower themselves to the man in the canyon and eventually bring a litter up to the top again.

They were all aware of the need to reach the man as soon as possible, but no one rushed. Safety required precision and attention to detail. They wanted the man to live, but not at the expense of any one of them.

Sheri started down first; then Tony set out, ten feet to the left of her. Experienced climbers and competitors on the climbing circuit, they descended smoothly and swiftly. The canyon walls were jagged but stable, providing plenty of hand- and footholds when necessary, though the two were able to glide down long stretches of the wall. Tony landed first, followed seconds later by Sheri. The others watched from the top as they surrounded the crumpled figure on the ground.

"He's alive," Sheri radioed. "Nonresponsive. He's lost a lot of blood. There's a head wound, but I don't see any ropes or a harness or other gear."

There was a pause, the crackle of the radio; then Tony transmitted: "This was no climbing accident. This guy's been shot. Right shoulder. He's got probable broken bones and the head injury. Get that chopper over here. We need to bring this guy up ASAP."

"Hannah, you ready to go?" Danny asked.

"I'm there." Hannah was already at the edge of the canyon, poised to begin the descent.

"Caleb, you and Vince take the litter and the vacuum mattress, and a helmet for the injured man. Ryan and Eldon, you set the high-angle rigging to bring up the litter. I'm calling for the chopper."

As soon as Hannah reached the bottom, Caleb and Vince set out, the litter and other equipment distributed between them, along with extra lines that would eventually be used to haul the patient in the litter to the surface. Eldon and Ryan took the belay position at the top and lowered them down the cliff.

Vince focused on keeping untangled and steady, and the descent happened so quickly he scarcely had time to be nervous. When he had unclipped from the line, he hurried to the huddle around the injured man.

"Get that mattress down here, and we'll shift him onto it," Tony directed.

"I've got the IV in," Hannah said. "I'll start a bag of saline. Somebody unpack a few chemical heat packs to help keep him warm." She keyed the radio and rattled off numbers for the man's pulse, blood pressure and oxygen levels.

Vince leaned in to get a closer look at the man. Maroon bloodstains painted his slacks and dress shirt—not clothing for a climb or a hike in the mountains. "Do you think someone shot him and pushed him down here?" he asked.

Tony looked up. "Either they pushed him or he fell."

"Do we know who he is?" Caleb asked.

"His wallet has an ID for Mitchell Patterson," Sheri said. "Do either of you know him?"

Vince stared at the man's battered shape, stunned. He never would have recognized Tammy's brother, he was so bruised and swollen. "That's Tammy's brother," he said.

"Tammy Patterson?" Hannah looked over her shoulder at them. "Of course. Mitch Patterson, the real estate agent." She turned back to him. "How did he end up down here?"

"That's for the sheriff to find out." Tony stood. "Let's get him in the litter and up to that helicopter."

They worked together to slide Mitch's body—which was fitted with the IV, an oxygen mask, and various splints and bandages—onto the vacuum mattress, which was then inflated to fit tightly around him, acting as a full-body splint. This was then placed in the litter. He was strapped in, along with heat packs, blankets, the IV fluids and oxygen tank.

The litter was attached to lines that hung down from a tripod at the canyon rim that helped to keep the litter suspended away from the canyon walls. Then Sheri and Tony began the arduous process of ascending the canyon walls while guiding the litter up between them.

Vince stood with Hannah and Caleb and watched the ascent. While the lines from the tripod would support most of the weight of the litter, the two climbers needed to hold it steady while navigating their own journey to the top.

"There's the chopper," Hannah said.

Vince listened and heard the faint throb of helicopter rotors. "Do you think he'll make it?" he asked.

She pulled off her latex gloves and tucked them in the pocket of her jacket. "He has a chance. I don't think he had been down here long when we got to him. We were able to stabilize him and ward off shock. But he has a lot of injuries. Probably some internal ones I wasn't able to assess. I couldn't tell you what his chances are."

When Mitch was safely to the top of the canyon, along with Sheri and Tony, Caleb and Vince helped Hannah gather the medical equipment and other supplies. They packed everything away. Hannah and Caleb ascended first, leaving Vince for last. He took out his phone and stared at the screen, even though he knew he had no signal here. He would need to contact Tammy and let her know what had happened to her brother.

But what had happened? Who had shot him and left him to die in this remote spot? He and his girlfriend had attended Valerie's memorial service a few hours ago—though now it seemed like days. The shooting must have happened shortly after that.

Fear lanced through him as another thought registered. Elisabeth was probably with Mitch when he was shot. What had happened to her?

TAMMY COASTED THE bicycle up to the front door of the condo and dismounted. The ride had energized her. Maybe she would start riding her bike to work. She wondered what Russ would think of that.

She took out her keys and unlocked the door, then wheeled the bicycle in ahead of her and left it against the wall in the front hall. She would need to find a better place to park it, but they would figure out something.

"Hello, Tammy. I was wondering what took you so long."

She froze, then slowly turned around to face Elisabeth. Or rather, she registered that the voice was Elisabeth's, but her gaze fixed on the gun in the woman's hand and refused to look away.

"Where's Vince?" Elisabeth asked.

"He had a search and rescue call. A climber fell in a canyon, up on Dixon Pass."

Elisabeth's laughter was another shock. "Oh, that's rich," she crowed. "Not what I had planned at all, but this might be even better."

Tammy forced her gaze away from the gun, but the expression on Elisabeth's face did nothing to calm her. The other woman was as sleek and put together as ever, with her long hair swept back in a low ponytail and the nails that rested against the gun sporting a perfect French manicure. But her eyes were dilated, her mouth fixed in a rictus of a smile. "How did you get in here?" Tammy asked.

"The first time I visited the manager's apartment, when I rented my place, I swiped a master key. I knew it would come in handy one day."

"What are you doing here?" Tammy tried to sound strong and in control. "And put away that gun."

"Who do you think you are, that you can tell me what to do? Now, get over there on that couch and sit down." She gestured toward the sofa with her free hand.

Tammy did as she was told, moving sideways so that her back was never to the other woman. "Where's Mitch?" she asked. "I saw the two of you at the memorial service."

"You didn't think I'd miss my own memorial service, did you?"

Elisabeth was V. Tammy had figured that out when she saw the gun in her hand. But did that also mean she was Valerie? "Where's Mitch?" she asked again.

"I left him at the bottom of a canyon, up on Dixon Pass. But apparently, my brother is helping to get him out. Or more probably, he's retrieving his body." She sat in a chair facing the sofa, the gun aimed at the middle of Tammy's chest. "That's inconvenient, but it will give us time to talk."

The idea that Mitch might be dead hit Tammy like a blow to the stomach. She wanted to protest that that couldn't be true, but she recognized the fruitlessness of arguing. She pushed the idea away entirely. She wouldn't think about Mitch right now. She had to focus on Valerie, and on keeping her from pulling the trigger. "What happened to you?" she asked. "That day on the camping trip, when you were ten?"

"I knew you'd have questions. I guess that's the reporter in you. Too bad you weren't around when I went missing. You strike me as someone who might actually have ferreted out the truth."

"What is the truth?" Tammy asked.

"I've been trying to tell you for weeks. My family—my mother and father and Vince—decided they didn't want me anymore. They were going to leave me up on that mountain to die. Instead, a man who was camping nearby offered to take care of me."

"The man kidnapped you," Tammy said.

"He didn't kidnap me. He did me a favor. I would have died without him."

Her agitation—and the way the gun shook in her hand—made Tammy nervous. She had to resist the impulse to argue. "What was the man's name?" she asked.

"Paul. Paul Rollins."

"And you're Elisabeth Rollins."

"Paul chose the name for me. Much better than Valerie."

"Where is Paul now?" Should Tammy expect him to walk through the door at any moment?

"He's dead. With him gone, I didn't have anyone left. Then I remembered my other family. The one who abandoned me."

Tammy bit her lip to keep from arguing that the Shepherds had not abandoned their daughter. Time to change the subject again. She needed to keep Valerie off-balance. "What happened with Mitch?" she asked.

"I needed him out of the way so I could take care of Vince and my parents." She crossed her legs and propped the grip of the handgun on her knee, her finger within easy reach of the trigger. "I would have liked to keep him around longer, at least until I had drained off more of his money. I thought I would have time to access all of his accounts before anyone discovered his body, but that may not be the case now."

"He loved you," Tammy said.

"So have the others." Her smile brightened. "I guess I'm just a very lovable person."

"I don't understand how Paul was able to keep you a secret all these years," Tammy said. "People were looking for you. Your parents hired a private detective. There were appeals in the media."

"Lies, all of it. If they were looking as hard as they said, they would have found me. Paul changed my name, sure, and he took me to a fancy salon and got me a good haircut—my first one. But the rest of me was just the same. It's not like we were living in a cave in the middle of nowhere. We lived in a beautiful house. We took vacations."

"What about school?"

"I was homeschooled. Paul had been a teacher, once upon a time. He taught me what I needed to know to help him in his business."

"What kind of business was that?"

That overly bright grin again. "Paul liked to say we taught people important financial lessons. We taught people to be more careful with their money."

"You conned people," Tammy guessed.

"*Con* sounds so crass. What we did required more finesse. We persuaded people to trust us. Most of them did."

"Is that why you're here now? Because you want money?"

"I have money, and I always know how to get more. No, I'm here for a different kind of payback."

Tammy swallowed hard. The gun, and the fact that Valerie had admitted to killing Mitch, indicated the payback could be a fatal one. "I'm not part of your family," she said. "Why waste your time with me?"

"Because Vince *looooves* you." She drew out the word. "The first time I saw you together, I knew it. He didn't care about me, his twin, but he's all gaga for you. Hurting you will hurt him. I thought at first that beating you up would be enough. You put up quite a fight, by the way. I can admire that, even if it made things inconvenient for me. But it also made me realize that a beating wasn't going to be enough. Vince can watch you die, then I'll kill him. It will be perfect."

Tammy choked back a moan. "What about your parents?" she asked. She didn't want more horrible details, but she needed to keep Valerie talking.

"I'll get them next, but no hurry. I won't have to sneak up on them like I did you and Vince. They'll be happy to open the door for their long-lost little girl. Then I can take my time deciding how to put an end to them and all their lies about truly loving me."

Tammy heard the hurt behind the hatred. What had Paul done to this young woman to damage her so much?

But she couldn't let sympathy blind her to the danger she was in. And Vince. Could she find a way to warn him before he came home and walked into his own death sentence?

Chapter Twenty-One

It was after seven when Vince unlocked the Escape parked at search and rescue headquarters. He had tried calling Tammy as soon as he picked up a phone signal, but the call had gone to voice mail after six rings. Maybe she was in the shower or busy with something else.

It was better if he gave her the message about her brother in person. Or maybe she already knew. That might explain why she hadn't answered the phone. She might be with her mother. Vince had told Declan and Ryker about Elisabeth as soon as he reached the top of the canyon, and they had radioed the information to the sheriff and started the search for her. They would have reached out to Mrs. Patterson and Tammy too.

"Vince, wait up!" He looked up and let out a groan when he saw Bethany jogging toward him.

"I don't have time to talk now," he said.

She stopped in front of him. "This won't take long. I just want to apologize for being so, well, awkward around you." She studied the ground between them. "I came to town to make a fresh start, right? I was trying to be all independent, going after what I wanted and that kind of thing? And I thought you were cute and nice and would be a fun date. But I should have realized you were already involved. I was so embarrassed when I found out you were already with someone. But I just wanted you to know I won't bother you anymore. And no hard feelings—I hope."

"Sure. No hard feelings." She looked so sad, standing there with her head down. Harmless, and probably lonely too. "Are you okay?"

She looked up, a forced smiled on her lips. "I'm fine." She shrugged. "Being alone in a new place is hard, but I'm starting to make friends."

"Count me as one of them," he said. "Me and Tammy."

The smile became more genuine. "Thanks." She took a step back. "I'll let you go now." She turned and hurried away, this time with her head up.

Vince drove to his condo and parked. Tammy had left the outside light on for him. Keys in hand, he moved toward the door. But it wasn't locked. Not good. Maybe she had forgotten in her distress over her brother, but with V still at large, it wasn't safe to leave the condo unsecured.

The hallway was dark. He left his jacket and pack on the hooks by the door, then almost fell over a bicycle. What was that doing there?

"Tammy?" he called.

"Vince, don't— *Ahhh!*"

He sprinted toward the living room but skidded to a stop when he saw Elisabeth standing by the sofa, one hand gripping Tammy's arm, the other holding a gun pressed to the side of Tammy's head. Blood trickled from Tammy's temple.

"Don't worry. I just tapped her with the gun barrel this time," Elisabeth said. "But if you don't cooperate, I'll shoot her."

"You shot Mitch," he said.

"Am I supposed to tell you you're a clever boy because you figured that out?" She sneered. "Vin, Vin, Vinnie, Vince."

He almost staggered under the weight of the knowledge that hit him then. Elisabeth was from Omaha, Nebraska. The town where his father had seen a young woman who looked like Valerie. She had shown up in Eagle Mountain about the time the messages from V began arriving. Her hair was darker than Valerie's, but she had the same slightly up-turned nose and the same dimple in her left cheek that he had. "Valerie, what are you doing?" he asked.

"It took you long enough to recognize me. I shouldn't have to tell you how insulting it is that you didn't even know who I was. Your long-lost twin. The one you had supposedly mourned all these years. Such hypocrisy."

"What do you want from us?" he asked.

Valerie looked at Tammy. "You see how he gets right to the point? He doesn't care what I've been up to for the past fifteen years. He just wants to know the bottom line. What will it take to make me go away again?"

"That's not what I meant," he said. "And I do care—"

"Shut up! Don't waste my time with more lies. As for what I want from you, that's easy. You and Mom and Dad—mostly Mom and Dad, but I blame you too, because you were their favorite and you didn't do anything to stop them—took away my life. The life I could have had, anyway. Now you get to pay with *your* life."

Vince glanced at Tammy. She was pale, but calm. Strong. "Let Tammy go and I'll do whatever you want," he said.

"Let her go right to the sheriff? I don't think so. No, you two are the buy-one-get-one special today." She shoved Tammy onto the sofa. "Sit down over here beside your girl-friend, and we'll talk about what happens next."

Vince sat. He wanted to keep her talking. As long as she was talking, she wasn't shooting. And every word bought a lit-tle more time for the sheriff and his deputies to figure out that

Elisabeth was V. She had shot her boyfriend and come after him and his family. "Why did you shoot Mitch?" he asked.

"I've already explained everything to your girlfriend. He was in the way of what I needed to do. Is he dead yet? I figured if the bullet didn't finish him off, the fall into the canyon would."

"He's alive," Vince said. "He'll tell the cops everything."

Tammy let out a whimper. Valerie glared at her, then turned her attention back to Vince. "By the time they find me, it will be too late," she said. "I know how to change my appearance and my name and melt into the background. Paul taught me all that."

"Who is Paul?"

Valerie sighed. "Again, I've already told Tammy. I don't like repeating myself. He's the man who saved me when my *family* threw me out."

"He was the camper you saw?" Vince guessed. "The one with the blue tent?"

"Again, you're smarter than I thought. And a hero to boot, climbing mountains and descending into canyons to save complete strangers. That surprised me when I found out. You were always such a coward. Too bad you didn't try harder to save me."

He started to reply, but Tammy squeezed his hand, hard. A warning not to upset Valerie by arguing with her? He squeezed back, letting her know he got the message. "That was you in the casino in Omaha, the time Dad saw you, wasn't it?" he asked.

"He told you about that, did he? I heard he came snooping around the next day, looking for me. But the manager had a thing for me, so he didn't mind saying he didn't know anything about me. I told him the guy asking questions was a creepy old man who was hassling me."

"Was it you who made those phone calls—the ones saying 'Help me' and asking for Daddy?"

She looked away. "I don't want to talk about that anymore. Stand up, both of you." She motioned with the gun. "Time to get this show on the road."

They stood.

"Oh, isn't that sweet? You're holding hands. But don't think the two of you are going to get the better of me. I've had lots of time to think about this. Now, get into the bedroom and take off all your clothes."

He and Tammy looked at each other with a mixture of shock and confusion. "Get going," Valerie ordered. "It's not like you two haven't seen each other naked before."

They went into the bedroom. "Clothes off!" Valerie barked. "Quit wasting my time."

Vince sat on the edge of the bed and began unlacing his boots. Slowly. Instead of sitting beside him, Tammy moved to the other side of the bed and took off her earrings. Good idea. The more space between them, the more difficult it would be for Valerie to watch them both at once.

Boots off, Vince turned his attention to removing his belt. He weighed it in his hand, wondering if he could use it as a weapon.

The gunshot was deafening in the small space. He jumped up and saw that Valerie had fired into the mattress. "The next one will be right in her chest if you don't get moving," she said, pointing the gun at Tammy.

He draped the belt over the headboard, then moved more quickly, shucking his jeans and socks, then peeling off his shirt, until he was standing in front of her in his boxers. "That's enough," she said. "I can always strip the body later." She turned once more to Tammy. "You lie down on the bed. Vince, you tie her up with those scarves." She indicated two scarves draped around the bedposts. "One hand to each bedpost. And do a good job."

Tammy remained standing, also in her underwear. "Why have him tie me up?"

"I'm setting the scene. Vince, depressed over the loss of his dear little sister, kills himself. But first, he kills you. After subjecting you to kinky sex."

Valerie's love of drama hadn't changed. But he didn't see any way out of doing what she wanted. He believed her when she said the next bullet would be for Tammy.

Tammy lay back on the bed. "Sorry about this," Vince said, as he knelt beside her and picked up one of the scarves.

I love you, she mouthed, and he nodded, unable to get out any words past the lump in his throat. He tied her wrist to the bedpost, not too tight but in what he hoped was a convincing knot. Then he moved to the other wrist.

"Comfortable?" Valerie asked. She moved to check the wrist Vince had just tied and made a tsking sound. "As I suspected, not tight enough. Just for that, you're going to get an extra bullet, Vince."

The teasing tone she used enraged him. He watched out of the corner of his eye as she bent over the knot, the pistol balanced awkwardly in her right hand as she used her ring and pinkie fingers to hold the scarf in place as she tightened the knot.

He left the other wrist untied and grabbed hold of the belt. The heavy buckle hit Valerie hard on the cheek, drawing blood. She juggled the gun and it went off, but the bullet hit the wall. Tammy yanked her hand away and rolled off the bed, landing hard on the floor. Meanwhile, Vince had lunged, both hands around the wrist that held the gun, until he succeeded in wrenching it from her. But she knocked it from his hand, and it fired again as it hit the floor.

He continued to wrestle with Valerie, struggling to subdue her. She fought with incredible strength, biting and kicking, scratching at his face and trying to knee him in the groin. Tammy raced from the room and returned a few seconds later with something in her hand. "Hold her still!" she pleaded.

But just then, Valerie bit Vince's hand, drawing blood. He drew back instinctively, and she lunged, over-balancing him. They both fell to the floor, her on top, both hands around his throat. His vision blurred, and he was sure he would black out.

Then he heard a horrible sound, like a knife cleaving a watermelon. Valerie's grip loosened, and she fell to one side.

Tammy stood over them, spattered with blood, the ice ax from Vince's search and rescue pack in her hand.

Pounding on the door reverberated through the house. "This is the sheriff!" Travis shouted. "Come out with your hands up!"

Tammy dropped the ax, and Vince staggered to his feet. He put his arm around her. "Come on," he said.

"I can't go out there like this," she whispered.

He reached back and grabbed the top sheet from the bed and wrapped it around her, then took the bottom sheet for himself. They walked into the living room just as the door burst open and Gage and Travis entered.

Gage took in the bedclothes and their state of undress and frowned. "We had a report of multiple gunshots at this address," he said. "And Mitch Patterson's car is outside in the lot. We believe his girlfriend, Elisabeth Rollins, tried to kill him."

"His girlfriend is in the bedroom," Vince said. "She shot Mitch, then tried to kill us. And her name isn't Elisabeth Rollins. It's Valerie Shepherd."

Jamie Douglas stepped in behind the Walker brothers. "You two can come with me," she said.

Tammy was shaking by the time they reached the parking lot, though the temperature was mild. Her eyes were glazed, her skin cold and clammy. "Call an ambulance," Vince said. "I think she's going into shock."

"One is on the way," Jamie said. "I've got a sweatshirt and pants in my patrol vehicle you can put on, Tammy, and Gage will have something that will fit you, Vince." She retrieved the clothes from the back of her SUV and started to help Tammy unwind the sheet when she saw the blood spatters. "Are you hurt?" she asked.

"That isn't my blood," Tammy said. "It's Valerie's." Then she broke down sobbing.

Vince gathered her close while Jamie radioed this information to Travis. More deputies arrived, along with an ambulance and most of Vince's neighbors. Tammy's boss, camera in hand, showed up. Vince only vaguely registered their presence. He held on to Tammy, smoothing her hair and murmuring, "It's going to be all right," over and over. As if by repetition, he could make himself believe it.

TAMMY SPENT THE night in the hospital, with Vince on one side of her bed and her mother on the other. She hadn't wanted to stay here, but the doctor had insisted it was necessary, then given her a sedative that made her not care anymore.

When she finally woke, sun streamed through the one window in her room. Vince got up from the chair where he had been sitting and came to the side of the bed. "How are you feeling?" he asked.

"I'm okay." She reached up and touched the bruise on the side of her face. It was tender, but the doctors had reassured her there was no lasting damage. She trembled when she thought of how much worse it could have been. "How are you?"

"Shaken up. But I'm going to be okay."

She turned to look at the chair where her mother had sat. "She went down to see your brother," Vince said.

Her eyes widened as she remembered Mitch. He had been in surgery when they installed her in this room last night. "Is he going to be okay?"

"He's got a long recovery ahead of him. Another surgery to pin his leg together. But he's going to be okay."

"And Valerie?"

"She's alive. You didn't kill her. You merely gave her a concussion. And saved both our lives."

Tammy's eyes filled with tears. "Your poor parents."

A tap on the door frame interrupted their discussion. Sheriff Travis Walker entered. "I stopped by to see how you're doing," he said.

"I'm going to be fine," Tammy said.

"I was just down getting a statement from your brother."

"What did he say?" Vince asked.

"He says the woman he knew as Elisabeth asked him to stop the car by the side of the road because she was feeling sick. Earlier in the day, she had surprised him with the news that she was pregnant, so he thought that was the reason she was feeling ill. He helped her over to the edge of the road. She pulled out a gun, shot him and pushed him over the edge."

"Cold blooded," Vince said.

"Vince has already given me his statement," Travis said. "Can you tell me what happened before he arrived at the condo yesterday evening?"

Tammy smoothed her hands over the sheets and tried to gather her thoughts. "I'll try to remember everything," she said.

Travis took out a recorder, recited her name and his and the time and date. Then she proceeded to tell her story, reliving those horrible moments when Valerie told her about Mitch and threatened her own life and that of Vince and the Shepherds. Vince held her hand while she spoke, keeping her strong. When she was finished, Travis shut off the recorder. "What will happen to Valerie?" she asked.

"She's in custody now but will be transferred to a mental health unit soon," Travis said. "The court will determine if she stands trial for the arson and three counts of attempted murder. Not to mention the thousands and thousands of dollars she and Paul Rollins have stolen over the years."

"Did you find out anything about Paul Rollins?" Vince asked.

"He was a former school teacher in Ogallala, Nebraska. He was fired after accusations of improper conduct with a student. A nine-year-old girl. He left town and fell off the radar for nine months, until he showed up with a girl he called Elisabeth. He introduced her as his daughter. They're suspected of being involved in various con games all over the country, in Mexico and the Caribbean. They targeted wealthy, older people with either investment or charity schemes. He apparently used Valerie to lull his targets into trusting him."

"Valerie said he was dead," Tammy said.

"He died two months ago of an asthma attack," Travis said. "He had a history of the disease, but when I contacted authorities in Omaha, I learned they are considering opening an investigation into his death."

"Do they think Valerie killed him?" Vince asked.

"I don't know," Travis said.

"She scares me," Tammy admitted.

"Whether she stands trial for the things she's done or is

committed for treatment, she won't be free to live on her own for a long time, if ever," Travis said.

"I'm trying to remind myself that she was hurt by what happened too," Tammy said. "Whatever this Paul guy did to her, it damaged her mind. I don't know if someone can ever come back from that."

"My parents are determined to help her any way they can," Vince said. "She's still their daughter, and they're relieved to know what happened to her, even if it hasn't resulted in the happy ending they're hoping for."

"One day, maybe she'll realize how fortunate she is to have them on her side," Travis said. He pocketed the recorder. "You'll need to stop by the office in the next day or so to sign this statement. And we may have other questions for both of you."

"Of course."

"Your condo will be unavailable for a few days," Travis said. "I can give you the name of a company that will clean it for you before you move back in."

"Okay," Vince said. "Thanks."

Travis took something from his pocket. Tammy thought it would be a business card for the cleaning company. Instead, he handed Vince a key. "You'll need a place to stay for a few days," he said. "Someplace quiet, away from the press and nosy neighbors. I have a cabin you can use. Up on Spirit Ridge. It's nothing fancy, but it's comfortable."

Vince stared at the key. "Thanks."

Travis left and Vince pocketed the key. "That was nice of him," Tammy said.

"He's a good man," Vince said. "He'll do right by Valerie, whether she deserves it or not."

"That cabin sounds like exactly what we need," she said. "When can I leave?"

"Whenever you want, I think," he said.

She looked toward the door. "I'd like to see Mitch, and I should say goodbye to my mother. What if she wants me to stay with her?"

"The hospital has an arrangement with a nearby hotel," he said. "She'll stay there until your brother transfers to a rehab facility."

She lay back on the pillows once more. "What a nightmare," she said.

He sat on the side of the bed and took her hand. "It will be a while before I can forget the sight of my sister standing there with a gun to your head," he said. "I came so close to losing you."

"You didn't lose me." She sat up and pulled him close. "And as awful as the next few months or years might be at times, you don't have to go through all this alone now."

"I know," he said. "That's the best thing to come out of all of this. Whatever happens, we'll get through it together."

Nothing he could have said would have meant more to her. She had broken off her relationship with Darrell because he wouldn't make a commitment. She didn't need a marriage proposal to believe Vince would be there for her. She trusted the connection they had would grow. They both knew loss, but out of that shared knowledge, they had found so much.

* * * * *

Don't miss the stories in this mini series!

EAGLE MOUNTAIN: CRIMINAL HISTORY

Twin Jeopardy
CINDI MYERS
December 2024

Mountain Captive
CINDI MYERS
January 2025

MILLS & BOON

INTRIGUE

Seek thrills. Solve crimes. Justice served.

Available Next Month

Child In Jeopardy Delores Fossen
Mountain Captive Cindi Myers

....

Cold Case Discovery Nicole Helm
Shadowing Her Stalker Maggie Wells

....

Special Forces K-9 Julie Miller
Fugitive Harbour Cassie Miles

Subscribe and fall in love with a Mills & Boon series today!

You'll be among the first to read stories delivered to your door monthly and enjoy great savings.

WE SIMPLY LOVE ROMANCE

MILLS & BOON

— JOIN US —

Sign up to our newsletter to stay up to date with...

- Exclusive member discount codes
- Competitions
- New release book information
- All the latest news on your favourite authors

Plus...
get $10 off your first order.
What's not to love?

Sign up at **millsandboon.com.au/newsletter**